Bounding
UP THE STEPS

DAVE TRANSUE

All characters and organizations appearing in this work are fictitious.
Any resemblance to real persons, living or dead, or organizations, is purely
coincidental. Characters, dialogue, incidents, and organizations are entirely of
the imagination of the author. For the benefit of the reader's understanding,
most of the stories and experiences portrayed are set before the year 1996.

BOUNDING UP THE STEPS

ISBN-13: 9781981733729
ISBN-10: 1981733728

Book interior layout design by Tara Mayberry, TeaBerryCreative.com

To the Lord Jesus Christ, King of Kings...I do not deserve His sacrifice and grace, but accept it with a humble heart and soul

To my darling wife, Christine, and to the two strong Transue men we raised...I love you to the moon and back

To Mrs. Susan Gatchell and Dr. Robert Iosue...for the positive influence you had on a young man so long ago

To those who took the time to read my manuscript and offer critical feedback, and to Sandy and Cindy, who believed in me when I was ready to give up...thank you from the bottom of my heart

To Jeff Piccola and the late John Shumaker...great men to whom I am forever grateful that you allowed me to be a small part of your impactful journey in public service

Finally, to the men and women in the Pennsylvania Capitol in elected and appointed positions—especially to the Piccola and Shumaker staffers I served with as a team—rarely do you receive thanks and gratitude for your service and sacrifices. It was the high honor and privilege of my life to work for the General Assembly...

ABOUT THE AUTHOR

*Photo Credit:
Sandy Transue Arena*

The author has over thirty-five years of experience in Pennsylvania politics, including service in several senior staff positions with the Pennsylvania General Assembly and with former Governor Tom Ridge as a deputy director. He managed several political campaigns, and volunteered in many others, including his first one at age sixteen. He and his wife, Christine, retired to live on the Jersey Shore to be near the Barnegat Bay and the ocean they love. They live with their rescue pit bull, Brownie.

TABLE OF CONTENTS

ONE

Farewell Capitol, Saving Gabriel

"**H**URRY UP, JACK. The boys will be here soon, and we can't be late for the party. A pressed white shirt and your tuxedo are on the bed. Before you argue about your tux being too formal for the evening, you're wearing it. A regular suit doesn't do justice to the night." In no mood to quarrel with Carolyn, my incredible wife for over thirty years now, I finished up in the shower. I toweled off and put my Army dog tags back on. The only time they left my neck is when I showered, part of my daily ritual for getting ready for whatever I might face, the odds slim of facing anything as demanding as my military training. The chain reminded me, too, that I had been in something much larger in purpose than myself.

I ignored the need to shave. In the last year of my work as a senior legislative staffer with the Pennsylvania General Assembly, I now sported a beard, very uncharacteristic, keeping my face clean-shaven and hair neat and trim for most of my adult life. Big Joe Curran, my father, had raised me this way. The new look with its speckles of gray appealed to me—perhaps a sign of wisdom and maybe licks from what life had dished out so far. Longer locks, naturally curling, I suppose were a signal to the world that I'd changed on the inside, too.

Big Joe rarely left my thoughts. Larger than life, he got his nickname from my mother, Annie Curran. Back when they dated, while walking the beach in Atlantic City, a large seagull slammed into Dad's chest. The poor bird—in shock from the blow—didn't harm my father, his chest strong and muscled as a man of six-four who took care of himself. Dad being Dad, an animal lover to the core, worried more about the critter's welfare than the impact on his body from a ten-pound flying objection hitting him at top speed. After the "seagull incident," as it became known, Mom called him "Big Joe." The name stuck through his adulthood.

Until the day he died, he'd labored and toiled for his family. The victim of smoking two packs of unfiltered cigarettes daily from the age of twelve, his lungs black and full of tar when he passed away in a North Carolina hospital, surrounded by my siblings and me as we watched him take his final breath. The last gasp of a miserable existence.

Dad's death affected me beyond measure since I'd spent my whole life trying to prove myself worthy of his praise and the hard lessons Dad imparted on what it took to be a man in a cruel world. The final night of Big Joe's time with us, I refused to go back to my hotel room. I talked to him, caressed his hair, wiped his head with a cold washcloth, even though he was unconscious and on heavy morphine to quiet the pain. A gut-wrenching cough, which should have brought up his damaged and weakened lungs, brought up blood and sputum that never ceased.

In the middle of the night, a nurse came in to stick him with more needles. *Utterly useless*, I thought. My temper flared, and I yelled in fury, "Get out. Can't you see he's dying? What's the purpose of sticking him again? No more tests or blood work!"

The nurse retreated, and I regret treating her so poorly. After all, there were medical protocols and orders to follow.

Dad never stopped to enjoy himself or the fruits of his endeavors, believing vacation or relaxation existed for slackers. I would not make the same mistake he did after pushing myself forward for thirty years in what had been an enjoyable and stressful life—the rough-and-tumble world of politics and public service.

Jack Jr. and Robert, our sons, used their key to enter the family homestead. Splitting expenses, they shared an apartment not too far away from our adopted hometown of York, Pennsylvania. We loved this town where trendy and quirky businesses lined George and Market Streets. The city, rich in history and known as the "First Capital," hosted the Continental Congress after it retreated to escape the British invasion of Philadelphia. The Articles of Confederation, America's first governing document, were written and adopted in the "White Rose City," a name derived from the storied House of York.

York had seen its fair share of challenges, including race riots in the sixties. Being a part of an urban renaissance movement where restaurants, the theater, and other conveniences were close by was a thrill. Carolyn and I liked to "people watch" as a form of relaxation and would pass time on a sidewalk bench, commenting on style, fashion, and mannerisms.

The city remained diverse in population and its housing charming with older Victorians, Colonials, and many brick row homes, dotting the landscape. York College sat on its southern border, providing sporting and cultural events to the community, and a constant vibrancy from having five thousand students on and around the campus. It made us feel young to be near the hustle and bustle of a prospering private institution of higher education.

More than anything, we wanted to raise the boys in a city so they would experience cultural differences and have roots, the latter something I had struggled with as a younger boy. The Curran family pulled up stakes every couple of years as I grew up—making us modern-day gypsies—embedded for only a year or two, depending on my father's promotions and mother's boredom with our housing. This almost constant movement made it difficult for my siblings and me to form lasting friendships. I vowed our sons wouldn't experience the same.

Well over six feet, our boys were handsome with darker hair and Carolyn's blue eyes and towered over me even though I was tall, too. Our oldest favored me with a leaner face and long nose, a trademark Curran feature. Also like his father, Jack's countenance conveyed a grave and mature essence. Robert resembled his mom, a tinge of red to his hair and a rounder face full of freckles. A smile seldom left his face and Robert's carefree spirit touched those around him.

Proud of the men they'd become, I was glad they could be with us for their old man's big retirement night. With them, a young African-American man, Gabriel, of bright but quiet intelligence, coming out of a self-imposed barrier erected to stop sorrow and deep personal hurt.

Gabriel joined us after his mother moved to Georgia to live with a boyfriend, abandoning the lad as he struggled to finish high school in his senior year. From flop house to flop house he traveled, living in dark alleys and abandoned dwellings—a small backpack and duffel bag his only worldly belongings. The young man's circumstances were much too close to my own. The wound from my mother walking out on our family reopened when he entered our legislative office one day fresh off the streets of York seeking help.

My heart raced. I broke out in a cold sweat as I relived my own trauma through his. *Get a hold of yourself, Jack, and call Carolyn,* I told myself. *This boy needs help.* After explaining the situation to my wife, without hesitation she said to bring him home where she made up a comfortable bed and fed Gabriel several helpings of spaghetti and meatballs. The poor kid, exhausted but with a full belly, fell fast asleep within the safe confines of our house.

Once he was out of earshot, I confronted his mother over the phone. "Isabella, this is Jack Curran. My wife and I live in York. Gabriel is living with us," I began.

"I haven't heard from him. How is he?" Isabella asked.

"He's okay now. Why in God's name would you walk out on him while he was in high school?" I demanded, forgetting further pleasantries.

"Don't you judge me, mister. Who're you anyway? I left Gabriel with a neighbor and some cash and didn't abandon him. My man got a job in the South, what was I supposed to do, stay behind? What's the problem? The boy's eighteen, you know..." her voice drifted off, revealing only the tiniest bit of remorse.

"This is the guy who took your son in, that's who I am. After the neighbor tossed him in just three weeks, he went to the mission, where someone tried to rob him one night. From there, he lived on the street until a pastor from a local church placed him temporarily. Your son has floated around ever since until he came into my office today. What's he supposed to do with no identification other than his school card? Can you mail us a birth certificate, so we can get him proper papers and help him find a job—can you at least do that?" Beyond exasperated at this point, a deafening silence from the other end was even more maddening. "Are you there, Isabella? Did ya hear me?" I asked her.

With a heavy sigh, she said, "I'm here and don't have Gabriel's birth certificate. I...I can't help you, I'm sorry, mister..." She hung up the phone, leaving Gabriel with us and no other history to work with. He became part of our family, subsequently graduating and finding a job. The terrible circumstances dealt to Gabriel by life could've brought him down. But he overcame them.

Twenty miles north of York was the place I'd worked many years in and around, Harrisburg, the city hosting the State Capitol Building and state government. Alive and prospering, the city is home to 253 members of the legislature, three thousand legislative staffers, thirty thousand state employees and bureaucrats, almost one thousand lawyers, and seven hundred lobbyists. Over twenty reporters covered how these folks interacted with each other through Pennsylvania's "legislative process," and the functioning of state government and its legislative, judicial, and executive branches.

I dressed in the formal clothes Carolyn had put out for me. She had her thick, reddish-brown hair pulled up in a bun and wore a black dress and tasteful silver jewelry to accentuate her natural beauty and bright, big blue eyes that portrayed a wonderful, youthful purity. Her good complexion required little makeup. Carolyn never needed heels, standing over five-seven.

Sweethearts since high school, she has always been my safe harbor. Tonight, and from the turmoil of my extended family and years in political service. There's no one I wanted by my side more than Carolyn. Earlier in the day, as we had made every major decision together in our marriage, we signed my state retirement papers, an irrevocable choice to turn away from the life we'd led for so long.

For some time, we had talked about my quitting as my health deteriorated, including several hospitalizations for chronic pneumonia. My doctors added more prescriptions for ailments I'd suffered from all my life with additional pills coming along in my twenties, thirties, forties, and early fifties to address new health problems. Like Big Joe, I had been hard-charging, relentless in my determination to succeed and provide for my family.

And while I shared most everything with Carolyn, I didn't tell her about a dark premonition that hovered over me. Like a black ominous cloud, it followed me during the day and into my nightmares. I couldn't escape the notion that I wouldn't have a long life to live, adding to the timing of my retirement and desire to enjoy life while I could. It was time for us to leave this venture, knowing our kids were self-sufficient. We had other dreams to pursue, and I had to do my level best to escape the early grip of the Grim Reaper.

The Curran gang climbed into the family's high-mileage, nondescript Chevy sedan, gray, that some would say matched my personality.

Cars were never anything but basic transportation for me. Jack Jr. offered to drive. He recognized my nerves were on edge, watching his mom squeeze my hand while rubbing my shoulder with her other hand as we sat together in the backseat.

We headed north on I-83, a road I had traveled on back and forth so many times I knew every hill and valley by heart. By habit, I glanced over to the various "hiding" spots the state troopers used to nab speeders even though my son had the cruise control engaged at the speed limit. He realized a ticket would be the hair trigger to my short fuse on an evening when it wouldn't take much for me to explode.

An old billboard (never replaced with contemporary advertising), which served as a landmark, caught my attention. In all his glory, the Marlboro Man sat on a handsome horse, ready to light his cigarette so he could enjoy the *great* taste that would be his. I wondered how many men followed his lead because they wanted to be that "guy." I chuckled, too, at the graffiti that marred this iconic American. In large letters—choosing the brightest fluorescent paint the "artist" could find—was scrawled "YOUR A PUSSY DUDE."

"What're you laughing at, Pop?" Robert asked me.

"The graffiti, son. Back in the day, the student newspaper editor called me the same thing. Kinda went to blows over it. That poor cowboy couldn't defend himself against an 'artist' lacking proper grammar. Funny if you knew how famous he was in my childhood." I tipped my imaginary hat to this rugged man; the last time he and I would cross paths again.

Snow blanketed the rural countryside. The soft glow of the evening sun, dipping below the horizon, seemed like a proper sign for the road that lie ahead in my life. As one of the last blasts of winter, I hoped the dawn of spring, a time for renewal of all things alive and green, would restore my soul. It had been scarred from too many political battles because I couldn't or wouldn't engage my own internal cruise control to take it easy and pace myself.

The great Susquehanna River loomed ahead. Once across, lost in deep thought, I said, "Slow down, son," as he used the exit marked "Capital City—Second Street" to enter Harrisburg. I was never a good backstreet driver; always at the wheel because life's circumstances had dictated so when my reality turned upside down as a teenager.

Fortunately, we found a parking spot on the street nearby to the offices of "Placid & Associates," home to my alter ego, and one of Harrisburg's most powerful lobbyists, Robert Placid. Before entering Rob's office that hosted my retirement get-together, Carolyn kissed me, whispering, "I'm so proud of you, Jackie. We love you." While my sons shared in that emotion, they were stoic and fearful that their parents were moving on to a new path.

Carolyn had a tissue ready as I wiped away a tear and blew my nose. I wasn't afraid to cry in front of my family and in public when my emotions couldn't be contained. While maintaining the facade of a serious exterior, mixed with a warm smile and booming laughter, the reality was something different. Sensitive on the inside and some folks would say thin-skinned, my profession demanded total and complete toughness that I tried to deliver at great personal cost to my well-being.

Before we entered Rob's office, I asked my family for a moment alone to gather my wits. I had pursued this goal with great focus and determination and now that it was here, I felt both triumph and a huge letdown. At the pinnacle of my influence, it was indeed time to cherish what I had accomplished in public service and politics and to thank God for the experiences He'd given me, and for the people He had placed on my journey.

Rob stepped outside, and his voice shook me from these thoughts. "Get in here, Jack. There are lots of folks waiting upstairs. Whatever you're thinking about can hold on." Carolyn got a big hug and Rob shook hands with Gabriel and both the boys, who he had watched grow up since their birth at York Hospital.

He, too, knew my mental state was more wired than usual. Rob gently guided me into his large conference room where a crowd waited to celebrate with us. Above the big window that framed the State Capitol Building in the background read a sign "Congratulations Jack and Carolyn."

As a staffer, I never served as the front man; the elected officials I worked for held that role. Humbled, I waved to acknowledge the applause of those gathered, pulling my wife up to my side since she deserved the real praise for dealing with the grueling schedule that drove me to work long into the evenings and weekends. And through more than a few missed holidays, we would rather not remember.

I surveyed the crowd of friends, associates, and members of the legislature who were there to wish us well. It seemed like only yesterday I began this adventurous career in politics.

TWO

Meet Henrietta Hoover

THIS EVENING was the culmination of a long struggle. In a pensive mood, I knew the time had come for another stage—the climbing and clawing uphill was over. Not before one last encounter, however, with a foe of many years: Representative Henrietta Zelda Hoover, an uncompromising conservative and the Joan of Arc of Pennsylvania's southwestern corner that borders Ohio. A few miles to the west and Hoover would've been a Buckeye instead of a proud Pennsylvanian. Originally elected as a Democrat, Hoover became a Republican in Ronald Reagan's second term after she realized her party no longer welcomed conservative Democrats. Her district had sent her to Harrisburg as a Republican ever since because of her feisty reputation.

Why's she here? I wondered. *To torment you one last time, Curran,* an inner voice answered. Hoover caught my stare of bewilderment and scowled at me. I let out a big laugh determined to one-up her, even though she usually got the best of our bitter exchanges over the years. *Not tonight, Henrietta. You won't get to me*; I tried to convince myself. *You will not ruin this evening.*

Unlike others in this gathering, Hoover had a champagne bottle to uncork for another reason. To celebrate final victory since we had tangled over school choice and other education-related issues for longer than I cared to remember. Henrietta never bent in her wish to seek perfection and rarely got anything in return other than the ability to keep her purity as a right-winger. I can't recall a single conversation when we agreed with each other. If I said, "Look at the blue sky." She'd respond, "It's green, Curran. You missed the serious dark clouds hovering overhead, you idiot." While I had moments of gloominess, Representative Hoover won hands down in that department.

As disagreeable as Henrietta Hoover was for me to deal with, at least her motives for being a constant obstacle had roots in her unique brand of conservatism. She and the Thirty-First President shared more than the same surname. But a strong penchant for doing nothing, or saying, "no, *nein, nyet,*" and, "go jump in a lake" for good measure.

Some of today's conservatives, like Henrietta, love to quote our hero, the Fortieth President, but, *in my opinion,* they ignore the pragmatic approach he used. Reagan recognized under our American governance structure the time to compromise comes if you want to get anything done. President Reagan often said: "If you got seventy-five or eighty percent of what you were asking for, I say, you take it and fight for the rest later."

From the earliest days of the Republic, give-and-take has been a requisite. Had conservatives of Hoover's flavor been members of the Constitutional Convention, I'm pretty sure it would've deadlocked, and the white flag of surrender hoisted, asking the British to take us back.

All too often the extremists in *both* parties allow "the perfect to be the enemy of the good," ignoring the wise words of a famous French philosopher. I have yet to see a "perfect product" produced by the legislative process. Reagan's and Voltaire's advice guided my approach to public service and served me well. Did I always advance the ball the yards I pushed for from the get-go? Hell no. Sometimes I gained just inches. Or retreat until we could regroup and try again.

How could I be totally miserable with her on such a grand evening? Without prompting from Carolyn (who tried like heck to bring out the best in me), I gave my old archenemy a little wave and smile. My gestures understood loud and clear as they were intended. *Here I am, Henrietta. Despite your best efforts, I not only survived but thrived.* Normally, I wouldn't be so conceited, but Hoover didn't conjure up real lightness and goodness in my heart.

She countered my phony friendliness with a furrowed face and pursed lips that signaled total contempt as her hands rested on her considerable hips. Henrietta wore a frumpy dark brown pantsuit; the color rarely varied. I don't think cosmetics ever graced her pale features. This signature move of hers, coupled with her curly black hair—rumored to be a wig that looked like Shirley Temple might've worn it—and spinster eye glasses, caused me to glance away. Henrietta had won our little contest of wills although it was good we hadn't traded nasty words.

As a lobbyist, Rob had to invite all the members of the legislature to the party, including Henrietta, whose attendance was for the sole purpose of dishing out the comeuppance she thought I deserved. This would be the last time I would have to interact with Representative Hoover, so my party was a hit for more than one reason. Another staffer or lobbyist would have to be her new target.

Most people not squarely and entirely in her far-right orbit avoided Henrietta like the plague, figuring her to be in the "no" column anyway so why waste time. One of the other guests present, a young senator for whom I had lots of respect, found himself in Henrietta's verbal grip as she quickly set to work on someone else. I heard her lecturing in that searing voice that had punished me for so long, "Do you know what the problem is?" I resisted the temptation to finish for Representative Hoover, anticipating the next salvo.

"The Senate has no respect for the House of Representatives, no respect, which is why nothing gets done." This legislator responded forcefully, assuring her of his chamber's total admiration. But she cut him off, changing subjects. "Why won't you guys move that union-busting bill we sent over last month? Show some courage! Kill the unions, and we defang the Democratic Party," she yelled. Bless this young member for having the patience to endure this diatribe.

As the host of the evening, Rob circulated about the room with great aplomb. While he cared for my family, he would not let a gathering like this pass without transacting business for his wealthy corporate clients. Dressed in a contemporary suit with a crisply pressed shirt, bold but tasteful tie, gold cuff links, and Rolex watch, the ensemble befitted his role as an influential lobbyist who got stuff done.

Overlooking the strategic State Street, Rob's office enjoyed a vista that ran from the Capitol to the Susquehanna River. In one direction, I gazed at the Rotunda Dome modeled after St. Peter's Basilica in Rome. Out the other window, the river that borders Harrisburg on its western front gently flowed by. While tranquil during my party, terrible floods over the years had shaped the city's citizens as gritty people.

Pennsylvania is a diverse state with the large Democratic cities of Philadelphia to the east and Pittsburgh to the west. A wide swath of territory, known as the "T," is where the Republican Party dominates from the Northern Tier of I-80 through Central Pennsylvania all the way to the Maryland border.

While the Southeastern suburbs of Philadelphia, where I came from, had been a given for the Grand Old Party (GOP) in the twentieth century, they are now a battleground between the two parties with the Democrats penetrating into something the Republicans previously counted on to offset the huge Democratic vote that comes out of Philadelphia by several hundred thousand more votes in statewide races.

I thought about the thousands of people I felt privileged and honored to work with. From seven governors of both parties, hundreds of legislators, business leaders, labor advocates, educators, doctors, reporters, lawyers, realtors, engineers, bankers, iron workers, teachers, indeed people coming from all walks of modern life.

Stop with the memories already, Jack. You must greet your guests, I scolded myself and plunged into the crowd. The trendy conference room had exposed brick walls, industrial iron beams, and stainless-steel surfaces that gleamed from the soft recessed lights set throughout the grand space. Rob scooped up the old building, which had lain dormant for some time, never sparing an expense when it meant impressing his clients.

Rob charged his clientele plenty, rumored to be retainers of ten-to-fifteen thousand dollars a month plus expenses. He had a cadre of young people, who left the legislative staff to join his lobbying firm, peddling their influence and connections for the widespread interests represented by Placid & Associates. His state lobbying registration statement a vivid demonstration of raw, overwhelming power and wealth. Gambling concerns, Fortune 500 corporations, unions, specialized manufacturers, Big Tobacco, and other entities that relied on his expertise and relationships.

I could be gregarious when needed and appeared confident on the outside. The reality: I'm really a loner filled with self-doubt, something that only family and Rob understand about me. While I enjoyed being around people, I could have easily been in the quiet of my den, reading a political biography or history, my faithful rescue pit bull JET by my side, providing all the comfort and company required.

To circulate in this well-appointed room, I needed to push myself, accepting the handshakes and backslaps from friends, colleagues, and a few people I recognized as worthy opponents, who, besides the scowling Henrietta, were checking to make sure I was retiring and this wasn't some sort of elaborate joke. Not a natural in working a room (something that comes easily to many politicians), I preferred smaller conversations and meetings rather than a large chamber.

These people were there for me, however, making it less challenging to flow through a room than a political dinner or cocktail party where plenty of strangers mixed about. Some political types can dive into any space and make mind-numbing conversation without a second thought. Not me. It was always awkward, and I strained to get in and out in whatever might be an acceptable time for the affair.

My retirement reception mirrored any gathering of politicos in Harrisburg with an open bar flowing with booze, several tables piled full of hors d'oeuvres, and a large floral centerpiece with enormous shoots of orange and yellow flowers I didn't recognize that dominated the room. A woman in a formal black dress and matching hat sat in the corner playing the harp. Her hands moved smoothly over the strings, oblivious to the surrounding crowd. Rob did everything first class.

THREE

My Best Friend Rob Placid

A WEB OF SCANDALOUS NEWS and gossip—that's what encompassed the shadowy side of the Capitol during my time there. Who was sleeping with whom, and who might be under investigation for public corruption—always the top categories of scuttlebutt. Pennsylvania has a long and unfortunate history of sordid and corrupt behavior. I knew *most* of the members, staff, and lobbyists to be honorable men and women doing the best they can to work together on challenging public policy issues—the annual budget always commanding the most attention of any legislative session.

Human nature what it is, inevitably, a few bad apples end up in the mix of thousands of people working in and around the Capitol. These folks garnered the headlines in state newspapers, the subject of whispers, too, at the legislative water coolers. The never-ending cycle of gossip and scandal motivated me to stay away from the Harrisburg bar scene, many times where this stuff generated from or occurred.

Early in my career, a few watering holes existed for the legislative crowd. Now Harrisburg has lots of liquor establishments on "Restaurant Row" that slices through the city on one of the main thoroughfares of

Second Street, running from the interstate to the neighboring suburban Susquehanna Township to the north. Italian, Irish, Greek, and good old American food available to the row's diners and lots of alcohol—always abundant for consumption.

Too much drinking, recognizable faces, and inappropriate behavior has landed many a politician or prominent lobbyist on the front-page of the newspaper, damaging banners taking a toll on reputations and the next election cycle. Social media and the fact just about everyone has a camera phone now has only heightened awareness of these behaviors.

Despite being burned out when I signed my retirement papers, I retained a sliver of passion and idealism about my life's work and respect for *most* of Pennsylvania's citizens serving in elected and appointed positions. So many serious issues, legislation, policy proposals, parliamentary procedure, debates, and so many funny stories to remember as I cataloged the memories that had consumed the waking hours and had interrupted many a night as the darkness closed in.

Many nights I didn't sleep, second-guessing my decisions and recommendations. Some staffers could leave the job at the Capitol at the end of each day. Not me. The work drove my thoughts and even dreams—why I kept a legal pad by my bedside to record the notions that poured from my subconscious.

To the day of my retirement, I remained mindful that my name never graced a ballot. My bosses subjected themselves to the electoral process. I didn't. Although at one time elective office was within the realm of the possible, I rejected it, recognizing I wouldn't see my children grow up. The officeholders I served answered to the voters and staff to them. As a manager of people over the years, I drilled this same principle into our personnel.

From the benefit of thousands of meetings, phone calls, emails, and speeches, the faces of friends and foes flashed through my mind as I stared at the beautiful green-tiled Rotunda bathed in a soft light. On top sat the Miss Commonwealth statue gilded in bronze. Below her, the American flag flew briskly in the crisp March air. A moment like this should be frozen in time as a postcard image I would remember forever.

Rob interrupted these thoughts. "How ya doing, buddy? Lost in thought again, I see." The bond we forged had endured since the two of us graduated from Ford College in 1986, forming a relationship that allowed us both to vent during the tough times and laugh during the victories. We remained close each working in his own way behind the scenes in Pennsylvania's capital city, taking decidedly different professional paths.

"A little nostalgic that it's all over for me, Rob, but I'll be okay." A night for toasting, we raised our glasses. "Thanks, man, for this. Can't take my eyes off the Rotunda where it all began for us so many moons ago..."

"Relish it, Jack. You earned it."

"Every damn bit of it, Rob. Look at Carolyn." Surrounded by friends, my wife's aura appeared different and more relaxed. For sure, she was a natural in any setting. After suffering through more chicken dinners and lousy banquets, a drill any spouse of a public servant understands all too well, she did these affairs like a pro. "There's visible relief on her face. What did I put her through?"

The moment too dark for Rob, he kicked into gear to shake me out of my somber mood. "Stop being an asshat. You took care of your family and gave them a good name. Now, please tell me that isn't Coors Light you're drinking, is it? There are several excellent craft beers to try, including from the microbrewery right here in Harrisburg." Rob and my sons liked to rib me about my choice of beer, believing I was too much a creature of habit. They were right. I liked my routines and planned no changes in my fifties.

"Yeah, it's Coors Light. I've been drinking this since my internship at the Heritage Foundation offices back in '85. As soon as I learned from the guys in the building that the Coors family supported conservative causes and the Republican Party, I haven't touched another beer." Rob had heard this response so many times before that I'm sure he tuned me out. "As much as you enjoy busting my stones, Robert, you'd be disappointed if I didn't stay consistent."

"Consistency isn't the right word, not at all. You're downright dull. No problem, though, I've put up with you for a long time. Somehow, we've made this friendship work as different as we are."

Rob Placid's last name connects well to a calm demeanor that courses through the eddies of a process that often gets fiery and fast-paced. Those with a faint heart or weak stomach should look elsewhere to apply their skills and talents. While we worked together, I envied Rob's even temper and laid-back approach but didn't begrudge his success. Many misjudged my friend's power and wealth as coming without effort and costs. I knew otherwise. Rob, also, paid a terrible price for the choices he made in life, including two broken marriages.

After several more swallows of beer, Rob got sentimental, too. Carolyn and I would pack up in a week to retire to our beloved Jersey Shore, having put our old Victorian home in York up for sale so we could move to our summer bungalow with its view of the beach, boardwalk, and tranquil bay, the only place where I would truly relax. Growing up for a while near the ocean, the powerful pull of the sea had never left me. The moment had come to return there.

Rob would miss our lunches. I was there for moral support even when we found ourselves on opposite sides of an issue—our fellowship deeper than any policy conflict or win or loss on legislation. Aware this was the only time I would usually take a lunch, we'd grab a hot dog from our preferred street vendor or visit my favorite deli, talking about the problems we faced, and the characters up on the "Hill" we interacted with daily. I suppose my dull life served as a consistency that Rob lacked in his, so we truly complemented each another. There was never a doubt about confidentiality between us.

"Hey, how 'bout we slip out and go to the Capitol? I wanna check out the Rotunda one last time," I said.

"We can't leave your guests, brother. You've got to keep making the rounds."

"No one will miss us for a little while. You're always telling me to be spontaneous, let's go," I insisted.

Out the side door we went as we walked towards where it'd all started for us. At the bottom of the steps, we paused to take in the view. "Did you ever think I'd make it to this day?" I asked Rob while laughing with my pal.

"I can't count all the times I watched you sweat this stuff, making it personal. I always told you to treat this as a marathon that first time we ran up the Capitol stairs together as young interns barely more than wet behind the ears," Rob said with a chuckle. I remembered the moment well when we first set eyes on the Capitol, bounding up the steps, so eager, so innocent, so clueless, nothing but book educated, excited to start the next adventure of our lives.

The memory would go with me to my grave and became a metaphor for the uphill journey that would follow. While Rob had approached our odyssey as a marathon, I'd always been the sprinter. The primary reason I was retiring while he had no intention of calling it quits. Rob enjoyed the immense influence he wielded in the legislature.

"Yeah, well, I beat you back then, man. Longer legs, dude, versus shorter stubs."

"I call bullshit but whatever, Jack. Not arguing as you exit the stage. C'mon, let's go in."

We checked in through security and sat on one of the marble benches that gave us a view of the inside of the Rotunda Dome. I continued in the reverie of how it had all started for us. "Remember my first job with Senator Jim Weigel as his chief of staff? I didn't think I'd make it. Talk about stress." Earlier in my career, a wealthy businessperson crossed the line when pushing my boss to support particular legislation. "That rich guy the senator and I met with intimated he'd give a campaign contribution to Weigel if he supported a certain bill. The senator threw him out of the office. It was a shit storm after that."

"Forgot about that. Okay, you should've reacted to that incident. Didn't law enforcement get involved and Kostantin Pokornin write stories for the *York Tribune* and *Harrisburg World*?" he asked. This circumstance was my first encounter with the famous Pokornin. Rob continued, "Still, you internalize stuff, and that's why you're a physical mess, my man."

"During the meeting, and after, my blood pressure shot up as the authorities sorted out the details. That was the first time I thought you'd have to pull the plug on me, Robert." We had this long-running joke that Rob would put me out of my misery if that moment ever came. As close as blood brothers, I didn't share with him the sinking feeling, however, that I felt my life would be short-lived. He'd lecture me about self-fulfilling prophecy, negative thinking, or some such nonsense.

My uptight manner made it the right time for me to hang it up. "Am I doing a good thing? I'm still relatively young." I'd paced around the house most of the night before signing the papers. It wasn't my nature to decide and let it rest. I had to poke and probe every decision and turning point. *No going back now, however. Damn the torpedoes, full steam ahead*, I thought, remembering a famous admiral's ballsy attack during the Civil War.

"You are, Jack. Now knock this shit off. By the way, I'd pull that plug in a heartbeat, Jackie boy, and sleep like a baby with a dry powdered ass that same night." Pretending as if he were pulling an electrical cord from an outlet, speaking in a heavy Irish brogue, Rob always kept it light for my sake. "All kidding aside. You know what your problem is, Curran?"

Here he goes, I braced myself, *he's going to talk about the stick being up a certain part of my anatomy*, a common theme since our college days when he first made this observation after we met.

"What's my problem?" I asked, rolling my eyes.

"Laddy, you never worked smart, believing you had to put more hours in this Capitol itself. I made the rounds in the evenings, meeting the members in a more relaxed environment. That's why I'm worth what I'm worth and why you're leaving on a government pension." Rob hurt me more than he intended.

I had to hit him back for this slight, so I mentioned one of Rob's conquests when we were interns conscious it remained a sore spot. I wanted to shift the focus away from my shortcomings and onto his. "Hey, whatever happened to that fiery red-head you hooked up with in the eighties, Russian or something, right?" I knew the answer but loved watching him squirm. "She went crazy that one night, banging on our apartment door, shrieking about you sleeping with her and dumping her. At least she didn't become an ex-wife, buddy." I had notched it up.

Rob visibly shuddered with the bad memory. "Have I ever mentioned you're a jerk off?"

"Once or twice," I said, smug and satisfied.

"Her name was Petra, and she was nuts."

"Yeah, she worked in the House, right, as a secretary, kinda big-boned and muscular? Not too pretty I recall."

"Now you're piling on, asshole. If you must know, security is what Petra did. Last I heard, she moved out to Montana or some rural state to teach yoga and sell natural foods, whatever that is. Every time I'd see her in the Capitol, I'd try to hide."

I imagined Rob lean and ducking behind one of the marble columns we sat by. The constant entertaining of legislators and clients over the years had caught up to his frame; his waistline bigger, for sure, than when we played flag football at Ford.

"Now that we're even, you're getting out at a good time. You and Carolyn will be beachcombers. Your body needs to heal, man. The Capitol Dome didn't collapse today when you walked out. It's survived since 1906 with thousands of legislators, staffers, and lobbyists calling it quits before you. Hell, it didn't collapse when Benjamin Walker retired. Not going anywhere with you leaving, Jack."

Walker was someone we both considered a friend. Before retiring, he was the most influential staff person in the Senate, known for working around the clock, ignoring the need to eat or sleep. Nothing of any consequence occurred in the Senate without Walker's knowledge or blessing even though he had never been elected to public office.

Rob and I had both clawed our way to success, having no wealth nor real strong political connections while growing up in Western and Eastern Pennsylvania, respectively. We were proud our success happened the old-fashioned way—through hard work, diligence, and education.

Placid's cell phone rang. "Dammit. I gotta take this. It's the big moving company I represent. Some in Congress are threatening to make life more difficult for the interstate haulers. This might take some time."

"No worries, bud. Do what you gotta do." As Rob stepped away for privacy, I had time alone to continue looking back. To cogitate on my tumultuous upbringing and how it so profoundly affected the course I took and the lens it established on how I saw public service. Mindful that this had not been a journey just about me, I remembered early mentors: Dr. Moran, Ford College's president, my business teacher Sarah Hahn, the Army, and the two legislators for whom I was proud to serve as their chief of staff—the capstone of my long political career.

Although an arduous task each day—because of exhaustion and weariness, it took every ounce of discipline I had—I'm glad now I kept a meticulous journal of these people and events, including notes of detailed conversations as they occurred. In my wildest dreams, I never expected to write a book. This is the story of a young man's journey in politics and his life experiences—experiences and events that shaped his principles and approach to public service. I hope you enjoy the tales as much as I loved living them.

FOUR

Big Joe and Annie Meet at the Park

THE SON OF JOSEPH AND ANNIE Curran, I was born in New Jersey, the fourth child out of five. Big Joe graduated from high school in Philadelphia, at once going to work as a storeroom parts clerk for Simpson Malley Smith (SMS) Corporation, a large truck manufacturer whose origins were in the Midwest. My dad didn't believe in college. His schooling happened on the streets of Philly. Higher education was only for fools and slackers, something my siblings and I frequently heard coming from his mouth, including when I left for Ford College.

Annie Fernsby, my beautiful mother, came from Abington, Montgomery County, a community close to the City of Brotherly Love. The belle of the ball in high school sought by many boys, she usually politely rejected their entreaties. Confident of her pretty looks and excellent athletic skills, a man would come at the right time. While many wanted her hand in marriage, Annie was in no rush, eager to expand her horizons beyond the provincial town of Abington.

Joe and Annie met in a park in Philadelphia by the Otto's Ice Cream factory, where Annie had landed a job after earning her high school diploma. A monkey had gotten loose from his owner, and a small crowd formed as the man chased the animal up into a tree. As my mom told the story, the onlookers pointed and cheered as the chimp evaded the slower man, performing tricks to the applause of the throng of people.

Joe Curran found himself smitten by Annie Fernsby's beauty and small-town manners. Sitting by a pleasant park fountain and enjoying the spray that provided some cool air and relief from the Philadelphia summer heat, they both laughed at the wiry monkey. Dad recalled he stumbled to say anything at first. Joe was a city kid. Here was a refined girl from the suburbs, different from any women he had dated in his Philly high school.

Tall and handsome, Dad had wavy brown hair, neatly trimmed around the ears and off his collar. A deep cleft in his chin distinguished him from other men. His initial awkwardness with Annie melted, a projected confidence soon wowed my mother. She'd not seen this in the high school boys who dogged her at the football games and dances. Mom says she knew right away that Dad differed from these other boys. More mature and in command.

Based on their recollections, I often imagined their early dating, what they wore, and what they said to each other back in 1949 when it all began for the Curran Seven. I'm sure Dad was in a starched white button-down shirt with a traditional solid-colored tie, gray slacks with a sharp crease, black wingtips highly shined, understanding that how a man dressed formed his image in the corporate world, where Big Joe was at the bottom rung. Just beginning his climb to success.

A bright summer cotton dress with matching gloves and hat helped highlight Annie's healthy complexion that needed minimal makeup. There's no doubt Mom was prettier than any other woman walking through the park that clear sunny day.

"That poor guy will never catch that monkey," Big Joe said as he leaned in toward Annie. He couldn't let her walk away from that fountain without making a move.

Feminine charms were her speciality when she desired to employ them. Batting her long dark eyelashes, Annie cooed, "He's so adorable." Pausing because she did not want the moment to pass either, she added, "Well, I'd better be going...I work over at the ice cream factory as a secretary and only get thirty minutes for lunch. I just started there and don't want to make my boss angry. Maybe we'll bump into each other again?" Annie wanted to leave the door open, something stirring in her about this young man.

Later, Dad remembered he couldn't let Mom depart without asking if she would join him for a Philadelphia Phillies game that Friday night. Joe enjoyed baseball. Annie felt drawn to this man and agreed to the date. After all, there was something remarkable about this guy, who carried himself with such authority he, like Annie, stood out in any crowd.

That night at the Phillies game, they grabbed hot dogs; Joe had a beer, Annie a Coke since she didn't drink alcohol. The Phillies played ball in Shibe Park, long before the construction of Veterans Stadium, where my parents taught me to love the game and my Fighting Phils, a passion I handed down to my two sons.

"My work at the company may be simple now, but I promise you I'm going places, Annie. I'm the first one to the storeroom in the morning and the last one to leave before the boss tells me to pack up," Joe said.

Mom took in this ambition, later telling us kids that Dad kind of terrified her with his swagger. Their conversation centered on his dreams and passion for achieving. Joe came from a modest North Philadelphia neighborhood where for most men the factories or docks were the only avenues for employment. Long before that work moved overseas under the guise of "free trade."

"Hang on to that idea, Annie. The cleanup hitter is at bat." Tall, brawny, and athletic, number four in the line-up took the first pitch. *Crack* went the stick. Up, up, up the ball shot. The crowd cheered for a home run. Falling to the left of the foul ball pole, Joe jumped from his seat and put his long arms up in the air. "I got it," he yelled. Annie didn't flinch as some people might since she competed in high school as a star athlete herself. Fans in their section applauded Joe's feat.

"This is for you, Annie, to remember our first date." Joe grabbed a pen out of his pocket, inscribing, "To Annie on our first date at Shibe Park, Philadelphia Phillies, 1949, Joseph." He was rewarded with a soft kiss on his cheek and a tear in Annie's eye. This ball now sits on my mantle, one of my most prized possessions, a symbol of their first date and love.

When the game finished, Big Joe asked for another date. "I have to see you again. I promise you won't regret getting to know me. I'm going up the corporate ladder. A sales position is coming open in six months." Like many men in the post-World War II generation, Dad had goals, and lofty plans—a beautiful and kind woman by his side made those dreams more enjoyable and possible.

While Joe missed fighting in the big war because of his age, he served as a sergeant in the Pennsylvania Army National Guard, enjoying the discipline and organization that came with military service. After Mom and Dad had divorced years later, she believed the military would have been a better route for Joe as he thrived in that environment.

Joe drove up every weekend to Annie's home in Abington while they continued to date. He slept on the sofa in the living room of the modest stone bungalow on Colonial Avenue, which housed Annie, her brother, sister, and their parents. And showered Annie with attention, courting her for marriage. They journeyed to more Phillies games, mixing in Saturday beach trips to the famous Atlantic City, where, after they splashed in the waves together, they would stroll the boardwalk, arm and arm, enjoying the cool ocean breeze and window shopping as vendors hawked their wares and carnival games. Occasionally, Joe would treat Annie to a push cart ride that would run the length of the boards.

Annie learned Big Joe had a terrible temper and swore like a sailor. Her strong Christian upbringing found this repulsive, profanity not permitted in the Fernsby household of the late 1940s. Later, after they married in a small Methodist church in the Fernsby's hometown, she discovered he had a drinking problem, too, and smoked cigarettes from a habit formed in his teen years. All bad qualities that caused my mother to regret saying yes to joining him at the altar in '50.

As a Christian, she made a vow before God and intended to keep her promise. Marriage, planning a family, and buying that first home in the suburbs is just what was expected in those years and in that culture. That's exactly the pattern my parents followed while married.

Big Joe's hard-charging work ethic and inability to relax without scotch and cigarettes as he pursued promotion became a part of their daily lives much to Annie's dismay and internal horror. Nine months after their honeymoon over a weekend in Washington, D.C., in a less than appealing motel because Big Joe earned little, Annie gave birth. Joe refused to take a longer vacation, saving what little time he had for his Army National Guard camp commitments in this period of the Korean Conflict. Several times during their first year of marriage, and a lonely pregnancy for Annie, she feared that Joe's unit would be called up for combat. A call to wartime duty never came, however.

FIVE

Annie is a Trophy, The Belt, Adeline, Turmoil and Trauma, Jack Withdraws

THE 1950s brought three children: Joseph Jr., William, and Emma. Big Joe spent the decade working to provide for his family, leaving little time at home. He rose from clerk, to salesman, to branch manager, and, finally, to regional boss, all headquartered in Philadelphia.

A devoted homemaker, Annie lavished love and attention on her children. But deep in her heart, she couldn't escape the gnawing notion she shouldn't have married Joe. While his confidence captivated her at first, she found him to be a flawed man. The allure burned off in his persistent pursuit of the American Dream. My mother became a trophy to be paraded around during corporate functions. In the family scrapbook from that era, many photographs show them dining in a stylish club or restaurant, extensions of Joe's entertainment responsibilities.

With a white dinner jacket on, Joe turned heads when he entered any nightclub with Annie on his arm. She wore a mink stole over her cocktail dress; her raven black hair radiated brilliant, an almost plastic smile planted on her face that bore a netted veil. Mrs. Joe Curran knew what her husband expected of her as he schmoozed his clients, colleagues, and bosses. And always the damn cigarettes in every picture. Other than Annie, everyone smoked—the suave thing to do before society learned how deadly the tobacco and chemicals are.

Mom's pregnancy with me, and the birth in 1965 of Carol, my baby sister, came as a surprise. After three kids in the 1950s, our parents thought they had the perfect family size.

Hailing from Scotch-Irish roots, my parents christened me "Jack Hudson Curran" after my great-grandfather on my nana Curran's side. My ancestor left Scotland as a fifteen-year-old in the late 1800s, immigrating to America for the promise of a better life. The first Jack Hudson lied about his age and enlisted in the Army, fighting in the Spanish-American War. His field manual, full of his musings and observations, portrays a man of great independence, a hot temper, and several descriptions of courage and bravery shown during battle.

At my grandmother's bended knee, she'd point to photographs of her father as a swashbuckling young lad. His hair the color of coal, something he and I shared besides our name. Barely old enough to shave, the pride he had wearing that dress uniform jumped off the pages of those rough and grainy black-and-white images. His namesake thrilled about seven decades later.

By her mid-thirties, Mom's beauty still shone brightly with splendid thick hair, full lips, and high cheekbones that framed her kind face. But her body had suffered after bearing five children although she somehow maintained a trim figure. Her pregnancy with Carol especially challenged her health, nearly ending both their lives.

One of Dad's many promotions required our family to move to Chicago (corporate headquarters). When Mom's water broke, she began hemorrhaging and couldn't wait for an ambulance to arrive. Big Joe scooped up Annie into his strong arms, rushing her to the hospital in his company car, ignoring all traffic laws along the way. He knew she and his fifth child might slip away as Annie cried out to God to save her baby. By His grace, both survived.

After Carol's birth, and a botched Caesarean, my mother's health fell apart. A succession of invasive surgeries left her weaker and weaker and the doctors piled on with lots of prescription drugs that carried terrible side effects. Carol and I went off for lengthy stays with our grandmothers; our older siblings remained behind with a nanny employed by Big Joe to care for them.

Our father always gave the family a lovely home. He withheld from us—time and affection. Big Joe's unrelenting drive for work, only made worse by alcohol abuse, made it impossible for him to share these qualities. A game of catch, attending school functions, reading to his kids, never happened in our formative years. Dad didn't bother with discipline, either, unless Annie signaled retreat.

She had to bear all the familial duties, plus mete out proper punishment that usually consisted of an antique wooden spoon to the fanny that stung and often corrected bad conduct. Risking Big Joe's temper with us wasn't wise and each night we were cautioned to be on our best behavior. We walked on eggshells when Joe came home; the safest approach as the five of us learned how to navigate around our father and his sullen moods.

The few times when Annie threw her hands up in the air, crying because one or more of us wouldn't listen—discipline and justice were dispensed by Big Joe with a belt to the butt, quick and stinging. My older sister, Emma, bore the famous Curran temper, too, and could be more stubborn than Big Joe. One time, Emma pushed Mom too far when she refused to go to school because of burned toast and runny eggs that the rest of us ate without complaint.

When our father walked through the door that evening, the belt came off. He moved towards Emma, his eyes ablaze with a look of frightening determination and anger for this breakdown of household order. It seemed as if he proceeded in slow motion when he pulled the leather off his trousers. The strap grew and grew in length. Joe stopped to crack it with a *snap* after he tugged it through the final loop. I hid behind our staircase in terror but also in gory anticipation of the beating to come since at a young age I didn't appreciate disorder either.

Emma took preemptive action against the belt. As a teenager, she stood five-nine, beautiful like our mother, only with blond hair. She raised up her leg and kicked Joe hard in the testicles, felling the giant who ruled his kingdom with an iron hand and expected complete obedience. Big Joe bowled over in intense pain, holding his genitalia while cursing at Emma and inventing new words none of us had ever heard before. Annie grabbed my sister and told her to run to her bedroom and lock the door. She moved to the fridge for an icepack, grabbing two aspirin from the kitchen cabinet along the way.

For several days, Dad had a dull, aching pain, the ice to that sensitive area a reminder of my sister's reaction to his leather whip. This marked the last time any of us suffered from the belt. None of us boys ever dared to stand up to Big Joe while we lived in his home. Emma had a certain stature in our family from this moment forward. Big Joe gave her a wide berth after this encounter.

When younger, Emma's dinner routine consisted of knocking over her milk onto our father's lap—when Joe would make an appearance for the evening meal—causing my older brothers to cover their mouths in muffled laughter. Joe's reaction was predictable. His face would get beet red as he jumped out of his chair. Dad would shout "sonofabitch" and "Annie" as if Mom had any way of anticipating when the moment would strike Emma to torment Big Joe. While we all feared our father, we also knew how he would react in certain situations. This "mistake" of Emma's didn't call for the belt. Tough but mostly fair described Dad.

Holidays were stressful in the Curran household. To this day, they are a challenge for me to appreciate because of the pallor that hung over our dwelling as we grew up. While believing in the Lord, Joe had no time for the extended celebrations of Christmas and Easter. Annie bore this responsibility as Joe ate in silence at our family table before packing up for work, leaving us to enjoy the festivities without him. A deep sadness enveloped my father, carried stoically, as he worked, smoked, and drank too hard, trying to forget whatever sorrows and demons he held within his soul.

One Christmas, however, Dad decided we *had* to visit his aunt Adeline after being badgered by my nana Curran that she hadn't heard from her sister in months. The reclusive, crazy aunt in the family, of all days, my father decides Christmas is the day to check on Adeline despite protests from Annie whose turkey dinner was pushed aside. He packed us into our large station wagon and we made the trip to Adeline's.

After Dad knocked on her front door for about ten minutes, she finally opened it a crack. "Who's there?" she barked out in her croaky voice that scared the hell out of me, only eleven at the time.

"It's me, Aunt Adeline, Joey." *I'm glad he lost that nickname along the way*, I said to myself.

The door opened slowly, and Mom tried to greet Adeline with a hug. Brushed off by a gnarled hand with veins that looked like cracking tree bark, the smell of an unbathed person overpowered us. I asked my mother, "Why does she stink, Mom?"

"Jack, mind your manners."

Aunt Adeline didn't seem to mind my outburst. She padded off to her corner chair, stained and tattered. Beside her lay a stack of *Reader's Digest* magazines, some intact, many cut to pieces. Around the walls were what looked like paper dolls she had fashioned with help from this iconic American periodical that became the material for her handiwork.

Big Joe kneeled by her side and I saw a glimpse of feeling from my father, who normally didn't show much emotion or sympathy. "Adeline, your sister is worried sick about you. Why aren't you returning her calls?"

"I'm fine. Tell her to stop bothering me," she answered. Besides the stench and exhibit of ghastly "friends" looking down at us from their perch on Adeline's discolored walls, I noticed open sores on her bare legs. Adeline was most definitely NOT fine.

Dad kissed her forehead and motioned that we should all head for the door. I couldn't wait to beat a path out of that frightful place. Dad's timing was sadistic for his wife and kids. But I give him credit for showing Christmas love for a woman in the throes of serious mental illness and neglect. Nana organized an intervention and Adeline received the care she needed in a nursing home. Not without a fight, however, since she, too, was the daughter of a war hero.

As my brothers grew up, pervasive drug abuse and loud rock music, two outgrowths of the '60s and '70s, invaded our home, too. Joe Jr. volunteered for the Marines after high school graduation. Doing so to flee our father's grip. This caused Mom even more anxiety as she prayed for his safety. My brother missed shipment to Vietnam, making it as far as Okinawa before serving stateside in San Diego, where pot reined free as the drug of choice.

On his return from duty and subsequent honorable discharge, Joe Jr. lived the hippie life, moving into a rat trap house he shared with other veterans. His long, unwashed hair, ear-popping music, and tattered clothes drew hard and fast battle lines between him and our father.

One of my earliest memories is being awakened by Mom's screams as my brother came home in the middle of the night, on drugs, boozed-up, and angry. At the bottom of our staircase he stood, yelling profanities aimed at our dad with the goal of enraging him to fight. It worked. The entire clan had moved out to the front porch of our handsome cedar Colonial to watch Senior and Junior throw fists at each other on the expansive lawn. The violence a poor substitute for love and understanding that did not exist between the two.

In between her sobs and making sure I was wrapped up in a big blanket against the damp air since pneumonia had struck me once again, Mom shrieked, "Stop it, stop it, both of you, please. Jackie, keep that blanket on you!"

Because he joined Joe Jr. in feeling repressed, middle brother William egged our older sibling on with, "Get him, bro."

Enjoying her ringside seat to the match since she fed off drama, Emma had her Barbie dolls join in cheering for the gladiators.

Through the narrow opening of the wool covering that encased me from head to toe, I wheezed out, "Don't hurt my daddy." Protectively, I hugged my baby sister, who bawled and bawled, too young to understand the bedlam going on around her.

I vividly remember Joe Jr. hopping into his hippie van, a 1960s Ford panel truck—held together with duct tape and chewing gum. With "Fuck you, Pigs," painted blood-red on the sides, my brother made a statement that further enraged Big Joe. Once Joe Jr. got behind the wheel of his rolling Woodstock, he chased Dad around the yard. If I hadn't seen it with my own innocent eyes, it could have been a British comedy television moment.

Rather, we were a messed-up family stretched to the limits of its bonds. We tried to cope in vain with the radical changes occurring in middle-class America after the calm and security of the Eisenhower era my father longed to return to. All his life, Big Joe never really left the 1950s.

Our patient neighbors in this upscale community had had enough and called the cops. If this turmoil happened in their homes, it didn't spill out onto the street, Curran-style. The police arrived. Long before Blue Lives Matter, they reacted to Junior's defiant statement and the donuts he made while hunting down my father. Drawing their weapons and a bullhorn, Joe Jr. finally stood down. The men in blue were all too glad to pin my brother to the ground. He ate extra dirt for good measure while the police twisted the handcuffs on tightly. Despite Annie's pleas, he was arrested for various offenses; in the end, getting off easy because Big Joe declined to press charges.

At a young age, I recoiled against this counterculture, shaping my conservatism in the early years. I sided with my dad and his haven of crew cuts, order, and discipline. While I didn't live through the fifties, I knew enough to join him in longing to return to the safety, security, and values of the post-war years. Dead serious, Big Joe blamed the decay of American society in the sixties to the arrival of The Beatles on our shores. He would describe in detail when they first debuted on the *Ed Sullivan Show* with their long, unkempt manes. The "Fab Four" radicalized the notion that men must keep their hair neat and clean. For Joe, this was the beginning of the end.

Just as the country turned upside down and rock-solid mores were no more, so did the Curran clan's family structure. Drug and alcohol abuse, a drug-selling conviction, extramarital affairs, multiple abortions, and sexual molestation, all would plague us. I would learn in junior high that our grandfather Fernsby was a monster, molesting my little sister repeatedly over a number of years.

Unbelievable rage overcame me at what had been done to her. Anger, too, that my parents had gone along for the "sake" of my grandmother in not exposing his perversion since she was unaware that her husband—an "upstanding" member of the community—was evil. Despite Carol's pleas to make him stop once she became old enough to understand, "cover-up" became the operative mode that protected my grandmother Fernsby while sacrificing tragically the purity, innocence, and safety of a little girl.

Only about nine and eleven at the time, I should have been more attentive to my mother's orders. Anytime we visited the Fernsby home, I had to go with my sister as the monster tried to lure her away from the rest of the family. I became the unknowing buffer against his wickedness. The "witness" to keep him from trying.

As big and vigorous as Joe was, I couldn't understand why he hadn't beaten this man into the ground. Later, I regretted the same after I learned the truth. In a way, I became complicit in the acceptance of this evil and struggle to this day to forgive myself for not standing up for my little sister. For not acting in place of my cowardly parents. Until I stared at my grandfather lying in his open coffin did I forgive him even though I had no feelings of love or tenderness for him. As a Christian, there was no choice to do so if I desired God's forgiveness for my sins.

With the Lord's grace and protection, my sister would rise above this, and other tragedies, to become a strong, accomplished woman. She started several successful businesses, using her many talents and later married a good, decent man. Together they raised wonderful children under a loving roof. Her willingness to talk about her abortions and the unspeakable horror of incest has helped others heal. An era of hiding molestation, which only permitted it to continue, is hopefully at an end in this country.

Blinding migraines became Annie's living hell for the failures of her marriage and the anger and chaos that surrounded our family during these years. She blamed the horrific pain on Joe's temper, smoking, and drinking. In those rare hours when Dad didn't work into the evening, he poured the scotch shortly after arriving home if he didn't stop at a bar first. Back at his desk by six or seven the next morning, somehow, he wasn't affected by the intense, persistent alcohol use.

Many days and nights, our mom would remain closeted in her bedroom. With curtains closed and lights off, a cold washcloth over her forehead, she tried to get relief from these headaches to no avail. We had no option but to carry on as best we could, contributing to the independence of the five Curran children.

Much like Annie, my survival instinct was to withdraw into myself to avoid the family conflict. One of the most dramatic outlets for a sensitive little boy whose body couldn't cope with the terrible stress and upheaval was to wet the bed at night. An uncontrolled, nervous bladder became a deep, dark secret. Before outsiders came into our home, the reminder rang out, "We do not discuss Jack's problem." More than anything, I sensed disappointment from Big Joe that his son had a "weakness." In time, while the turmoil continued around me, puberty corrected this condition. But not without horrible, unspeakable shame that little Jackie was the runt of the family—with most of my adult life spent trying to prove otherwise.

I stayed in my room as much as possible with my cherished books, bringing an escape to somewhere, anywhere, but the Curran homestead. Drawn to history and political biographies at a young age, I lost myself in the experiences and events of others. I saw life through the lens of the great people I read about. Douglas MacArthur, Teddy Roosevelt, Abraham Lincoln, Henry the VIII, Amelia Earhart, Harry Truman, John Adams, to name only a few.

An entire collection of the *Hardy Boys*, a gift from my nana Curran, recognized the need to read as if it were part of my very essence—as important as the need to breathe. A sponge, I couldn't get my hands on enough books. Never imagining that someday my passion for reading and history would shape my philosophy, political beliefs, and approach to helping elected officials govern.

College would be my ultimate escape from my parents, Fernsby grandparents, and older siblings. But that lie ahead in the future.

SIX

Antiques from the Ghetto, Racism in Suburbia

IN THE LATER YEARS of the Joe and Annie Curran story, Dad tired of the corporate culture, yearning to be his own boss without the piles of paperwork and hassles of managing people. He and Annie started an antique business out of a small garage. But like everything Joe did, the new enterprise became the singular purpose. The boys had to help in the family endeavor, and this is where I discovered more about Dad, the man.

Only eight at the time, one early Saturday morning Dad entered my bedroom and shook me awake. "Get up, Jack. Time to go to work."

"Daddy, I just want to sleep," I answered, while rubbing my bleary eyes.

"No time for that, son. Clean up and get some dry clothes on." I was never allowed to forget I woke up wet each morning.

At that point, Mom came down the hallway. "What're you doing, Joe? Let Jackie get some rest. You know how prone he is to pneumonia and bronchitis. I don't want him out in this cold weather."

"He needs to be toughened up. You've made him a sissy and let him stay in his room with all those...books." Joe mentioned my books with contempt. "Jack's going to learn how to be a man. His weekends belong to me now."

"No smoking in your truck. He's too fragile."

"Enough, Annie." Dad flashed Mom the "look" that meant no more arguing. She relented as she usually did. After throwing on some winter play clothes and eating a bowl of cereal at a record pace because Big Joe was impatient, Dad lifted me up into the big truck that served as the rolling headquarters of "Wine Press Antiques," so named for the vintage farm tool that graced our wall for as long as anyone could remember. At virtually every weekend thereafter, unless on my sick bed, I'd go to work with Big Joe until graduation from high school.

While my grade school buddies threw a football around or played Little League or basketball, we'd be searching for old junk. That precious time away from doing what kids normally do gave me little chance to explore and develop any athletic skills until high school. When that time came, I chose to run, drawn to the track and open road as a loner—just me against my body, the fatigue, and the enemy of the clock. Joe never attended my athletic events to cheer because he wasn't wired that way.

Back in those early days of Wine Press Antiques, the routine didn't change much. The Schuylkill Expressway ran along the river and we used that road to head to the neighborhoods of North and West Philadelphia, the streets familiar to Big Joe from growing up there and working for SMS when he sold trucks. Seeing my father's boyhood home, a narrow brick row house at the corner of Eleventh and Lehigh in North Philly and how Dad burst with enthusiasm describing the stick ball he and his buddies played in the alley by the little house brought us closer as father and son. I connected to the Little Joe he reminisced about, not too much older than I was at that time.

The communities had changed a great deal, but my dad was comfortable wherever he traveled. This first exposure to deep poverty would have a lifelong impact on my thinking as a human being; later as a staffer to public servants. As we drove through the old city, combing the area for antiques, I saw run-down row homes and parks filled with debris. And cars, factories, and warehouses long ago abandoned.

During the hot summer months, it was routine for fire hydrants to be opened illegally as residents splashed around in the streets, trying to escape the brutal heat. That oppressive oven affected us during the day. But each evening, we were blessed to escape to a lovely suburban home via one of the bridges over the Delaware River to New Jersey. Eventually, a house at the seashore would be the ultimate luxury Dad provided.

The people we encountered had little reprieve from poverty and sweltering heat or numbing cold. Dad could be tough. But he had a deep connection with the men, women, and children of these neighborhoods. The color of a person's skin didn't matter to him—another lifelong lesson imparted to all his kids through quiet example.

With no contacts in the antique business when he launched this venture, Joe would stop at the corner junk shops dotting these communities, buying whatever might be available and networking further with the owners of these small city enterprises. Often, we would knock cold on row home doors if the "odds and ends" stores didn't bring success. Little did I know at the time how much I learned simply by watching Big Joe in action. The art of negotiation taught by one of the masters of the form—Joe Curran.

Dad had a standard opening pitch: "I'm an antique dealer. Do you have any old furniture, pottery, crocks, Depression glassware, trunks, or clocks you might want to sell? I have cash." Most of the time, the owners would open the door, and Joe would find something to buy. And I would see poverty on the inside and squalid conditions that no person should ever have to live in.

Each trip's goal: fill the truck to unload back at the warehouse. From there, the stuff would be cleaned, cataloged, and sold at retail, auction, or to wholesale dealers. These same dealers scratched their heads about where Dad located his inventory. His answer was always truthful—North and West Philadelphia. The typical reaction: a shake of the head, a quizzical look, and maybe a question of, "Joe, why would a white man dare drive around those neighborhoods?"

More talkative during these times than at home, Dad loved his truck and those Philly streets. We would talk about the poverty in the city and I could feel his deep empathy for people trapped with scant hope. And a sorrow that his beloved city had changed so much from once being an industrial giant and port of origin for the Northeastern United States to a struggling urban center that hemorrhaged jobs, population, and vitality.

At one of the junk shops on our route, Dad chatted with the owner about the Philadelphia Phillies, one of his few passions besides work. Gunshots popped out nearby. Dad grabbed me and tossed me hard into the truck, yelling, "Get down, Jack."

Terrified, I stuttered, "What'sss...hh...hhappening...Daddy? What's that noise?"

"Never mind, son. Just stay hidden," as Dad revved up the engine to speed off to safety away from the random bullets flying around. On the way home, Big Joe explained that a gang war had erupted on the block.

I recall asking my father, "Can I tell my friends in school what happened?"

To a little tike, a street battle had to be shared now that we were safely out of range of the gunfire. Dad chuckled and told me to keep quiet, realizing our mostly white school district wouldn't even begin to understand drugs, gang warfare, and gun violence. In the suburban neighborhoods where I grew up, the biggest problem kids had was making sure the neighbors' windows didn't get hit during street ball.

Through the basements and attics we would crawl, searching for old stuff to buy. Besides the skill of negotiation, I learned about the antique business itself and developed a good eye for finding value. Dad and I also bonded because of this special time together, more so than my brothers (who were back at the warehouse) or my sisters (the girls weren't permitted to work in the family enterprise since Big Joe didn't believe in equal rights).

Sometimes, I didn't dodge the cockroaches and fleas that infested many of the places we visited. Coming home with flea bites one Sunday, protestations from Annie on this condition fell on Joe's deaf ears. "Joe, look at Jackie's arms and legs. They're red and inflamed." Mom shook her head in obvious disgust, bent over as she said this, gently rubbing ointment over my small limbs that had been scratched raw and oozed with pus and infection.

"He'll be fine, Annie. He needs to be taught how to be a man." That he did in his own hard and unsympathetic way. Carrying on was Dad's expectation. Ignore pain and inconvenience and work without complaint. Just as he did every day, around the clock, so that his family would have a comfortable life—the only model I had available to follow when my turn came.

Big Joe would drink plenty of coffee. A cigarette always burned between his long fingers while we listened to *KYW News* on the truck radio. I would absorb Big Joe's reactions and opinions on the issues of the day further shaping my values. The time with him allowed me to look beyond my daddy's temper, drinking, smoking, and foul moods and I found my first hero in life—as imperfect a man as he was. Dad was quietly a religious man, who loved his wife and kids. Articulating that love other than through his deeds was another matter.

While Joe didn't want to pay any more than necessary, many times he'd buy something even if the homeowner had little stuff to sell or the profit wouldn't amount too much. The calls would pour in before Christmas and Big Joe would make a special trip to Philly, so his customers would have cash to purchase holiday presents for their children. Big Joe gave back to the city he so dearly loved.

One of our regular suppliers was known as "Big Sweet." A tall, lovable, African-American man, Sweet operated a small junk shop in North

Philadelphia. He had a son, Howard, about my age, who also worked with his dad on the weekends. I enjoyed stopping by Big Sweet's shop knowing Howard would be there while our fathers conducted business, haggling with each other over the price of the goods. Their routine changed little.

"I'll give you fifty for that whole pile, Sweet. Cash is king." Dad would pull the bill bearing U.S. Grant out of his pocket and wave it in front of Sweet.

"Nah, Joe, that won't do. The way I figure, there's at least a Franklin sitting there. Don't force me to tell folks in this neighborhood how cheap you are." Sweet was no dummy, and these guys did this dance during every visit.

A feigned grimace or long pause might follow Sweet's counter and Joe would respond, but not without Sweet believing he just might walk on the purchase. "That's a tight margin, Sweet, but I think it'll work if you throw in that little wood table over there and make it eighty bucks." No doubt Dad had this same tactic used against him when he sold trucks. Only back then, Big Joe had to throw in floor mats or a free oil change to seal the deal. Sweet and Joe would arrive at a middle ground and load up the truck until the next time they haggled and danced.

That shop was one of the neatest places for kids our age to play. The front sidewalk had piles full of wares. Through the not-so-well-lit space—a small bulb or two dangled from the plaster ceiling—an open courtyard connected the buildings with little natural light penetrating, giving it an eerie canyon effect. The smell of a dead cat would've stopped any adult dead in their tracks, but not two boys who didn't care if they stumbled upon a decaying feline, bird, or rat's nest (I'm not kidding!). Loaded with a cornucopia of furniture, auto parts, appliances, and kitchen items, plenty of places allowed for hide-and-seek.

These short stops didn't permit much playtime, so we convinced Joe and Sweet for Howard to travel home to New Jersey to spend time with me. Summer weather brought a whole week for playing, swimming, and enjoying the openness that Howard had never experienced. His only world that shop and a courtyard surrounded by asphalt, concrete, and piles and piles of junk. Their small apartment sat to the rear of the property.

To generate extra cash, I also had a newspaper route. Howard borrowed Carol's bike to help deliver papers the first day of vacation as we arose around six. The dawn dense with fog, our bundle seemed heavier than usual from the morning dew. Mom promised a big breakfast of pancakes, sausage, and chocolate milk as an incentive to get home sooner.

Almost finished for the day, we joked about being able to taste Mom's meal. One of my customers—let's call him "Harry the Bigot"—came out to his front lawn maintained in such a manner that Harry must've been retired. A little older and wiser and I would have recognized what the black lawn jockey displayed next to his porch meant.

Gesturing with his hands, Harry the Bigot yelled obscenities and words I didn't understand—all this aimed at Howard. The final words he hurled, "Don't come back here again." Crying, we pedaled the bikes back to my house, the remaining papers ditched on the road near this bastard's property. About ten years old, the word "frightened" doesn't do justice to the terror we experienced.

What seemed like an eternity in reaching the safety of the Curran castle, we ran in the front door. Mom greeted us and realized something was very wrong. "What's the matter, honey? What happened? You boys are home and safe." By this time, we were both sobbing, so she grabbed a washcloth to clean us up. "It's okay. Calm down. Mom is here." I had never been so scared in my life. A stranger, this evil asshole had said nothing when I delivered his paper until Howard helped that day.

Annie's soothing voice and the washcloth eventually did the job. She asked again, what happened? "A customer shouted stuff. He said words I don't know," I said, breaking the silence.

Howard added, "He used a word my daddy says is bad. Starts with the letter 'N.'" I still didn't understand what the heck Howard meant since that word *never, ever* entered the house of Joe and Annie Curran.

Kneeling, Mom said, "Okay, boys. I understand what happened. He's a terrible, terrible man, and that is a horrible word. Jack, you're not to deliver a newspaper to him again, do you hear me? I'm calling the company to remove him from your route, and I'm notifying the police." Mom kissed Howard on the forehead, hugging him against her comforting body. "Sweetheart, we love having you here. I'm so sorry this man hurt you." While I didn't grasp what Howard was going through, my heart ached for him as his small body shook, releasing more emotions as time went on.

"Jack, don't tell your father where this man lives. The police can handle this." Annie believed Big Joe would take matters into his own hands.

Howard never stayed with the Curran family again; his visit cut short because he'd been so traumatized and treated so poorly in his first foray into white America. Had Annie given Big Joe all the details about the incident, I'm sure our neighbor's vocabulary and outlook on race relations would've been corrected with a broken knee cap and jaw, perhaps more.

SEVEN

Divorce, Carolyn and Jack Meet,
First Kiss and Togas

WHILE JOE AND ANNIE deep down loved each other, that love wasn't enough to keep them together, particularly in the face of our family strife, turmoil, and Big Joe's bad behaviors. Mom learned to live without Dad being around much, leaning on her children and sister for comfort and solace. With the older kids out of the household and married, Annie wanted more from life and volunteered as a "candy striper" at Abington Memorial Hospital.

In 1979, we'd left New Jersey and returned to Abington since Annie wanted to be closer to her sister and her parents. If the Curran clan didn't move because of Big Joe's promotions, the U-Haul truck showed up because Annie wanted a new home, hoping a change, new scenery, new furnishings, and decorations would improve family life with Joe. It never did.

Multiple relocations became a crutch to try to escape and leave behind the conflict that surrounded the Currans. After we came back east from Dad's posting to Chicago, we lived in Willingboro, the woods and lakes of

Tabernacle, and Sea Isle City, before we returned to Annie's hometown, just as I had started high school at the Jersey Shore.

The Curran children were used to this pattern of changing schools and behaving like gypsies. Big Joe always told us it would build our "character." Anytime our father said this, one of the Curran kids would say we had plenty of "character," something that all of us inherited from Big Joe.

At Abington Hospital, Annie met a doctor, beginning an affair that led her to leave Big Joe, an event that would conclude the final act of ripping the Currans apart. Carol and I were the biggest victims since our older siblings had moved out by this time. One day, Mom pulled me aside in the kitchen of our brick split level, facing a lovely park in Abington, to break the news of their divorce.

Mature at a young age, the family joke became "Jack's ten going on forty," also the age at which I devoured the entire *World Book of Encyclopedias*, cramming my brain full of much useful and useless information.

Mom and I were close. As her most sickly child, I battled asthma, bronchitis, and pneumonia since birth. Sometimes the infections were so bad, my eyes would ooze yellow and green pus as an outlet for the overwhelming poison my body contained. Mom hugged me many nights, praying to God for relief of my breathing and health problems. Her faith never wavered. One of the ways she loved her kids was through prayer, which continued until the day she passed away to be with the Lord.

"Jackie, I have something to tell you," Mom began as she started to cry. To acknowledge divorce and an affair was difficult stuff to share with a teenager. Deep in conflict with her Christian values, Mom's words rocked what was left of my "safe" world. "Daddy and I have been miserable for many years, and you know how my health has suffered. I'm drowning, son. I've decided to leave your father."

Even though I didn't see much affection between them for many years, it never occurred to me they might split. Of course, I was doing my own thing in school activities, running cross country, winter, and spring track. And I had begun my political adventure (more on that to follow).

I objected at once. "Mom, you can't do this now. Carol has two more years until she graduates. This is my final year in high school. You've got to wait to leave Dad. When we're both out, do what you have to do." Selfish on my part, I didn't care. Whenever Joe and Annie demanded we move, we did so. Back in Abington felt right like I had put down roots after all those relocations for Dad's promotions or because Mom sought a change to make up for the defects of their marriage.

"The decision's been made, Jack. There's nothing to discuss." Said with an assertiveness that Mom rarely had. After raising five kids and putting up with Joe's behavior for thirty years, she wanted her life back. Plus, there was now "the doctor," as he became known. "There's more, son. I met a physician at the hospital. His name's Doctor Antonio Carpella. He's rented an apartment for me in the school district. I want you and Carol to come with me. Daddy can stay here. Or we'll sell the house, and he can find his own place."

I erupted, something rare in my interactions with Annie. "How the fuck can you do this, Mom?"

Rarely did anyone use the F-bomb, including Big Joe, who had plenty of other tried-and-true Anglo-Saxon curse words to use. The moment didn't call for restraint or empathy. The floor had fallen out below Carol and me and I remember thinking, *We're locked in a funhouse at the circus with no exit door from this horror of hell.*

Mom slapped me hard against the face. She thought about grabbing the trusty wooden spoon, but at my full height of six-two, muscled from working for Joe and conditioning for sports, the spoon would have been of no effect. "Watch your mouth. I'm your mother, and you will not use that language with me. You'll have a beautiful place to live and can finish out at Abington. I understand you're furious right now. This thing just happened, and I'm not fighting it any longer. Your father's hands aren't clean, either," Mom yelled. She wasn't allowed to have the temper of the other six Currans.

In a cold fury, I stared back at her. From somewhere deep inside, I summoned the will to hold back the tears from the searing pain to my cheek and the enormity of what had just happened. Almost as if I knew from this moment on I had to have tremendous discipline, a mere slap nothing more than a small distraction and road bump to be dealt with.

With hatred in my eyes, I snapped, "This is fucking bullshit, Mom. There, I said 'fuck' again. Gonna hit the other cheek? I'm not going with you. I'm staying right here with Dad, and Carol can remain, too. I'll take care of her since someone has to keep this family together now that you're bailing on it."

Defiant, I resolved not to let Joe and Annie—and their drama—screw up my life. I had dreams of college and into politics after that. *Damn my parents for their mistakes,* my insides boiled. This wasn't Christian behavior, but they hadn't been faithful and were selfish in not sticking it out a few more years for my sake and Carol's.

In between the sobs that followed my line in the sand, Mom shared more details I didn't want to hear. "Your father's a cheater. There were several secretaries that Daddy pursued, and I never said anything. He hasn't told you about your illegitimate half-sister, has he? How about that? How do you feel about your hero now? Your father wasn't always working, you know, during those long hours away. You have to come with me, Jack. Don't hurt me like this."

Annie had internalized Big Joe's infidelity along with his other bad behaviors. I knew instinctively how to damage Mom. Taking a stand with Big Joe became the weapon of revenge against wrongdoing and the decision to wreck our household.

With the walls closing in and the news my life had turned upside down, I stumbled out, slamming the kitchen door behind me. Plus, I had another sibling. *When did this happen and where's my new sister?* I asked myself. My beat-up, blue '67 Chevy Malibu with a leather top and eight-cylinder engine sat in the driveway, an escape when things got tense in our home and my chariot away from the mess of Joe and Annie Curran. I jumped in, revved the gas hard, and left tire marks on the cement, scaring the hell out of Mom. *Let 'em worry about me for a change*, I vowed, although they seemed locked into themselves, giving Carol and me only a mere thought.

After this kitchen talk, the turning point in my young life, Mom left and took Carol, only fifteen, with her. Annie continued to be distraught I wouldn't go with her. I refused to abandon Big Joe. Nor would I visit the apartment since Carpella paid for it. She tried to have me over, but I held the moral high ground and suppose that moralistic tendency guided future challenges and decisions as well. Nor did I want to risk running into the doctor, afraid of what I would do if given a chance.

Big Joe's depression, present for many years, deepened. And while Dad continued to work hard, any shred of joy left his life with Annie gone. She filed for divorce based on promises the doctor would leave his wife. Perhaps the lack of a prenuptial prevented departure from "Mrs. Urologist." Rumor had it, the doctor had his hands full with her high-maintenance, uppity behaviors. Carpella didn't walk out, and the affair ended after Annie issued an ultimatum.

Joe kept the refrigerator stocked with beer and wine to supplement his scotch but nothing else, forcing me to fend for myself during that year, bumming meals off friends and eating lots of McDonald's fast food. Thank God for the kindness of several mothers in the neighborhood, who pitied me and made sure I ate a decent meal occasionally.

Several weeks after Annie walked out on Big Joe, I summoned the courage to ask Carolyn Gianella on a date. We met in our sophomore year. That first day is seared in my memory. I'd just moved into the Abington School District in October of '79 and didn't know the mammoth high school building yet, having relocated from a much smaller building while being schooled at the Jersey Shore.

After health class, I saw this beautiful girl with thick reddish-brown hair down below the shoulders, lots of freckles, and a figure I couldn't help but notice. As students shuffled about in the crowded hallway, I asked for assistance. "I'm embarrassed to admit I can't find my next class. My family just moved to Pennsylvania from Sea Isle City. The guidance office didn't bother to give me a tour of the building. Go figure. The name is Jack," as I handed her the class schedule.

"Sure, I'll take you to that room, follow me. I'm Carolyn." I felt at ease with her. She had soulful blue eyes that along with an adorable smile tugged at my heart like no female ever had. As we walked side by side, Carolyn caught me glancing over to check her out.

With only a few dates in middle school under my belt—if you can call meeting a girl at the gym dance a "date"—I was shy with girls. Your mom calling you "handsome," primping your hair, and telling you the acne in full bloom all over your chin and forehead is a sign of maturity, doesn't count for much either. "Awkward" is the only way to describe these dances. The guys on one side of the room, gawking at the girls on the other side. I was never that guy who ventured out to the middle—not caring what the other boys thought of his lousy moves. The girls responded to this bravery by giving him a slow dance partner all night long while the rest of us looked jealously on.

To celebrate our senior year, our class assembled on the football field to have a picture taken for the yearbook in the form of "82," the year of our graduation. This pivotal point meant we'd arrived as big-time seniors. One couldn't help but feel the excitement as we high-fived each another to mark this milestone. I sought Carolyn out. While I had buddies from sports, I wanted to be with her for this photo—the cute girl, smiling anytime we saw each other in school or at football games. We raised our arms up for the picture, cheering as a class at our collective accomplishment.

Once the all-clear sign came from the photographer who snapped the still from a big cherry picker (several takes had to be tossed out because of the guys raising their middle fingers), I reached over to kiss Carolyn full on the mouth, capping this perfect moment. Her first real kiss and mine, I stood on top of the world. And then blushed. *Is she gonna slap me for an overly aggressive action?* I asked myself in a panic.

Carolyn's hair shined a luxurious auburn in the bright sunlight. She threw her head back and giggled. "What took you so long? I've been on edge for you to make a move for two years. Now are you going to ask me on a date or what?" Carolyn can cut through the nonsense better than anyone I know.

"There's a toga party tonight to celebrate the big photo. How 'bout I pick you up at your place at seven?" *Animal House* had debuted several years before, and toga parties were a cool thing to do. Although not thrilled with the idea of our first date with sheets as the attire, Carolyn didn't quibble and said yes.

Mom left linen in the hall closet and I found a neutral color to fashion a makeshift toga. In my drawer, I located a pair of basketball shorts to wear underneath. I left myself bare-chested, vainly wanting to impress Carolyn. Pleased with the look as I posed in the mirror (including checking out my biceps), I drove the old Chevy over to her place.

The Gianellas lived in a pleasant enough brick ranch with a neatly kept lawn—rockers and plants adorned their small front porch. I observed that their home sat in a nice neighborhood. But not nearly as fashionable as Annie's taste demanded. *What a snob you are, Curran,* my conscience pricked. *Raised by Annie, I can't help it. She never wanted to just keep up with the Joneses; she had to beat them,* I replied to justify these awful thoughts.

As I approached their painted red door and rang the bell, I realized how ridiculous I looked in this get-up. Mrs. Gianella welcomed me in, asking if I wanted a soda, while I waited for Carolyn to finish getting ready for the party.

Their home's décor appeared outdated. I saw yellow brocade, floor-length drapes that covered the windows. While dusk out, I couldn't help but think they resembled World War II blackout curtains. I doubted much natural light penetrated their thickness. Wrapped over each piece of furniture—crinkling plastic, the kind I remembered sticking to uncomfortably whenever we visited my nana Curran.

Nana had this weird habit of putting cookies in her clothes dryer. I would ask Mom, "Why are the snacks always in the dryer?" she'd just shrug and say something about freshness. The afternoon snack, intertwined with Nana's huge brassieres and other underthings, usually remained untouched as a real downer for a kid's appetite, though. But back to the Gianella family.

Finally, after scanning the area, my eyes locked upon Frank Gianella. He sat in the corner of the living room in a large overstuffed chair that clearly had seen better days. A big cigar stuck out of his mouth. With curly gray hair and matching mustache, Mr. Gianella's unusually bright blue eyes did not twinkle when we made contact. Instead, they registered suspicion. Gianella was a blue-collar machinist, proud of the work he did with his hands.

Here stood this kid with a sheet wrapped around him, picking up his baby daughter for her first date with a boy. I subconsciously tightened the toga, feeling naked in front of Carolyn's father, glad at least the shorts were on, wondering whether I should cover my bare chest with my hands.

A confident young man, very arrogant now that I look back, the irony of picking up Carolyn wearing an outrageous outfit, while trying to have a conversation with Mr. Gianella, came crashing down on me. Her dad didn't fall for any attempt at chit chat or pleasantries. He grunted when we shook hands after giving me a quick up-and-down. Quickly returning to his television program, *M*A*S*H*, Gianella behaved himself only because Carolyn and his wife asked him to.

They told Gianella of my plans to go to college and enter politics, something this blue-collar worker didn't find appealing in a young man dating his baby girl. The impression he formed—unfortunate but understandable. Dressed ridiculously in a bed sheet, he didn't know how hard I'd worked in Big Joe's antique business. Dirty hands came with the job. Politics had taken hold of me for a different path than he understood. Or would want Carolyn involved with.

EIGHT

FBLA, Nixon Lunch Box, First
Campaign and Inspired by Reagan

ONE DAY WHILE WALKING the school hallway with my friends, I noticed a flyer announcing the next meeting of the Future Business Leaders of America (FBLA). I stopped to read the poster. Still the new kid on the block at Abington High, I asked Daniel and Sam about FBLA.

"Bro, it's a club for girls. All the secretarial majors are in there. Don't bother with that shit. Stick with sports," the more vocal of our group, Sam, noted.

From a business family, the idea intrigued me. One day after school, I walked into the club's meeting place and stopped dead in my tracks. Forty-two females stared back at me, including Mrs. Sarah Hahn, a woman in her early thirties with a kind face and welcoming way. "Come in, come in," Mrs. Hahn said. "We're just getting started."

A friend from history class, Michelle, sat in the back row with an empty seat available next to her so I headed that way. At least I knew someone in the room. "Jack, what're you doing here?" she asked.

"Thought I'd check it out," I whispered, conscious that as the new kid I shouldn't interrupt the advisors as they discussed the club's agenda.

"Sam and Daniel said something about being a girls' gig, but wow, they weren't kidding."

With a smile, Michelle said, "Well, I guess it's your lucky day. You have a harem." Little did I realize at the time that this club intended to spur on entrepreneurialism would help be a link to politics. It gave me the opportunity to develop leadership skills and network statewide with clubs across the Commonwealth.

The scruffy hair on my face signaled to Mrs. Hahn something wasn't right. After a club meeting one day, she asked about my home life. Pre-divorce, I would have never dared to go without shaving since that's how Big Joe raised his sons. "Please standby for a couple of minutes so I can talk with you," she said. Once the other students departed, Mrs. Hahn posed the question I'd been avoiding from everyone at school, deeply ashamed by the break up. Back in those days, divorce was not as common, and none of my friends came from broken homes.

"How're things at home, Jack, is everything okay?"

Wound up like a top, with the anger and hurts held in and no one to talk with, I covered my face and broke down crying. A compassionate woman, Mrs. Hahn listened more than anything as I poured out my sorrows. She was a shining example of the selfless devotion that thousands of educators show each day as they teach, nurture, and care for pupils under their charge.

Another teacher's actions directly sparked my interest in politics when she entered our social studies class one day. Her name: Patricia Norman. Diminutive at only four-eight, one did not dare challenge her authority over the classroom. She scared me and everyone else in our class. Miss Norman gave us a choice during the 1980 election year. Read a book from the proscribed list and do the usual book report or volunteer in a political campaign.

I had done more book reports than I cared to remember. *Why not volunteer?* I mused. My teacher provided me *both* the Democratic and

GOP contact information—although I would never have volunteered for the other party. I grew up knowing both my parents voted for Barry Goldwater in '64. Not too many people admitted to this choice back in those days.

Only sixteen years old, I picked up the house phone and called the Republican county commissioner's campaign to volunteer. The GOP candidate, Kenneth Robinson, faced a popular Democrat for our local congressional district. The Democrat, Miles Lawrence, had won in 1974 after the political disaster of Watergate and Richard Nixon's resignation, a terrible year for Republicans nationwide.

Watergate reminds me of a photograph Annie kept as a memento, I suppose realizing there might be a political career in my future and maybe I'd want this for posterity's sake. Nixon had resigned in August of '74 and I cried like I had lost my beloved dog. Ten years old and what am I distraught about but "Tricky Dick's" departure?!

My version of a security blanket—the Nixon lunchbox I proudly carried to school each day. With the Thirty-Seventh President no longer in vogue, Annie packed my lunch in a simple brown bag that first school day after his resignation. I noticed immediately. "Mom, where's my Nixon box?"

"The President's gone, Jackie. We'll get you a new lunch box, not that they'll pattern one after Gerald Ford. He's so dull and clumsy. How about something safe like Superman or Spiderman?"

Even at a young age, I didn't like change and threw a temper tantrum about the lunch box. Annie's answer to calm me down and "retire" the box with dignity: a little ceremony—captured by the photograph I found among her treasures.

We'd gathered in the attic where the Nixon box would rest along with lots of dust and moths. Dressed in a makeshift military uniform, Carol had a large kitchen pot on her head that doubled as a helmet with my old air rifle serving as her side arm. I wore a green shirt, pants, and black Converse sneakers—my outfit for when we played "Army" in the neighborhood.

Annie opened the formalities by reciting a scripture, "Then He said to them, 'Render therefore to Caesar the things that are Caesar's, and to God the things that are God's.'" (*Modern English Version*, Matt. 22.21). Even during a fantasy event she'd organized on an impromptu basis, Mom managed to work Christianity into the mix. On cue from her, I played "Taps" on my little kazoo—at least something close to that military tune. Annie tossed the lunch box into an old trunk and we officially moved to the Gerald Ford era. But back to the 1980 campaign.

Despite the GOP machine mounting vigorous contests each cycle, Lawrence appeared on the ballot for his fourth term in Congress. He and his staff excelled at constituent work, which allowed him to cast votes not always in sync with the conservative views of his constituents. Deeds like aiding with passports, assisting veterans with their care, and arranging tours to the U.S. Capitol and White House had built up a reservoir of good will and voters gave him a break from liberal votes they didn't agree with.

With all my political wisdom as a fresh-faced teenager, I was sure 1980 would be different. Reagan had the party and country galvanized after the debacle of the Jimmy Carter years. Mom saved another keepsake; this time a copy of a letter I penned to Carter in '77 at the ripe age of thirteen, imploring the President not to give back the Panama Canal. In my mind, built with American treasure, ingenuity, and the blood of many men who labored and died, the canal stood as a symbol of American greatness.

The campaign seemed glad to have a youngster to do the grunt work that young aides do. For the first trip to the office, I carefully shaved, showered, and put on my only jacket and tie. The trusty Chevy Malibu, my chariot again to a new world—the county seat of Norristown. Whatever task needed to be done, I did it, drawing attention from the candidate and his inner circle.

One night, Robinson's top aide pulled me aside. "Jack, would you like to go to a party get-out-the-vote rally?" he asked. "The headliner is Ronald Reagan."

"Are you kidding? He's my hero. I'd love to go." Now I needed to muster the courage to ask Big Joe for money to buy a new three-piece suit and red tie so that I would be dressed right to listen to the GOP presidential nominee.

In a rapturous state, Reagan, like my father, seemed larger than life. If political heaven exists, I found myself in it. Tall, handsome, confident, kind, and dignified, the governor articulated his formula for getting the country and economy back on track, while confronting the growing Soviet menace, emphasizing free market principles, limited government, and a strong national defense, music to my young conservative ears.

In that instant, at that rally, it was just "The Gipper" and me. I remember the appeal to my heart, stirring a profound passion for America when he said: "Freedom is never more than one generation away from extinction. We didn't pass it to our children in the bloodstream. It must be fought for, protected, and handed on for them to do the same."

Ronald Reagan had unbounded optimism about the future of the United States. For him, America's best days lie ahead. Not behind us. He awakened the "better angels of our nature" as the Republican Party's first President wrote in his 1861 Inaugural Address. Even more energized after that rally—pushed forward by Reagan's words and deeds—I went door-to-door with my candidate, stuffing envelopes, and putting up yard signs. The start of many political campaigns that would follow throughout my adult life.

Election Day came. I spent thirteen hours driving around with Commissioner Robinson and one of his staff as we visited polls to greet voters and election volunteers. Around noon, the commissioner and congressman bumped into each other at a polling place in the district.

Congressman Lawrence had a button on, taunting the GOP for the three earlier times he beat the machine. It read "THE FOURTH MIRACLE." Like waving a red flag in front of a bull, the button enraged me. I got close to Lawrence and said, "You're going down today. Enjoy the rest of your term."

The congressman, too stunned to say anything back to this mouthy teenager, shuffled away. The commissioner's staffer taught me a lesson about political etiquette and manners. "You just embarrassed Commissioner Robinson. If you want to continue in politics, choose your words more wisely. Whether you like him or not, our opponent is a United States congressman. Now cool it."

Despite Reagan's landslide, the commissioner lost. But I caught the political bug and informed the two public school teachers who had inspired me (Hahn and Norman) that I wouldn't be studying accounting in college but instead political science and politics with plans to go to either Washington, D.C. or Harrisburg thereafter. One of the thousands of kids with the same dream because of Ronald Reagan's inspiration. Much as Jack Kennedy captivated the youth of the sixties, Ronald Reagan did the same for many in my generation in the early eighties.

NINE

*What's Wrong with You, Emma Captivates Main
Line Cocktail Party, Shut up and Listen Joe*

MONTGOMERY COUNTY COMMISSIONER Kenneth Robinson
hadn't forgotten about my interest in politics and wanted to meet
in his office at the county courthouse. I pulled out that same three-
piece suit and conservative red tie, looking forward to seeing him in his
inner sanctum.

Outside the commissioner's office sat his trusted assistant Mickey,
who'd been kind to me during the campaign. While we waited, she asked
about my interest in politics. "You're in high school. When I grew up,
teenagers weren't conservative. We were liberal and mad as hell because
of the Vietnam War. What's wrong with you, why aren't you hanging out
with kids your age, why aren't you raging against government injustice or
pushing for changes to the drinking age?" she asked all this with a smile
but with validity since I was such an oddity.

In retrospect, I was so serious sitting in that richly appointed office
with a suit, tie, and the comforting crew cut. I spewed out my beliefs in
Ronald Reagan and the conservative policies he'd be putting into effect
in 1981 and didn't mention sports or hobbies, going right into political

mode, even babbling something about twenty-one being an acceptable age for alcohol consumption. Mickey must've thought I was a big nerd. Guilty as charged.

Mickey ushered me into the commissioner's office. Warmly greeting each other, Robinson asked to see me to do something novel by appointing me to sit on a county advisory council for public transportation. I used two kinds of travel then: walking or riding in the old Chevy. For sure, I knew squat about commuter rails or buses. That didn't deter me from saying, "Absolutely, I want the appointment." In public service at age seventeen! Running down the courthouse stairs, I shouted out, "I'm on my way," as I waved in my hand the official appointment papers the commissioner had given me when we took a photo for his newsletter.

As the only high school student involved in this way, I attended all the meetings. In business attire to make sure I blended in, I asked many questions and interacted with the men and women of this council. They were amazed at the confidence of this young man—who carried himself as someone much older. With little knowledge of public transportation, I took rides and copious notes about what I saw as positives and negatives and reported these observations back to those in charge.

My high school buddies ribbed me that I was missing out on the parties and fun. But I didn't care. The future and the political pathway that hopefully lay before me—that's what I focused on. And an inner voice reminded, demanded, *You must succeed despite what Annie and Joe did to the family.* That same voice echoed around in my head that I had been a runt and sissy as a younger boy; still fighting to show others, especially Big Joe, that I'd left that part of me behind.

The commissioner continued his political activities, thinking he might want to make another run for Congress in '82. Commissioner Robinson gave me a complimentary invitation to a cocktail party a wealthy friend of his planned to raise big dollars, so Robinson's war chest would be full if he plunged in again.

Emma heard about the invite and asked if she could go with me to the party. There I was a seventeen-year-old. On my arm, my twenty-two-year-old gorgeous sister who wore a tea-length dress, her blond hair piled high, wearing antique earrings and heels Annie provided for the occasion, adding to Emma's natural height of almost six feet.

Fortunately, I had the presence of mind to ask my older brother William for use of his classic, forest-green British convertible to travel to the fundraiser after he gave me a few lessons on a manual transmission. With the top up since Emma didn't want her hair disturbed, the two of us pulled into a large circular drive for this mansion on the Main Line of Philadelphia.

Intimidated, I gazed up at one of the largest homes I'd ever seen. Not Emma. Before I made it around to open her door, she headed towards the manor to make her appearance known. A valet accepted the car keys. In my most important voice, I said, "Listen, be very careful with the car. Here's a fin for your troubles." As an employee, he couldn't tell me what he really thought about this cheesy line and this cheesy kid.

A butler—someone later called him "Seymour"—opened the mammoth walnut door. Dressed in traditional black garb, Seymour greeted us rather haughtily, asking for our names as he gave me a look; I'm sure thinking to himself—*This kid doesn't belong here.*

"Jack Curran, guest of Commissioner Robinson," I said, putting my hand out aggressively, sensing this man thought we were not of the right class. Even at that age, I had a good ability to read people and their non-verbal cues.

"Let me check the list, sir." Seymour dropped the "sir" in a lower voice. His distaste was evident. Nor did he bother returning the courtesy of a handshake. "Yes, I've found your name, please follow me." Close on Seymour's small heels, Emma prepared to make a grand entrance by checking her makeup in a hallway mirror. I was in awe of my big sister and glad she towered over the snobby little servant, who only reached up to Emma's shoulders.

Once in the huge room, where over one hundred people mingled about, I whistled and muttered, "Look at this, Em." Both impressed and revolted by the ostentatious display of enormous wealth, I recalled the host was a trial lawyer.

From ambulance chasing, he graduated to a couple of big product liability cases that earned millions of dollars in fees and a steady stream of business after that. I'm sure he put the ladder manufacturer and all the retailers that carried the "defective" item out of business. Hundreds of jobs gone—with a forty percent fee for this attorney's troubles—perhaps because some dumb oaf over 375 pounds stood on the top step and took out himself and maybe his wife (struggling to hold the ladder below) when his considerable weight shifted and down he went.

Across the room, I spotted the host with Commissioner Robinson. He wore a toupee—noticeable from fifty feet. *With all his riches, why doesn't this lawyer have a better rug covering his head?* I wondered. The counselor's taste centered on a Louis XIV motif dominated by gold-gilded mirrors, daintily carved chairs not for sitting, oil paintings that were of French or Italian landscapes, statuary made from various materials, luxurious silk draperies that could've graced Buckingham Palace or the Vatican, and a floor-to-ceiling marble fireplace with menacing lions on each side.

For a moment, I envisioned these felines morphing into the owner of this monstrosity and one of his partners, growling at each other, as they reviewed pending work. *Not that slip-and-fall case. The other one against the big drug company. That's where the money is. Imagine the cable ads we can run.* Beady-eyed and ready for the next killer jury decision, I blinked my eyes several times to lose the vision, and mumbled, "You read too many novels, Curran."

A white baby grand piano sat in the corner of the space. Dressed in all white—the intent obvious that the piano player blend with the instrument to make a seamless transition—the pianist played soft music to allow the guests to chat with ease. With the flair for the dramatic, Emma walked through the room and leaned against the musical instrument as if she planned on reading a part for a movie and expected Humphrey Bogart or Cary Grant to light the cigarette taken out of her clutch purse.

Emma knew her beauty, height, and the ruby-red dress she modeled would command attention, particularly against a white backdrop. The sashay worked as planned. After all, Annie had raised her. And Mom was the queen of corporate functions.

All eyes turned towards Emma. No man there could avoid being drawn into her presence, and every woman seethed at the glamour and allure she projected. Emma disappeared among a circle of admirers and left me to make small talk and appear older than the high school kid I was.

Later, I'd tired of all these wealthy people, asking the same questions of why I was present, how did I know the commissioner, where was I planning to go to college? "Penn with Villanova your fallback we hope," the repeated add on. My insides wanted to shout out, "Higher education will be in the school of Big Joe's hard knocks and nothing else!"

My sister had to be dragged out of the party. "I've had enough, Em. The food's not that good, and there are lots of phony baloneys here. Should've decked the server when he asked whether I wanted a 'Roy Rogers' or not. To be a smart-ass, I ordered a scotch neat. 'Bartender Douche' shook his head after I didn't produce identification." I said all this while grabbing her arm.

"Three men asked me out, Jack, including one guy who wants to go on a cruise and set me up in an apartment in Center City Philadelphia near his law firm. Can you believe it? Of course I said no, but how fun to be ogled over. How come you're not having a blast? Joe and William are so right; you are boring." Emma gushed all this out.

Not impressed, I said, "I'm sure you enjoyed being pawed by these guys, sis. Let's get out of here. These people are incredibly annoying. And, no, this isn't that special. Commissioner Robinson saw me here. I'm done with this museum called a home." I ignored the dig about my personality as if my brothers were something to be emulated.

This cocktail party wouldn't be the last time I suffered through a fundraiser nor the final moment when I'd feel challenged on fitting in. The Curran family was comfortable but certainly not wealthy by any means. Throughout my career, I'd be forced to deal with rich people, who liked flaunting their money, expecting the political system to kowtow to their whims because they were big-dollar givers.

As Carolyn and my friends applied to higher education, going to college was deep in my heart. No one in the family had done so back at least five generations to my great-great-grandfather, Joseph. If I hoped to maintain any sanity, I had to leave Abington and Joe and Annie and the family drama with it.

Big Joe wouldn't commit to helping pay for higher education, however, or even allow me to go. Dad had always made it clear to his kids that college was a waste of time. He wanted me to work in the family business after high school—as Junior and William did. The world of antiques wasn't a mystery after ten years and I wanted nothing to do with dirty old stuff or Big Joe's furniture truck. What I'd give now, however, to have another day to ride around with him, to talk to Dad again about the challenges I've faced, to share in the quiet satisfaction he received from a hard day's work.

One night, Mom came over to the house. She knew by this time Big Joe was probably at his usual bar, Beatty's Roast Beef and Beer. I poured my troubles out to Mom and shared my dreams about going to school and getting involved in politics even though she'd heard these goals before. Very proud of me, she was upset I struggled in this manner because Big Joe's stubbornness stood in my way.

Annie hadn't talked with Joe in months. They avoided each other with the divorce just about finished. The last time Mom had been over, she went into the attic and discovered Dad had tossed her wedding dress and their photo album. He wanted no reminders in the house of her or their marriage. Mom did something very uncharacteristic, worried because I was distraught. Annie picked up the phone and called Beatty's to have Big Joe paged.

Joe sat at the bar stool reserved for his use and came to the bar phone after the bartender yelled out, "Joe, there's a lady on for you. No, I don't know who it is. Not your secretary, big guy."

"Don't be an asshole, Sean. I'm a good tipper in this joint. Hello, who's this?"

"Joe, it's Annie. Jack and I are at the house."

"What the hell do you want, Annie? I already gave an arm, leg, and both testicles in the divorce, more than that piss doctor gave you. Can't a man be left alone to drink?"

Annie launched. "Shut up and listen, Joe. Jack's going to college and we'll both support him as best we can. Working in the business isn't part of his plan. Now swallow your hatred and do the right thing for Jack. Remember your dreams at his age? I do. No one dared stand in your way." Annie said this with a ferocity I'd never seen, shocking both Dad and me. Big Joe felt like he no longer knew this woman he'd courted over thirty years before.

Joe uttered in a low voice, "Jack can go to college but shouldn't expect any help in paying for it. I don't have the money. He'll have to figure it out himself." Dad not only didn't believe in higher education but had raised his brood to be financially independent, just like his parents raised him. And their parents before them and so on.

"There's cash stashed away, hidden from me in the divorce, you're too smart not to. At least you're letting Jack go from the business. Bye, Joe." Dropping the phone back down on its cradle, Annie turned to me. "You won't have any further problems with your father. Get going with what you need to do. I'm not sure how I can help other than providing spending money. Have the peace to attend college, my son." I hugged Mom, crying with relief and joy.

I continued to struggle to forgive Annie for the affair and walking out. Intellectually, I knew she'd been a drowning woman because of Joe's bad habits and workaholic drive. But my sense of morality and responsibility just couldn't let go of what she'd done. For me—both now and back then—marriage is something you stick with, no matter what, especially if kids are involved. While mine isn't perfect (because of my many faults), God blessed me with a kind and loving woman who shares my values of faith, country, family, hard work, thriftiness, modesty, and honesty.

Without taking out substantial student loans backed by the government, I couldn't have gone to college. After this episode, I decided to join the Army Reserve to serve my country, generate more funds, and to please Big Joe since he, too, had served. I starved for his attention and approval.

TEN

Army Boot Camp, The Cookie Monster

CAROLYN AND I GRADUATED from high school in the spring of 1982, both of us with plans to go to higher education. I chose Ford College in the western part of the state, a small, affordable school with the added benefit of being almost five hours from home, the two most important factors in my decision. Carolyn had her sights set on staying closer to the Gianellas and picked West Chester State College (now a university). Through those four years we dated on-and-off. But getting through school first was the priority. Even when dating other women, Carolyn's picture remained on my dorm-room desk, a symbol of how she stole my heart in high school.

The day after my eighteenth birthday, I signed the six-year enlistment to join the Army Reserve and shipped out to Fort Jackson, South Carolina for boot camp and nine weeks of intensive indoctrination the summer before college. As trainees, we lived in an open barracks; bunk beds neatly lined up and across from each other, fifty of us to each building. Survival depended on teamwork, a lesson learned early as we faced the Army's singular goal: to break down our civilian core and remake us into soldiers all within a matter of one summer.

Physical training, or PT, at 0415 each day set the right tone for this test of our character. Although that first morning of rolling out of the bunk with five minutes to "shit, shower and shave," as our drill sergeant so crudely put it, shocked us trainees from our slumber. The PT uniform consisted of gray shorts, brown tee-shirt, a jock, white crew socks, and cheap sneakers. After PT, we wore forest-brown camouflage Battle Dress Uniforms, the brown tee-shirt again, brown boxer shorts, and green wool socks (coarse to the touch and usually soaked with sweat). Black combat boots were the default footwear. Until broken in, we had sores on our feet and ankles.

At the end of each day, all the guys huddled around to shine those boots, talk about mail from home, or how training had been that day. I love to sing so the tunes we learned rolled off my tongue; the other men followed my lead and deep bass voice, a time when our drill sergeant would leave us alone to spit shine without being hassled.

Carolyn faithfully wrote me several times a week and would sign her name with a heart symbol and a smooch from her red lipstick. A dab of subtle perfume wafted up as soon as I opened the envelope. The smell made me homesick and the other word starting with a "H" and ending with a "Y." The reader can fill in the blanks.

Meals were about three or four minutes each with little time other than to wolf down the gruel the cooks had prepared that day. There were grits—lots of them—with a hard pad of butter that would only melt if you took a blowtorch to it. Like a weathered old dog turd, the "sausage" needed to be mixed in thoroughly with the pancakes or French toast to form a food pyramid. Not on the approved USDA diet by the way. Despite their different shapes, these flour concoctions felt like pressed board against the teeth and tongue—washed down with ample swigs of imitation syrup so it slid down your throat to avoid laceration.

Lunch and dinner weren't an improvement. Cow patties, some sort of potato served out of large industrial cans, and either peas or carrots, the fare provided for our voluntary servitude. Due to heat and humidity that never quit, the pint of chilled milk provided at each meal went down like we were Bedouins, taking our first drink after crossing the Arabian Peninsula. Woe to anyone who asked for something not dumped onto your tray as we shuffled through the chow line. The reply remained consistent: "This ain't a Howard Johnson's, Private. Move along and be grateful Uncle Sam is feeding you this slop." Even the cooks couldn't deny how bad the food was.

We marched a lot, shouting out cadences not always politically correct since the genders stayed segregated at that time. I loved every minute of it: the camaraderie, discipline, training, and ideal I was part of something much larger than myself. Only three weeks until I'd be standing at parade rest on the graduation grounds with the platoon and our drill sergeant—we counted down the days. But something happened that almost gave me a ticket home before that big day.

Assigned to "fireguard" one night with another soldier, I had pulled the duty to watch over the hastily renovated barracks. Constructed of all wood, the buildings would burn down within minutes if they caught fire. Reconstructed because of the Reagan defense build-up of the early eighties, how cool that my hero Ronald Reagan, was my commander-in-chief! The President ran on a platform of achieving peace through strength so that the Soviets would recognize America led the Free World again, defending freedom, ready to challenge the expansion of communism before Reagan won the Cold War.

Charlie (C) Company was headquartered high on "Tank Hill" where thousands of soldiers had been prepared earlier in the century for the fight against the Nazis and Japanese. A large water tank marked "Fort Jackson" stood as a majestic and tall symbol for the thousands of men and women who'd lived on that steep hill comprising nothing but small roads, barracks, pine trees, and sand. Lots of it.

Somewhere along the way, the Pentagon decided Tank Hill could be mothballed until President Reagan ramped up the military. We were the first company through those old barracks probably since Vietnam, housing another generation of Americans ready to confront a new threat to freedom and democracy. How do I know this? The toilets didn't work, and the light bulbs blinked on-and-off, forcing contractors to come back to try to fix problems from sixty-year-old buildings loaded with knob-and-tube wiring, old-style fuses, and rusted out pipes.

"Tinderbox" is too subtle a way to put how quickly our barracks would've burned in a fire. While men slept, two people in each building of C Company needed to be on watch to guard against such an occurrence. One of us sat at the top of the second floor stairs—the other at the entranceway to the barracks itself to make communication easy. To break up the monotony, I wrote this letter to my father, who had done Basic Training thirty-five years before me in Fort Indiantown Gap, Pennsylvania. In what can only be called chicken scratch at best, compared to Big Joe's distinctive cursive writing that no doubt won him awards in his Philly elementary school, I began describing my military journey.

Dear Pop, Well it's 2:00 in the morning at good ole Fort Jackson. I can see out the window the water tank all lit up (I suppose the lights are to warn off low-flying planes?). About the only landmark around here to speak of and the reason we call this place "Tank Hill." Probably wondering why I'm writing before the crack of dawn, right? I'm on fireguard, remember how shitty a duty that is (I'm sure back in the day you had the same thing!)? The silence is deafening, broken up by guys farting and wrestling with their bunk mattresses, I guess because of nightmares. You wouldn't believe the conversations they have in their sleep—some shouldn't be repeated! The snoring and chirp, chirp, chirp of the crickets never stop, and occasionally someone stumbles by me to take a piss. At least I'm not on KP (Kitchen Patrol, the guys who clean up after the cooks). What a lousy job that is. Those guys need to be up soon to start their shifts, so I'll rouse them by kicking their bunks. Supposedly, the grease pit needs to be cleaned out. I hope to avoid that stinky duty. Whenever someone falls out of line, that's one of the threats by the drill sergeants, "The pit needs to be emptied." Maybe there isn't such a thing, but it sure smells like it near the mess hall where they serve our so-called "chow." Today, we marched over to the tear gas chamber. Really nothing more than a tin shack where they pipe that stuff in. We walked in with our gas masks on and then the drill sergeant ordered us to take the mask off (he left his on!). Tough way to learn the thing works, huh?! My eyes burned, and I hacked up a lung or two and raced for the door to get the hell out once they gave us the signal we could leave. Earlier in the week, we threw a live grenade, and I worried that my shitty arm wouldn't clear the wall and you and Mom would be burying me (joke). I'm getting good at the rifle range since we do that just about every day (no joke). There's also some mean cadences probably handed down through the generations (maybe you can remember them for your next letter). A few guys are having a hard time and can't seem to adjust to keeping their bunk and locker squared away. Not me, thanks to the rule you imposed—keep your room clean! Time to go, Pop. The other guy on fireguard is hollering he found something, not sure what that means, but he's annoying me. Real bossy German type, by the way. Love you much, your son, Jack. P.S. Next week is bivouac. I won't be writing you from the woods. P.S.S. Don't tell anyone in the family, especially Mom if you run into her, but the last time in the field, I tripped and fell into a mound of South Carolina red fire ants that didn't appreciate having their home disturbed by a big lug like me. Huge welts all over my arms. Just a badge of honor to be worn down here, at least that's how the medic treated it when he cleaned me up and gave me some industrial-looking salve to put on.

"What do ya want, Schmidt?" I asked my buddy of German heritage, who could have been the prototype of Hitler's Aryan race: tall, blond, blue-eyed with a clear complexion. Unabashedly jealous of him, it looked like a zit had never blemished that perfect face. He had peach fuzz and didn't shave every day, something the rest of us had to do religiously—the five o'clock shadow a sure giveaway to the instructors that a blade hadn't touched skin in twenty-four hours. "I'm writing a letter to my father."

"You gotta come down here, Jack. I'm trying to save you some," he said.

"Save me what? I'm not supposed to leave the floor. What's so important?"

"Blow me already, Curran. Just get down here and quit asking questions like you're a trained CIA interrogator."

Schmidt was in the office our drill sergeant used on the ground floor. Sergeant First Class Manuel Ortiz was a man of shorter height but muscled and sturdy. Tattoos covered the biceps of each of his ripped arms. A clipped black mustache added to his tough persona that conveyed the message: "Don't mess with me." And, of course, he had the wide-brimmed hat reserved for the Army's drill sergeants. Like the other men in my platoon, I feared him. His word was law. He never had to repeat himself.

When I entered the office, I spied Schmidt in the top drawer of our sergeant's desk. "Look what I found," he said, in between munching on a large pack of Oreo cookies. For six weeks, we had gone without snacks or sweets. Once I saw my friend chowing down on those cookies, I lost all self-restraint and grabbed a handful. Between the two of us, we put that entire package away. Satisfied, sitting on the floor of our drill sergeant's office like pigs finished at the trough—with loud burps to prove it—we realized we had taken and eaten his cookies. But there wasn't a Wawa available down the street to buy a replacement package.

"Shit, what're we going to do? Why the hell did you go into his drawer in the first place?" I asked my buddy as if my hands were clean in the theft, panic setting in at once. In such times, my breathing becomes labored. I grabbed for my inhaler that never left my body.

Private Schmidt, my comrade in stupidity, wasn't taking the fall alone. "You jumped right in, Curran, eating faster than me and now you need your puffer. What the fuck? Hopefully, he doesn't even notice his food is gone. Watch the barracks for a couple of minutes, and I'll go hide the package under one of the abandoned buildings close by." While our company's barracks had been renovated, many unused billets stood nearby; perfect for us to conceal the evidence of our dastardly crime.

How could I be so stupid? Sergeant Ortiz would go into his desk and know someone took his cookies. We'd be charged with a crime and kicked out of the Army. The only thing we could do—wait, hope, and pray the hammer wouldn't fall. Down it came on top of our heads that next morning.

After breakfast, before we marched out to that day's training, Ortiz ordered the entire platoon into formation. This was it. Scenarios of doom and punishment rolled around in my head.

"I wanted an Oreo cookie because my stomach growled with hunger. Unlike you unworthy dirt bags, I don't always get three meals a day. The whole package of cookies is missing and now I'm hungry...and pissed off. Who went into my office, into my desk, and stole my cookies? If the culprit doesn't step forward, I'm punishing you all. Rise and fall together, right? So, what's it going to be? Is someone man enough to step out?" Sergeant First Class Ortiz asked in a long Southern drawl, dragging out the syllables and words, which only made the pit in my belly grow larger and larger. I felt like hurling the sausage turds and those left over decadent delights—black-and-white icing saucers that no person can resist—that were making their way through my digestive tract.

Big Joe and Annie raised us to accept the consequences for when we'd done wrong. And my conscience burned. I couldn't allow my comrades to be blamed. Without looking over to the instigator of this mess,

Herr Schmidt, I stepped out of formation, barking out, "This private stole your cookies, Drill Sergeant." My so-called friend didn't step out. I alone stood there—a proud Scots-Irishman versus the cowardice of the representative of the German people.

"Private Curran, you're in for a lot of pain. The rest of you fall out until I'm finished with this 'cookie monster' here." The platoon quickly dispersed—relieved they weren't part of this escapade. I spied my fellow thief, Schmidt, entering the barracks; his head down. *You pimple-less, shave-less coward. My ancestor fought the Spanish for America while yours goose-stepped for the Kaiser,* I said to myself. "I will not turn you in, Curran. You've been a good soldier. The incredible brain fart you had could ruin your military career if I pursued charges."

Relief flooded over me. But I wasn't in the clear yet and didn't dare peer into his eyes, remaining at attention, looking straight ahead, trying to keep my shaking hands steady and my wobbly knees from clicking. I clenched my buttocks together to make sure the cursed cookies didn't unwillingly appear.

Ortiz continued, "You will pull KP every morning until graduation and will be my permanent road guard, too. You can also knock out an extra fifty push-ups every day until graduation. Consider yourself lucky this is all I'm doing to you, cookie monster," he said this with the slightest grin. While angry, he probably thought it was kind of funny I'd taken his snack and had stepped out so quickly. I'd done nothing wrong up to this point so he also was no doubt shocked.

A few guys had been in trouble, not this soldier. One of the men had even been sentenced by a judge to boot camp. Either join the Army or go to jail, the stark choice this kid faced. He ended up discharged and sent home after two weeks of training, unable to adjust to military life. With the scuttlebutt coming back that the judge sent him away to the state penitentiary.

I would gladly do KP—although I hoped the pit didn't need scrubbing—I did enough of that on Big Joe's "antiques." And be the "road guard," who wears the vest running ahead of our marching formation to stop traffic at each intersection we passed through. After all, I had to work off those wicked Oreos. "Thank you, Drill Sergeant. This private apologizes for taking your property," I said, keeping it short and simple. Saying anything more might cause him to change his mind. As a would-be politician, brevity suited this audience.

"After your push-ups, cookie monster, fall out and stay out of my sight." That name stuck until graduation. Each time he said it, the smile got a little bigger. When I look back on all the idiotic things I'd done in my life, this one ranked up there towards the top. Because of my craving for sugar, I almost got booted out of the military. Imagine what a dishonorable discharge would've done to my plans to enter politics?! That dream never far from my thoughts, even during tough Army training.

South Carolina in mid-August, our graduation time, was unbearably hot and humid. Even after eating all those cookies, I lost fifteen pounds, bringing my weight down to 145. Lean, muscled, and ready to fight, I was proud to see Big Joe in the crowd. Dad and Mom patched up their differences long enough to make the trip together and brought along Carolyn and Carol. After the ceremony, Dad patted me on the shoulder and said, "Son, I'm proud of you, and my grandfather would be proud, too."

With a lump in my throat and misty-eyed, I got out, "Hooah, Pop." Praise from Big Joe happened so little. I began to feel like I was redeeming myself from the bookworm and bedwetter who had embarrassed his father. And the mention of Corporal Jack Hudson, a Spanish-American War hero, made my enlistment and the arduous training worth every minute.

Later, while reading *Time* magazine in the fall of 1984, I saw one of my Basic Training buddies on the cover as part of Time's coverage of the Grenada military operation that freed American students and stopped

Cuban intervention. After camp, he'd gone on to infantry school at Fort Benning, Georgia; then called to duty in that small Caribbean island. Proud of him, our commander-in-chief, and the country I served, America roared back from the destructiveness of Vietnam and the Carter years.

ELEVEN

Go West Young Man, All Alone,
Curran is a Stooge

A SMALL, FRIENDLY COLLEGE, Ford emphasized that its professors and administrators interact closely with students. On a former golf course, it was an idyllic setting for learning. A tiny creek—bordered by many willow trees that seemed to whisper, "It's safe and peaceful here"— meandered through the campus. Its rolling hills had the greenest, the lushest grass I'd ever seen. With perfectly manicured boxwood hedges, and several misting fountains placed at strategic locations throughout the grounds, students had plenty of places to study and congregate together, or just to lay out in the sun or throw a football around. A colorful postcard I received in the mail, capturing this tranquil scene, caught my eye when searching for where I hoped to attend.

An "upgraded vehicle," a 1973 Mercury Capri faded lime green with rust spots all over it, served as new transportation for the trip to Ford. A bad clutch made it difficult to shift gears. At the top of my lungs, I yelled out, "Go West, young man, and grow up with the country," famous advice from Horace Greeley in the 1800s that worked for this young man in the

1980s. With little to my name except the absolute determination to succeed, escape from Abington was the theme that day.

Before my early morning departure, I searched around for an eight-
track tape and popped in my favorite Bruce Springsteen album. The volume cranked up so high the Merc's windows rattled while I sang along to
lyrics that seemed like they were written from one Jersey boy to another.
They touched my heart as I harmonized and experienced feelings of freedom and liberation. I couldn't have been happier to be away from chaos as
I headed towards my future via the Pennsylvania Turnpike, shouting out,
"Bye-bye to the Currans and hello Ford."

When I arrived on campus and found the freshmen dorm, I realized I
was alone. Other students bustled about with their parents and siblings.
Busy unloading their vehicles or decorating their rooms, the sound of
laughter and pride filled the air, the landmark of making it to higher education a family triumph to be celebrated, not scorned. *You're an orphan,
Jack. Get over it and stop the pity party. Deal with the reality,* I thought to
nudge myself along. Hyperactivity would be the tonic for shaking off
the intense sadness and isolation experienced during those first few
hours at Ford.

The college employed resident staff and our floor assistant told his
charges to call him "Killer." For a dorm that housed two hundred boys
on their own for the first time with complete freedom, Ford had chosen
its people well to keep us collectively from destroying the place and each
other. Perhaps Killer, as an African-American man who bench-pressed
a cool 225, understood loneliness. He saw me juggling boxes, shuffling
along the hallway with shoulders slouched. Without a word, he helped
me move in. Later that day, he invited me to dinner in the cafeteria, while
most of Killer's other freshmen dined with their parents and family. When
it seemed like Jack Curran faced the world alone, I will never forget his
kindness.

With no hesitation or doubt, I enrolled in political science and dove right into campus life. A bulletin board in the dorm announced that freshmen student senate elections would be held in a few weeks. I snatched a petition and approached the election with all I'd learned in the failed congressional race, including touching the voters, in this case Ford's freshmen students by knocking on every dorm door at Ford with the goal of meeting as many newbies as possible.

Thirteen candidates ran that year, and I polled sixty-seven percent of the ballots cast; the others split the remaining thirty-three percent. One of the other candidates, a young man from Sharon, Pennsylvania, Robert Placid, also enrolled in political science. He won the election, too. But didn't put in nearly the effort I had, later telling me he'd laughed at this somber young man, who seemed like he had a "stick up his ass," working way too hard for a student government position. We formed a lifelong friendship from this first encounter.

Through student government, I drew the attention of Dr. William Moran, Ford's president. Moran and the Board of Trustees held a forum each year for us to air grievances, real or imagined. With my big victory, the upperclassmen asked me to make the presentation. That same three-piece suit still fit, and I put it on and prepared charts and handouts for the changes we wanted. I recall "important" things like expanded visitation hours between the gender-segregated dorms and a remodeling of the pub where many students congregated.

One of the most impactful relationships of my young life began. Dr. Moran and I met often, including with my election to president of the student government the end of my sophomore year. Unheard of at Ford, the post was usually reserved for an incoming senior. Moran's door remained open to students, and I marveled that he seemed to be everywhere on campus, club and sports events, art exhibits, musical affairs, and simply holding court in the cafeteria where he sampled the same food his students ate.

Rob and I became involved in the Greek system, pledging together. He convinced me I needed to lighten up and let the little hair I had down, the crew cut now even tighter because of the Army. One day as young brothers, we picked up the kegs for the fraternity house party that Thursday night. College security didn't bother with these parties (so popular on campus) if the noise stayed at a low roar. After loading the beer in my car, I told Rob we had to swing by the student government office to handle a "pressing" matter, something Rob pushed back against.

"There's nothing there that can't wait. We joined the fraternity to relax a bit. Let it go until tomorrow," Rob urged.

"Five minutes only," I said as we pulled into the parking spot by the student union building that housed the office. As Placid waited, four large kegs sat in the back seat and hatchback of the car. College security passed by and spotted the beer. I should've just put a sign on the car "I HAVE ILLEGAL BEER" since our guards weren't the brightest bulbs in any chandelier!

Both of us got written up for having alcohol on campus, a serious violation, since it was technically prohibited. Brazen for having the beer in plain view, we deserved the citation. Or more accurately, I invited the punishment since Rob wanted to drive right to the house. The one security guard enjoyed being a rival of mine, and I couldn't stomach his look of sheer delight at nailing the student government president for a major infraction.

The next day, I went to see Dr. Moran to talk about an agenda item and entered his office with a short wave and, "Hi there." Nothing occurred on campus without his knowledge and watchful eye. One of Moran's routines included a perusal of the security reports each morning to keep his finger on a significant pulse of college life.

His scalding response: "Don't 'hi there' me, Jack Curran. I read last night's report. What you and Rob Placid did in such disregard of our rules is outrageous." Moran was angry and had every right to be. I'd been arrogant to pull this stunt while serving as the student government leader. He continued, "You're in an important position. You will apologize to your peers at the next student government meeting. You also will attend the next Faculty Senate meeting to apologize to the faculty and administration. Last, you will write an open letter for publication in the student newspaper to say you're sorry to your fellow students. None of this is subject to debate."

The shame profound and palpable, I accepted this admonishment with, "I'm so sorry, sir." A valuable lesson about setting an example while holding office had been learned. While only a student government position, I tucked this incident away, trying to conduct myself in later political positions with dignity and integrity—not always successful, I'm sad to admit. Dr. Moran didn't hold the infraction against me. As an educator, he used the transgression to shape me and my character.

In the middle of my term as president, the student newspaper installed a new editor. The new chief was radical and differed dramatically from his predecessor, a friend of mine and an ally. Overnight, student government went from positive headlines to spiteful, demeaning prose that attacked everything we did. His goal appeared to be to chop off the head of the student establishment.

Confident in my ability to win people over, I scheduled a sit down with my adversary—on his turf and terms. While we shared the same first name, Jack Weaver didn't fit the demographic of Ford. A commuter living on his own, he was much older than the rest of the student body. With tattered clothes, longer hair, and a scruffy beard, we were opposites in every way.

When I entered the newspaper's office, he pointed to a metal folding chair that faced his disorganized desk. Piles of papers towered over each other along with a tray filled with cigarette ashes, the only items on the table top. On one of those towers of disorganized sheets lay a file folder marked "Curran." An unflattering mug shot, taken during a student government meeting when I was pissed off about something, stared back at me with the note scrawled in bold letters "WEAK AND IMMATURE." He eyed me with caution as I began to try to charm him, willing myself to ignore his scribbled observations.

"Thanks for the chance to get to know one another, Jack. You're new to the paper and campus activities so I thought I'd introduce myself, talk a bit about student government, and the projects we're working on with the administration to make life better for our fellow students. Perhaps we can meet every week or every other week for these kinds of chats." Perfecting my diplomatic "Can't we all get along and play nice together" approach, I hoped to win over Weaver to bend him to my will.

Jack lit up a cigarette and took a long drag on the death stick, blowing the smoke through his nostrils with such force I thought something else might come out along with the toxic chemicals wrapped in paper. His peepers narrowing, Weaver asked me, "How old are you, Curran?"

"Listen, I'm asthmatic, put that out, please." *I'm at a disadvantage already,* I thought, as I coughed and tried to get some clean air down into my lungs. The man disgusted me and our meeting had just begun. He stubbed the cigarette out in an exaggerated manner and waited for an answer, his chin now resting on his hand as if to telegraph complete contempt.

"I'm twenty, but what does that have to do with anything," I snapped. "I was elected earlier than anyone else has been in my position but assure you, I've earned my stripes to be student government president."

"At your age, you barely know how to wipe your ass, Curran. Ten years ago, I protested the Vietnam War, burned the American flag, and threw rocks at the cops! I know how to take a stand. Have you ever opposed the administration on anything? Name one disagreement? I bet you can't."

"I have older brothers, Jack, who did the same things. I remember the war and lived with the terrible conflict it caused between my siblings and my father. And guess what? I sided with my dad. Your style is not my style, and I've gotten a lot of shit done with more in the works. If you're looking for me to organize some ridiculous sit-in and ask the women on campus to burn their bras in protest, you got the wrong guy. We're finished here, Weaver."

As I rose from my chair, he sneered with laughter, purposely showing that I couldn't irritate him. But he did just fine poking this bear. "Thanks for coming to the office, Curran, or should I say, 'President Curran.' You're a pussy by the way."

The rage built to a crescendo as I came around Weaver's desk while maintaining constant contact through my brown burning pupils and snarled, "What did you say?"

The editor didn't flinch and maintained his gaze. "I said, 'you're a pussy.' Want me to spell it for you in case you didn't participate in the grade school spelling bee."

"Let's meet off-campus, Weaver, and we'll find out who the pussy is. Fuck off." Of average height with scrawny arms, I bet he hadn't been in a gym for years, if ever. Jack might have been the type to know the martial arts but, at that moment, I didn't care. He could *Taekwondo* my ass all he wanted. One takedown and my muscle and extra weight would settle things.

Who is this guy to challenge my credentials and leadership? I thought with an unchecked massive ego. After all, elected the top dog on campus, I worked harder than everyone else, sacrificing time, missing parties, trying to avoid romantic relationships. I had built up in my mind a self-inflated importance, and this fellow student sensed it. Or maybe he was just a jackass. Maybe both. Fists clenched, I left the office as Weaver's laugh rang in my ears.

In a foul mood already from four days of incessant rain and nasty weather that had flooded one of the college's lower parking lots—the tiny creek became a raging river—I shook off my poncho as I sat down at the president's desk. I had stopped first in the student union atrium. The latest edition of the newspaper, placed neatly in a stack in a plastic rack marked *The Ford Gazette*, screeched out "CURRAN A STOOGE OF THE ADMINISTRATION."

Dammit, why doesn't the editor have a front-page story on the damage the campus sustained from this storm? Surely that's more newsworthy than my approach to student governance. I wonder if I can collect all the stacks of papers to enforce some censorship on this out-of-control hippie. Nah, too crazy and narcissistic.

Rob's timing couldn't have been worse when he walked into the student government office, interrupting my stream of consciousness. "What's going on, Jack? Wanna grab a beer later?"

"Did you see this story in the paper? That sonofabitch." Echoes of Big Joe ripped at my conscience as I hurled across the room a paperweight Dr. Moran gave me when I became president. It smashed into little pieces and I knew I had gone too far. Rob calmly grabbed the paper and scanned the news item.

"The guy is a buffoon," he began. "Chill, Jack. Your actions speak, not this nonsense. I have people we can get to write letters to the editor. We'll attack this clown and defend you. Don't worry, we'll turn up the heat. Seriously, let it go." Right, as always, I had overreacted to the criticism. What did I expect as an elected leader, undying adulation? Or maybe I expected to be carried around on a sedan chair by the masses?

Without Rob's prompting, supportive letters poured into the paper. As I crossed campus going about my business, classmates shouted out, "Keep up the good work" and "Don't sweat it, bud." And the one I appreciated the most, "Weaver's an asshole, Jack."

In our weekly breakfast, President Moran made light of it. "I held this office during the war, Jack, and he's dead wrong. The antics Weaver took part in fail. Besides, if you're a stooge at least you're my stooge," he said this with a wink, and we both laughed.

About a month after the damning headline, I announced two projects of significance, including more commuter parking and selection of a new food service vendor for the next school year. Weaver grudgingly printed the announcement, burying it on page five of the paper below a story about the college's sewer plant achieving recertification from the state. Probably his way of equating my achievements with human shit that would continue to be safely flushed and scoured.

After my successful term and "retirement," I focused on finding internships, knowing I had few political connections and experience would be important to secure a job after graduation. President Moran talked with some professors and made some phone calls after asking me the direction I wanted to take. Two internships arose from our discussions: a Washington, D.C. program that coupled classes at Georgetown University with internship placements; and a position at the Pennsylvania State Capitol in my senior year.

TWELVE

Jack Meets Jack, Shoving Match
over Israel and Palestine

WITH THE WINDOWS DOWN and the radio blaring out a tune, I sang along, oblivious to paying attention to my directions to the nation's capital. Despite missing my exit off I-495, I was in a terrific mood. Ready for the next challenge.

Placed with a group called "Citizens for Conservative Priorities and Common Sense," an organization established to lobby for President Reagan's policies, I went to work each day at the heart of the conservative movement—in the Heritage Foundation offices. Under the tutelage of the full-time staff, I contacted the grassroots to urge them to call or write Congress on such Reagan priorities as supplying funds to the rebels fighting the communists in Angola and for the Strategic Defense Initiative (SDI), or "Star Wars" as Reagan's critics labeled it. The organization's leadership, in close touch with the White House, coordinated efforts with the administration's agenda.

Working for my hero's priorities, the first trip to the Capitol Building found its way into my diary that day. Given a stack of flyers to deliver to each congressional office—this in the days before fax machines or email—when I found Jack Kemp's office my heart beat faster. One of the founders of supply-side economics, Kemp co-authored the tax cuts that President Reagan had endorsed in his 1980 campaign to jump-start an economy reeling from high inflation and unemployment and skyrocketing interest rates.

Congressman Kemp and a visitor had just wrapped up a conversation when I walked in. Besides Reagan, Jack Kemp served as a model for what I hoped to emulate in public service. Several of his books on restoring the greatness of America sat on the Curran bookshelf, well-worn and marked with notes. The congressman articulated conservative principles but with a special outreach to minorities. Kemp asserted that through education and greater economic opportunity, the nation can lift populations that have not experienced the American Dream, a view I've always shared.

A strong policy focus remained the cities and urban decay and his record was all about compassion and addressing poverty and despair for those left behind. Did this strike a chord with me because of the experiences I had in Philadelphia during the 1970s? You bet. Later, I did my best to use the public service platform available to legislative staff to address the same priorities.

Kemp put his hand out to shake mine and asked me where I hailed from and what I was doing in Washington, D.C. For a few minutes we chatted, and my confidence grew around a man who projected an aura of leadership. Alone with one of the GOP's national leaders, I had something to share but hesitated. "Congressman, during the 1980 campaign..." I paused momentarily for the right words.

"Yes, Jack, go ahead." Kemp had this hushed, gravelly voice, well developed in the countless football huddles he led, probably used to drawing out people who might be intimidated by his presence. A handsome guy with silver hair, the legendary athletic quarterback for the Buffalo Bills filled any room with charisma. Next to him in a huddle, one could imagine how he dominated the group, inspiring teammates or colleagues onto victory, perhaps playing through injuries that took a toll on his body.

"During the Detroit convention, I sent a telegraph to Reagan," I paused again, unsure of whether he cared what this young Republican did or not.

"You followed that gathering?" Kemp inquired as if he had all the time in the world to chat with me.

"Every minute and the news coverage, too," I said. "The message to Ronald Reagan expressed disappointment he selected George Bush instead of you as his running mate." There, it was out.

"Good of you to do that, Jack. Things happen for a reason though. The President needs me here on the 'Hill' to support his agenda. Young warriors like you have to keep the faith, too." The congressman knew Reagan required critical congressional help for his policies meant to transform the country and felt comfortable enough in his own skin to serve as one of the most valuable backup quarterbacks to "The Gipper," America's first-string star.

An aide entered with a Kemp-authored book and a pen for the congressman to write an inscription that read "To my friend, Jack Curran, All the best, Jack Kemp." Cherishing this, I would keep the book in a prominent place in each of my offices in later years.

International in scope, the program had students from all over the world in residence, including young people from Europe, Asia, and the Middle East. One of my roommates came from a wealthy Lebanese family. With envy, I watched when he parked a rather garish, yellow Cadillac convertible next to my car that belonged in a junk heap.

Israel holds a special place for me as a Christian. They share American ideals of freedom and democracy and remain the only ally America can rely upon in the Middle East. The United States had intervened in Lebanon in 1984 to broker peace between warring factions while asserting American power in the face of growing Soviet influence in that region.

Akil (or "intelligent" in Arabic) lived in this area and experienced firsthand violence. He had a different perspective on Israel. With my feet up on a coffee table, reading through *National Review* while sipping on wine from a box of red kept in our refrigerator for guests, one of my favorite columnists had written a piece on the constant attacks Israel endured in the Gaza Strip and on its northern border. Akil sat down in a comfortable chair in our living room and began bantering with me. Educated at American University in Beirut, his English was flawless.

"What are you reading, Jack?" he asked, starting a conversation. I liked time alone, irritated to be away from the story. Usually, we got along well, joking back and forth.

"About Israel, Akil, and the recent rash of terrorism it has endured from the Palestinians. That Yasser Arafat's a thug and criminal." If I hadn't been annoyed, maybe I would have been more circumspect and not so blunt. Absorbed in reading, filters on proper *Miss Manner's* behavior were nowhere in sight.

"What do you know about the Middle East other than what you read in a biased opinion piece?" he heatedly asked. "The Israelis are the aggressors. They have illegally occupied lands given by the British and UN to the Zionists. The Palestinians are merely defending themselves."

"Rocket attacks and bombs that blow up innocent civilians. You call that 'defensive' in nature? I don't think so, Akil. Israel's owned that land all the way back to the Old Testament when God promised it to Abraham and the Hebrew people. After what the Nazis did to the Jews in the Holocaust, they deserve...they need a safe place. I know my history."

"Rubbish. The Palestinians are the rightful heirs, and the Holocaust didn't happen." I knew these "deniers" existed, but never up close and personal like this.

Incredulous, I replied, "Never happened? Hitler and the Nazis gassed, shot, burned, and tortured six million Jews, Akil." I emphasized each horror for effect. "Where did all those people go, besides to a horrible death? C'mon. You're better educated than that." I snorted with derision.

"How could you understand the death and destruction Ariel Sharon (Israel's Defense Minister in the early eighties) perpetuated on the Lebanese population? I saw the aftermath of the massacre they presided over with my own two eyes and you read in a magazine about the Middle East. You make me sick. American arrogance and ignorance at its worst." By now, Akil spit out his words, yelling something in Arabic that sounded like a curse. I learned later it translated into "you shit." Hovering over me, I stood up, and we were nose-to-chin since I towered over him.

"How dare you, Akil! You're in my country on a guest visa. I'll give you American arrogance." I shook my fist. All the provocation needed to start a pushing war. Surprisingly strong, Akil more than held his own.

One of our roommates entered the fray to separate us. His wise words were, "There are three more weeks together in this apartment, guys. Neither of you will solve the Middle Eastern conflict."

While the D.C. experience was rich, and I loved Georgetown, the Capitol Building, the museums and memorials, and took in everything that great city offered, I was one of thousands of young people, trying to have an impact and felt like a small fish in a vast pond. Reagan's governing philosophy, in line with the Tenth Amendment of the Constitution (widely ignored by lawmakers and the courts), centered on returning governance to the people and states, reversing years of liberalism and an "almighty" federal government that intoned it alone knew the answer to every problem. The states were, and face an uphill battle to remain, the laboratories of experimentation, emphasized repeatedly by guest speakers brought in to lecture on various subjects.

So, I set my sights next on Pennsylvania's State Capitol, the second of the internships Dr. Moran secured for me. The Commonwealth seemed a more likely place to dig in as a public servant hopeful.

THIRTEEN

Jack and Rob Storm the Capitol, What about Children, Tony Molinaro

BOUNDING UP THE GREAT CAPITOL STEPS along with Rob, it became a race on who would get to the top quicker. I won that day, but did I? The Bible tells us, "Again I saw under the sun that the race is not to the swift." (Ecc. 9.11). Our competition that day was no different. While I won the physical contest to the top of that small granite mountain, Rob became the actual victor. Still in the arena, mixing it up, doing battle for his clients, while I write the story of our journey together from the quiet of my den.

After the race, we paused to catch our breath, winded but exhilarated. Eager to begin an internship with Senator John Young, the chairman of the Senate Education Committee, President Moran knew him through their interactions over higher education public policy. Placid had an internship in the House Republican Caucus so we found a cheap apartment to share expenses the spring semester of our senior year.

The first time through the revolving door of the State Capitol, Rob and I were awestruck as we gazed up into the beautiful Rotunda. Vibrant murals adorned the ceiling, stain glass windows depicted various scenes from the Commonwealth's rich history, and gold-leaf paint covered much of the surface. Straight ahead—a majestic marble staircase, with magnificent statues on each side that held beautiful glass globe lights.

Always recognized as one of the most handsome capitol buildings in the country, this was our new home, albeit temporary. Little did we know that permanent would replace temporary. We stopped before going our separate ways and read the plaque encased in the glazed tile floor. "Here Stood, Theodore Roosevelt, President of the United States, October Fourth, 1906—The Day He Dedicated This Building."

Rob took the right hallway to report to the House, and I went in the other direction to present myself to Senator Young's office. Passing a long row of wood doors, mahogany and rich in color, I read each of the senator's nameplates, which listed their district number and the counties they represented and memorized these names. Intuitively, I knew they would be important later.

Straight ahead, I found the elevator and took it to the third floor. Even little details like carved door knobs and the elevator itself, which had the same gold-leaf paint and plexiglass sheathing to protect the art work since the lift doubled to carry cargo in between floors, impressed me. Pennsylvania had spared no expense in building the General Assembly's home to conduct the peoples' business.

Several pamphlets about the history of the Capitol's construction noted that graft and scandal swirled around the project. Some of those involved in the erection of this magnificent edifice got jail time. Another notch in the Commonwealth's long sad history of graft and scandal.

The chairman's office was easy to find and two secretaries in the outer area greeted me. Two other staffers outside the chairman's personal office said hello and pointed to a smaller intern desk in the corner of the suite where I would work. Noticing the heavy-toned walnut paneling from the 1970s, the interior of the office didn't match the grandeur of the hallways and dome. Later, the Capitol Preservation Committee supervised the restoration of each Capitol office to their original splendor. The added touch of a complete ban on smoking cheered non-smokers and protected the priceless artwork from decay and ruin.

That first day, Senator Young met with Benjamin Walker, counsel to the majority leader. The senator asked that I join the meeting. A former special education teacher, Young did not project a commanding presence. While handsome in a rough backwoods kind of way, his once straw-colored hair had turned to a chalky shade. A kindness surrounded his soft brown eyes. Unassuming and soft-spoken in manner, Young reminded me of several educators at Abington, who did their jobs quietly and didn't seek fanfare. Hailing from rural Pennsylvania as he did, Young mirrored the qualities of the constituents he represented. Known as a workhorse in the Senate, not as a showboater.

Senator Young made introductions. "Jack, meet Ben Walker. He's an important guy in the caucus and here to talk with me about education bills I'm being asked to list for committee consideration." A methodical man, the chairman cared deeply about education. I shook hands with Walker, the first of many interactions we'd have in the years to come.

Nothing short of brilliant, Walker was scrawny and chain-smoked cigarettes and drank black coffee to keep his body supercharged to serve his single client—the Senate Republican Caucus. A thatch of sandy blond hair swept across his high forehead. Inquisitive gray eyes the window to a brain that whirled like a computer. Despite Walker's dominant position in the staff hierarchy, his haphazard dress demonstrated his interest in getting the job done than in playing the part. This contrasted with other staffers who focused on appearing influential through meticulous and expensive attire, and who didn't always have the brain power to match their wardrobe.

Caught up in the wave of education reform sparked by the publication of "A Nation at Risk," the GOP administration wanted changes to public education in Pennsylvania. I had read the book in one of my political science classes, absorbing its assertions that American schools were failing. The report provoked a serious discussion on education at the local, state, and federal levels.

With only the limited experience of public education from good suburban schools, I didn't agree with the report's conclusions at the time. Once I became more familiar with the failures of public education in urban areas, I'd become a champion of choice in education to free families trapped in bad schools.

Senator Young sat in a powerful place with his appointment by the president pro tempore to be the chairman of the Senate Education Committee. In Harrisburg, chairmen alone decide a committee's agenda and what is voted and not voted. A chairman decides the order of bills and amendments to consider during a meeting, influencing the flow of discussion and vote outcomes.

Governor Walter Van Dalen—a Republican and a no-nonsense former corporate executive from the Allentown area—demanded that Chairman Young support state testing of schoolchildren, the capstone of his reform agenda. His secretary of education and legislative director pushed Young hard, too. Their boss wasn't one to take "no" for an answer and this proposal would be a sea change for Pennsylvania's public education system.

For the first time under the governor's proposal, student assessments would analyze pupil knowledge in the core areas of English and Math at certain key grades. Up to that time, Pennsylvania had a proud tradition of learning governed by locally elected school boards. Educators were given broad latitude and discretion in curriculum choice and assessments while the administration's ideas ran counter to that thread. Since then, both the federal and state governments have consistently chipped away at this autonomy.

A new Harrisburg testing scheme was unpopular with both the teachers' union, Teachers for Fairness (TFF), and school boards, the School Directors Association of Pennsylvania (SDAP). These organizations possessed powerful voices anytime the General Assembly considered any primary education proposal. Senator Young also heard from conservatives whispering in his ear that they didn't like the Commonwealth interfering in the province of locally controlled education.

"Ben, I'm getting a lot of pressure from Van Dalen and his folks to list this testing bill. They're squeezing my balls hard. The governor profiled this idea in his budget address. He's asking for authority to test students along with a big appropriation to administer the program." Young's distaste was apparent as I watched him make a face describing the governor's new program. Governors of both parties typically use the annual budget speech to the General Assembly to highlight not only financial matters but important policy priorities they hope to carry out in the upcoming fiscal year.

"I've gotten the same fucking calls, Senator, from the administration," Walker admitted. As the most instrumental staffer in the Senate Republican Caucus with a reputation for intense loyalty to the twenty-six senators that made up the caucus in the fifty-member Senate, Walker was super smart. And his memory spanned over thirty years of staffing the assembly. Chief executives came and went. But Ben Walker remained there with the job of protecting his caucus when controversial topics were under discussion. State educational testing clearly fell into this category.

Walker continued, "The governor has no shot in the House with the Democrats in charge and you know how demanding he and his people are. They expect the Senate to move the agenda. I've pushed them off as much as I can, Chairman. Perhaps we should hold public hearings to give the school boards, union, and other groups a chance to go on record and kick up the dust to slow the governor down. It will give us time to develop compromises in the event there aren't enough votes to pass the initiative. Or we might have to put testing into an omnibus school code."

The Pennsylvania Public School Code of 1949 is a massive body of work that details how Pennsylvania governs public education. If the Senate moved on the governor's idea—and couldn't pass the bill by itself—it might be slipped into the "school code," via a much larger amendment. This amendment, as part of a much broader bill with many subject matters relating to education, would draw less attention that way. Whether at the national or state level, this method of hiding bills inside other larger bills is a time-honored way to confuse the voters and rank-and-file legislators.

Another favorite Harrisburg maneuver is to couple a controversial issue with the annual funding provided to schools, making it difficult for legislators and interest groups to oppose. If they do, money for school districts may be jeopardized in the event the legislation falters because of that opposition.

Before Senator Young could respond to Walker's suggestion, I intervened in the conversation. Profanity seemed acceptable at the Capitol. I figured in my head, *When in Rome, right?* "Who the fuck does the governor think he is, anyway? After all, the General Assembly's a co-equal branch of government." After less than a day and some political science classes, I was suddenly an expert.

"I'd rather you not talk about Governor Van Dalen that way, Jack," Senator Young said. Walker merely raised an eyebrow in response to my intemperance. "Okay, where were we? Hearings, right? I'll commit to a couple of hearings, and then we regroup. We're taking our time on this. The state has never tested, and it's not a good idea to pit school districts against each other. The union's been in, and I've gotten calls from teachers in my district. This issue doesn't smell right." Young and the union were close, and their lobbyist had been in several times to push back against the governor's plan.

Pennsylvania's chief executive hated the union since it had poured millions of dollars against him in his re-election campaign. But TFF failed to knock him out. The old saying by Ralph Waldo Emerson applied here. "When you strike at a king, you must kill him." They didn't defeat him at the ballot box. Now Governor Van Dalen had a second term to exact revenge on TFF. While the governor proclaimed education reform a priority, he and his people had a reputation for toughness. State testing became a way of poking the union in the eye while taking the high ground of "accountability in public education."

It would not be easy to pass the plan over the opposition of TFF, however. Besides their massive political action committee (PAC), they could galvanize teachers, who would often call legislators from break rooms during the school day after they received a union alert. The union gave not only dollars in campaigns but bodies—a valuable commodity in election contests. Teachers would work the polls, man phone banks, and put up yard signs against candidates that crossed the union.

Damn good at what it did, I always respected TFF for their prowess and savvy. In strategy and tactics, they were normally several moves ahead of everyone else, including legislators and staff. I count myself in this category. Even back then, as a fiscal conservative, the power of TFF disturbed me. The start of thirty years of battling against them on education reform or any change that threatened the status quo they guarded for their members.

As if a student in Senator Young's classroom—conscious especially of my screw up using profanity—I raised my hand to ask a question. "Yes, Jack. What is it? You don't have to ask for permission," Young chortled, flattered I treated him as a classroom teacher.

"Senator, it seems like we've spent most of this meeting talking about..." I equivocated, fearing I might offend Young further on day one of the internship.

"Speak your mind. Ben and I don't want yes men on staff, do we, Ben?" Walker dipped his head in assent.

"Well, we've talked a lot about politics and adults working in education but not as much about the kids. What about children and their interests?" I inquired with innocence, not that far removed yet from time spent as a student in a public education classroom.

"We tend to do that in this building. Who is for and who is against—we jump right to that question in any legislative analysis. I've got grave concerns about what this means for learning. Ben and I just skipped that part since he knows of my love for education. I believe that testing might overshadow everything else and crowd out real nuts-and-bolts teaching. What's on the test and how to pass may become more relevant than anything else. Thank you for pulling us back to the students."

The chairman's prediction proved correct: standardized testing has overpowered learning and shackled teachers and administrators, empowering bureaucrats instead, *in my humble opinion*. These unelected employees sit in offices and cubicles in Harrisburg and Washington, D.C., overseeing this massive and expensive enterprise that all states *must* follow.

Other than taking a standardized test my school district selected (I remember the Stanford Achievement Test, for instance), somehow, I received a decent education. Today's educators and pupils face the monotony of hours and hours of teaching and testing around a multiple-choice exam, scored and analyzed from far away of the actual halls of learning.

The senator wrapped up the meeting and charged the staff with organizing the public hearings to be held during session days to maximize participation of committee members. Scheduled by the General Assembly on Monday through Wednesday of most weeks, by holding the hearings in the Capitol on session days members can dash in and out. Multiple conferences, meetings, and conversations back in their offices with lobbyists, constituents, and the various people drawn to the Capitol Building is a daily routine for members and their staffs. Most members return to their districts on Thursdays and Fridays.

Even though a Republican, Young wanted the Democrats—along with his own members—in attendance. He worked well with the minority chairman and counted on Democratic opposition as he tallied up a tentative vote. Between their twenty-four votes in the Senate and understanding some members of his caucus were close to the unions or school boards; he could kill the plan.

At the very least, Young could attempt to make it insignificant and inconsequential. Another state program established and funded—without any real purpose until another governor came along to expand or scrap it, depending on their political ideology.

Time for lunch so Rob and I met in the cafeteria, buzzing with members, staffers, lobbyists, constituents, and tourists. Placid worked for the Republicans in the House. As the minority caucus, unlike the GOP in the Senate, they didn't control the committees or floor calendar. As a result, they were mainly reactive to whatever the Democrats did in the House. Rob landed a research position with the House GOP Policy Committee; established to generate Republican ideas and policy as a foil to the Democrat majority.

As we waited in line for a hamburger and soup, Rob described his new boss, Representative Anthony Molinaro. "Tony's from Hanover, York County, and is articulate, smart, and partisan. He walked us through a platform that focuses on fiscal conservatism and legislation to crack down on crime. It's our job to flesh out the concepts and language." I leaned over the table, listening intently to Rob talk about this House member. "Molinaro's been tasked by the caucus whip, Noah Johnson, to put together a series of proposals. The members will unveil these next month on the Capitol Rotunda steps, followed by press conferences around the Commonwealth. Tony's hard-charging. But as he told us about Johnson, it sounds like this guy is the real pit bull for the caucus in attacking the Democrats." Usually even-keeled, not today—Placid was excited to be staffing "Tony."

With keen attention, I picked up on the informality of the House and asked, "You call the representatives by their first name? The Senate is so formal. I wouldn't dare call Senator Young by his first name. Even Ben Walker, the Senate's senior staffer, calls him 'Senator or Chairman.'" We ate our food and shared more observations on this first day in the Capitol Building; both of us wanted to pinch ourselves that we'd made it and were part of this exciting atmosphere.

Invited to join the other Republican staffers for drinks after work, Rob asked that I come along. I resisted. Not that I didn't enjoy being with people. On the surface, I had a natural personality. But preferred reading and preparing for the next day's work, setting a pattern to follow for the next thirty years. Rob insisted we meet in the Rotunda after work, and I reluctantly agreed to go with him to the bar. As my alter ego, his ongoing purpose: to make me learn to relax or to remove that "stick" he said was up my rear end.

FOURTEEN

Capitol Gossip, Kostantin, First Assignment

THAT NIGHT AT THE BAR a big crowd milled around since this club attracted the Capitol gang. Rob introduced me to his new friends from the House Republican Caucus. At once, they highlighted the differences between the two bodies. "C'mon over to the House, Jack. It's much more fun than the Senate. We pass lots of bills and have anywhere from ten to two hundred amendments filed against legislation on the calendar. It's laughable the Senate considers an avalanche of changes, a handful filed," Jeb said, the apparent leader of the group.

After only one day on the job, I felt the need to defend my employer's honor. "In the office today, the pace of the Senate versus the House came up when someone mentioned a two-hundred-page-jobs bill you guys sent over last week in a bum rush."

"That's a damn good proposal," Jeb replied. "We made it more business-friendly through floor amendments. They are too quick to condemn what we pass and just fucking lazy about work and public policy."

With both hands held up in a sign of "I surrender," I'd offended my new friends. "Whoa, guys, I'm not saying that. Only repeating what I heard. They claim to be much more 'thoughtful,' taking the time necessary to shape legislation. Said the House only wants to please special interest groups and popular demand by passing lots of crappy bills to generate press releases and news articles."

Jeb didn't appreciate this lecture, countering, "We don't see it like that. What they call a filter, it's more like 'burial by the Senate.' With the Democrats in control this session, we're glad you guys stop bad, liberal shit. Last session when the GOP was in charge, the other chamber killed as many Republican bills as they're doing with the House Democrats in the majority now. Nothing ever fucking changes with the Senate. Nothing." Jeb shook his head in disgust. Inwardly, I liked the reference to "you guys," and the way it made me feel to be a part of the upper chamber's deliberative culture.

The conversation highlighted a good lesson about the inherent tensions built in between the chambers. House members represent over sixty thousand people, running for election every two years. Senators have a quarter of a million people in their districts with longer terms of four years in between elections.

With an expanded term, senators have the luxury of not being as responsive as House members are to their constituents. They may cast controversial votes earlier in their terms, hoping the electorate forget these decisions by the time re-election rolls around. The twenty-four-hour news cycle has only fostered and emboldened politicians who know the public's attention span is short and shifts with the story of each day.

"What's the deal with the senator's DUI? There's been a rumor he's a drunk. What do you know about it?" Jeb asked, providing my first taste of Harrisburg gossip. I wasn't in the habit of reading the *Harrisburg World* and hadn't yet encountered their long-time Capitol beat reporter, Kostantin Pokornin. Around the Capitol's hallways, he lurked. Before him lay a treasure trove of gossip that led to salacious reporting and big headlines to help sell newspapers.

"Yeah, I heard something about that. Really don't know anything other than what I read." Rob stifled a laugh as he watched me try to bullshit my way through the conversation.

Pokornin stood only four-eleven with a massive pot belly and a pock-marked face probably formed from severe acne suffered during his teen years. A flop of jet black hair sat on top of his rather bulbous head, most days his pelt uncombed and unruly. Kostantin's personal hygiene left something to be desired. Anyone he interviewed wanted to flee from the stench of body odor and bad breath before Kostantin even began his usual hard line of questioning.

What he lacked in physical stature and cleanliness, Pokornin made up for in persistence. Kostantin struck fear in the hearts of many politicians who believed he hid in the shadows of the building even when he wasn't around. Pokornin came from an old school of yellow journalism, breaking the story on this senator's DUI.

All hours of the day and night, Pokornin, who had no outside life or family, trolled about. Late one evening, he spied the senator stumbling through the Rotunda. Apparently drunk from a good time downtown, a lobbyist had probably entertained the legislator. His loyal staffer was present to make sure he got to the office safely, so he could sober up for the next day's session. The staffer would alert Senate Security, who would leave the member alone on the office sofa to sleep off the alcohol until the Senate opened.

Once Kostantin knew the legislator had a drinking problem, he filed this away in a brain packed with trivial until needed for another day. That time arrived when rumors circulated of the arrest of a legislator for drunk driving. Journalist Kostantin Pokornin thrived on gossip with a network of people that fed tips to him. Expert at sorting fact from fiction. Often the lines between the two blurred to write titillating copy.

Pokornin started as a hawker of papers on a busy New York City street corner before promotion to be a stringer in the newsroom. His mentor, Oscar Jez Pollak, a crusty and disagreeable chap himself, taught the young lad the ropes before Pokornin moved to Central Pennsylvania to become a legislative reporter under the initial tutelage of Lorranzo DiMatteo, a tough and respected journalist who knew his way around the Capitol. The two sometimes shared a byline on major stories.

Kostantin Pokornin maintained a Rolodex of folks from law enforcement. In a voice that wheezed all the time because of the pressure 250 pounds squeezed on his diaphragm, Kostantin placed calls to multiple sources. Is the rumor true? Did this senator drive drunk? His hunch paid off when he confirmed the crime had occurred in Harrisburg as the member drove home to his suburban apartment. Legislators stay in hotels or often share rooms with other lawmakers since they must be in town during session days. For many members of the General Assembly, it's simply not practical to commute while in session.

Once again, Kostantin beat others to a juicy story. The Senate Republican leadership acknowledged the DUI and indicated the senator would be placed into rehab at once. They knew from his staffer (who had tipped off leadership) there was a problem. From an earlier trip to the wood shed, they'd told their colleague to lay off alcohol. He ignored the admonition.

The indiscretion, embarrassing to the caucus, forced the president pro tempore to remove the legislator from the committee responsible for vetting all bills dealing with the Liquor Control Board and booze establishments. Pokornin highlighted this angle that the senator sat on the group that established the rules and regulations for the consumption of alcohol and hit this soft pitch out of the ballpark.

We finished up drinks and Rob and I bid our new friends goodnight to walk back to our basement apartment on one of Harrisburg's small alleys downtown. The accommodations, woefully outdated, had thankfully come furnished. At a couple of hundred bucks a month, the price was right. Both of us were grateful to have put a notch in our belt, getting through day one as interns at the State Capitol.

Early the next morning, I donned my winter gear to go for a run. I dressed quietly so Rob could sleep. Not a morning person, he'd probably be asleep when I returned. I jogged down Locust Street towards the Susquehanna River, noticing a beautiful park and path that ran along its banks. The air blew cold, the river frozen, so I didn't exert myself too much as I fought a strong headwind. The time alone was a release when I let my mind relax from the almost constant thoughts of finishing up college and moving to the next stage of my life. I'd been setting goals since my sophomore year in high school; blessed by God that the plan was falling into place.

Around Division Street, about a mile and a half into the jog, I turned up towards Third Street to go back through the city's brownstones and small businesses. I passed people walking their dogs, bundled up against the frigid weather. A driver in a rush to get to work hit an ice puddle—formed in a pothole that could've swallowed the entire Curran vehicle—dousing me with arctic liquid. *No wave of sorry, didn't see you, or can I give you a lift home?* I noted as I resisted the urge to flip this guy the bird.

I observed that folks in Harrisburg weren't any nicer than in Abington. The people of Watsonville (Ford's host town) spoiled me. Citizens said good morning to one another, men held doors open for the fairer sex, and "paying it forward" was a well-established practice before it became a bumper sticker. *Maybe hosting state government has made these folks hard and cynical,* I mused, now chilled to the bone as my teeth chattered from the icicle bath. I began worrying about whether this would bring on the dreaded bronchitis and pneumonia, an ongoing curse upon my body.

As I approached the State Capitol, I again found myself in awe to be interning in this building. The steps called out my name: *Curran, Curran, see if you can beat yesterday's pace.* With my best Rocky imitation, I ran up them like a gazelle, taking two at a clip. When I reached the top, arms up high in the air, I answered back to the granite edifice, *Not bad, eh?* Turning around, I looked down the breadth of State Street all the way to the Susquehanna. I'd enjoy this gorgeous vista for years to come.

At a slower pace, I returned to the apartment and discovered Rob had made coffee and was in the shower. I'd stopped for a copy of the *Harrisburg World* at a newsstand. The proprietor was an older African-American gentleman. He gave me a wave and cheery good morning—his politeness seemed to be the exception that morning—as I paid for my paper. To avoid the ignorance exhibited the day before over the DUI, I scanned the daily paper, a new habit that began because of that incident.

Drenched and cold, I peeled off the layer of sweats, Army wool hat, socks, supporter, and running shoes and grabbed for my bathrobe and asthma inhaler, shivering from an apartment barely sixty-two degrees because Rob and I couldn't afford heat. I sat at the small, rickety kitchen table. After taking a puff of medicine to clear my airways, I enjoyed the aroma and warmth of the freshly brewed coffee in the Ford College mug I cherished. The liquid heat would have to suffice until the shower was mine and the pulsating hot water brought up my body's core temperature.

I leafed through the paper and noticed an article about a computer company that had allegedly bribed Pennsylvania's State Treasurer to win a significant accounting contract. The trial in federal court was under-way, and those charged were claiming their innocence. Finished with the news, I perused an entertainment blurb that Dionne Warwick and friends had the number one hit in America. "That's What Friends Are For" heightened awareness of AIDS at a time when the country wasn't that serious about the killer disease. I checked the NBA scores to see how the Philadelphia 76ers had done the night before. An avid Philly sports fan, I remained loyal to the region where my ancestors had come from since the 1850s.

The hot shower felt good, and I dressed eager to hit day two as a Pennsylvania Senate intern. Around 8:30, I arrived at the office and went to the small desk. A note from Young's chief of staff asked me to research proposed legislation sponsored by the Dean of the Senate Senator Michael Madison. In his ninth term as a senator, Madison was a Republican from my part of the Commonwealth. I'd read about him in our local papers. A Navy officer in World War II, voters elected him to the General Assembly in 1948.

"Charismatic, intelligent, and hardworking" described this legislator who'd seen it all in Harrisburg, including the arrival and the departure of eight governors from both parties. The cane that propped him up also served as a makeshift gavel. Anytime he needed to draw attention to himself, whether in a committee meeting, his office, or the caucus room, down the stick went.

The senator and his staff provided services to their constituents— second to none. One of many reasons the Republican bosses in the old man's district didn't dare oppose him. Madison wasn't from the machine and stood as a proud maverick. He took orders from no one. Senate leadership couldn't count on his vote either, particularly on issues important to labor, a key constituency for Senator Madison.

With the Senate divided twenty-six to twenty-four along party lines, the Dean enjoyed this pivotal role and used seniority and his independent streak to get his way with the leaders. The threat of joining the Democrats on controversial votes did not need to be voiced. But was understood.

As a veteran, this legislator championed military and veterans' causes, including the reason for sponsoring the bill I would research. Senator Madison's proposal had support during this time of Cold War with the Soviet Union. Since the country had moved to an all-volunteer military at the end of the Vietnam War, the senator's legislation compelled school districts to give recruiters personal information on graduating seniors. With no draft in place, recruiters faced a challenge to provide a steady supply of soldiers, sailors, marines, and airmen for the military's needs.

Opponents of the bill included school boards, and the teachers' union, Teachers for Fairness. Harrisburg and Washington, D.C. are infamous for passing unfunded mandates to require public schools to do various things without funding to implement the requirement. Instead, the burden is foisted on local property taxpayers. In this manner, Representative "I'm for good schools" can proudly point to the mandate in his or her summer newsletter. What's unspoken here? "I made you, the local property taxpayer cough up the dough, instead of the state."

Under Madison's bill, schools would have to compile these lists of graduating seniors at their expense, the primary reason for school board opposition. The union opposed the legislation on pupil-privacy grounds—joined in the fight by the Civil Liberties Council of Pennsylvania (CLCP), a self-appointed watchdog that fights for constitutional rights.

The idea frightened me as a conservative who fears a larger government and understands privacy concerns. Yet I supported a strong national defense and knew recruiters struggled to make their quotas to staff the robust military Reagan was building. What I thought didn't matter though. Analyze the bill and start the vetting process. That was the job at hand, regardless of my personal views.

If asked for an opinion—or if I felt compelled to protect my boss—I would have provided it. And anytime afterwards when I staffed future legislation and policy decisions. Once a decision happened, I staffed it. Period. Research of this nature was meaty stuff, and I jumped into it, appreciating the chance to staff a controversial bill.

FIFTEEN

Agnes, Ennis, Dean of the Senate

CONCENTRATION IN A BUSY OFFICE is difficult and the internship my first exposure to the concept of multi-tasking, critical to any staffer's success in the General Assembly. I pulled out a legal-sized pad to jot down ideas on how to approach the research, a successful strategy in college and my student government days. At the top of the list: examine the relevant federal and state laws that might impact upon the issue. Second, talk with the interest groups supporting and opposing the proposal, something I knew Senator Young wanted when he called it the first question of any legislative analysis. Third, I needed to meet with Madison's staff on what they saw as possible pitfalls if the chairman scheduled the bill and what they estimated the rough vote tally in the committee might appear to be.

If Chairman Young listed the legislation, we'd move to a more refined count. Never, ever, does one go into any vote without knowing the outcome—sometimes those tallies don't work out when members flip, failing to tell the chairman or leader of their reversal. Yes, legislators can be unpredictable and do change their minds.

The Senate Archives was on the ground floor so I figured this would be a good way to start the research. Plus, I needed quiet after a morning of phones ringing non-stop. Before I went in through the mahogany door, I grasped the brass knob and felt the raised seal decoration make an imprint on my hand.

Along each aisle inside were stacks of glass-enclosed bookcases with volumes of legislative journals, complete sets of the Pennsylvania and U.S. statutes, court cases, the Pennsylvania regulatory code, and plenty of books on the Commonwealth's rich history—an extensive array of works for any would-be researcher. Across the room, I spied a large mahogany conference table with sturdy empire-style curved legs—outside a door marked "Senate Caucus Room." Later, I learned that this space was limited to the majority members of the Senate and senior staff; their deliberations private and not open to public or media scrutiny.

Interrupting my gaze around an older woman, who sat at a reception desk, asked if I needed any help. Her nameplate read "Agnes Bonneville." Probably in her late-fifties, she had streaky blond hair, bright orange lipstick, and dangling gold earrings. To top off the look, Agnes wore a puffy white blouse and tight pants that didn't flatter her figure nor did the get-up sync with the formal appearance of the room. Acting as if I'd done this for a long time, I introduced myself, "Jack Curran, an intern for the chair of the Education Committee. Pleased to meet you."

"Ms. Bonneville's my name. Call me Agnes. What can I do for you, young man?" I noticed how she'd stopped flipping through a scandal rag that sat on a pile of tabloids, along with nail polish, a can of hair spray, one of those balls squeezed for stress relief—although I doubt the ball got much use based on first impressions—and what looked like a cheap bottle of perfume. I sniffed the air and detected a faint fragrance that wafted about as it clashed with the musty odor of old tomes.

The perfume Agnes wore wasn't on the list to be researched that day, so I ventured on. "There's a research project Senator Young wants me to do and I need help to understand the volumes here. To be honest, the room's a little intimidating. If you can show me how to understand better the Pennsylvania and federal laws, that'd be a good start." *Perfectly reasonable ask,* I thought with satisfaction.

In a clipped fashion, because she seemed anxious to get back to the tabloids, she said, "Wish I could help you, Jack. I'm here to watch the phone and greet visitors. Our director and his assistant are out, but you can stop back tomorrow. Help yourself through the bookcases. Just make sure you put everything back the way you found it." Agnes emphasized this last point. I noticed the "news story" on top of her pile featured *Dynasty* television stars, Linda Evans and Joan Collins, in a knock-down catfight.

"Much more weighty stuff than my research," I said under my breath in a smart-ass way.

"What'd you say? My hearing isn't as good as it used to be."

Watch yourself, Jack. Too early to be making enemies, I reminded myself. "Oh, sorry. I asked if you could at least skim over the necessary information with me and I'll take it from there?" Jack Curran didn't give up easily even though this lady might be three times my age and likely had sat in this space longer than I'd walked on the earth.

As the phone rang, she went to pick it up, saying with finality, "Not my job," and then answering, "Senate Archives." My first taste of the legislative bureaucracy that didn't move as fast as I liked, regardless of how much I may want to push or whine.

Determined to keep going, I found the federal statutes related to educational records and pulled the state military code, spreading the stuff out at the large conference table. The door from the caucus room opened, startling me from my intense study of the law. In walked a tall woman, thin and rather statuesque, who carried herself well in a chic designer suit. Her flaming red hair and freckles drew attention to her as she moved through a room. Not pretty in a conventional way, more handsome than anything else, she was in a great hurry and barked at Agnes, who had her own moment of fright from the intrusion.

Quickly, Agnes stuffed the magazine under a manila folder apparently kept ready for this purpose as she tried to appear busy on research work. "Yes, Ennis, how can I help?" the Evans and Collins catfight would have to wait.

"Agnes, get Senator Jones. He's wanted in caucus immediately. Tell his staff we're discussing his legislation on banking fees. Members have questions." Ennis's tone made me involuntarily sit up, too. As she passed me on her way back to the caucus, Ennis turned and stopped to tap me on the shoulder. "Don't sit at this table while we're in caucus. The members need privacy and don't want to be overheard by outsiders. Move over to the other spot behind Agnes." Ennis left despite the finger I raised as I began to ask a question to no avail.

I proceeded over to the table by my new friend, not sure what I'd done wrong. "Agnes, who the heck is that? Man, she's a powerhouse, isn't she?"

Agnes stared into my eyes for over thirty seconds, obviously wondering if she could trust me. Finally, she answered, "That's Ennis O'Reilly. Works for this place as a policy person. Rumor has it that she came up from Washington's capital building and is a distant cousin to one of the senators from Philly. Don't mind her. That's just her nature. She don't mean nothing by it. Ennis is real skinny like that because she moves so fast." It was abundantly clear through her words and actions that Agnes tried to stay out of Ennis's way.

"Is she a lawyer?" I asked, already doubting whether I had the necessary drive and intelligence to keep up with such a force of nature like Ennis.

"No. Seems to always be juggling lots of papers and telling people what to do though." Note to self: *Keep out of Ennis's way.* Evidently, I had a lot to learn about Harrisburg and the various personalities that made the legislature work.

After relocating to a safer table, I read through relevant law and made copies and returned to Young's suite. Before calling the interest groups, I scheduled an appointment with Senator Madison's staff to understand better the reasons for introducing the bill.

The senator's office was in the new East Wing of the Capitol Building. Constructed at great expense to match as much as possible the existing structure, it had also seen controversy as the original 1906 building had. Democrats, who were in the majority in the House, launched a probe of the thirty million dollars spent on the granite material for the East Wing, dubbing the alleged scandal "Granitegate." As with so many other investigations here and in Washington, nothing ever came of it.

Senator Madison's office wasn't hard to find. I opened the glass door to enter his cavernous and well-furnished suite and provided my name to the receptionist. She ushered me into the senator's private office instead of to "Matt's" desk for the meeting we'd arranged. I wanted to wipe the smirk off his face while he lounged in the chair by Madison's side, his one leg up over the arm of the reproduction, "antique" wingback in what I thought was a disrespectful way.

"Uh, hello, Senator, my name's Jack Curran. I thought Matt and I were meeting about the, uh, legislation." Not ready for the Dean of the Senate, I fumbled around for words.

"You're meeting with me. Have a seat," Madison ordered. His eyes narrowed further as if he were conducting a cross-examination in a courtroom. "Who're you and why hasn't Young moved my bill yet?" he asked.

As the senator spoke I fixed my attention on the cane, wondering if he'd take a swipe with this old hickory stick that had a large decorative deer on top. The senator's uncommonly large hand covered the stag when not rapping it against his desk for emphasis or to subdue an opponent into submission.

The room spun, I struggled to focus, finally replying, "I'm an intern for Chairman Young, Senator Madison. He asked me to put together a review of the military recruiters' bill. I can't answer the question on his intentions for the legislation." *Oh shit*, I said to myself. This man was only the second member I'd met in the Senate, and it had to be someone who'd served in this body almost twice as long as I'd been alive.

Madison's face crinkled up as he bellowed, "An intern?! Do you believe this, Matt, Young's got an intern working on my bill? I don't even rate an entry-level researcher."

"Snickering Matt" clasped his hands behind his head, smiling broadly, pleased with the ambush he'd set. "Senator Young's had plenty of time, Senator Madison. Hard to understand the lack of respect for the most senior member of the Senate."

"Matt the Hatchet's" well-placed words added fuel to a fire already raging, and the Dean continued. "Tell Young I'm insulted he didn't come here to talk with me, sending an intern instead. Tell him I'll be speaking with leadership about amending my bill onto something else on the Senate calendar since Young wants to kill it. Make sure he understands the veterans' groups will know he's the hold up on their legislation. They're a power not to be trifled with, you know. Got all that?" he demanded.

Irate, the senator's words spewed out to where a projectile of saliva shot out of his mouth, landing hard on my chin. I didn't dare ask for a hanky to wipe it off. Since he was an old Navy officer, I should've been at attention in front of his desk being only a mere sergeant in the Army National Guard.

My notepad had lots of scribbles, so I could convey the message with complete accuracy. I had a false start with my voice that emitted an unintelligible gurgling sound; that's how rattled the old man had me. On a second try, I said, "Senator, I'm so sorry, uh, for the misunderstanding. I know Senator Young's interested in the legislation and I'll take the message back." Kill the messenger. No doubt, I wasn't the first one to experience Madison's wrath. Nor would I be the last.

"Do that," Senator Madison hollered. "Warn Young I expect the bill listed pronto." He brought the cane down hard on his desk, *bang,* and I jumped in the chair, startled with his intensity. The new rut on the surface of his furniture a visible sign that our meeting was over. "Get me Ben Walker on the phone right away," he yelled out to his receptionist. The large hand waved towards the exit to dismiss me from his court. "Go already, young man, what're you waiting for?"

Incredulous the senator's staffer had let this go down the way it did, I ran out of his office, thinking—*You old coot.* I learned the hard way Madison's staff operated like this—in a perpetual "we gotcha" state with both staffers and lobbyists.

Young's office became a refuge away from Madison and his lackey and I felt like crawling under the little desk. *If today's representative of how Harrisburg works, it's time to apply to law school,* I determined.

Calls to the interest groups and Department of Education awaited, so I got back down to business and had pleasant and productive interactions that helped settle my nerves. My preference would've been to brief the senator and his chief of staff in person, but they were out of the office. Thank God for my typing teacher at Abington, Miss Peterson, as my fingers pounded away smoothly at the keyboard of a borrowed word processor available for staff use—well before the days of Windows and desktop computers—and explained via a memo what I'd learned.

The Department of Education had pointed to a federal law that governed student privacy and records. They believed the law would permit the Commonwealth to give parents the choice of removing their children from the list provided to the military recruiters without violating this federal statute. I saved the best for last and reported almost verbatim the Madison encounter—I left out the spit landing on my prominent chin and the dent in his desk, believing those details to be "un-senatorial," and unworthy of mention in a formal document that I had no idea how far it would circulate.

SIXTEEN

Saving a Cross-Dresser

DESPITE THE ENNIS shoulder-tapping and ass-chewing I got from the Dean of the Senate, I was pleased with the day's accomplishments. A little after five, I started home to the apartment. *A burger and Coors Light to celebrate; that's on the menu for an otherwise good day,* I decided.

As I made my way up Third Street and passed the Fulton Bank Building, one of the taller structures in Harrisburg, my reverie ended abruptly when I spotted a large African-American man beating a smaller African-American woman as she lay on the icy sidewalk curled up in the fetal position. Severely hurt, her whimpers and the sounds of horrible pain were barely audible against the wind that whipped around the corner of the building. Cars drove by, and people continued about their business, just another day in Harrisburg, apparently.

Without hesitating, I scurried to the scene and jumped on the man's back. As a big guy at six-two, and in decent shape from lifting at the gym, I knew at once he outmatched me. This man—we'll call him "Damien" since his real name remains unknown—was ripped and over six-five. He had diamond earring studs in both ears. An offensive, perverse tattoo on his neck prompted me to pull my head away, repulsed by the image.

Somehow, I restrained his arms. But that didn't stop Damien. His black dress boots—they must've been size thirteen plus—became his available weapon to kick this poor lady. Howling at the top of his lungs, the blows to her body caused her to cry out for mercy. And still, Damien assaulted her.

His mammoth fists were weapons employed to swat back at me like I was a pesky mosquito buzzing his ears. "Get the fuck off me, you cracker. You crazy. This ain't your business," he hollered. Over time, his aim improved, and his fists caught my ears, lips, and finally my nose as I held on. Damien arched his long torso to try to remove the nuisance on his back while punching repeatedly. I clung to him like a cowboy on a raging bull; his powerful legs never ceased pummeling and pounding his victim.

Blood poured from my nose and lips and my face swelled up as if it were a cooked marshmallow. I yelled out to bystanders, "Don't just stand there, call the police. This maniac's going to kill her." A business owner heard the cries for help, came out, and returned inside to his establishment to dial 911.

After what seemed like an eternity, the cavalry arrived and pulled me off Damien. Wobbly like a rag doll, I staggered over to the curb to sit down. The police knocked this bad dude to the ground hard, slapping on the handcuffs, no doubt trying to give him a little taste of the pain he'd inflicted. As the only witness willing to talk, the cops took my statement. Everyone else pretended they'd seen nothing. The ambulance also arrived to treat the woman, bleeding badly from her head.

I couldn't help but notice her skirt hiked up far. The poor lady also lost her dignity because of this perp. The cop saw me staring at the victim. "You do realize, she's a man. Didn't you notice the Adam's apple? It's a sure tell." It took all the discipline I had to respect "Officer Obvious" and hold back my palm from smacking him in the forehead. *In that split second to act, I should've focused on that body part*? I asked myself. "He likes dressing in women's clothes, and they're in a business relationship," the man in blue continued matter-of-factly. *Like it matters she's a woman or not,* I wanted to say as a scolding but kept my swollen lips shut.

Instead I asked, "Do you really think I had time to notice the plumbing under her skirt or a moment to check out her throat before I jumped on psycho-killer over there?" I pointed at my "new pal," not making it easy on the cops as they shoved him into the backseat of the nearby cruiser. "I did right here," I said, exasperated. "Why do I feel like I'm on trial for being the 'Good Samaritan?'" I asked. The officer shrugged. For him, there wasn't a good answer. Just another day in a city neighborhood.

"Let us treat that face," the medic said, thankfully saving me from further interaction with the police. I shook my head no, and he said, "Okay, your choice, but you should see a doctor."

The apartment was close by. Once inside, I collapsed onto our ratty sofa and tilted my head back. I used a towel to stop my nose from bleeding. Ice in a plastic bag helped with the puffiness from the multiple hits to my battered mug. A couple of aspirin, taken with a swig of beer, admittedly not the best combination, I fell asleep once the adrenaline from the fight wore off.

Rob came in and woke me up with a few shakes. "What the hell happened, Curran? You look like shit."

Startled and groggy, I mumbled, "Thanks." Rob got me a glass of water, and I told him about the pimp, Damien, and his pummeling of a cross-dressing man—apparently his prostitute—and my rather pointless intervention.

"This may be one of the dumber things you've ever done, Jack. That man could've killed you! Let me take you to the hospital, okay? Something might be broken or there might be internal bleeding."

"What should I have done at that split second, genius? None of the assholes milling about helped the lady. And no hospitals. I don't have medical insurance, remember?"

The last thing I needed was an expensive doctor's bill. The discussion that would follow with Big Joe wouldn't be a pleasant one since he made it clear after high school we sank or swam on our own.

"Calling the cops would've been enough. I know you're named after your great-grandfather, the war hero, but this stunt is beyond ridiculous. Unlike him, you were unarmed." Before cell phone days, Rob was right. I could have entered one of the businesses to dial 911. "The pimp might've been pumped up on drugs with a weapon. What if Damien, as you call him, had turned and shot or knifed you? I'd be calling a funeral director instead of talking with you about the hospital," he said.

"No time to think it through, Rob. I figured 'mad dog' might kill her, or maybe she was a man, I don't know, it's a blur now. Just let me rest, all right? You've made your point." Still foggy from the blows to my head about what I'd seen and done—and what the cop had mentioned—had me twisted around in a loop over gender identity. My head pounded and only wanted sleep.

"You're batshit crazy, Jack Curran. 'He saved a cross-dresser...' How's that for an epitaph?" Rob concluded, making me feel even lousier than I did.

SEVENTEEN

First Legislative Success, Senator Schwemmer,
Toppling the Boss George Dimple

WHEN I REPORTED TO THE OFFICE the next morning, I made up an excuse that I had gone to the YMCA for boxing lessons and hadn't protected against an upper cut—not wanting to repeat the story of "Crazy Curran" leaping on a big dude's back. Yet Rob wasn't so quiet when we met up with his friends from the House for lunch. They ribbed me about being both a hero and an idiot.

Senator Young and his chief of staff arrived in the afternoon. They called me into his office and the senator began, "Jack, I read through the material you wrote. Look, you did nothing wrong. The old man's well-known for using these tactics. I'll list his bill for the next committee meeting. Ben Walker and I talked it through and Ben calmed Madison down after the tongue-lashing you got. Once the military recruiters' bill comes out of the committee, he'll move onto something else. Good work."

"Thank you, Senator. I'm a big boy and just glad this didn't cause any problems."

"Not at all. Okay, work with the staff here, and you can go with them up to the Legislative Reference Bureau to have an amendment prepared for me to sponsor. The change will allow parents to remove their students from the 'list' if they worry about privacy. Based on your conversation with the union and school boards, I'm going to make the military pay for the administrative costs districts will incur to give the lists. That should at least make them neutral on the bill. By the way, what the hell happened to your face? I hope the other guy looks worse."

"Boxing lessons, Senator. From now on, I run and lift weights only. Never was much of an athlete," I quipped with a slightly crooked grin, hoping he wouldn't ask for more details.

Thrilled to be on the ground floor of a bill's consideration and movement, Young's staff took me to meet with one of the attorneys to have the amendment prepared. Together, we came up with the necessary language and where to place the changes in the bill.

Time for my first committee gathering to witness Senator Madison's bill move through the initial step of many to come in the legislative process. Chairman Young opened the discussion after rapping the gavel. "This meeting of the Senate Education Committee will now come to order. The clerk will call the roll." The committee comprised seven Republicans and four Democrats, and all members were present for this meeting. "Out of respect to the good gentleman from the Southeast, the chair calls up Senator Madison's military recruiters' legislation. Senator, please come forward and give us an overview of why you sponsored this bill."

Unsteady, Madison rose from his seat in the front row. An aide attempted to help the Dean but was swatted away with the cane. Senator Madison ambled toward the witness table, probably the hundredth time he'd be testifying for legislation. As he sat down in the comfortable swivel leather chair, he coughed, and the senator ordered his underappreciated staffer (not Matt) to "fetch me some water."

Faithful to the Philadelphia accent he was proud of, "water" was pronounced *wooder*. Born and raised in the City of Brotherly Love, now representing one of its older suburbs, the senator loved its traditions, including the annual Mummer's Parade, where he learned as a little boy to strut down Broad Street on New Year's Day. I tried to imagine the wizened and leathery old codger as a young 'un; his whole life ahead of him as he performed for the crowds, colorful feathers gracing his head and body. Maybe the early adulation of the masses caused Madison to pursue a political career; the sound of clapping and cheering addictive to many would-be politicians.

After swallowing the drink, the senator began in his distinctive twang. "Mr. Chairman, thank you for the courtesy you offer to an old man and veteran." Dressed in their American Legion and VFW uniforms, the crowd of veterans supporting the proposal loved it. Senator Madison belonged to them. "The country faces yet another threat, this time from communism and a Soviet Union bent on expanding its footprint around the world. This legislation will help our military meet its recruiting goals by providing lists of graduating seniors from Pennsylvania schools. I appreciate the work the chairman's office did in preparing an amendment, which I support."

Senator Young had watched this type of performance before and remained impassive in expression and words. "Thank you, Senator, for those most cogent remarks. I offer Amendment 0561 on behalf of the gentleman. The military will pay the administrative costs schools may incur in providing the lists and the amendment allows parents to opt-out their students to protect privacy rights. The change will bring the proposal into compliance with federal protections. Is there a second?"

Known for conservative views, the senator from Lancaster hoped to run for Congress someday. Support for the military was ideal for highlighting for the folks back home, so he raised his hand to second the proposed change. "The Chair thanks the gentleman from Lancaster. Is there any discussion on the amendment before the committee? Seeing none, may we cast a unanimous vote for the proposed change?" Chairman Young looked over at the minority chair, who signaled he had no objections.

"Thank you, the amendment is approved. The senator from Lancaster now moves the amended legislation, seconded by the gentlelady from Uniontown. Before the committee is the modified bill. Is there any further discussion?"

Before Young could call the final vote, one of the Democratic members sought recognition. Looking through the Senate handbook that listed the senators with photographs, I noted Senator Stanley Ionesco came from a small town close to Pittsburgh. The photo did far more justice to his appearance than sitting only twenty feet away from him. Gaunt and pale with narrow rat-like eyes and a beak nose, Ionesco slouched down close to the table as he prepared to talk. The sight of him made me ponder the wonders of democracy. *Is this the best the voters can do—sending this tower of power to the Capitol out of several hundred thousand plus possible candidates in the region to choose from?*

"The Chair recognizes Senator Ionesco." I heard a groan from two Republican staffers I recognized from moving about the hallways. Apparently, they anticipated his move to come. At this point, Senator Madison, a shrewd tactician from many legislative battles, stared hard at Ionesco—almost daring him to oppose the legislation.

"Thank you, Mr. Chairman. The amendment improves the bill," he said in a thin and reedy voice. "But it's important to note for the record that the Civil Liberties Council of Pennsylvania remains opposed for privacy reasons and believes the bill is unconstitutional. I will support the legislation but only to move the process forward and reserve the right to oppose the measure on final passage." As he sat back in the chair, this Democratic senator squared his shoulders, a sign he was pleased about positioning himself on both sides of the issue.

"The Chair thanks the gentleman. Senator Madison, you wish to be recognized?"

"I do, Mr. Chairman. Senator Ionesco, thank you for that unwavering support. The thousands of veterans represented by the organizations present, thank you as well. I'm sure they'll inform their members in your district how you voted today for national defense." A titter ran through the audience as Senator Madison said this, causing Senator Ionesco to react with a scowl. Wisely, he chose not to take Madison's subtle challenge—the puff in his chest had disappeared, however. On a roll, the old warrior continued, "I know the gentleman understands the courts decide constitutionality, not the Civil Liberties Council of Pennsylvania. At least that's what they taught me in law school a long, long time ago although I note the gentleman is not an attorney."

The veterans applauded this line vigorously, and Chairman Young asked for order from the audience by banging the gavel several times. "Thank you, Senator, for that valuable civics lesson." Such a subtle sense of humor that made the point without being offensive; I loved it. "Okay, the clerk will call the roll on the amended legislation. Are there any negative votes? Seeing none, Senator Madison's bill is reported to the floor, as amended." After the meeting, the senator's chief of staff explained the legislation would be considered quickly by the full Senate since Madison sat in a pivotal position as a swing vote in the caucus.

After this weighty stuff, Rob and I settled into a routine, using those intern days to meet as many people in the legislative process as possible, soaking in as much as we could with graduation from Ford fast approaching. On the way home one day, I stopped by Rob's office and met his boss, Representative Tony Molinaro. Impressed with this guy, he was a hardcore Republican, very smart, who spoke with passion about the issues I cared about as a conservative Republican.

The next day, as I got on the elevator to head back down to the Senate Archives, I encountered a new senator and recognized him from my trusty pamphlet as Senator Dalton Tabner Schwemmer. Short and fat, a tuft of grayish black hair sat on each side of his head slicked back like the greasers from the fifties. His shoes appeared like they had been buffed with a chocolate bar.

Schwemmer reeked of smoke. A not too fashionable pipe stuck up from his shirt pocket as if it were a periscope. Not so good recollections of grandfather Fernsby—the monster—over washed me as the stink conjured up memories of the Prince Albert tobacco tin Pop-Pop carried around. We nodded hello to each other as I hacked into my coat sleeve.

While riding the elevator down, Senator Schwemmer pulled out a long black comb—the kind you had to have in middle school tucked into your back jean's pocket if you wanted to look "cool"—and groomed the tufts of hair. I watched in disgust as tiny snowflakes of dandruff slowly drifted down on my pant leg and highly shined black shoes. *Why couldn't they land on the senator's slummy footwear instead?*

We reached the ground floor at last. After you I gestured to give me time to shake off the debris left behind and to take in some fresh air once he departed. Later, this same legislator would be at the center of allegations that caused all of us to receive "training" because of his alleged behavior.

When I arrived at the Senate Archives, I said hello to my new pal, Agnes—she and I having reached an understanding of how staffers need to leave her alone with the tabloids she enjoyed so much. I pulled the Pennsylvania Manual (an encyclopedia on the Commonwealth's government) from a bookshelf and old microfilm copies of the *York Tribune* to read about Tony Molinaro's background. Curious how he got his start, several photos of the representative showed a handsome man of over six feet with a sharp nose and a thick mane of black hair. One close-up picture revealed a scar, about two inches, that covered the bottom of his chin, probably the result of a childhood bike accident or such.

Elected by the voters in 1980, his colleagues chose Tony as a member of leadership while only in his third term—apparently impressed with his abilities. Highly personal between the members with the elections held behind closed doors, leadership positions are much sought after since they bring extra pay and prestige than service just as a rank-and-file legislator. Molinaro went to Duquesne Law for his degree. He practiced law in York for several years before deciding to run for the House. Tony's political start was anything but smooth.

Back in those days, George Yoder Dimple, an old-time boss, controlled the GOP. He did so as an attorney whose official title for the party was "Counselor." Party chairmen came and went but Dimple ruled the York County Republican Party for over fifty years through an understanding of party rules and a network of politicians who owed their allegiance to him. Molinaro and Dimple would intersect in a way that George would remember until the day he died, an old man over one hundred when many mourners came out to pay their respects.

From articles I read and from later detailed recollections Tony shared directly with me, Molinaro wanted Dimple's help in being appointed to the Hanover Borough Council. An opening became available through a resignation. Civic-minded, the council appointment would enhance his standing within the community and legal circles.

But first, he had to swallow his pride with a visit to the party boss to "kiss the ring." One day, Tony walked from his law office in York to Dimple's well-known unofficial headquarters, a small rather seedy bar several blocks from Market Square, the heart of downtown York.

A long-time arrangement with the restaurant's owner, Gus, allowed Dimple to use the bar and one had to get past Gus to meet with Boss Dimple. Only five-nine, his muscles bulged in the old-style, gabardine uniform he consistently wore. A scar ran the length of his left cheek, the wound suffered during a fight that resulted in paralysis for his opponent. Rumor around York was that Gus had served in the Merchant Marine and a brawl broke out between him and a shipmate during an arm-wrestling contest. Gus was just the man to protect Dimple from unnecessary guests.

After Tony entered the bar, offensive and conflicting smells of stale beer, body odor, and cooked sausage—the latter a fare that Gus put out for regular customers to eat—assaulted his senses. Since cleanliness was not one of the owner's goals, Molinaro's expensive leather shoes went *squish, squish, squish* against the floor as he approached Gus, waiting with a wary eye.

"I'm Tony Molinaro, a local lawyer and loyal Republican. Here to see Mr. Dimple. Pleased to meet you, Gus." A friend had briefed Tony on proper bar protocol.

"Wait here." Gus, a man of few words with a limited vocabulary, didn't bother to shake Tony's hand.

Gus motioned that Tony had the green light. Dimple sat in his usual booth in the corner of the poorly lit back room and Tony noticed the aged party boss poring over that day's *York Tribune*, scraps of paper with notes on them strewn about. Molinaro introduced himself even though he was sure George Dimple recognized him through the county courthouse.

Dimple looked up and asked, "What can I do for you, young man? I knew your father and helped your mother get a secretarial job with the school district." An old pro at setting the right tone for any meeting since George already knew of Tony's interest in the open council seat, Dimple wanted to remind Molinaro of the earlier good he'd done for Molinaro's family.

"Mr. Dimple, my parents always spoke highly of your leadership of the party. I came here to seek your blessing and aid in filling the vacancy open on the Hanover Borough Council. The mayor and several council members say they're waiting to hear who you will support for the position. I'm practicing law in York and want to get involved in the community through public service and I intend to volunteer more in the party. You may recall I worked in several key contests before going off to college and law school." Molinaro hoped all this would be enough to convince the old man to be for him.

Hunched over and back to reading the paper, Dimple spoke in a lower tone now, out of habit so he could not be overheard. He came from an old school you never knew who might be listening even though Gus kept the area clear. "You have a bright future, Molinaro. I want to see you get more involved in the party in the upcoming presidential election. We could use articulate fellows like you speaking at local rallies for our candidate. I've promised that position to Henry King, a faithful party man for many years. His insurance business is struggling, and he needs more visibility. Get more active, and we'll talk again," he concluded. With that, he tried to dismiss Tony from the booth. The way needed to be free for others coming through the bar to seek his support for favors and he had yet to finish the day's paper.

"Henry King's a party hack," Molinaro blurted out, already developing a reputation for calling it the way he saw it, regardless of who he might offend. "Hanover's council needs visionary thinking to help the town pull through challenging times. Please reconsider your position."

George Yoder Dimple did not like having to repeat himself, and his white eyebrow arched in obvious annoyance. "I've made my decision. Check back in a year or two." Just about anyone else would have let it go with this dismissal. But not Anthony Edward Molinaro. When he set his sights on something, nothing deterred him. Tony realized the vacancy appointment would not go his way without the old man's support.

As he left the bar, Molinaro decided to jump into the upcoming race for the House. The incumbent had announced his retirement. Already two other men signaled an interest in running, including Hanover's mayor, Boss Dimple's protégé. If Molinaro couldn't serve on the borough council, he'd run for the General Assembly and defeat Dimple at the ballot box.

Tony always attributed his win to knocking on doors throughout the district, victory coming the old-fashioned way of wearing out shoe leather. He, his lovely wife, and a few key supporters outworked the party and the other two campaigns to win the Republican nomination, assuring victory in the fall in the GOP district. Molinaro would later recount with a twinkle in his eye that his public service career would have been short-lived—and the party spared a contentious primary—had Dimple recommended him for the borough council appointment.

The win marked a major defeat for George Dimple and the party machinery he controlled. Not long after, Dimple retired from politics— the floodgates of opposition now open once others realized the boss could be defanged.

This guy is indeed the real deal, I marveled. I continued reading old cop- ies of the *York Tribune* and came across articles that indicated Molinaro supported abortion choice and served as a leader of that movement. This gave me pause since I opposed abortion, an early lesson that not everyone in the GOP shared my views. It helped me better understand about the party being a "big tent" on abortion differences.

NINETEEN

A Door Opens, The Interview,
Senator James Channing Weigel

FORD COLLEGE BECKONED that we return for graduation. Rob's internship with the House resulted in a job offer because his abilities and demeanor were so impressive. Nor did it hurt he'd been going out for drinks most evenings with the staffers working for the Policy Committee.

In a different position, I possessed glowing reviews from Senator Young and staff, but there were no openings in the Senate Republican Caucus where jobs were much harder to secure since the upper chamber used far fewer employees as a smaller institution than the House. After graduation, other than my Army pay and the little spending money Annie sent, I'd have no funds. The student loans would come due with no home back in Abington to return to—Big Joe and Annie lived in separate apartments with no room to spare. My older siblings didn't have extra space either.

Rob's place, leased for after graduation, was a place to crash and while I appreciated the charity, I needed to find a job, and quick, or I'd be sleeping on his sofa and working at McDonald's, or in another minimum wage position until paying work became open in the Capitol. Convinced this was my path after the terrific internship experience with the chairman, I prayed for God's help. Once again, the Lord guided and provided. He never failed to open doors in the past; doing so this time, six days before graduation from Ford.

Young's chief of staff left a message for me at the student government offices, the only contact number available for personal use. The note said to call; a position had opened on the staff for the senator representing the York area. Using the rotary telephone on the old desk when I was student government president, I called him back. The opening literally just happened, and he'd be faxing articles from the *York Tribune* as background if I could find a fax machine to receive them. That technology still very much in its infancy, I proceeded to Dr. Moran's office for suggestions. Thankfully, he had a fax and his secretary kindly stood on alert for the material.

The next day, I picked up the articles and noted they were written by Kostantin Pokornin since the *Harrisburg World* and *York Tribune* were sister papers. With great interest I read how the senator's staffer abused the Senate's taxpayer-funded expense accounts, entertaining himself and his friends on the government's tab at the most upscale restaurants in Harrisburg. Pokornin scooped everyone else in the Capitol newsroom with this sensational story.

Follow-up stories specified that the legislator in question, James Channing Weigel, had called the staffer into the office, and demanded honest answers about the expenses. Rather than fessing up, the staffer tried to assert the lunches and dinners were for "business purposes." The senator fired him on the spot, and the Senate required restitution or the authorities would bring charges for misusing taxpayer funds.

Why would he breach his boss's trust and that of the taxpayers? I asked myself. This guy worked in a senior position as Weigel's chief of staff. My experiences: two internships, the county transportation advisory council, and one political campaign. *How did I fit into all this?* When I reached the chairman's chief of staff, I asked him, "I see Pokornin broke a huge story after I left, but how does this impact me?"

"Senator Weigel asked around for resumes, and we sent yours over. Young followed up and spoke with Jim yesterday. Senator Weigel likes your experiences, especially the military, and wants you to call for an interview. The boss gave you a stellar review, too." Young's chief of staff never used more words than necessary. "Let us know how you make out. Good luck, Jack." He quickly hung up the phone, and I realized he had lots of important business to tend to other than helping me find a job. Their reputations were on the line when they'd vouched for me to Weigel. And I wasn't about to let them down.

I stopped for a moment to thank God for this opportunity and for watching over me—as He had ever since Annie walked out earlier in the decade. My next call was to Carolyn. Dating again, the sound of her voice caused me to choke up a bit. There's no one I wanted to share this good news with other than Carolyn Gianella. I explained the broad strokes of the development in a shotgun fashion. My style when overly emotional. "Baby, you won't believe it. A senator wants to interview me in the Capitol...for a chief of staff job...me, in a top position. Can you believe it?"

"Jackie, I'm so happy for you. How did this happen? Where in the Capitol?"

With more details filled in, I told her I longed to hold and kiss her at graduation. Carolyn would drive out to Ford, along with Joe, Annie, and my siblings, to witness the first Curran ever to graduate from college.

Carolyn and I said goodbye, and I gained my composure. Next, I placed a call to the senator's office and spoke with Gloria West, his executive assistant. Senator Weigel wanted to see me in the Capitol tomorrow at ten-thirty; could I be there? Without hesitation, I answered absolutely, realizing that meant a departure by six in the morning to make sure I arrived on time for the interview.

Rob was in the campus pub when I gave him the good news. Crossing through the Quad, I greeted classmates along the way and my next stop was Dr. Moran—rooting for me to land a job since he knew of my family circumstances and the uncertainty that lie ahead.

At the crack of dawn, I shaved, showered, and put on my suit, clasping my dog tags and chain since they were a good luck charm of sorts. Thankfully, the old Merc started for the trip on the Pennsylvania Turnpike east to Harrisburg, where I found a parking spot on Third Street, across from the Capitol. Seeing the building again that I just knew I had to work in, my heart quickened as I ran up the steps on this gorgeous May morning, itching to meet with the senator.

In a jubilant mood, I went through the revolving door twice like a kid on a carousel ride. The Rotunda's breathtaking view was before me again. To the day I walked out, I never tired of its magnificence and pinched myself to be so privileged to work in Pennsylvania's Capitol. In the hustle and bustle and stresses of each day, it is all too easy to forget the honor that comes with serving as a legislative staffer.

Turning left, I retraced the steps taken back in January for the start of the internship. On the right, I passed the Caucus Room and Senate Archives. With twenty minutes to spare, I stopped in to ask Agnes about Senator James Channing Weigel. She responded quickly as was her habit. "Nice man, Jack. Says hello to the common folk like me. Some of them are so snobby and can't be bothered with us little people. Very rich from what I hear. Gloria West is the big wheel in that office so be friendly with her. That's about it."

Agnes and I were now buddies, and the internship provided the friendship with her to gain valuable insights on Weigel, the man. "That's so helpful. Is it okay if I give you a hug?" I asked with great gratitude. This receptionist now dear to me gave her assent, and we hugged although I now smelled of her perfume with an interview right around the corner.

From the bookcase, I pulled Senator Weigel's bio and learned he had been raised in York, building from the ground up a string of successful auto dealerships known as "JCW Motors." "Jim," as he was called, was well-known in the region for his charitable and community efforts that flowed from having a thriving business.

Little did I recognize at the time about his rivalry with Representative Tony Molinaro and how their intersection would impact me. The two had battled for the GOP primary nomination and Weigel won, despite Tony's legislative experience and better-known name. In the general election, the Republican nominee stuck to traditional themes of limited government, lower taxes, and tougher penalties to deter crime. While Senator Weigel lost his native York since it'd become heavily Democratic, the Republican suburbs and rural areas voted for him in a landslide.

With this information tucked away in my mind, I took the elevator up to the third floor to Senator Weigel's office and drew in a deep breath to steady my nerves as I opened the door. In the reception area sat a woman in her mid-forties or so. Tasteful makeup with a skirt, tight cotton sweater, and high heels—her hair coiffed carefully—gave the overall impression of a confident professional. She introduced herself as Gloria West, the senator's assistant, and had me sit down in the anteroom and offered me coffee and that morning's copy of the *York Tribune*. "Senator Weigel is on the phone, running a bit late, do you mind waiting?" I responded that my schedule was open. Like opportunity knocked elsewhere.

About fifteen minutes passed as Gloria typed, smoked a cigarette, and answered the telephone, which rarely stopped ringing. The pace reminded me of Senator Young's office, fast and chaotic. At last, I overheard the senator buzz Gloria over the intercom to show me in. Here was my big moment. My first real interview in the Capitol Building. Senator Young secured this meeting; now I had to sell Jack Curran, would-be legislative staffer.

I walked into Senator Weigel's office and he stepped around a big walnut desk, greeting me with a warm handshake and genuine smile. In his late-fifties with thinning gray hair parted over, a soft twinkle around his azure eyes at once set any visitor at ease. The senator's suit coat was draped neatly over a rack and he wore brown suspenders, which I later learned were part of his daily fashion. Snapping these straps before he sat back down, I noticed this same nervous habit when I began working for him.

Weigel carried himself with an air befitting his role as a state senator and exuded confidence—but not arrogance. I observed a wall filled with awards and plaques honoring him for community and charity work. A brass desk lamp with an automobile on top and "JCW Motors" emblazoned across the side provided little light in the rather dim office.

The senator initiated the conversation. "Have a seat, Jack. Thanks for coming in."

"I'm really grateful for the opportunity, Senator, and brought my resume for your review. I'd be glad to answer any questions you or your staff may have." The one-page bio, printed on classy off-white stationery, had been scoured by several professors and Dr. Moran.

"Your resume's impressive for such a young age. I've spoken with your former boss, Senator Young. Ben Walker also thinks highly about his interactions with you. I know all about you," he emphasized this last part. I wondered whether a background check had been performed, not that I had anything to hide. Stunned, my mouth dropped. While I lacked much interview experience, something didn't seem right. Where were the questions about strengths and weaknesses, goals in life, why I wanted to work for him, the usual grist in a job interrogation? Weigel didn't lead with any of that.

"Senator, I'm gratified by their recommendations," I said. What else could one say to the unexpected?

Weigel's large hand went up to silence me to discourage further conversation. "Jack, I need a chief of staff right away with two busy offices and eleven staff you'll manage. I like your background and the way you carry yourself. When do you graduate and when can you start?"

Finally questions I could answer—although not the expected ones. "On Saturday, Senator. I can begin on Monday and have a friend who starts in the House then. Until I find a permanent place, I can bunk with him."

"Good, Monday it is." Weigel didn't waste any time. We hadn't even discussed salary. The senator buzzed Gloria into the office. "Gloria, Jack joins us on Monday at twenty thousand a year. Please send the Chief Clerk the necessary paperwork and get Jack a parking space assigned. Perhaps the Chief Clerk's office can see him now to sign his forms." I'd been with him fewer than five minutes and would start on Monday and didn't dare interrupt the senator—thrilled with the compensation. Weigel could've offered less for that matter.

"Okay, Jack, thanks for coming in. See you next week." Senator Weigel arose from his desk to shake my hand, ready to move to the next appointment or phone call. I prided myself on moving fast, but this guy was intense and why he'd been such a successful businessman.

"You won't be sorry, sir. Thank you." Shaking his hand firmly, I turned to follow Gloria out. Weigel's assistant told me how to get to the next destination, and I bid her goodbye.

A job, and not just a researcher's job, but the chief of staff. *What the hell do I know about running an office and managing people?* I vowed that no one, absolutely no one, in the senator's office or maybe on the entire Capitol staff would work harder than Jack Curran. Gainfully employed in the arena I'd pursued with such vigor and determination, I thanked the Lord. Following that with a loud *whoop* in the hallway, I pumped my fists into the air with pure excitement, unrestrained and joyful.

TWENTY

Frank Gianella Says No,
Graduation, Smoking Weed

GRADUATION FROM FORD COLLEGE was a proud day although Big Joe grumbled because of the work he'd miss from an overnight stay. Resentment of higher education had been shelved for just that day. Besides the Currans and Carolyn, Mr. and Mrs. Hahn made the trip. As much as anyone, I owed my success to my teacher's encouragement and compassion.

When I walked across the stage to receive the diploma from President Moran, I wanted to hug him. Protocol wouldn't allow that so a firm handshake between us, and a wink from him sufficed. He'd done so much for me.

In a great hurry for the last five or six years to get to the next stage of life, compiling a mental checklist of things to do along the way: High school and political activities—check; Army—check; college—check; a job in politics—check. Now came the time to propose to Carolyn with a means available to support us.

With the little money I had saved up, and a payment plan through a jewelry store located not far from the college, with Rob's help and a better eye for style, I purchased a modest quarter-carat diamond engagement ring for over five hundred bucks. While a small rock, I'd bought it for my high school sweetheart, planning to ask Carolyn to marry me in front of the family at the celebration dinner after graduation. Joe and Annie and my siblings loved Carolyn as someone now as much of a Curran as any of us.

But first I had to surmount a huge obstacle, her father, and the formality of permission to marry Carolyn. From a pay phone, I called the Gianella home before the big commencement day. Frank Gianella was not talkative or friendly. Not much had changed since that first moment we met when I picked his daughter up in a toga—and that one is squarely on me. While we weren't close, I respected him as Carolyn's father and a good man, who had worked hard to support his family.

Placing the call, I chatted warmly with Mrs. Gianella before asking if "Mr. G," as I called him, had a moment to chat. Down in his basement shop, working on a metal project, the timing was less than ideal. Mrs. Gianella told him to be "nice" before he picked up the telephone and acknowledged the call. "Mr. G, sorry to bother you. There's something important I need to talk with you about."

"I'm busy working in the basement, Jack. Can you speak with Carolyn's mother about this?"

That would have been my preference to talk to her or anyone else for that matter. No retreating now. "No, sir. This one needs to be with you."

"Okay, what's up?"

"Tomorrow I graduate from college and start a job on Monday with the Pennsylvania Senate. Now that I have the means to support your daughter, who I love very much, with your permission, I'd like to propose to Carolyn at my family's dinner for graduation Saturday night." Over and over, I'd practiced this little speech; hopeful my approach would win him over. It didn't.

For what seemed like at least a minute, silence ensued on the other end of the line, except for the chewing of the big cigar that remained permanently in Gianella's mouth. "Carolyn's my little girl. This engagement is way too quick, and I don't want her to get hurt." He probably wanted to add that he'd come for me, shotgun in hand if need be.

"We're ready for this step, sir." This resistance wasn't unexpected, but I struggled to keep my voice level, never appreciating when anyone tried to hold me back from a goal. "I love your daughter and promise I will always care for her."

Frank Gianella didn't appreciate my persistence. "Look, Jack, you've asked and got my answer. I don't like this interest in politics you have and don't trust politicians. This isn't a good life for my daughter or the life I hoped for her." Now I went silent. "Are you there, Jack, did you hear what I said? I work with my hands. That's what's real and what I know. The world you're in is foreign to me."

"Sir, I hear you loud and clear. At least things are out in the open..." I went from calm to barking in less than thirty seconds. "For the record, I've worked with my hands, too...in my father's antique business, hard and dirty work for ten years, washing grimy glassware, scrubbing roach shit off filthy china closets, and wire-brushing old iron pots till my fingers bled, not to mention hauling furniture down the stairs of narrow row homes and back to our workshop. All of this in all kinds of crappy weather." Enraged, my chest thumped harder and harder. *Why do I have to justify myself to this man?* "I wanted to do this right, but if you don't give us your blessing, I guess we move forward without it..."

He clapped over the phone, prompting me to smash "Ma Bell's" plastic telephone receiver against the little metal stand that held the phone book. A deep dent formed as a testament to our dented relationship. "Nice speech. What do you want, pity you worked hard as a kid? Boo-hoo. Don't marry Carolyn, Jack. Not a wise move. I'll talk with my daughter to make my feelings known."

No further point to the conversation without going beyond a step that would've been disrespectful to my future wife. "Thanks for your time. So long." Gianella said something in reply, the big cigar muffling what could've been more than a goodbye. The relationship with Carolyn's father would never be right, and I suppose we had at least one thing in common—stubbornness.

Undeterred by his rejection, at the celebration that Saturday night, getting down on my knee I proposed to the love of my life, the person who'd been there for so many key moments. I again felt like a man on top of the world, reminded of our first kiss at the photo at Abington High. Cheers and catcalls erupted from family and friends as I drew Carolyn in for a deep and passionate kiss.

Because of the reaction by Frank Gianella, we decided on a short engagement period with a wedding date planned for August at Carolyn's church in Abington. Protestant like my family, as an Italian-American I'd wrongly assumed Carolyn to be Catholic. The Gianella's church was not too far from where my parents had married; and while their marriage didn't last beyond thirty years, it felt right we would marry in the closest thing the Curran family had to a hometown: Abington, Pennsylvania.

After the graduation parties concluded, Rob wanted to meet for one last blast. Some of our fraternity brothers were getting together at the frat house so Rob, Carolyn, and I headed over there. Carolyn showed off her engagement ring to the other girlfriends. I got teased from my brothers as the first one of us with plans to get hitched. A couple of the guys had steady relationships, casually discussing marriage; others like Rob planned on remaining bachelors, at least for a while. The house quickly became packed, the noise level rising, all of us knowing this goodbye had to be put off as long as possible.

In honor of our engagement, Rob picked up Coors Light and wine coolers for the women. As a former president and the acknowledged social leader of the fraternity, Rob climbed on one of the dining room chairs and had the stereo turned down to propose a toast to the brothers of the Class of '86. Eight of us joined as freshmen. We would go off to adulthood, jobs, marriage, children, and, for some of my brothers, divorce, and then remarriage. Most likely the next interesting chapters of our lives.

A sad time we lifted our drinks to each other, reminiscing about the stupid stuff we'd done, somehow surviving the antics we engaged in. In speech after speech, sealed by throwing red Solo cups into the living room fireplace, we vowed to stay close, trying to convince ourselves that everyday life and pressures after college wouldn't interfere with our strong bond. But deep down, we realized it would.

The fraternity taught me how to have fun; the only time I relaxed was when hanging out with my brothers. They also forced me to make choices in life, including about drug use. That memory not a good one. Repulsed by the substance abuse of my older siblings, I avoided pot until my sophomore year. My girlfriend and I had just broken up. Several of my brothers were smoking weed when I entered the fraternity house as a younger brother back then.

"Hey guys," I waved to them, walking through the living room in a hurry to get past the illegal drug activity.

"Why the long face, Jack? C'mon, chew the knob with us." Our lingo for catching up with one another.

"I don't want to interrupt. Jaclyn dumped me so I'm a little down right now. Going back to see Nick to have a beer with him." He was my best friend in the fraternity besides Rob and I hoped he'd cheer me up after losing the only serious girlfriend I had at Ford. Beautiful on the outside and inside, Jaclyn's smile had a way of uplifting my otherwise gloomy outlook.

"Nick's not here. Have a seat, brother." One of my pledge brothers named Willie yanked me down to sit with the three of them as they huddled around a big bong that intimidated the crap out of me. Willie continued egging me on, knowing I appeared to be on the moral ropes. "This is way better than beer, Curran. C'mon, join us."

"No way, guys. That shit's not for me. I'm not touching it. I've got a career in politics to think about." Never far from my thoughts, I wanted nothing in my background that might be a problem or impediment, particularly if I ever ran for public office. Intuitively, I knew drug use could be an issue, although this was before several politicians admitted to recreational use and the public doesn't seem to care now along with other immoral activities that mattered in another time. A better time for public decency.

"Yeah, we're aware, Jack. You've told us over and over about your plans. Just a few tokes. Won't hurt you, bud. No one will ever know...," Willie assured me. He thought I didn't notice the wink, but I did.

Tired and not expecting Jaclyn to dump me, I should've kept walking. *Why not? What's the harm? Who will know as Willie said? If I can't trust my fraternity brothers, who can I trust?* These were my thoughts as I considered their tempting offer.

Around the coffee table we sat. Unlike a former president, I inhaled once, and then again and again. My vision blurred. The bong grew with each toke—warped and menacing. The instrument before me morphed into an anaconda, springing to life, ready to digest me as a living sacrifice on the altar of illegal and immoral drug use.

"That's it, Curran," Willie said, in control of the moment. "Now you're relaxing."

After about twenty minutes, I giggled uncontrollably and yelled out, "I see monkeys, brothers. Give me a banana for the little guys." From a snake to primates, I had landed metaphorically in the Amazon rainforest.

"There's nothing there. You're not used to the wicked stuff, are you?" Willie asked.

Rob, my rescuer and always true blue, came through the front door. After a quick survey of the entire scene, he questioned our stoned brothers. "What the fuck did you guys do? You know he doesn't smoke pot." Pulling me up, Rob guided me towards Nick's room. "Sleep this off, pal. I'll deal with you assholes later," Rob warned our fraternity brothers, shaking his head in disgust. Willie merely laughed as I stumbled along. His hands held up in a show of "who me?"

In the final haze of the marijuana cloud, I remember one of the guys taunting that my political career would be over now they had the "goods" on me for trying drugs, the earlier assurances long forgotten. While they were only kidding, it only added to how disappointed I was with myself for breaking down and smoking pot. A terrible headache and hangover the next morning, my punishment for being so weak in the first place. The silver lining is that I never had a desire or moment when I ever contemplated drug use again.

TWENTY-ONE

Panic on the Pennsylvania Turnpike, Flowing
White Robes, I'm not from Sodom and Gomorrah

HUNGOVER FROM TOO MUCH CELEBRATING with the guys and gals during the last hurrah, I slowly packed up the '73 Mercury Capri with the entirety of my belongings: clothes, a trunk of memorabilia, photos and awards, stereo and albums, all my Army gear, and a couple hundred dollars given at graduation. Living simply, I owned little. I counted on Carolyn, who had better taste, to furnish whatever we chose to be our home. Until then, I would continue a Spartan existence.

East on the turnpike I traveled to my new home of Harrisburg, excited about starting work Monday morning. I would miss Ford, President Moran, and my fraternity brothers. The campus served as a sanctuary; my safe place away from the drama and tumultuous years of the Curran family. Other than the Capitol internship, rarely had I left its confines with no house to return to back in Abington.

A bittersweet time, the car stereo distracted me at such moments. I popped into the slot one of the "must play" tunes anytime we hung out at the college's neighborhood bar. With the window down, I sang along. The tears began with lots of memories of the best four years of my life.

Despite my confident exterior, I was nervous about serving as a chief of staff at the young age of twenty-two. And my very last work in that arena was as an intern. *Eleven people and two offices in a highly charged political environment? What was I thinking?* Doubt crept in, destructive and insidious. A knot soon formed in my stomach and my bowels cramped up. *Should I turn around? Maybe Dr. Moran has an entry-level position on campus, and I can stay within its safe walls? How do I stop this panic?*

I swung the wheel over to the side of the road and got the door open just in time. The stream of vomit represented all those emotions—the alcohol from last night no doubt contributing to the turmoil. My soul ached with loneliness. A fresh wave of nausea overcame me, and I had to fight the urge to go. With no portable potty in sight, I wasn't about to use my military training to find a tree on the roadside and go with a leaf as toilet paper. My drill sergeant's advice at once came to mind, "Make sure you don't grab for poison ivy."

At the next rest stop, deeply unsettled about whether Harrisburg should be my destination after all, after a trip to the restroom, I found a pay phone and called President Moran at home. Thankfully, he answered. "Dr. Moran, it's Jack Curran, I can't make it at the State Capitol." Hyperventilating, spitting these words out, I needed to hear that soothing voice.

"Jack, calm down. Take a deep breath," Dr. Moran said. "Tell me what's going on."

"I'm so lonely and miss the college. I'm not ready to manage an office, Dr. Moran. Maybe this political thing is a mistake after all...is there a job on campus for me?" I asked in a childlike way.

"Listen to me, Jack. You're ready for what lies ahead. Mrs. Moran and I are very proud of you, as are your professors. This job is just the next step in your journey. You'll be fine." My breathing became more even, and I thanked someone who'd been the closest thing to a second father to me. In some ways, President Moran was more of a dad than Big Joe—so removed from my daily life. "Call me anytime. We're all cheering for you, Jack. Bye."

Reassured my destiny lie ahead on the eastern banks of the Susquehanna, not back in Western Pennsylvania, I finished the ride. Once I found Rob's new apartment, I unpacked and ironed a white shirt and got my suit, tie, and shoes ready for work—the first day in a job in politics. My goal finally secured.

Senate Security let me in Weigel's suite the following morning because I'd arrived at the Capitol before everyone else (a pattern I would follow for most of my career). The legislative bureaucracy had yet to assign a key or identification card, so I read the paper while waiting for the senator's staff to arrive. Gloria came in; soon, several other female staffers followed. All of them seemed excited about my hire. From their cryptic remarks, I gather my predecessor didn't treat the staff with much respect. This put added pressure on me to make sure I rebuilt a team that desperately needed leadership and high morale after the scandal from the previous chief of staff's misconduct.

Gloria showed me to my office on the ground floor. Separated from Weigel and the rest of the team with space at a premium in the Capitol Building in those days, an old storage room converted into "cubicles" served as my first work space. Shared with three other staffers, I noticed the plaster ceiling appeared to be hanging loosely in places and smelled a musty odor coming from the large heat pump that dominated the outside wall (causing extra use of my asthma inhaler!). While not even Class B office space, I shook off the feeling of being assigned to work in a dumpy oversized broom closet.

With this room as my headquarters in the Capitol, I soon learned that most days I would run up and down three flights of stairs since Senator Weigel called us to his office all day long. He kept the staff and me hopping—used to having a large contingent of salesman and service people at his beck and call when he ran a massive automobile enterprise.

After settling in, Gloria buzzed me to come upstairs, saying we had to go over scheduling with the senator to sort through the multitude of meeting requests and invitations to community events he received. Monday morning was the time set aside to stay on top of the significant volume coming into the office. A people person, Weigel said yes to as much as possible. The staff had to keep up with his schedule, plus handle meetings on the senator's behalf with constituents and lobbyists. We also covered local meetings and speaking engagements when the senator couldn't be in attendance.

Gloria and I entered the senator's office with the scheduling folder. Weigel greeted me as if I belonged for years. "Good to see you, Jack," he said. "Sit down, sit down, there's work to do," he motioned to one of the two side chairs across from his desk. Over the course of nearly a decade, I would spend countless hours in this chair as his closest strategic and policy advisor even after leaving his employ.

We sorted through the pile of requests and came to a speaking engagement in rural Adams County—outside of the senator's district—from the Women Against Alcohol (WAA). Vivian Ulrich, the president of the group, hailed from Weigel's area and wanted the senator to come out to their meeting place, an old church campsite, to give a legislative update on the Liquor Control Board and underage drinking. The real goal of the WAA remained temperance. Short of a return to Prohibition 2.0, they cared about measures in the General Assembly that would make drinking alcohol more difficult for adults and impossible for minors.

"Jack, I can't do this speech. I have a town hall meeting Thursday night in the northern part of the county. You must cover this," Weigel said as he removed his eyeglasses. My immediate thought: *You're throwing me right into the deep end of the swimming pool.* Time to sink or swim from his vantage point, and he wasn't giving me any arm floaties to cheat with.

"Um, Senator, I haven't had the chance to research alcohol issues. Is there anyone else on the staff that might take this one until I get a little more settled in?" I tried hard to worm my way out of this responsibility. Jim Weigel saw right through me.

The same twinkle that'd probably helped sell many automobiles responded to my nervousness and doubt. "You'll be all right. Susan is an excellent researcher. Ask her to put brief talking points together and then open for questions." He assured me, "There's nothing to speaking to a group like this." Gloria chimed in it wasn't doable for the senator to attend the town hall meeting and this event. That settled it; off to Adams County to speak to an ultra-conservative organization. A living relic from Prohibition times.

As I turned to leave Jim's office, he asked, "Jack, you will live in my senatorial district, right?"

We hadn't discussed this at all in that brief interview. "Senator, uh, I'm staying with a friend in his apartment and planned to get my own place here in Harrisburg. I want to be close to work."

Weigel shook his head. "No, that won't do. As my chief of staff, I need you to live in the district. How else can you understand the people I represent other than by residing in the area? When not here in the Capitol, you'll be working in my office on North George Street in York." Okay, none of this came up. A long commute from York to Harrisburg wasn't mentioned, nor did I talk with Carolyn about the need to live in York.

On the first day of work, how could I argue with the boss? "Sure, sir, okay...understood. My fiancée and I get married in August, and we'll find a place down there then." That settled that. We would live in York, an area I knew nothing about.

Thursday evening came quickly. With just four days as a legislative staffer under my belt, I left our district office and drove to Adams County using Route 30, a busy road that narrowed to two lanes once it cleared the more populated areas. Off the highway to a smaller country road, I made my way to New Berlin, the destination not too far from that small town, deep, very deep, within Pennsylvania's Bible Belt. The asphalt country road I followed soon led onto a stone path. The Mercury Capri bounced and jostled towards the nondescript concrete building with peeling paint and weeds growing around it. Cars parked nearby the only sign the area hadn't been abandoned long ago.

Later, I'd "treat myself" to a black 1981 Ford Fiesta—the old Capri fetched two hundred bucks from a teenager that demanded I toss in the newer car mats to sweeten the deal (Big Joe would have been proud of his negotiating skills!). Woefully underpowered and boxy, the tinny Fiesta seemed like a sad stepchild to the Volkswagen Golf I really wanted but couldn't afford.

When I parked the car, for some strange reason, I locked the door. The hill people weren't about to jump me for the Merc and the ten bucks in my pocket. But old habits are hard to break.

With no soul in sight except the host, Vivian Ulrich, who had exited a side door to greet me, my first reaction was that of flight. Vivian had long gray hair, kept just below shoulder length. Her rouge and lipstick were applied heavily and unevenly; the bright eyeliner caked on accentuated her large Doe-like eyes. A flowing white robe adorned her body and a large gold cross lay across her chest. I had to force myself not to jump back in and continue driving—there was no hiding from the WAA in Pennsylvania's backwoods, however. Creepy. It would get worse.

While we waited at the front of the church hall, I nervously read and reread my notes, pretending to listen to Vivian's small talk about the goals of their organization, how many members they had, and how much her members were looking forward to my talk. A procession of older women—also in flowing white robes—entered, carrying long lit candles with cones to prevent the wax from dripping onto their withered hands. Since Vivian had dimmed the lights, my dark suit contrasted against their white robes as the room glowed from the uneven candle flames.

I knew they were harmless, but I'd experienced nothing like this, including at the churches my parents raised me in. One of the few residual benefits from the various "Annie and Joe moves" included attending different churches with different experiences. But nothing prepared me for this experience that seemed straight out of maybe *The Waltons* or *Little House on the Prairie.*

The ladies moved to the three front rows of chairs as Vivian stepped up to introduce me. The old gal still had a spring in her step; I suppose thinking she'd pulled in a much bigger fish than little ole me. In a higher-pitched, bird-like voice—I imagined her singing in the church choir—she began her introduction. "The WAA is happy to have Mr. Jack Curran, Chief of Staff to Senator Jim Weigel, with us tonight. Senator Weigel called me personally to say he has a town hall meeting previously scheduled and promised his aide would represent him well." *You have way too much confidence in me, Weigel*, my inner voice said, *sending me to speak before a group like this.*

"Mr. Curran just joined the senator's staff and told me he is originally from the suburbs of the big and worldly city of Philadelphia. We won't hold that against him, will we, ladies?" the women joined Vivian in giggling.

What an awkward moment. "I'm from Abington and many places before that, not Sodom and Gomorrah," I wanted to yell out!

My host for the evening concluded, "After he updates us on the Liquor Control Board and underage drinking, Mr. Curran will take questions. Please join me in welcoming Jack Curran." Mrs. Ulrich put her unlit candle down to applaud. The rest of the WAA members tapped their hands deftly, having nowhere to place the lit candles.

Well, here you go, Jack, you wanted this life, I reminded myself. I had plenty of public speaking experience. And had come a long way from the little boy at the church Christmas pageant whose hands couldn't stop shaking as I tried to read my part. I willed my legs to stop quivering; the iron black music stand that held my notes my anchor that evening.

Looking about, I spotted a small brass cross that sat on an oak table. *Please be with me, Jesus,* I prayed.

Then I dove in. "Thank you, Mrs. Ulrich, for that warm introduction." The ladies were pleasant enough, but "warm" stretched the truth for sure. When one is in politics, exaggeration is expected, however. As I glanced over at my hostess, I knew the line stopped at "Mrs. Ulrich" and not "Vivian."

"As Mrs. Ulrich indicated, Senator Weigel has a previous engagement and sends his best wishes to the WAA. He and your president have had many positive interactions, and the senator appreciates the important work you do promoting alcohol abstinence." I silently thanked Susan for giving me excellent talking points. In those days before the internet, she was a first-rate researcher.

I'd heard of the WAA but thought it to be extinct before Weigel sent me to the hinterland of Adams County, where the organization flourished, fighting to uphold a culture from a far simpler and more decent time. "In this period of decaying morals in the country, throughout its history, the WAA has been a force for clean living and healthy families. The Commonwealth of Pennsylvania has a strong tradition of controlling alcohol sales through the establishment of the Liquor Control Board, or LCB, one of two states in the union that controls the distribution and sale of liquor through state-owned stores."

As a free market Republican, I wanted to shout out, "It's archaic." But that wasn't my place. Weigel supported retention of this system of alcohol control, and I had to represent him, not my views—not the last time I'd have to defend a position I didn't hold. This is one of the fundamental quandaries of being a good staff person. Give advice and recommendations. But be prepared to carry out instructions and positions you may not agree with. Where it really gets difficult is when those positions conflict with your conscience or moral values.

I continued, "The LCB system is more consumer-friendly; the result of reforms to add credit cards to the stores, an extension of hours, and locations made more convenient for Pennsylvanians to buy liquor and wine. Several votes to abolish the system and open the sale of alcohol to private sector entities failed. I'm pleased to tell you, Senator Weigel is opposed to privatization of the LCB." The ladies blew out their candles and applauded this line.

Loose now, although I found it harder to read my remarks without the candlelight, the single exposed bulb overhead couldn't brighten a cupboard let alone a decrepit church property, I was on a roll. Sweat poured down my arms and perspiration dotted my forehead from the evening's humidity. The building lacked air conditioning or fans and the stale air magnified the scent I recognized could only be toilet water. One of Annie's closest friends—we called her "Auntie Bess"—seemed to bathe herself in it.

Oh, what I would've given for a glass of water. Or better yet, a shot of Jack Daniels with a beer chaser. But that would've been like letting loose a loud fart during church.

"On underage drinking, one proposal appears to be on track to pass the General Assembly, and the governor has said he will sign the bill if it reaches his desk. For any underage drinking offense, a minor would lose their driving privileges with progressively higher penalties for later offenses. The thinking is that a young person's driver's license is one of their most prized possessions. The threat of a suspension will be a huge deterrent to underage drinking."

I talked about underage drinking a bit more and threw statistics in about how Pennsylvania ranked against surrounding states. Susan found data that showed we did a better job at alcohol control even though I doubted this "control" worked. Or was necessary. It seemed to be nothing but a huge inconvenience to consumers and a sop to the unions that upheld and benefitted from the system protecting workers whose wages and benefits were far higher than what private sector retail outlets paid.

Vivian led the group in further applause and stepped back up to the front for questions. One of the oldest women present stood up. *Probably someone who'd lived through the experiment of the Eighteenth Amendment and the 1920s,* I mused. "My name is Mrs. Horatio Geiselman," she began. "Thank you, young man, for the update." I felt like I should have been in diapers, holding a rattle as she addressed me. "While I'm glad the effort to privatize the LCB failed, I am disappointed the senator, and others are making it more convenient to buy alcohol. We should make it more difficult, not easier," said Mrs. Geiselman. "Credit is not a good idea... force *them* to spend the cash in their pocket rather than using their plastic conveniences." Clearly, Mrs. Geiselman believed purchasing liquor to be a sin and drinkers were of questionable character.

To let this sink in, she paused and concluded with, "Men will run up credit cards with booze purchases, harming women and children, depriving them of food and clothing!"

With that grand most sexist statement, she sat down to enthusiastic applause acknowledged with the slightest bow. Any movement more than tiny for Mrs. Horatio Geiselman, a.k.a. the possible daughter of Methuselah (the oldest recorded man from the Bible) and we would have been rubbing her back with Icy Hot ointment, chanting in *Sanskrit* for a miracle with holy incense burning for good measure.

Her many wrinkles fascinated me, and I had to force myself to concentrate. I answered, "Thank you, ma'am, for that observation. All I can say is that the current system is a compromise between those who want to open sales altogether and those who want to make it harder to buy alcohol. Our system isn't perfect. I think we can all agree that having only seven hundred stores is far preferable to having five thousand." I threw out a big number, having no idea how many private outlets would exist with privatization, hoping the threat of that many potential new liquor joints would calm them down (politicians can and do make numbers up!). It did. My ancient questioner seemed to be satisfied.

After several more questions, the group clapped again. Mrs. Ulrich escorted me to the exit, promising she would call Senator Weigel to give him a good report. I thanked her and fled to the car once the church door closed and I was safely out of sight. Transported back in history to an uncomplicated time and age, I was glad Weigel made me attend this out-of-body experience, knowing it would make a great journal entry I entitled *"Fourth Day in Senate, 1920s Style."*

TWENTY-TWO

Marriage, Jack and the Prostitute, Racism in the Capitol, Attempted Bribe

CAROLYN AND I MARRIED in August. I survived her father's evil eye at the altar with the help of a shot of whiskey Rob provided from a flask he discreetly slipped out of his tux pocket to steel me through that difficult part of the ceremony. During a five-day honeymoon to Bermuda, we swam, ate delicious foods, drank lots of white wine, and made love, tenderly, passionately, without reservation—as only a husband and wife can truly do.

Carolyn thankfully forced us to wait. But I lacked the strength to say no as an incoming junior—before we started dating—when I lost my virginity.

My buddies and I rented a dump at the Jersey Shore for a week to celebrate the end of school. Our female next-door neighbors, ironically, came from a town near Abington. They asked if we wanted to join forces, sharing booze, food, and suntan lotion at the motel pool. Beautiful, wild, and in their early twenties. Sounds like nirvana for seventeen-year-old boys, right?

"Barb" and I slipped off from one of the raucous parties. The more seasoned of the two of us took the lead, guiding this half-frightened kid through the act that lacked love or emotional connection and lasted less than four minutes. Recovering from a hangover the next day, guilt and my Christian values took over. I could hear Annie's voice echo around in my head with what constituted the sex "talk" in the Curran family, "Keep *it* in your pants until you're married."

I found Barb at the pool, stretched out and lounging in a skimpy bikini. The fluorescent lime of her two-piece is not the only thing she radiated. Sexual passion briefly overcame me, and I momentarily forgot my reason for the visit. *Concentrate, Curran,* my brain waves struggled to say as my hands went to shield the front of my black swim trunks. Saddling next to her, I apologized for our fling.

Barb's response burned me harder than the sun's rays and my face showed it. "For what? I know it was your first time. We had sex, Jack, because I'm attracted to you. That's it. What are you some kind of choir boy?" she asked. YEP.

The newly wedded Currans decided on a comfortable brick townhouse in a redeveloped section of York, not far from the Codorus Creek, as our first home. Close to the water ran a lovely walking trail. The Central Market House, a venue of fresh flowers, meats, vegetables, and some various cultures where one could sample different foods, stood nearby. There was something special about being a part of the urban renewal efforts of the city. Although finding myself face-to-face with a prostitute while tending to the garden one day is not what I expected from such a cosmopolitan life.

Rather than the gentle aroma of the flowers planted lovingly by Carolyn, my olfactory senses were assaulted by an offensive fragrance, not CHANEL No 5. Admittedly, I'm not a perfume aficionado, but this scent brought tears to my eyes and burned my nostrils.

Gazing up from the weeds—waging what seemed like a losing battle—a leggy woman, who didn't need the spiked high heels she wore,
greeted me. A sable leather skirt left nothing to modesty and the streaks
of crimson in her black hair screeched "Red-Light District." The knot at
her belly button tied off a bejeweled shirt held together by a silver clasp—
reminding me of the formal antique sterling silver napkin holders Annie
used to entertain with. Maybe payment tendered from a cash-poor customer? Stamped on the side of her long torso: a dragon tattoo with yellow
and orange flames shooting from its mouth the name "Sophia."

Sophia's hazel eyes were friendly enough once you got past the over-
painted face. "Do you like my perfume?" she asked me. "It's called '*Odeur
de lavande pour dames.*' That's French for 'Lavender Scent for Ladies.'"
Sophia beamed with pride at her linguistic talent although I'm not sure
an actual Frenchman would've approved of the translation.

I mumbled something about the perfume being "nice," while I tried
to hold my breath.

"What're you doing?" Sophia inquired, one of her spiked heels now
rested on the split rail fence I'd installed to give our property a boundary.

My head down to avoid the "view" I had from Sophia's new provoca-
tive position, I answered, "Weeding." The dandelions became tougher to
yank out as if the roots were determined to remain in the ground to avoid
the stench from her "perfume." Inside my head, a voice warned: *This isn't
a welcome wagon call, Curran.*

"You live here alone?" my sweet-talking new acquaintance probed
with a sultry smile highlighted by cherry-red lipstick.

"Honey," I bellowed out with more lung power than I ever had before,
"Come meet the neighbor." Turning back to the raised flowerbed, I sighed
with relief, gulping in fresh air now that Sophia had left, deciding I wasn't
worth more than a minute of time. I did a quick calculation and figured
she'd lost a couple of bucks in missed revenue just in our brief encounter.

Summer had passed, the leaves were just beginning to turn into a vibrant canopy, and the air began to cool late in the evening. I'd survived June, the busiest time traditionally in the legislative schedule since the fiscal year ends on June 30 of each year. Sometimes, the legislature and governor miss the July 1 budget deadline, spilling over into the Independence Day holiday, occasionally well beyond that.

Carolyn concentrated on creating a stable home life for me after the many years I had gone without experiencing this kind of tranquility. She decorated, cooked, and listened to me each evening as I shared with her daily life at the Capitol before making my journal entry. She knew the little break we had enjoyed would soon be over as I prepared for an expected busy fall session when we returned to action in September.

A typical session day at the Capitol: fast-paced, fun, crazy, stressful, and depending on the voting schedule for that day, could go long into the night. I had done many all-nighters, weekends, and holidays, rarely working from nine-to-five daily. Legislative life demanded it. Until the last couple of years of my career, I thrived on the pace. After the exhilaration of these sessions, I'd come back down, physically and emotionally spent, until catching up on sleep and eating better foods.

Many a night, we'd wolf down pizza or crackers, rushing around to meet deadlines and put out fires that happen as members, administration officials, staff, and lobbyists clash over challenging public policy issues. And reporters chase about demanding information when many times there's no concrete news to share. Human nature what it is, tempers flare, separation occurs, and cooling off begins. Everyone can move on until the next crisis erupts and then it starts all over again. We were like hamsters on a wheel, the elusive "carrot," or resolution of conflict, many times out of reach.

We'd been through several long session weeks that fall with each day blurring into the next. In the last stretch of Governor Walter Van Dalen's second term, a Democrat would succeed him by defeating his

GOP lieutenant governor. Half the Senate was up for election and the entire House. There was much to do before the session ended. All members, including Senator Weigel, had their wish lists of legislation they wanted to enact.

Lobbyists scurried about, working to advance priority items or hoping to defeat bills and amendments. Sometimes using the clock is an advantage for opponents, knowing that all bills not enacted die on November 30 of an even-numbered year. January brings a new session, a blank slate to write upon for two years and so on.

Tuesday of a session week came—usually the most hectic day of each week, much of the action packed into that day. On Monday, members are traveling into Harrisburg from their districts, and on Wednesday, they return home. This detailed notation from the senator's schedule was an ordinary Tuesday for us, reflective of Weigel's pace, and of the General Assembly overall:

7:30–8:00-Reception by Community Colleges (Susan)

8:00–8:30-Legislative reception by Realtors (Jack)

8:30–9:00-Legislative reception by School Nurses (Jack)

9:15–9:30-Meeting with staff to review morning's committee meetings

9:30–10:30-Consumer Protection and Professional Licensure Committee (Susan)

10:15–10:30-Photos with school groups-Rotunda

10:30–10:45-Meeting with law enforcement officials to discuss Judiciary meeting bills (Jack)

10:45–11:00-JCW return phone calls (Gloria/Jack)

11:00–11:30-Meeting with Department of Transportation to discuss district road and bridge projects (Jack)

11:30–12:30-Judiciary Committee meeting (Jack)

12:30–1:00-Lunch from Capitol cafeteria-JCW/Jack review of legislative priorities and Senate calendar

1:00-Session begins

1:30-Meeting of Appropriations Committee called from the floor (Jack)

1:45-Caucus

2:15-JCW calls Jack to Senate Archives to discuss bill under review in caucus

3:00-JCW meeting with Senator Pumfrey and constituents (Jack)

4:00-Senate session resumes

4:25-JCW put on Temporary Capitol Leave

4:30-Meeting with Businessman from Erie area (Jack)

4:45-JCW returns to Senate floor

7:00-Session Concludes

7:00-Reception by Insurance Industry (Susan)

7:15-JCW conference with Ben Walker

8:00-JCW attend community event in York (Jack)

For the senator and our staff, we were like whirling dervishes, rarely resting, usually running about to stay on pace with the demands of the schedule. Either one of our employees or I would attend these meetings and events with Senator Weigel. All the while lobbyists, who didn't have appointments, continued to stop in, asking to see either Weigel or staff. On top of this activity, the phone never ceased ringing. Constituents expected their calls to be answered and staff to respond to concerns and issues.

Two meetings are noteworthy from this typical schedule, one of which resulted in an explosion from Jim; the other, with another senator, who used offensive language in front of us and his constituents.

Senator Caddock Pumfrey, an older man with a pencil-shaped mustache, had a reputation for being obnoxious with his fellow members, staff, and lobbyists. The senator maintained a different persona back home—warm and friendly. This member was a legislative "Dr. Jekyll and Mr. Hyde." One personality in his district, and the other coming out in the Capitol.

Pumfrey wanted Senator Weigel to come to a meeting with his constituents to talk about law enforcement since Jim had developed an expertise in these issues, especially because of his appointment to the Pennsylvania Crime Prevention Commission (PCPC). Weigel asked me to join to take notes and address any follow up that might be needed. Dread hovered over me because of Pumfrey's reputation for berating staff people. For months, I stayed away from this senator. His team had confided in me on how abusive Pumfrey could be.

One time, while meeting with a staff member, Pumfrey didn't like waiting for his aide to find the relevant section of state law. Many of Pennsylvania's statutes are difficult to locate and challenging to read, depending on the subject matter. In a rage, the senator ordered him to go to the Legislative Reference Bureau at once. The poor guy said verbatim, per Pumfrey's order, to the attorneys there, "I'm an idiot and can't read state law. Senator Pumfrey wants you to teach me how to read a bill and law." To describe this legislator as "mean" was an understatement—his office a revolving door of staff, who couldn't bear the abuse for too long.

Pumfrey's constituents were upset that the crime commission hadn't awarded a grant for their community's efforts to combat crime. There simply weren't enough funds to go around, which is why the program had to be competitive. Commission staff briefed Jim on the deficiencies of the grant application and Weigel tried to explain why the town didn't receive an award, suggesting that the group persevere and apply again in the next funding round. Senator Weigel also offered to visit their area to see firsthand what the town confronted.

Performing for his voters, Pumfrey interrupted Jim by telling him he had to come to the area to see how a "particular race had taken over." Senator Pumfrey used a very offensive word at that point and I'd never heard this word in casual conversation, let alone in the State Capitol. All of us, including the senator's constituents, sat in stunned silence for a moment. The only sound audible: the gasp I involuntarily let out.

I leaned over and whispered to Weigel, "He shouldn't be using that language, Senator." My murmur wasn't as quiet as intended. Blame my deep, booming voice that doesn't have a "low" setting.

Senator Pumfrey turned his bald, egg-shaped head; the first time he acknowledged my presence. Like the color of coal, Pumfrey's eyes bore into me, lifeless, betraying nothing, except unrestrained scorn for an underling. Perhaps at a younger time, those eyes conveyed kindness and joy, but not now. The senator asked me with dripping contempt, "What did you say?"

Senator Weigel didn't want to embarrass Pumfrey in front of his constituents because of senatorial protocol but came to the rescue before the situation could escalate further. Jim interjected, "Caddock, let's focus on the grant application and its merits, okay?"

Pumfrey didn't let go and retorted, "Your aide doesn't know his place, Weigel. I'll be talking with leadership about his attitude. They will fire him."

The mention of possible termination, my obligations to Carolyn and the career path I'd pursued for so long flashed before my eyes. I didn't sweat for more than twenty seconds as Jim Weigel wouldn't stand for being threatened and could face a bully like no one else. "No need to, Caddock. Jack works for me, not leadership. I don't believe you want this incident discussed in a public light, do you? The offer to tour your town still stands. Thanks for making me aware of the grant. C'mon, Jack." Weigel stood up, beckoning me to join him as he headed for the door.

With my head lowered in shame, I apologized as we walked back to the office. "I'm sorry, sir. My father wouldn't tolerate that crap in our household. Do you want me to apologize to Senator Pumfrey?"

"No apology needed. You tried to whisper and didn't lose your temper. I wanted to let Pumfrey have it. Your interruption worked. It made the point and got us out of there," the senator said all this with a low chuckle. Weigel didn't have a bad bone in his body and had no tolerance for racism. Moments like these made me so proud to work for him.

The second meeting that day occurred with a wealthy businessman from the Erie area who wanted to see Senator Weigel about legislation he and his company supported. I joined Jim. Admittedly, both Weigel and I were tired. And somewhat ill-tempered by the time this meeting occurred—four-thirty in the afternoon—of what had been a long day among several session weeks, also demanding. Since we both commuted from York on session days, the days were even longer with travel time.

After exchanging pleasantries, this company owner explained the details of the legislation and why his industry supported it. He then made the mistake of indicating that Senator Weigel would be backed by this man's group *if* the senator supported the bill. Vague, he never mentioned a campaign contribution or amount. But enough was said for Jim to erupt as my notes show—his face and ears became red and his lips quivered with rage.

"Before you say another word, get out, get out now! No one mentions monetary support connected to a vote. No one." Weigel's long, crooked finger pointed to the door. "Jack, open the door so I have a clear shot to throw this fool out." I leaped out of my chair and rushed like a man on a mission to open the door, stumbling over the carpet since I could be a real klutz when stressed.

In shock, this guy probably had little experience in these matters, thinking Harrisburg conducted business in this way. "Senator, there's been a misunderstanding. I...I wasn't offering you anything. I only wanted to convey that if you supported us, our industry would be supportive of you." Even so, there's a fine line between a bribe and general support.

"What's in that briefcase, cash? Get the hell outta here now. Do not come back to this office." By now, Weigel was shouting. Beyond rattled, this small-time tycoon tried to shake our hands. Jim wanted none of it.

Once he ran out of our office, the senator asked to see Ben Walker. When they talked later that evening, out of an abundance of caution and to satisfy Jim more than anything, Walker suggested we report the matter to the proper law enforcement authorities. We did the next day.

Later that afternoon, Gloria answered a phone call from Kostantin Pokornin of the *Harrisburg World* and *York Tribune*. Someone had leaked information of the meeting's contents to Pokornin, likely coming from one of his many sources in law enforcement.

This super-sleuth reporter stalked us, including waiting outside the office door. Pokornin knew Weigel would have to use the restroom at some point. Jim relented and called Kostantin into the office after we strategized how to handle the interview.

"What can I do for you, Kostantin?"

"Senator Weigel, how big was the bribe?" Kostantin wrote his story before the interview began—he just needed to fill in the blanks.

"I was not 'bribed,' as you say. The man I met with intimated there would be support coming my way if I supported a certain bill. I literally threw him out of the office before the conversation could continue. That's what happened. Nothing more."

"Why the referral to law enforcement? Must be more to this than that, Senator." Pokornin wanted to nail another politician's tail to his wall of shame. Wasn't happening.

"I made the referral based on the advice of counsel. Law enforcement will determine the next steps." Weigel's signs of irritation showed as I sat in the corner taking notes.

"Well, Senator, this isn't the first time you've had problems so forgive me if I'm skeptical. That's our job in the Fourth Estate." Pokornin hissed these words towards Jim. From my spot over eight feet away, I caught a blast of Kostantin's bad breath. I could only imagine what the senator experienced across the desk from this journalist.

"That situation is over. It's old news. The two have nothing to do with one another. If there's nothing else, I have an appointment waiting. Good day." Our strategy: schedule Pokornin for only five minutes with a group of constituents to mark time in the lobby area as the excuse to wrap the meeting. It worked.

"Well, okay, Senator, I'll be keeping an eye on you and your office. Where there's smoke, there's fire," he said this as he shuffled out the door on his way to bird dog another story.

Gloria came in right afterward with a spray can of air freshener at the ready. She knew Kostantin had left more than just bad will behind. Eventually, law enforcement concluded that enough detail didn't exist to warrant further action. After that meeting, we never closed Jim's inner office door. A staffer always present as a witness as our added precaution to ensure transparency.

TWENTY-THREE

Oral Sex is Illegal, Superman and
Toenail Cutting, Bertie and the
Village People, Racism Defeated

NOTHING PREPARED ME for my encounter with Elizabeth Beverson when she came in seeking the senator's help with a constituent "problem" that troubled her and Mr. Beverson. Indeed, I used profanity, especially while serving in the military, and discussed sex with my Army and sports buddies in nothing but crass locker room talk. Yet a hippie taught me a thing or two one day long ago when she walked into our office.

Just another constituent case to resolve. Or so it seemed when I put my hand and business card out with the official introduction. "Jack Curran, the senator's chief of staff, how can I help you?"

"Hi, Elizabeth Beverson, very pleased to meet you. I live in the senator's district," she began. "We need Jim Weigel to intervene on our behalf." Assisting constituents with their everyday problems was part of the job and Weigel expected the team to offer top-notch service.

We were to treat citizens with the utmost respect in the process. As I took in her appearance that day, I had to stifle a laugh by pretending to sneeze into my sleeve. Elizabeth responded with "Gesundheit." No "God bless you," an early tell for how the conversation would go.

She had long black hair down to her waist and a peace-symbol barrette that helped part her curls evenly down the middle. Complemented by hip-hugging jeans and a bright tie-dye shirt, I envisioned her partying at Woodstock some seventeen years before as Jefferson Airplane, Joe Cocker, and The Who jammed away. And sex, drugs, and whatever else broke out during those three infamous days of rock-and-roll mayhem.

"Thanks for taking the time to visit. The senator's in a meeting, but you can tell me what's going on and what we can do to assist." Legal pad at the ready to take notes, she began her story.

"Earl and I engage in oral sex often, and I've heard the act is illegal. We had no idea government regulates sex between a couple. Confirm this, please, and tell the police not to bother peeping in our window. The cops should have better things to do than trying to catch us." These words popped out of her mouth as nonchalantly as one would talk about the weather or that day's stock market results.

My pen froze somewhere around "oral sex," and I was glad our receptionist sat within earshot. "To be honest, I'm not sure, uh, whether it is or not—"

Cutting me off, she exclaimed, "Speak up! I can't hear you. Are you afraid of discussing sex? Didn't you have sex ed in school? What're they teaching young folks now?" Elizabeth had me on the run.

Crossing my arms in a defensive gesture, I responded, "Yes, I did, Mrs. Beverson."

Back in those days, our gym teacher taught health. "Mr. R" had little training in the subject. A crusty, old Marine with a square jaw and white stubble hair, he seemed to live, eat, and sleep in his sweats, always in the school colors. Mr. R's method of teaching the subject—he said nothing about "sex"—was to tell the class to open our textbooks and not ask questions. One wise ass, who would "innocently" put his hand up and pose a question about something on page forty-three of the text, for instance, sought more lurid details. Mr. R would yell at the student to pipe down and exact revenge in the next gym period when that kid became the group target during a fun game of "bombardment."

"I doubt the police have that much time, uh, on their hands to be, uh, trying to enforce this law if it, uh, exists." Generally an articulate person, the Beverson woman had me tongue-tied.

"Hold on, young man," Mrs. Beverson was in her early forties or so, "we need to know the law. I'm not interested in your opinions. Earl and I just want the facts." Mr. Beverson, or "Earl," didn't join her, but she carried the concern of two people rattled that their sex life wasn't safe from the intrusive watch of "big brother" government.

"Okay, Mrs. Beverson. Give me a minute," I said, stalling for time. "We have a copy of Pennsylvania's law back in the conference room. Please make yourself comfortable, and I'll return after I check it out." I rushed out of the lobby, my armpits soaked with sweat. I asked our receptionist if she would mind taking water to Mrs. Beverson, so I could compose myself. She had a big smile on her face, watching me squirm. By now, the entire staff understood me to be a grave young man.

Well stocked with all the books I needed, the conference room became a temporary shelter away from extreme embarrassment. First, I checked Title 18 of the Crimes Code. Nothing concrete there, at least from a cursory review. Then I called one of the attorneys on the Capitol Legal Staff with whom I'd become friendly. Forced to say the words "oral sex," the lawyer was too much of a professional to pile on. She found the right language and flagged it for me to find in my copy of the statute. To my surprise, this act remained a crime under Pennsylvania law.

Oh boy, I get to show this to Mrs. Beverson. Her source proved accurate. I used the copier in a vain try to buy more time. *Perhaps she's left by now,* I hoped. She hadn't. "Uh, Mrs. Beverson, the information is correct. There is, uh, a statute, on the books, uh, addressing this, uh, sex act." I handed her the copy, avoiding eye contact. Instead, I focused on the people walk-ing by our district office since we sat at a little table that looked out onto the sidewalk through a big storefront window.

Mrs. Beverson reacted with way too much enthusiasm to this con-firmation, smacking her fist against her palm. "Ha, I knew it. I told Earl we're lawbreakers. But he doesn't care as much as I do. Said one after-noon, 'the cops might learn something if they're watching.'" From my reflection in the window, I noticed I'd moved from red in the face to a plum wine hue with her explanation of Earl's mindset and the imagery that suggested of the guys in blue, stalking the Beverson's home on some great stake-out. Donuts, telescope, and battering ram at the ready.

Elizabeth's rants got louder now that the truth blared out in the open and she added, "You inform the senator we expect him to sponsor a bill to do away with this silly prohibition. It's none of the government's business what Earl and I do in our bedroom." I had to agree but would not draft any proposal for Senator Weigel to introduce that would free up an old taboo addressing oral sex. Or I'd be the second chief of staff to be fired from his office.

Each bill introduced is accompanied by what's called a "co-sponsor-ship memorandum," circulated to each senator along with the proposed legislation. Usually the goal is to get as many co-sponsors on your bill as possible to prove support. I imagined myself sitting down at the computer to write this memo, quoting the rationale for the current state law (maybe consulting with Vivian Ulrich of the WAA for why it originated to pro-tect the morality of Pennsylvania's citizens), as I explained why Senator Weigel considered the proposal to be important. *Let oral sex rein freely in the Commonwealth*, I would write.

There's no doubt we'd become the laughingstock of the Capitol, fod-der for the water cooler talk that goes around the building each day if we foolishly responded to her concern. These documents are part of the public domain. Kostantin Pokornin would grab a copy of the material and wave it around in his pudgy hands for some juicy purpose if nothing else to show in a news story that the state legislature was out of touch. The headline would read "LEGISLATURE CLUELESS" with a subtitle "WEIGEL FIXATED ON SEX." The obvious theme would be people are struggling to find housing, jobs, education, and health care while the emperor Nero (in this case, Weigel) fiddles and Rome burns.

To signal the end of the meeting, I arose from my chair and guided Mrs. Beverson towards the exit door. "I'll be sure to brief the senator on our conversation and show him a copy of the law and I know he'll consider your concern." "Oral sex" wouldn't be coming out of my mouth again. Once was enough.

With one last try at lobbying, she retorted, "I expect him to do more than that and expect a phone call after you talk to him." At least she didn't plan on coming back. I could tell her over the telephone easier than in person this wouldn't be a priority item for Jim Weigel. A notion flashed through my mind I should send her over to the Democratic representative's office so that his staff would have to deflect her but rejected the idea as mean-spirited.

"Thank you so much for coming in, Mrs. Beverson. Please don't hesitate to contact us again if we can be of any assistance." I stretched my hand out doing my damnedest to sound like these words were sincere. I waited a moment until she got out on the street. As I turned back into the office, Gloria and our receptionist laughed at my expense. Gloria promised to make time on Jim's schedule to "brief" him on this latest constituent case. "You earned your pay today, Curran," I mumbled to myself as I went to the bathroom to towel myself off.

I vowed early in my career to keep notes of characters, besides Mrs. Beverson, that crossed our threshold never dreaming I would write a book, happy I had kept this chronicle. Most of the people seeking aid truly needed it; some had serious mental illnesses, and while their stories were sometimes amusing, their real circumstances weren't.

We had many poor people from the streets of York, pleading for help in finding housing, food, and clothing. My heart burst for them, a reminder of the poverty I saw years before in Philadelphia as a young, impressionable child. A staunch Republican, it troubled me that so many suffered in the healthy economy of the eighties.

Affirmation for me that a quality education is the key to economic opportunity; different school choices the pathway where traditional public education fails or doesn't address the needs of individual children. These tragic cases were a vivid example, too, of how much the breakdown of the family structure had spawned poverty, drug and alcohol abuse, domestic violence, and overall despair.

Even the most colorful characters deserved respect although sometimes it was tough to keep a straight face. We had a habit of tracking the moon cycle; the loonier cases appeared to correspond with the full moon phase of that month.

In a red cape, spandex tights, and black boots, "Superman" insisted he had special powers. All he wanted was an audience to vent against a government Superman asserted had implanted tracking devices within him. The Central Intelligence Agency and Interpol were favorite targets as this super hero lowered his voice, so he would not be overheard talking about the vast conspiracy that existed against him.

I remember him stressing that if he became upset, toothpaste would come out of both ears. This would be the outcome from having the devices inside him, monitoring his movements as computers watched Superman's every move. I found myself fascinated with his lobes, watching carefully, wondering whether Crest or Colgate would make an appearance.

I was kicked in the "keister" by Mr. Keister when he called one day during one of those cycles when the moon appeared in the sky at its largest and brightest phase. Our phone lines were ringing off the hook and I drew the honor of answering Mr. Keister's call. "Yeah, I need my toe nails clipped," he yelled.

"Pardon me, what do you need?" I asked, sure he wasn't calling for personal hygiene help. Note to self: *Get your hearing checked!*

"What are you an idiot? I said, 'I need my toe nails cut.' Don't the taxpayers pay your salary? Weigel's newsletter said to call for help."

"Yes, it did, Mr. Keister. Yes, I'm paid by the taxpayers. Wanted to make sure I heard you right."

"You heard me. Now are you going to cut my nails or not?"

We were known as a staff for going above and beyond. But this demand set a record. We also had a reputation for being innovative and resourceful. I asked Mr. Keister a few questions and learned that because of his weight, he could no longer reach his feet. "They're long and gross and I live alone," he added for my benefit. After a few phone calls, we found a church with a volunteer willing to assist Mr. Keister, following the Lord's example when the Son of God washed the feet of His disciples as an act of love and servitude.

York had a small gay community that wanted an audience with Senator Weigel. They had grievances revolving around discrimination based on sexual orientation. The senator wasn't one to avoid a tense situation, but this event gave him pause. Gloria passed the invite off to me to attend a forum sponsored by a church in York that had gay congregants. Furious at Weigel for putting me in this spot, I was in no position to argue. He had made me his chief of staff at the young age of twenty-two, and this was the life I'd signed up to lead.

The evening came much too quickly, and I braced myself for when I entered the sanctuary—ignorant, naïve, and not sure of what to expect. Greeted by the Reverend Cherie Clark, she appeared to be in her mid-forties with short gray hair, cut severely with bangs straight across the forehead. Dressed in black pants and a black shirt with a traditional white pastor's collar around her neck, she was warm and gracious. Reverend Clark offered coffee as she explained that the church catered to York's gay population; aware that there were churches in York that might not be as welcoming.

As we entered the room, I did my best to walk like John Wayne, figuring I had to exert extra masculinity. As if these guys might be interested in me! About twenty people filled the pews, mostly males. While respectful, a few of the men dressed like the Village People ready to perform their signature song. This caused me to drop my voice down lower an octave or two. The pastor served as the moderator of the forum. I told myself, *Time to listen, Jack, and shut your pie hole.*

I heard stories about gay men, severely beaten, targeted they felt because of their orientation. There were tales of discrimination in the workplace and within the healthcare industry of insurance and visitation rights to loved ones. I couldn't answer many of these concerns. Like a broken record, I promised over and over to brief the senator on their plight.

One citizen didn't appreciate the reply, and I don't blame him. He identified himself as "Bertie," a large man in a yellow dress, pink sneakers, and a gold necklace that covered the prominent opening of his dress, revealing a forest of black chest hair than I could ever sport. Bertie wanted a response on why Senator Weigel didn't support the extension of Pennsylvania's hate crimes statute to include sexual orientation as a protected class.

The law protected anyone who was the victim of a crime because of their race or religion. And applied an extra penalty if they were assaulted, and the court found "hate" involved in the offense. In these cases, this necessitated evidence of the perpetrator's thoughts when they committed the crime. Did they target the victim because of the characteristic they had or exhibited, or because the victim was "in the wrong place at the wrong time?"

Bertie asked, "How can Jim Weigel not support this good measure to protect people victimized just because they are gay? A group of thugs assaulted my boyfriend and me outside a gay bar up in Harrisburg. How can you stand there and defend the senator's position?"

Weigel represented mostly a Republican area outside of the City of York, including conservative areas south of the city. At that time, voters down there had no interest in supporting the extension of the hate crimes law to gay or transgender people. But I was on the hot seat, forced to defend Jim's position, a view I privately agreed with though. For me, any assault is repugnant, and the criminal should be punished, regardless of the victim's background.

"Thank you for sharing your experience with me. I promise all of you; I will let the senator know about tonight's concerns." Challenging to defend Weigel in this forum, there was no question I had to. "May I call you, Bertie?"

"I guess." He wasn't going to make this easy.

"Bertie, Senator Weigel doesn't believe in creating a division between straight and gay people for law enforcement and the Crimes Code. His preferred approach is to make penalties tougher for any assault, regardless of a person's sexual orientation. Senator Weigel's been a staunch advocate for police and wants them to have the tools and personnel needed to make our communities safer." Forced to think on my feet, Weigel and I had never talked about his position at any length so I made this up on the fly.

"That sounds great on paper but doesn't make me, or anyone here tonight feel any safer. We're a target because we're gay; do you understand that? You're a big, strong, straight guy. How could we expect you to know what it's like for us?"

I blushed at this characterization but pushed on. Time to go with my gut and be more personal. I'm not sure Jim would have approved. Even so, the senator wasn't there being grilled, and defusing a tense situation had to be the goal. "I do understand. Not everyone shares your view that the hate crimes law should include sexual orientation. Many of the senator's constituents believe otherwise." The crowd groaned with this answer.

But no stopping now. Although attitudes and mores have changed since I said this way back in the day.

"I want to share a personal story on what I encountered so you at least know I understand firsthand what's going on. Besides reporting on your concerns, I will also tell the senator what I'm about to say. Only my best friend and wife know of this. It's not something I've ever wanted to talk about with anyone else because I'm not looking for any credit."

In some length, I described the beating I saw and had intervened in and the cop's reaction to my intervention. I made sure the attendees knew I didn't care whether "she" was a man. Someone beaten in broad daylight on the streets of Harrisburg compelled me to act. Period. I risked being accused of pandering. I hoped my passion and sincerity would come across though. Silence ensued for about thirty seconds. Bertie then applauded. Others soon followed. Reverend Clark thanked me for attending. The group seemed satisfied a servant from the government listened to their concerns.

Senator Weigel was *not* in a listening mood when he summoned Gloria and me into the office one Monday morning. "Did you two read in the *Saturday Tribune* about the racial attack on that couple? Reverend Smith called me about it. His church organized a vigil in response. I attended and promised we would mount a repair effort to their house."

The couple and their three children had recently moved to a white suburb, Prenkleton, to escape the city environs. Racist thugs vandalized their home, including painting swastikas and pouring fuel oil around the foundation. Something had disrupted the attack before they could light a fire to the accelerant; otherwise, the family probably would have perished. An outpouring of love from the community enveloped this family, including attendance by Senator Weigel at the vigil organized by an African-American church.

"Senator, that's noble; but how're we taking the lead on getting their home repaired?" I asked, realizing after I opened my mouth that the question was in vain. In no mood for questions or debate, racism revolted this man—something he and Big Joe shared.

"I know an extensive network of contractors in this area, Jack. A day will be scheduled, soon, and volunteers and handymen will do whatever needs to be done to repair and make that house livable again. In the process, we'll take care of all the other work on the family's to-do list. I intend to send a message to the bastards who did this." His chin jutted out as he said this, the great Weigel determination evident and debate out of the question, not even from his chief of staff.

That force of will came from Weigel's mother whose maiden name was "Channing." Jim proudly referenced his middle name anytime he could. The Channing family had operated a lucrative sawmill and related enterprises in nearby Waynesboro for several generations. Fiercely independent, they dominated the town until "progress and advanced technologies" closed the operations. "Gloria, find an open day on the weekend that works for my schedule. That's the day to target for the clean-up. Jack, you and the rest of the staff will be there as workers. No excuses from anyone, got it?"

"Yes, sir," I said. When the senator was in rapid-fire mode, it was our job to do, not to question.

"Get Susan in here so I can dictate a rough press release. Also, Gloria, get Robert Krol on the phone. Since he's a general contractor, I'll ask him to donate the materials and have folks on the work site to supervise the rest of us. Make sure you keep Reverend Smith posted on the details of the project," he said. The senator concluded, "Let's get going. There's work waiting."

We sprang into action. In less than a month, the house sparkled new as if the attack had never occurred. At the public dedication ceremony that followed with Reverend Smith presiding, Senator Weigel spoke powerfully, without notes, with loving words for the family and condemnation for the evil involved in the assault on these peaceful people. Even

Kostantin Pokornin wiped away a tear as Weigel talked and the family huddled around him grateful for his leadership and compassion. Carolyn and I cried, too. She had volunteered on the workday to support the family, hugging me tightly when she saw their children, realizing if the fire had ignited they could have perished.

The story doesn't end here. In the 1992 election battle I write about later, the husband and wife—both registered Democrats—called Senator Weigel at home after reading his opponent's negative campaign material. They volunteered to cut a radio ad and their gratitude poured out in the sixty-second commercial, demonstrating the essence of a man, a public servant who widely quoted and believed in the scripture that tells us, "But do you want to be shown, O foolish man, that faith without works is dead?" (James 2.20).

TWENTY-FOUR

No hablo Inglés, Yolanda Rossi, Amen Boss

"WHY, JACKIE, does it always have to be you?" Carolyn asked as I gently tried to break the news I'd be working in a ghetto in Philadelphia at election time. Courage or foolishness? Looking back on a lifetime of experiences and adventures, I suppose I've blurred the fine line many times, leaping first to step into a breach where others may hesitate to act.

"Honey, I realize it's hard to understand but there's no one else who can go from our office. The party needs people down there and I'm a guy. Those neighborhoods don't frighten me as they do others. Do you want me to send Susan to work the polling place? I won't do that. Once I find a pay phone, I'll call you during a break in the action." Carolyn worried about my safety. But I wasn't budging. Not the last time I'd fail to heed my wife's advice.

Campaign time had arrived, and the Senate Republican majority continued to be tenuous with the Democrats only needing to flip a seat or two to take power and control. Senator Weigel and I were on the way to a suburban Harrisburg location for an election briefing over the lunch hour. Weigel took me to these off-campus events because he valued my

opinion and believed in making sure I continued to grow as a legislative staffer. While never voiced, Jim served as a teacher besides being a
demanding boss.

A nondescript motel with fake plants in the lobby was the location
of the meeting. Before finding the conference room where campaign
staff conducted the briefings, we passed Senator Caddock Pumfrey. I
avoided making eye contact and Weigel and Pumfrey merely nodded to
one another.

Each Republican senator was asked to come in to make them feel part
of efforts to keep the majority and to "squeeze" them at the end of the
meeting for what usually amounted to a substantial campaign contribution from their own campaign committee to the caucus campaign committee. Weigel would not be the exception. Often more generous with his
campaign dollars than I ever agreed with; raising money in York County
and Central Pennsylvania could be challenging so I wanted to be cau-
tious and prudent with Weigel's expenditures.

Greeted by the top leaders of the caucus and senior staff, they introduced us to an intense and dumpy looking man in his mid-thirties.
Overweight and perpetually out of breath, "Bill," as he asked to be
called—no last name was provided, adding to the mystery of where he
came from—worked as a campaign strategist. In a mostly cryptic fashion, he wandered about the briefing.

This left me somewhat lost as he walked us through the most important race that fall. The leadership wanted to retain a seat the GOP had
won the year before in a special election that occurred because of the
death of an incumbent Democrat from Philly. Typically outgunned and
outspent in that city, the GOP would usually ignore a race like this one,
but the advantages of incumbency gave us *a shot* at a win.

The caucus candidate, a young female, had already made enemies in
the Senate from childish and immature actions, but there was no question the time had come to rally behind her candidacy for re-election. In

the balance: the Republican Party's grip on the Pennsylvania Senate during a period when the Democrats continued to control the House and the Governor's Mansion.

After guiding us through the challenges of the Philly race, the leaders stepped back, preferring to let Bill be the heavy when it came time for the "ask" and how much the caucus expected Jim to cough up in campaign dough. "Senator Weigel, you're not up this cycle," Bill began. While I didn't yet have a lot of campaign experience, my stomach flopped around, knowing what was coming. "The caucus noticed you have a little over fifty thousand dollars in your campaign committee. Each rank-and-file member is being asked to put up at least ten thousand dollars for our final efforts to retain the majority. That should be doable, right, Senator?"

Jim didn't intimidate easily, having built an automobile empire that required him to read people across the table as he successfully closed many deals. The senator turned to our top leader and said, "I'm a team player. You don't have to lean on me. I'll talk with my campaign treasurer and have a check sent within a day or two." Jim had no choice but to contribute and they recognized it. The "ask" continued, however.

"One more thing, Senator," Bill said. "We need bodies to work on Election Day. The party has little apparatus on the ground so we're asking offices to consider sending volunteers, who'll have to take vacation leave." This is where stupid completely took over for me.

At that point in my career, the leadership team, other than Ben Walker, barely knew me. To impress them and prove my stripes as a team player, too, I spoke up. "No problem. Sign me up," I said too eagerly.

Weigel gave me an odd look. He realized the Philly neighborhoods in this senatorial district were crime-ridden and tough. He and I had never discussed my childhood and familiarity with these Philadelphia streets. We really had no reason to. "Are you sure, Jack? Let's talk about this, and we can tell Bill later," he urged.

Bill wheezed with a *hoot*. "Sucker" must've been written all over my face. "Senator, he'll be fine. Jack, we'll get the details to you of where to report." That settled it. Philadelphia-bound to work in a rough community. But it didn't faze me in the least. I'd ridden around those streets with Big Joe as a kid. Which led to the disagreement with Carolyn when I broke the day's news.

The next week, I packed up for an overnight stay in the City of Brotherly Love and reported to the polling precinct. The neighborhood had long ago transitioned into mostly a Spanish-speaking community. Bill had assigned a white, suburban boy to be an election watcher and worker. But I suppose he had no choice since the party remained short of volunteers, especially people of color.

My first mistake: showing up in a suit and tie—standard attire in Harrisburg—but not for this polling place in an old storefront with steps before the days of handicapped accessibility. I checked into the front table to introduce myself to the judge of elections and we had an immediate language barrier. My suspicion is he spoke English, but "Judge Angel" would not make it easy and answered, "*No hablo inglés.*" The judge shrugged his shoulders and returned to the work of getting the tiny place ready to open by seven o'clock.

How the heck do I guard against fraud and corruption, notorious in Philadelphia, with such an obvious language problem? I wondered. There remained a job to do, so I figured I should at least get outside to hand out palm cards with our candidate's name on them (thankfully in Spanish). I left the cluttered and crowded storefront.

My foray into Philly electoral politics reminds me of a story told by an old Philly GOP politician. He had seen many scandals during his years battling the Democrats, who enjoyed complete control over Philadelphia's election machinery. According to his tale—it happened earlier in his career—he arrived at his polling place around ten minutes after the poll opened. He asked the judge of elections how many voters had cast their ballots up to that point, so he could begin making an accounting. The answer: "seven hundred." Incredulous, he asked how that many people could have voted in such a short period of time. Without missing a beat, the judge's response: "You missed the rush." And who says dead people don't vote. But back to my own experience.

Shortly after the poll opened, Bill greeted me while making the rounds to check on the campaign team. I couldn't help but notice the donut crumbs in Bill's unruly brown beard. In another life, Bill might have been a bass guitarist for ZZ Top—his shaggy fur and appearance clearly not the benchmark for his compensation. Not a moment passed before he blasted me after he rolled down the car window just enough to hear him, but not enough for someone to jump him. Street smart, Bill wasn't a fool.

"What the hell are you doing in office attire, Curran? You should be in jeans and a sweatshirt. This isn't a suburban, lily-white precinct, you asshole." I blushed with this screw up. "There's no time to get changed. At least loosen that tie and take off that overcoat." Unseasonably warm out, I shed the coat and suit jacket and rolled up my sleeves. Bill pulled away, leaving a blast of exhaust behind from his 1980 Chrysler K-Car— his way of reinforcing how little he thought of Jack Curran. I got down to the business of promoting the candidate as best I could.

A little around ten, I felt as futile in my efforts as when one does when trying to push the ocean back with a broom. A big white Cadillac pulled up to the curb and double-parked, ignoring how little room remained on the narrow city street. The driver, a heavyset man who we'll call "Frankie," labored to get out of the car. Frankie opened the rear door and I swear he should've blown a trumpet to announce the queen's arrival. Out stepped a woman in her sixties or so with ivory hair teased up into a shockingly bad perm that screamed the 1980s. Her thin lips needed thick red lipstick for fear they'd be lost under a nose much too big for her face.

Despite the nice weather, she wore a fur coat and lots of gold jewelry. Watching her, I knew at once to pay attention to this woman in charge of something as she walked up to me instinctively knowing I didn't belong in Philadelphia. "Who're you?" she demanded, biting off the words as she asked the question.

"Jack Curran, pleased to meet you." Annie's emphasis on manners didn't flee me, even when electioneering in a Philly slum.

With disdain, she looked me over and continued with an accent I recognized as from South Philly. "Why're you here and where're you from?"

Thinking it would impress her, I explained, "I'm from Harrisburg, working for the GOP." Wrong. Proper Jack should've just blurted out, "I'm with the government, and I'm here to help."

She put me in my place quickly. "From Harrisburg? We don't need outsiders here. Get back into your car and beat it." She moved away with one last look of contempt, rapidly turning the charm on for the Democrat workers that outnumbered me by seven-to-one as they formed a tight ring around this Philly celebrity. *Who the heck is this woman?* I asked myself.

I should have let it go but letting go rarely happened with me. "I have every right to be here," I yelled over.

The queen didn't bother to respond as she whispered something to the gang of seven. The most imposing volunteer she had within her entourage—we'll call him "Salvadore"—came over my way. My buddy Sal tried his best to intimidate me into leaving. His presence cast a large shadow over where I stood. Shaken, I struggled to control my bowels. Where were Big Joe and Big Sweet when I needed them to ward off Salvadore?! Somehow, I stood my ground, but courage and bravery were not the reasons. "Paralysis" is a more accurate description.

A long day in Philadelphia with over thirteen hours spent at the tiny polling place. I took the results to the campaign headquarters after the poll closed, tired and weary. Our candidate lost my precinct by a four-to-one margin and in the end lost re-election by a significant percentage.

Fortunately, the caucus picked up a seat in Western Pennsylvania in an upset that saved the majority.

Despite screwing up with my attire, Bill and the senior staff gave me credit for hanging in there and for standing my ground against the city's Democratic boss—Yolanda Rossi. Little did I realize I had encountered a legend in the city. My stock rose after that day as the story went around— exaggerated as the Harrisburg gossip mill does—that Yolanda's thugs had jumped me after I spit on her high heels, after the initial confrontation.

Any credit I had banked with Senator Weigel soon evaporated after my trip to Philly. We found ourselves locked in a rare disagreement over Weigel's resolve to fight the state parole board over a bureaucratic procedure that stood in the way of justice prevailing for one of his constituents.

Mrs. Matilda Gascho—sole guardian of her grandson—lost Bray to a horrific crime. The young man had just gained his driver's license and was on the way home from an evening church event. At a busy intersection in York County, a repeat drunk driver, who began drinking around three o'clock that afternoon, broadsided Bray's 1977 bright orange Toyota Celica, killing the boy instantly. At the scene of the crime, the perp blew a .23 blood alcohol level. Because of previous convictions, a jury found the driver guilty of "Homicide by Vehicle while DUI" with a maximum sentence imposed of ten years.

Covered extensively by the *York Tribune*, this high-profile case preceded Jim Weigel's election to the Pennsylvania Senate. Under the Commonwealth's criminal statutes, half way into his sentence, the offender became eligible for parole and that's when my senator went into action. Friendly with the Gascho family for many years, Senator Weigel was not only aware of the tragic circumstances of the case, but of Matilda's decline following Bray's death. She suffered a stroke that confined her to a wheelchair. With grief and trauma so deep, Mrs. Gascho refused to leave her apartment, relying upon friends and neighbors for care and support.

Pennsylvania law allowed for the victim to provide "input" prior to any parole decision (victim's rights have since been strengthened considerably thanks to the tireless work of victim's advocacy groups and leadership from Tony Molinaro and other legislative champions). That input didn't consider a situation like Mrs. Gascho's, however, and I became the bearer of this news to Senator Weigel.

"Boss, you asked me to follow up with the parole board about Mrs. Gascho's testimony as a victim and they got back to me," I began.

"What'd they say, Jack?"

"Well, since Mrs. Gascho can't appear at the parole offices, they'll take a written statement from her."

"That woman has suffered enough. Dammit, Jack, Matilda wants to tell her story in person. You understand she won't leave her apartment for fear of traveling on the roads. The board is going to have to take her testimony there," the senator insisted.

"The board says the law doesn't provide that option, Senator. Should we really be interfering in this case?" I asked, usually a voice for caution and restraint, respecting procedures and authority instead of challenging the status quo when the need cried out for it.

"Interfering? Really, Jack? You buy this nonsense. It's certainly within the spirit of the law for them to accommodate a victim that finds herself wheelchair and homebound. You go back to the board and tell them I'll be holding a press conference unless they figure out how to take Matilda's personal statement at her home. Her trauma needs to be part of the record." I began to object and stopped after Weigel gave me the "look" of no more debate.

I asked Susan to write a media advisory announcing a press conference on the York County Courthouse steps to discuss the Gascho parole case. Emblazoned across the top, I wrote "DRAFT." I faxed this bombshell to the parole board with a note to call me. The board's legislative person did so almost immediately as I knew she would.

"This is highly irregular, Jack. We are more than willing to accept a written statement. We'll take the extra step that a loved one or friend can read it to the assigned hearing examiner. That's got to be enough," she emphasized.

"Sorry, Shirley, my boss is adamant that won't do. We are not asking for anything illegal. Take her statement in her home because of her infirmities. No one will criticize the board for recognizing the circumstances of Mrs. Gascho."

"Our lawyers disagree, Jack. This kind of accommodation could taint the parole decision if the board denies parole."

"That's ridiculous and you guys need to ignore the attorneys and find some common sense. She wants to speak in person. Hasn't our constituent been through enough. I'm telling you I will launch that media advisory, and you guys can deal with the fallout from Senator Weigel's press conference. Good luck with an interview with Kostantin Pokornin. We'll be cheering for him and I'll give Pokornin whatever he needs as background. Count on it."

The parole board relented. They knew their bureaucratic inflexibility would be magnified across the pages of the *York Tribune*. Maybe beyond that media outlet.

Fast forward to Mrs. Gascho's modest dining room where we had gathered. Hunched over in the wheelchair, she wore a faded sunflower-patterned dress. In a more carefree time, Matilda shared her memories of wearing that same dress as she held Bray's little hand to walk to a neighborhood park. We strained to understand her since she slurred her words because of the stroke's effects.

I pictured this lovely woman laughing with her precious boy as they enjoyed watching the bees dancing from flower to flower; the summer air heavy with the smell of freshly cut grass as the song birds chirped a happy noise to one another. Girls chanted riddles as they jumped rope and boys climbed the jungle gym, rough-housing with each other. Matilda released

Bray's hand as he rushed to join the fun. Life was good for grandmother and grandson.

I shook my thoughts away to focus on Mrs. Gascho's "day in court." As she relived that horrible night's events from the knock on the door by the police to the meeting with the undertaker who had the difficult job to make Bray's once handsome face presentable for the funeral that followed. She shared with the hearing examiner—and a court stenographer whose job was extra hard because of Matilda's incapacitation—that Bray had been active in his church youth group and local fire company. Liked by everyone as a good kid who did well in school and remembered the lessons of life lovingly taught by his grandmother Matilda.

Through her sorrowful eyes, a window to happier memories, I saw her dreams for Bray of graduation from the fire academy, planning a life of service to save others. And, perhaps, marriage to his high school sweetheart. I couldn't help but selfishly think, *What if this had been Joe and Annie Curran experiencing this horror, testifying to the lost potential of their son Jack Curran?* Bray would have been twenty-three, my age as I sat there with tears in my eyes.

Towards the end of her gut-wrenching testimony, Jim turned to me. With his free hand—the other held Matilda's as Weigel willed his tremendous moral strength and fortitude into her being—the senator patted my shoulder. The gesture conveying all it needed to: *Now you understand why I pushed so hard, Jack. I knew what needed to be done for justice to happen, for an old woman's voice to be heard.* With a slight nod, I communicated back: *Amen, Jim.*

TWENTY-FIVE

Old Lady on the Street, The Power of Talk Radio

TWO YEARS INTO MY TENURE as his chief of staff, Senator Weigel stood for re-election to another term in the Pennsylvania Senate and won by the biggest margin yet, facing an opponent who ran on traditional Democratic themes in what remained a solidly Republican district. Everywhere Jim campaigned, and during official functions, citizens confronted him about the need to reform Pennsylvania's property tax system. Not a new issue in Pennsylvania; for years, governors had attempted to move the ball forward on this thorny public policy problem. Local taxpayers heavily fund public education with property taxes the backbone of their contribution to public schools.

The last straw for Jim: eviction of a ninety-two-year-old woman—forcibly removed by sheriff's deputies—all because she couldn't afford her tax bill. Photos of her kicking and screaming were splashed all over the *York Tribune*; in fact, making news across the country.

The senator appeared regularly on a conservative talk radio show in the region, striving to keep a decent relationship with David Cortes, the host. Loud and flamboyant, this political gadfly enjoyed a strong following and called our office immediately after the incident, demanding that

Weigel participate in his show to talk about the injustice of the eviction. David knew it would be difficult for Jim to duck the invite. He was right. Jim agreed to be a guest, never one to avoid a nasty political fight.

"Senator, thank you for coming on to discuss a national tragedy. Sheriff's deputies dragged an elderly woman from her home...her home, Senator Weigel, which she and her deceased husband paid off a long time ago. Now because of a grossly unfair system of taxation that house is gone. As a people, we're nothing but indentured servants for the government. What're you going to do about this?"

In a measured tone, Weigel began, "I appreciate the chance, David, to visit the program to talk about property tax reform. I join with your listeners, and all Central Pennsylvanians, at being appalled by what happened to this poor woman. I've been an active proponent for change since being elected to the Senate." Cortes wasn't about to let Weigel explain the nuances of a complex issue. He rarely waited for his guests, especially legislators, to explain the vagaries of the legislative process. This broadcast wouldn't be the exception. David had a hot topic and wanted action, NOW, not next week, next month, or next year.

"With all due respect, Senator Weigel, as much as I can muster when there's an old lady on the street, we don't wanna know about your stance." Virtually wailing over the radio now, "We wanna hear how to prevent this catastrophe from happening again."

As I sat with Jim in his office, I saw the telltale signs of frustration and anger and grabbed a legal pad to write, *I realize it's hard but must keep calm.* I held this in front of Weigel and he waved me off, irritated I'd distracted him. Easy enough for me to urge patience, I wasn't under attack from a grandstander—who never let the facts get in the way of a good argument!

"Let me finish, David, please. The rage is understandable. I'm outraged, too. But we must translate that into legislative action. I'm one legislator of 253. What may work for me and my constituents, doesn't necessarily help members and their voters in other regions of Pennsylvania."

"No excuses, Senator. People are losing their homes. I have a press release here from the governor and the House majority leader that condemns what happened to this homeowner. In the statement, they call on the Republican Senate to agree with the plan they put together to shift reliance away from property taxes to income. I don't pretend to understand all the details, but the idea sounds better than what we have at present. Where do you stand?"

"We're just sorting out this massive proposal. While the governor and Democratic House support it, the Senate has just seen it. Two hundred pages, very complicated, and we haven't caucused on the bill yet. The shift away from the property tax makes sense. And the assessment reforms, too. I want to listen to what my colleagues also have to say and whether we have the votes or not." Not a bad answer as I gave Weigel a thumbs-up for giving himself a little room to maneuver.

Cortes demanded, "Why haven't you analyzed it yet, Senator? The bill passed yesterday. There's one day left in this session, right? The time to act is now, again, no excuses." David wouldn't let Jim off so easily. As a member of the media, he had a job to do. As much as those in public service may gripe about the news media—and I've done my fair share of bitching—having a free and unfettered press is a key part of keeping those in power grounded, honest, and accountable to the voters.

With a small sigh, Weigel conceded, "Yes, David, the session's almost over. Again, the Senate just got the bill. I'm inclined to support it, however. When we hang up, I plan on checking in with my leadership to see if we can't get the legislation on the voting calendar. That's the best I can do for now, okay?"

The radio host snapped at Jim. "Not good enough, Senator Weigel, but let's take some calls to hear what folks have to say. I'm sure they're as angry as I am." David knew how to tee up his audience.

After being pummeled by five callers, Jim had had enough. Ready to support the bill after the program, the senator asked Gloria to get Ben

Walker on the phone, so he could report on the show and get feedback from the top staff person. Broadcasts as controversial as this one always generated a flood of contacts from our constituents. I convened a meeting to brief the staff and go over basic talking points on how to respond to questions about the Democratic plan.

As I returned to my desk, I found a message to call Bruce Bauer, a special assistant to the Senate Republican leadership. Just about everyone on the Senate staff felt intimidated by Bruce. Wrong for me to feel this way, I didn't like his appearance since he wore wrinkled and ill-fitted suits that didn't help his cause as a tall man, almost six-seven. Shirttails often out, flapping around when he walked the hallways, his height allowed Bauer to dominate any room.

As a Yale man and Rhodes Scholar, originally from New York, he answered to all the Senate Republican leaders but was particularly close to the president pro tempore. They met at Yale while the pro tem served as a guest lecturer there.

While very smart and articulate, one couldn't call Bauer handsome. Hair dark and combed over to hide a bald spot, he had unusually large ears. A recessed child-sized chin added to his odd appearance. I returned Bauer's message, and he asked me to come up to his office on an upper floor. Never summoned there before, the timing made it clear Bauer had listened to the show. When I entered his office, a large copy of *War, Politics, and Power* by Carl von Clausewitz sat prominently on Bauer's desk—apparently the guiding literature for his approach to governing.

Over his shoulder, a large framed photo graced his wall. The president pro tempore sat at his large masculine table, with Bruce behind him, a powerful image of their closeness and alliance. Joining this image were his academic credentials. Along with Yale and his Rhodes bona fides, this staffer also had a law degree from Columbia (although he did not practice). *I'm about to match wits with this guy with my little ole Ford degree,* I worried.

Bauer wasted no time in blasting me about the radio show. "Why did Weigel commit to supporting that tax reform bill the Democrats amended? The governor wants that. We don't. Weigel has to backtrack on that."

"What did you want Jim to do?" I countered. "We have this elderly lady, from York County no less, evicted from her home as the Democrats move this plan. Cortes wouldn't let it go."

"Yeah...well you should've stopped him from going on the program." *Here we go, the Harrisburg blame game is in full-blown mode.*

"I'm not able to let him go on or off the show, Bruce. Jim regularly appears on Cortes's broadcast and couldn't hide. Our constituents are pissed about this eviction. Senator Weigel is on the phone with Ben Walker right now asking what the plan is."

Snapping the cap back onto the pen in his hand as if to stress the point, his voice getting louder, Bauer shouted, "I'll tell you what the plan is. Nothing, absolutely nothing, will happen with that bill. The clock expires tomorrow night, and the legislation will be dead. Leadership expects the caucus to hold the line—that's the plan. Any further questions?"

For good or bad, no one bullied me. Senator Weigel appeared to be ready to vote "yes" on the legislation so I needed to watch his back. "We'll see what Jim does. I'm not able to say whether he holds or not after that radio show. Senator Weigel has been on record for supporting tax reform since his first election. You guys better have contingency plans ready." That's as far as I could or would go. Anything else would undermine Jim Weigel's position.

The meeting ended on this down note. As I climbed the steep stairs to the third floor to report to Weigel on the conversation with Bauer, I sensed we were on a collision course with the leadership. Not only did we have this prominent eviction, and now a radio show that had Jim on the record for supporting the governor's proposal, but Weigel had a reputation for working well with the Democrats. On occasion, he bucked our leaders to work across the aisle. Because of his warm personality and genuine thoughtfulness, the other party liked Jim.

Elected in 1986 by a razor-thin margin, the Democratic governor made property tax reform a signature issue in his campaign. With help from the Democratic majority in the House, he pushed through this complex overhaul of Pennsylvania's local taxation system, the hallmark being a shift from property taxes to a personal income tax. Many believe income is a better measure of one's ability to pay for our public schools and local services than a tax levied on an artificial "assessed value" that may or may not be in tune with the market value.

House strategists found a low-profile Senate bill the Senate had passed previously. It gave tax breaks to widget makers that pledged to continue producing their widgets in Pennsylvania. The House inserted this massive reform, sending the bill back to the Senate for what's called a "concurrence" vote, an up or down vote with no amendments permitted (the rules have since been changed to allow a chamber to amend on concurrence). Enough legislative mumbo-jumbo, though.

Based on Jim's call with Ben Walker, and my meeting with Bauer, we realized Senate Republican leadership stood opposed to the legislation. My first real taste of nothing but raw partisan politics at the worst sickened me and pricked my conscience. Not naïve enough to believe the GOP to be alone in this behavior—the Democrats were just as guilty of blocking Republican ideas because they didn't come from their caucus when they were in power.

The father of our country warned in his Farewell Address: "The alternate domination of one faction over another, sharpened by the spirit of revenge, natural to party dissension, which in different ages and countries has perpetrated the most horrid enormities, is itself a frightful despotism." Such wise words for the ages. But promptly ignored after President Washington uttered them as the Federalists and Jeffersonian Democratic-Republicans battled for supremacy in his twilight years.

Had a GOP governor pushed this reform through, we would have had a different conversation, running the bill after fine-tuning it to deal with whatever concerns our members had instead of putting up road-blocks because the Democrats had sponsored it. Various reasons were invented on why the proposal had insurmountable flaws. The real reason for Republican opposition—to prevent the Democratic chief executive from achieving victory two years into his first term. Republican leaders feared to give him a platform in his re-election year, 1990, to which the governor could point to a successful overhaul of local taxation, something he'd promised to do in his 1986 win.

TWENTY-SIX

Bucking the Party, Punishment, Governor Calls, Trapped

"**H**OW DID CAUCUS GO? Is leadership still opposed?" I asked Jim. He didn't seem himself. The senator realized what had to be done but also understood the shit storm coming his way.

"Not good, Jack. But we can't let this moment pass. It's the closest we've come to real tax reform in years. Four of us are bolting the leadership, including on procedural motions." The third rail of legislative politics, vote your conscience on substantive policy, ideological, or district concerns, but stick with the leaders on the procedure. Or suffer the consequences for undermining leadership.

An example of a procedural motion is a "Motion to Adjourn," which can be a powerful tool to end a floor session when the leadership wants to shut off debate on an issue. The expectation on such a motion is that the rank-and-file members must stand with the leaders and support this move. This "stand with the leadership no matter what" differs from when a vote occurs on the underlying subject of the legislation or amendments.

Members can and do bolt the leadership on substance, especially if they perceive the leaders' direction to be contrary to the wishes of their constituents or their own personal views and beliefs. Or for some political animals, a vote in opposition to leadership may be necessary to survive the next election cycle.

"Did they specify what the punishment would be for joining the Democrats?"

"Don't be ridiculous," the senator said. "They know it'd leak out to the media thirty seconds after caucus finished. You know how some of our members are blabbermouths with what goes on behind closed doors. On the phone immediately with their favorite reporter or lobbyist, sharing details to curry favor."

Leadership has enormous power and clout, controlling committee assignments, and office and staff allocations, including ultimate control over doling out of "WAMs," or Walking Around Money, discretionary grants given to each member to support community endeavors in their district. While these awards went through an executive agency for "review," they were rarely denied since the leadership of each caucus had the ultimate say on distribution.

The unspoken understanding: buck your leaders and risk losing your WAMs. Jim believed in using the grants to do positive things in his district, especially to support nonprofit entities that assisted the poor in York. But being deprived of the funds wouldn't deter his support for property tax reform and the greater good.

Many times, I can remember the actual check (made payable to the nonprofit or municipality) being delivered to our office for the senator to present personally to the recipient. Regular executive agency grants are never handled in this way. Besides serving as a carrot-and-stick with the rank-and-file, WAMs gave incumbents a powerful tool to influence re-election through the positive goodwill generated by handing out checks. They have since been abolished primarily due to ongoing budgetary pressures and the leadership of each caucus has lost a forceful method to control unruly rank-and-file members.

Over the loudspeaker, we heard, "The Senate will return to session immediately."

"Well, this is it, Jack. Time to put on my big boy pants."

"The staff and I'll be up in the gallery, rooting for you, boss. We're proud of you."

The Democrats had four Republican votes in their pocket and humored the "paper majority" that found itself powerless as the clock ticked toward midnight—the expiration of the session. Rising for recognition, the president pro tempore led the GOP opposition. A rarity, he usually limited his public role in the chamber to presiding over the Senate when the lieutenant governor (of the opposite party but empowered by the Constitution to preside) wasn't available to do so.

Regal in manner, the president pro tempore stood tall and erect, not quite like his protégé Bauer, but still more than average. Unlike his subordinate, this senator's clothes weren't off-the-rack but impeccably tailored. Rarely did he need notes when he spoke. An engineer by training, he helped design several skyscrapers in New York, projects befitting the size of his self-esteem. This bona fide member of *Mensa* didn't suffer fools easily. The senator's once black hair had turned pure white—which added to his elegant appearance.

A coal miner's son, his father immigrated as a child from Italy. The family raised him to be their American success story. He didn't disappoint. Christened "Marco Corvi," every Tuesday the president pro tem hosted the Italian Caucus in his office for lunch; the gathering helped build his power base.

Ben Walker pulled out of his bag of tricks every motion possible to defeat this tax reform bill, including a Motion to Adjourn, which would have stopped the bill dead in its tracks. Other challenges centered on what's called "germaneness," or a motion that the House changes conflicted with the original subject of the legislation passed by the Senate. Another parliamentary assault questioned the constitutionality of the tax reform proposal, arguing that the bill's proposed changes conflicted with Pennsylvania's Constitution.

Conveyed in a dramatic fashion with the pro tempore removing his Brooks Brothers glasses to make each point, every effort failed because the Democrats had the four Republican votes, joining all Democratic senators. But the GOP stalwarts had one last Hail Mary to try. Only in the legislature would this attempt pass for acceptable. Recognized to speak for a final time, the Republican leader stood and paused. He looked at his four colleagues—traitors at that moment—giving them an opportunity for redemption before it was too late. The four held their ground. "Mr. President, point of order."

The lieutenant governor, presiding to ensure the flow of the debate went the way of the governor and his fellow Democrats, was a hearty Irishman and the kind of guy to have a beer with. He answered, "The gentleman will state his point."

"Mr. President, we assert the chamber's wall clock is wrong. It's after midnight according to our watches (said before cell phones and desktop computers keyed on the Atomic Clock). Therefore, Mr. President, the session has expired, and the Senate must adjourn. Constitutionally, there is no time left to consider the legislation in question." His loyal GOP colleagues clapped for the gentleman's ingenuity.

The four renegades remained silent and stone-faced. From my seat in the gallery, I watched Jim as he made notes on his legal pad. The largest move of his career to date, his outward calmness in the face of bitter partisanship set Weigel apart from many of his fellow senators.

Drama was not the sole preserve of the Republicans alone. The lieutenant governor looked over at the wall clock, stared at his watch, called an aide over to gaze at his watch, and then answered, "No, it's fourteen minutes to midnight, Senator. Of course, you may challenge the ruling of the Chair." He proclaimed this confident his decision would be sustained because of the Republican crossover votes.

"We do so, Mr. President." The final moment for party discipline had arrived. One last determined look from the president pro tem warned the "turncoats" not to join the Democrats.

"The clerk will call the roll." After all the names had been called, the lieutenant governor announced the vote. "The ayes are twenty-two, the nays are twenty-eight, the motion fails, and the body has sustained the ruling. The chamber's clock is correct." Like I said, only in the legislative world does it take a parliamentary decision to confirm that time is accurate.

The Democratic leader jumped to his feet and called out, "Mr. President, for a motion, please."

"The Chair recognizes the Democratic leader." From Pittsburgh, the leader grew up on the streets. What he lacked in book intelligence, he made up for in common sense, street-smarts, and the ability to tell bawdy jokes, an exceptional talent when trying to bring colleagues around to his point of view. This Democrat became famous as an amateur boxer before entering politics. While the leader had a natural personality, he didn't suffer fools either.

"Mr. President, I move the Senate do now concur in changes by the House to the Senate legislation, therefore adopting this necessary tax reform proposal and sending it to our governor for signature."

"There being no further debate, the clerk will call the roll." With bated breath, we waited in the gallery, scribbling the votes down to see if anyone had switched.

"The final vote on concurrence is twenty-eight ayes, twenty-two nays, and the House will be so notified." With a flourish, the lieutenant governor signed the legislation and off the messenger sped so that the speaker of the House could sign the bill. The governor, the last stop in the process, stood ready to affix his signature to make the bill a law of the Commonwealth.

At that moment, members, staffers, lobbyists, and reporters exhaled. The drama was over. Tax reform would happen if, and it was a big if, the voters approved. Because the legislation hinged on a change to Pennsylvania's Constitution, the electorate must be given an opportunity to approve or disapprove via a ballot question—the case with any constitutional amendments. Without the constitutional amendment and the necessary voter approval, the ability to implement the tax reform changes would be null and void.

As a staff, we remained at work until around four o'clock that morning, assisting Jim in preparing talking points and a press release on why he'd bucked the party's leadership and why he believed this measure to be better than the present system that forced older adults from their homes. I struggled to stay awake on the ride back to York.

Quietly entering our townhome, I made my way to the bedroom and lost my balance after hitting the cedar chest Carolyn kept at the foot of our queen-size bed. "Sonofabitch, dammit to hell, I hit that stupid thing every time I come home." Somehow, my exhaustion and lack of coordination in the middle of the night was Carolyn's fault.

Carolyn turned over and rubbed her eyes. "What time is it, Jack?"

"It's almost five, honey. My knee is throbbing."

"Don't be a baby. You'll be fine." My wife rolled over and tried to go back to sleep.

Bone-tired, I undressed to my boxers and tee-shirt and climbed into bed. Too wired to sleep after the emotional roller coaster of the past day, I tossed and turned. My mind raced with what a new day would bring. Sure that punishment would come because of Jim's independence, I experienced a full range of emotions. From pride in the senator, to fear of what the leadership could do to us, to being demoralized as I watched from a front row seat raw partisan power in action.

After about thirty minutes, Carolyn reached over to turn the lamp on by her side of the bed. "Okay, Jack, what's eating you? I can't sleep with you flopping around. Spill it out, what happened last night?"

"I made the wrong career decision, babe. I'm exhausted, but don't see a way out. I just don't think I have what it takes to be a good chief of staff. Too damn sensitive in this job even though I try to be tough. Is this really what I signed up for...this horrible partisan game? What do I do? I'm in a bottomless pit." With my head buried in Carolyn's bosom, she gently rubbed my neck. What could Carolyn really say?

Circumstances were not as simple as they once were. Married with a home and children under discussion, there seemed to be no way out. "Trapped in a job" summarizes the overwhelming feeling experienced that night. Not the last time I'd have these sentiments and this internal wrestling with my conscience and career path and whether I had the toughness to compete in a dog eat dog political arena.

The punishment from Senator Weigel's vote began in earnest the next day. If you think a sandbox fight with toddlers is messy and silly, it is an ice cream party compared to what some adult legislators do when payback time comes. When Jim arrived at the Capitol at lunchtime, someone had moved his parking space to a less desirable area. I recall right under a tree where lots of birds congregate, appropriate for the avian shit we found ourselves in. There was nothing to do but ignore this pettiness.

An influential senior staffer paid an unexpected visit to explain that Jim's office renovations—in the planning stages for months—were now "on hold."

I remember Weigel's classy reaction. "It's okay. Do what you have to do." Senator Weigel wasn't willing to play their game. His shabby suite became a badge of honor, proof he had stood up to the leaders to do the right thing.

Our day brightened when Gloria interrupted with word the governor's office wanted to speak on the phone with the senator. Jim picked up the line. "Please hold for the Governor," his secretary had placed the call.

"Senator Weigel, I'm calling to thank you for your help and courage. I realize you got hammered by your leadership for voting with me." Many on our side of the aisle didn't like the governor, but I did. A stand-up guy in my estimation, I appreciated his strong pro-life stance that put him at odds with his own party that supported abortion rights without question or limit.

"It was the right thing to do, Governor. We're putting material together to get out to my constituents. I plan on an editorial board visit with the *York Tribune* to push them for an endorsement of the spring referendum. We've got to keep the momentum going, Governor."

"Agreed, Jim. My public relations folks will be all over this, and I'll be getting out around the state to urge a 'yes' vote. Before I go to the next call, Senator, is there anything you need?"

We had hoped they'd ask but hadn't negotiated anything beforehand for Weigel's vote. Jim didn't do business that way. Yet, if asked after the fact, we had an answer ready. "Now that you ask, Governor, there's something...I've been pushing this new computer system for law enforcement, and I'm getting nowhere with my leadership because of the cost. After this issue, they definitely won't help."

"How much, Jim?"

"One million to start. And an appropriation thereafter until the system is fully upgraded. It will make their work much more efficient and allow them to catch a lot more bad guys."

"I'll talk with my budget secretary. Shouldn't be a problem to work that into next year's fiscal proposal. If your people need anything on messaging for tax reform, have them get in touch with my special assistant who's running point for me. Thanks again for all your help, Jim. Take care."

The governor hung up, and we had the computer system the senator had been unsuccessfully pushing for several years. While Senator Weigel hadn't asked for anything for his stance, Harrisburg can be very transactional. You want my vote; I must get something in return is the model *some*, not all, legislators follow.

The governor's tax reform plan would go down in defeat that following spring—rejected by the voters by a three-to-one margin. Because the scheme was so complicated, it was difficult to explain and sell but easy to create doubt and fear against the proposal. This became the classic, it's better to stick with "the devil you know than the devil you don't know." As I write this from the solitude of my home—almost thirty years after this failed effort—the battle in Pennsylvania still rages over how to more fairly pay for public education and local government services. And worthy of reminder, seniors are still losing their homes because of an impossible property tax burden.

Designed to help the elderly more than any other voting bloc, ironically, senior citizens came out in droves to vote "no" on the proposal. A moment when Pennsylvania could have had substantial reform went down in flames. Out of favor with his leadership, there was no question Jim Weigel would keep going for some of the biggest challenges we would yet face.

TWENTY-SEVEN

George W. Bush, Willie Horton, Jack and the National Anthem

GLORIA WAVED ME PAST her desk and into Jim's office. I'd paused before entering since he was on the telephone in what looked like an intense conversation. "Who's Jim talking with?" I whispered.

"Tony Molinaro. Something about Vice President Bush's eldest son visiting for a campaign stop on behalf of his father. That's all I know."

Bush sought to be the first sitting vice president to be elected president since Martin Van Buren won election to succeed Andrew Jackson. Despite the Iran-Contra affair, President Reagan remained popular and Bush hoped to run on "The Gipper's" coattails to become the Forty-First President of the United States.

Senator Weigel's conversation was wrapping up. "Okay, Tony, I'll be there. Whatever you need me to do. Yes, thanks for including me. Bye." Regardless of the tension that existed between the two men because they'd battled for the Republican nomination, they worked together when the issue called for it.

I sat down in my usual chair as Jim finished writing notes on a legal pad. He looked up with an eyeful of concern. "That was Tony." I nodded yes. "He's organizing a campaign event for Vice President Bush in a few days. His son, George, is coming to Pennsylvania to highlight the *Willie Horton* television ad and Tony will be the emcee of the affair. Molinaro wants the York County Delegation in attendance and I promised to be there."

"What's the concern, boss? Something's bothering you."

"That spot is controversial, Jack. I represent the city and many minorities. The ad's been labeled 'racist.' I'm usually a loyal party guy but I wish they'd use Bush's son for some other purpose. Way too divisive for my taste."

The spot played on a furlough granted by Michael Dukakis when he served as the governor of Massachusetts. It showed convicted murderer Willie Horton, an African-American, who did not return to prison, but committed heinous crimes while out on a weekend pass. Meant to portray Governor Dukakis as "soft on crime," the ad proved useful in raising concerns about the Democratic candidate's judgment. But it also stirred contention, passion, and animosity.

Weigel put aside his reservations and invited me to join him at the press event held in a large room over in the House of Representatives. Tony did his usual good job managing the various pieces of an affair like this one and Weigel remained silent. He stood there as a backdrop along with several other legislators and politicians. The future President, George W. Bush, spoke about his father's qualifications and attacked Dukakis as too liberal for America. The ad aired as planned.

Before the event ended, however, a horde of Democratic and leftist activists tried to overwhelm the room. House Security successfully contained them and barred the doors. We waited anxiously for the Capitol and State Police to arrive to remove the crowd from the hallway outside while we remained barricaded in.

My journal entry from that day reads: *While confusion occurred around him, Bush appeared unflappable—but irritated his schedule had been impaired, asking several times when the hallways would be free to allow his departure. I'm sure he had other stops planned. Never a fan of George H.W. Bush, I continue to believe Jack Kemp should've been Ronald Reagan's vice president as the true ideological heir of Reagan. Jack would run now as president with a different campaign message. It would be more inclusive yet still deeply conservative focusing on energizing free enterprise and education to lift people out of poverty. Will never forget my meeting him as an intern! I'll hold my nose and vote for Bush's old man. No choice but to do that with Dukakis as the D nominee.*

But I'd be less than honest if I didn't admit how exciting it was to be in the room with George W. Bush, Tony Molinaro, Jim Weigel, and many other politicos. Trapped with no exit until the cavalry came to the rescue, my party passions and loyalty ran high. I got lost in the moment. Was the political spot "racist" and unfair? I didn't think so at the time but respected the viewpoint of those who thought so. The furlough program was fair game as a wrong-headed policy, although if memory serves it'd survived between Republican and Democratic administrations in Massachusetts (the only state to go for George McGovern in the '72 presidential election).

The original spot that profiled Willie Horton—produced by an independent organization, and the Bush *Revolving Door* television ad—embarrassed the Democrats and inflamed racial passions. Why Senator Weigel remained reticent since he represented a large minority population in York. Using the furlough as the Bush folks did made for an easy political play and allowed them to avoid discussion of the significant issues facing the nation at that time.

In another obvious ploy to bring over conservatives, like me, who remained dubious about George H.W. Bush's credentials as a conservative, his campaign also attacked Dukakis for opposing mandatory recitation of the Pledge of Allegiance in our schools. Like the furlough program, they dangled this "red meat" issue for the Republican base. Bush and his folks profiled this and furloughs to make him palatable in the GOP primaries and to rally the faithful behind the vice president in the General Election. The tactics worked.

Eventually, our rescuers reached us. No arrests were made that I recall. The protest stayed largely peaceful other than some pushing, shoving, and lots of banging on the ornate mahogany door that protected us from the angry throng.

I had my own American flag encounter the following spring when a senior staffer invited several other junior staffers and me to go to a Baltimore Orioles game at the old Memorial Stadium. He found a lobbyist to sponsor the trip and apparently wanted to get a group of us younger guys out for a ball game and camaraderie. I went because I love baseball, proudly wearing my well-worn Phillies cap and Mike Schmidt jersey Big Joe gave me during the 1980 World Series championship. Carolyn took advantage of my absence to return to Abington to be with the Gianellas for an overnight visit so all was well.

We were having a great time pre-game. Then came the National Anthem. The announcer asked us to rise as a teenage girl prepared to sing from home plate. Our section stood, removed our hats to honor Old Glory and the country, except for a couple in their twenties, who remained seated, drinking their beer. Oblivious to the two minutes it takes to remember how special our nation is.

After she sang the last note, I could feel my blood pressure rising at this slight to America and all those who value freedom. I belted out in my deepest and sternest voice, "You are supposed to stand for the National Anthem. Where's your decency and respect?"

The guy turned and gave me the finger, his universally understood reaction and opposition to my fierce patriotism. As I contemplated a response, our host reached over and grabbed my arm. "What's the matter with you, Curran? We're at a baseball game. Can you please let it go?"

I called Rob the next day to relay what happened. He responded true to form. "Jack, you gotta stop trying to fix stupid. When are you going to realize that?" I was never invited back to any social gatherings by members of the Senate senior staff after this incident.

TWENTY-EIGHT

First Argument, You've Become Big Joe,
Riots, The Mouse and Prison Tour

ANOTHER LATE DINNER and Carolyn was unusually quiet. We'd been married for several years. While she had made some friends at her job and with neighbors, my better half experienced significant loneliness. I continued to work at a relentless pace. Each night, I'd walk around and think about a problem or issue at the Capitol. Energy during those years almost limitless—four or five hours of sleep met my needs.

Not Carolyn, however. A light sleeper, many nights she'd lie awake because of my pacing, while the television aired whatever broadcast at three o'clock in the morning. Usually, a shopping channel as background—costume jewelry, trinkets, and kitchen gadgets hawked by models with plastic features and the inflection of permanent enthusiasm, regardless of the junk they had to peddle.

So busy and focused on my career, I missed all the signs of her unhappiness, and took for granted she'd deal with my hectic schedule and inability to leave work behind at the Capitol. Carolyn was giving me the silent treatment at dinner. To start a conversation, I opened a bottle of her favorite wine. Well beyond alcohol resolving her loneliness and my selfishness, I went to give her a kiss. That's when she let me have it.

"Jackie, we never see each other at normal times as most couples do. The job consumes you. You've become Big Joe. I try to support you, but that only encourages more bad behavior." Bawling, tears streamed down Carolyn's lovely cheeks. "Flabbergasted" best describes my reaction. Her frustration had been building for several years. And I hadn't seen the signals.

"I thought things were great. We have a beautiful home and the weekends together—"

Interrupting me, she wouldn't allow me off so quickly. "Weekends? You mean when the session doesn't spill over or Jim doesn't need you to go to a weekend event. It's always something. Your wife is never first in this marriage; the Senate and Senator Weigel are. I've had it and will not go along like Annie Curran did for thirty years." Carolyn had pushed the Big Joe and Annie buttons hard, which only she could do. After all, she'd suffered through their divorce with me. Carolyn now had my full attention.

"I'm so sorry, honey. I love you so much. All I ever wanted was for us to be happy. I've been on this crazy ride, ignoring your needs...I never sought to be my father, believe me." I said this not only to convince her but me. *Aren't you following the only male example you have for how a marriage should work, Curran?* I probed myself. I drew her close as she convulsed harder into sobs. I'd hurt the most important person in my life, expecting love and loyalty to be there, regardless of how hard I worked. "Baby, please forgive me. I'll do better and pack up earlier in the evenings and leave time for coffee in the morning. Don't give up on me, not you. You're my whole world."

Our phone rang, the timing awful. I went to answer it when I should have let it go. It was Senator Weigel. In an urgent voice, the senator said, "There's a riot underway, Jack, at the Camp Hill prison right now. Meet me up at the Capitol in forty-five minutes so we can talk through how I'll respond to this." Jim hung up the phone quicker than I could reply yes or no.

I couldn't make eye contact with my wife when I broke the bad news. "That was the senator. Camp Hill prison is rioting, and he needs me. I don't know what to say, Carolyn. These riots are huge. I'll try to be home before eleven."

She wiped away her tears and her breathing became steadier. With a sigh, Carolyn Curran gave in—at least temporarily. "We can't even have an argument without that man and the Senate coming between us. Go to the office, Jack. I'll finish eating by myself, and we'll continue this conversation later. You will put boundaries on Jim, the staff, and the Senate." Carolyn didn't have to say, "or else." Understood, loud and clear. She'd gotten my attention, and I felt rotten leaving her in this state.

Quickly dressing in something more presentable than blue jeans, I hopped in the car for the now familiar route of I-83 North. I had time to think about my marriage, work, and the immediate problem of riots at the prison. Selfishly, I worried about the effect this riot would have on the workload when my thoughts should have been about what the guards and law enforcement faced.

After arriving at the Capitol, I put the television on in Senator Weigel's suite to catch up on the breaking news. The uprising had erupted in the open yard while the inmates milled about. The perps attacked one guard and then the chaos spread with many guards overpowered. The prisoners now controlled the prison. Officers had been taken hostage and fires raged. A secure holding cell now held the men and women, who had before detained the cons. Contingencies in place for such an event called for the dispatch of a highly trained unit of the Pennsylvania State Police.

At that point, Jim entered, talking fast and discussing how he needed to get on top of this. As a local senator with expertise because of his service on the crime commission, he would have to answer to the press. "Draft a letter, Jack, to the chairman of the Judiciary Committee, copies to the Central Pennsylvania Delegation and to the caucus with a press release to go with the correspondence. We need to launch an inquiry right away about how this happened." The legal pad I borrowed from Gloria's desk had scribbles all over it and I knew we needed Susan to work on a news release with Jim in such a "take-no-prisoners" mode.

Before doing so, I had to be the voice of caution. "Senator, maybe we let this unfold a bit before you jump in feet first. We don't have all the facts. Wait until the departmental leadership has answers," I urged him. "I think we need to take it slow."

Pennsylvania had a notoriously overcrowded prison system, something Jim knew from his work on the commission and he believed that to be a core reason for the riot. "That's exactly why I'm getting involved," the senator said. "And why the Senate must get out front. To find out the facts, figure out what caused this, and how we prevent it from happening again. I don't want a debate on this, Jack, start writing. There're prisons across this state that also might ignite at any time," Weigel emphasized. "I have no confidence the leadership has this under control."

On the phone that night with Susan, we crafted the documents Senator Weigel wanted for release in the morning. That next day, the State Police moved in to retake the prison. It turned out to be only short-lived. While the inmates were put back into cells, not all the units were secured, the locking mechanisms broken during the first uprising. Guards warned prison officials the jail wasn't safe but prison leadership ignored advice from those on the ground. As the officers attempted to lock down the facility the next evening, the second riot began. Because of the broken locks, the inmates got out, rioted, and took charge of the prison, setting more fires, and seizing new hostages along the way.

Once again, the State Police quelled the riots, and regained control. This time permanently. Over one hundred guards and seventy prisoners sustained injuries with half the facility destroyed. Finger-pointing began at once on what caused the disturbances: overcrowding, understaffing, poor conditions, improper mixing of violent and nonviolent inmates, and an overall lack of leadership by those charged with running the state jail. All cited as triggers.

Jim's instincts proved right. He became part of the loyal opposition's response to the Democratic administration's excuses and, frankly, incompetent actions during and after the riots. Because of his quick reaction, Weigel positioned himself as one of the media's go-to guys for comment. The uprisings made national news. Republicans, in control of the Senate, were determined publicly to demand answers from the Democratic governor's administration. Events occurred one year before his expected re-election campaign—perfect to highlight to gin up voters and regain Republican control of the governor's office.

Mostly a non-event, the hearing we launched turned out pointless. The smoke from the fires could still be seen as the Senate committee, including my boss, grilled the prison leadership. As I feared, they had few answers this early.

After our inquisition, the committee demanded access to the jail. At first rebuffed by the governor's folks saying it was still too "dangerous" for outsiders to be entering the prison, the administration relented after we found a law that guaranteed legislators the right to visit state prisons. At the time, I didn't try to hold Weigel back. He had toured jails before and wouldn't be stopped from visiting Camp Hill, wanting it to happen at once—not in weeks after things had been cleaned up.

My first time entering a prison as I accompanied the senator, and one that had just suffered through two riots. *Unnerving* is how I described in my journal the sounds of the solid bar doors locking. The *clang* the first sign of the loss of freedom. The guard accompanying us, barrel-chested and sturdy as a California redwood, used his huge biceps to pull on the door for good measure; the *clunk*, the final sound of confinement with the inmates. No escape possible until the officer in the block tower pushed the button leading to the outside world.

Once inside, a small man welcomed our group. Mousy in appearance, he introduced himself as the Deputy Secretary for Security Arnold Diffenderfer. From black horn-rimmed glasses, to a pocket protector, down to the brown Hush Puppies that covered his feet, this individual didn't engender a sense of "security" with him in charge. In close to my senator's ear, having learned the lesson from my audible whisper that backfired with Senator Pumfrey, I joked that our guide looked like a "mouse," my lame attempt to break the fright of the moment. With a low chuckle, Jim told me to pipe down.

"Come this way, please," said the Mouse efficiently, as if he were showing us Disney World. Instead, it looked like the wreckage from the set of a new reality television show, *Riots Gone Wild.* "Over at that spot," the Mouse pointed, "is where the first fight broke out." Above us, I spied guards in the towers, rifles at the ready for any mischief the inmates might've been plotting. And that gave me some comfort.

"The dripping you notice results from the helicopters that dropped large vats of water over the prison. We did that to extinguish the fire and disorient the prisoners. It also served as a diversion before the troopers broke in." I was pretty sure the Mouse wasn't within ten miles of the facility, directing copters, firefighters, and the State Police when chaos reigned. But what did I know?

"Okay, look to the right through those windows. That's what's left of the main cafeteria. We're still cleaning up the mess." The destruction reminded me of a famous food fight scene from the first R-rated movie I had watched with some buddies while in high school. But this damage was real and not some fraternity fantasy.

"Senators, you asked to walk through a cell block to talk with the inmates. Over there is Block B. The riots didn't touch it. Besides, those prisoners are all nonviolent," the Mouse assured us.

Annie's manners never left me. Amid this damage, I asked the Mouse, "Sir, what's the difference between violent and nonviolent offenders?"

He deflected the question over to the guard whose nametag read "Ivan Gabor." Ivan merely grunted something about the length of their sentence determined their violence potential. *Doesn't sound too scientific a method*, I noted.

"Right this way, ladies and gentlemen, Officer Gabor will take it from here." Ready to retreat to his office, the Mouse seemed satisfied his tour guide duties were over.

Before he had a chance to depart, I raised my hand but this time I dropped the pleasantries. "Excuse me, aren't you going in there with us?" I'd be damned if a deputy secretary didn't have to walk through if I was forced to enter what were in my mind the gates of hell.

The Mouse's cheeks flushed pink, and he muttered, "I don't go in the blocks, the inmates make fun of me." Now I felt like a toad for my boorish behavior. "You'll be okay. Remember how they got the name 'convict,' it stems from 'a con job' because they're all 'innocent.' I'm sure they'll try to convince you of that. Good luck."

Ivan seemed glad to be rid of Deputy Secretary Diffenderfer—flashing us his pearly whites as the Mouse hastily strolled away. Officer Gabor pointed that we could go inside after he opened the outer gate. An even sturdier door closed behind us and a wave of renewed panic set in. "Senator, are we safe in here? I'm not so sure. Kind of claustrophobic right now. What's the plan if they riot again?" the questions tumbled out of me.

Jim answered in stride, "We're surrounded by guards and state troopers, Jack, and Officer Gabor's right here. Relax and show no fear. Convicts sense that. Follow my lead and stay close." Despite his assurances, I lacked confidence the officers had control of the jail and thought as we walked through the building, we'd make a great prize as hostages. Why else would the Mouse retreat as he did? Jim had no such emotions or views. I prayed silently. *Please God don't let me become someone's bitch boy.*

Weigel walked up to prisoners, clothed only in boxer shorts, and asked, "Were you part of the riots or injured by them? What do you think of conditions here and your treatment by the guards?"

Weigel's admonition to stay close forgotten, I wandered off in the cell-block now mesmerized by my temporary confinement and the long row of symmetrical iron bars. The further I moved into the block, the stronger the odor of unbathed men—mixed with some sort of cleaning solvent—assaulted my senses.

A prisoner beckoned me over to his cell, yelling for my attention. *Do I go over or remain in the middle at a safe distance? How do I not display fear when I'm scared shitless behind bars in a prison that rioted barely six days ago?* As nonchalantly as possible, as if strolling through a rose garden, I walked over and said hello, out of place in a suit and tie, conversing with a white, middle-aged man clothed only in his underwear and a tee-shirt.

"What're you guys here for?" he asked.

"We're from the Senate Judiciary Committee, trying to get to the bottom of what happened," I said. *Why do I always sound so damn formal, like I'm testifying, instead of talking with a jailbird in an iron cage? Tone it down, Jack.*

"Lots of shit wrong, man," he said. "This jail's jammed full, and the guards they treat us like crap. I'm not supposed to be locked up, anyway. Didn't commit the crime they accused me of. I'm innocent." *The Mouse's weak try at prison humor rang true after all. Plus one for his knowledge of the prison he's in charge of.*

"What're you in for?" I asked him, figuring that to be the age-old question to pose.

"Arson. The man said I tried to burn down an empty warehouse for a friend of mine who got the insurance cash," my new prison friend said. "I've got two more years to go before parole. Do you think you could take a look at my case? Maybe you can find a new angle for me to go free? I have a file on it right here." *Arson, a nonviolent offense? I wondered. What are the violent crimes if this guy's unlawfulness is considered petty?* One more check mark on the list for why this tour was an awful idea.

Nervously looking around for the senator, the time had come to move on. "I'm sorry. I'm not an attorney and can't help you. Thank you for sharing your story though and answering my questions."

"Thanks for nothing, man." He gave me the middle finger to cap off his anger and frustration. But I had no power nor would I ever dream of trying to second-guess a judge and jury.

While a made-for-television photo opportunity, we learned nothing new from the tour. A symbolic move more than anything, we ensured that the governor and his people understood that the General Assembly wanted to be a player in the aftermath of the riots. We wanted cooperation and a seat at the table as solutions were developed to address the poor conditions of Pennsylvania's prison system.

The latest challenge for the office couldn't have come at a worse time for our marriage. I tried harder to have breakfast with Carolyn and to be home for dinner at a more reasonable hour. The demands of serving as a chief of staff to Jim Weigel didn't quit though. My health suffered. But I didn't complain to Carolyn; that would only make the situation more trying.

The nurse's office at the Capitol a frequent stop with my blood pressure at high levels, I was only twenty-five and a ticking time bomb. Like Annie, migraines also struck, my body's way of coping with stress. The doctor put me on two daily pills to control both my blood pressure and my inability to slow down. The asthma puffer became a more frequent crutch since stress always aggravated my breathing. Unless I eased up, the doctor counseled, my health would continue to get worse.

TWENTY-NINE

No Budget/No Pay, Saved by the Paper Clip,
Memory Loss, School Vouchers, Little Jack

I T WAS 1990 and the Democratic governor stood for re-election. The
GOP put up a weak pro-choice candidate from Philadelphia, infamous
for putting his foot in his mouth, describing the incumbent chief executive as a "redneck Irishman from Brighton Heights." Unlike most traditional Republicans, this nominee ran mostly to the left of the Democrat
on abortion, and other social issues. He took a licking as the governor
won his home area of Western Pennsylvania in a landslide and even
Central Pennsylvania, usually a GOP bastion, went the governor's way.
Thank God for the secrecy of the ballot box since I voted against my party's nominee, preferring a conservative, pro-life governor to the liberal
Republican candidate.

Although technically "balanced" that year, the budget comprised
tricks and smoke and mirrors to give the illusion that expenses equaled
revenues. By making onetime transfers from funds that had accrued sur-
pluses, the die was cast for a huge structural deficit of one billion dollars
for the 1991 fiscal year.

As a nation, we were at war with Iraq, the first Desert Storm, with the President assembling an international coalition to drive Saddam Hussein out of Kuwait. My unit heard rumors of possible activation. Massive call-ups of the Army Reserve and National Guard occurred, primarily in supply and transportation units, since the Regular Army found itself deficient in these areas. While I served in a field artillery unit, we believed the call would come if the war lasted longer than expected. Still, we trained and remained in a high state of readiness until the combat phase concluded. Prepared to go, I drew up a will and power of attorney, ensuring that Carolyn understood our finances.

Commonwealth government remained divided, with a Democratic governor and House, and a Senate that continued under the control of the GOP. The July 1, 1991 budget deadline passed by and state workers were not paid as a result since Pennsylvania lacked legal spending authority. Many state employees lived in the northern part of Senator Weigel's district so we had a political problem on our hands. Personally, the impasse couldn't have come at a more challenging time for Carolyn and me. Pregnant with Jack Jr. (due in September) with our townhome for sale, we had our eye on a larger Victorian on the other side of York, closer to York College.

Since state workers were not paid, there were rumors our pay would stop, too. To break the news of our lost compensation, Ben Walker called a special staff meeting, never a good sign. In his usual calm way, Ben gave the word. "Even though the legislative accounts are separate, and staff could legally be paid, the leaders have decided that until the budget is resolved, we will not be compensated. But you'll be expected to show up for work." A collective groan filled the room.

While a wise political decision we share in the pain of the thousands of state employees affected, it meant sacrifices, too. Carolyn and I had been thrifty, with savings to cushion the blow, but the same couldn't be said for many of the secretaries and clerks, who lived on much less than a chief of staff's salary.

Bruce Bauer jumped in. "Listen, people, we don't want to hear your griping. We're going without pay, too. Now's the time to pull together and be good soldiers. That's what our bosses expect." More catcalls went up from the back of the room in response to this little pep talk.

A fiscal conservative, Weigel wanted to hold the line on taxes and spending. But he found himself in a difficult spot politically. State workers rallied at the Capitol at least weekly, and they were angry, chanting ugly things as they marched on the building. The *York Tribune*, its sister paper the *Harrisburg World*, and other newspapers across the Commonwealth attacked the General Assembly for the budget impasse as a failure of fulfilling its primary responsibility of passing one by the deadline.

Along with the two senators from Dauphin and Cumberland Counties, who represented even more state workers than Senator Weigel did, the three legislators introduced legislation to avoid what we called "payless paydays." By putting the last year's budget in place automatically if the General Assembly missed the July 1 deadline, employees would be paid. The bill contained a provision forbidding legislators, the governor, and cabinet from receiving compensation in the event of an impasse, politically popular in Central Pennsylvania, but not with the leadership, who wouldn't move the trio's proposal.

The final budget enacted in August of 1991, addressed a one-billion-dollar structural deficit and filled it with a three-billion-dollar tax increase that Pennsylvania's business community felt the hardest in higher taxes paid by corporations and small businesses. These new levies crushed the Commonwealth's business climate and job creation.

Democrats put up the lion's share of the votes since their party held the governor's office. In return, they demanded much greater spending for "investments" (as they liked to call them) in education, job training, and welfare, in exchange for their tax votes. One of those Democrats from

Philadelphia ghost voted by inserting a paper clip into the voting mechanism on his desk so he would be recorded as a "yes" vote and could leave for a family vacation. Without that paper clip, the massive taxes wouldn't have passed since this legislator became the 102nd vote needed.

Republican leaders in the House and Senate were loudly criticized for sticking up just enough votes to aid the Democrats with the passage of the final budget and tax increases. One of the most vocal critics: Representative Tony Molinaro. He had taken a hard line against the spending and tax hikes, and what he believed to be a total capitulation by the top leaders.

During this same period, the Senate passed a comprehensive school voucher bill, an early predecessor to school choice programs that would follow. These included a hugely popular scholarship program funded by business tax credits, charter schools, and a more parent-friendly home school law.

Under enormous pressure from the local Catholic diocese to support the voucher bill, Senator Weigel had mostly followed the lead of the school boards and teachers' union on education policy in the past. But not this time. I also lobbied Jim, believing the public education establishment's monopoly had to be broken, especially to help low-income families whose districts failed to educate these kids, despite the significant state resources provided to them.

Courageous, Weigel bucked opposition from the union and school boards, as one of the few legislators from Central Pennsylvania to support vouchers. A firestorm of criticism and constituent calls and letters from teachers in our district followed his vote. We answered every call and every letter to explain why Jim had supported school choice. Representing the York City School District as he did, Weigel was concerned about the lack of options available to families in that perpetually troubled entity.

During this time, we noticed the senator had more and more difficulty with his memory. Gloria and I reminded him of things we'd discussed before. We had to be more precise with the schedule, speeches, and background information. This further challenged the team given an already large workload.

Jack Jr. came along during this time of work turmoil. I always struggled with separating job responsibilities with pressures at home. That summer of chaos at the Capitol detracted from what should have been a joyous moment for the Curran family. While I remember the great pride I had in watching the birth of our first son, I also made a whopper of a mistake when Carolyn went into labor.

I had taken part of an afternoon off for a cookout Rob hosted at his Harrisburg townhome, bringing Carolyn up from York so she and Rob might catch up, too. When her water broke during the barbecue, she whispered, "It's time to go, Jack. My water just broke." The doctors must've miscalculated Little Jack's expected due date by several weeks as neither of us expected labor to begin this soon.

Panic and stupidity set in when I asked, "You mean it broke now? What do we do? Should you sit down?" I forgot the birthing classes and the books I read each night before falling asleep.

Once again, Carolyn remained the calm one. "Yes, my water broke. We should leave for the hospital, but there's time. The first baby always takes—" Interrupted by a contraction, she didn't finish the sentence. I kicked into high gear and guided my wife to the car and then remembered a project at the office that needed my direction to the staff, well before cell phone days would have permitted multi-tasking. With a quick detour to the Capitol, I rationalized, *It's on the way to the interstate and what does a few minutes hurt, anyway?*

While in labor but not so much so she didn't recognize my move, Carolyn snapped, "What're you doing, Jack? Don't tell me you're heading to the office."

In front of the Capitol, I found a parking space and assured Carolyn with a pat on her arm, "I'll just be a minute, honey."

When I entered our suite, I hastily gave Gloria instructions on an unfinished project and told her Carolyn was in labor and waiting in the car. Without hesitation, Gloria smacked me in the back of the head. In mild pain, I yelled, "*Ouch*, why did you hit me?"

"For Carolyn. She's in more agony than you can ever imagine. Sometimes I think you're worse than Jim. He wouldn't have left Diane in the car during labor. Get out of here now!" I ran out the door and told my wife what Gloria had done. Good she replied as she whacked me even harder on the back of the head. The second *ouch* of that day.

THIRTY

Year of the Challenger, Lame Duck

AFTER LITTLE JACK'S BIRTH, I dove into getting ready for what would be the most difficult re-election year that Jim and I would experience. The year was 1992. "Toss out the bums!" the clarion call of the electorate. President George H.W. Bush found himself challenged by a young, moderate Democrat in Bill Clinton and by an independent businessman in Ross Perot.

Much like the current political culture, incumbency mattered little. Voters wanted to support candidates that attacked the status quo in Harrisburg and Washington, D.C. Jim had a strong record of achievements. But coming off the 1991 budget impasse (and the anger of state employees), the controversial school voucher vote, and having a significant health issue of memory impairment, we faced the "perfect storm" that year.

Fortunately, Senator Weigel had challenged the establishment, including that tax reform vote when he bolted the party. By highlighting this and introducing other bills to address legislative compensation, always a sore spot in Pennsylvania, and pointing to successful efforts by

Weigel to save tax dollars by eliminating wasteful patronage jobs, we cast
Jim rightfully as a reformer.

But the Democrats smelled blood in our district. The caucus and
Republican State Committee were concerned, too. The area's demo-
graphics had changed with the city becoming even more Democratic.
The inner suburbs were now a toss-up between the parties, plus we had
lost some strong Republican areas because of redistricting. Jim's district
became more compact due to growth in the outer suburbs. Rumors of
Weigel's decline also had spread. Too many lobbyists, legislators, and citizens noticed the senator's memory lapses despite our efforts to compen-
sate and hide the health problem as much as we could.

The Senate Democrats recruited a young man, Thomas Stanton-
Fisher, to challenge Senator Weigel. A lawyer, his practice floundered
from a lack of business and visibility. Election to the state Senate would
bring a pay raise, better benefits, and higher recognition and influence if
he continued practicing law while serving as a senator.

For the benefit of the reader, rank-and-file legislators in Pennsylvania
currently make over eighty-six thousand dollars per year with a generous
pension, and health care benefits more lucrative than generally offered in
the private sector. Not in line with public opinion, I'm of the view that our
legislators should be adequately compensated given the sacrifices they
make to serve and the grueling schedule most legislators maintain. Do we
want only the wealthy to be able to serve? Cut the pay and benefits and
that will be the result.

Our advantage in re-election: Senator Weigel's likeability and the
tremendous respect he'd earned from his business and community work
and for his accessibility and responsiveness as a senator. Jim was careful
to maintain a strong Republican voting record, matching the opinions of
the people of York County closely.

Stanton-Fisher challenged Weigel to a series of debates across the district because he'd heard the rumors of Jim's declining health and wanted

to put him and his record under the spotlight. It would've been folly to expose the senator to one-on-one encounters where he might potentially commit serious gaffes that could tip the race. Instead, we agreed to several community-sponsored events of joint appearances, consisting of opening remarks and questions-and-answers from the audience. This would give the *illusion* of debates, without a head-to-head confrontation, where Weigel might falter because of his failing memory.

Terribly torn seeing the senator in this condition, I recognized there was no way he wouldn't run again for re-election because of pride and how much Jim loved his job. But maintaining his legacy and dignity concerned me. I sensed this would be the last hurrah. If we got him through this "Year of the Challenger" in a district that had become more competitive, he'd have to call it quits, either at the end of the term or during the next four years.

Did my conscience bother me we hid the truth from the voters about his medical situation? You bet. I struggled with my ethics and with my loyalty to someone I loved and honored but pushed ahead, regardless. If Senator James Channing Weigel suited up for the game, I had to be there, too.

As Jim's top guy, still at a young age, I continued my management responsibilities during a chaotic campaign. The office didn't shut down because of a tight election and citizens expected excellent service. Staff morale was in the pits, too. Our team knew the boss wasn't doing well, worried about the election outcome and their jobs if Weigel lost, and I had to be both a manager and a cheerleader. Whatever doubts I had about Weigel running and winning, I kept to myself, chewing up my insides from holding that stress and the burdens of juggling an office and campaign.

Politics abhors a vacuum. Weigel let his campaign infrastructure atrophy since the last re-election in '88 and several times during campaign meetings that wandered with no purpose, I'd ask, "Who's in charge of the overall effort?" Jim had no answer nor did his titular campaign chairman. Unacceptable, given a strong opponent and toxic political season. As a result, I stepped into the breach and assumed overall responsibility for directing the political effort. Everything I'd learned from that first campaign at age sixteen to volunteering in several more campaigns, I called upon to manage Weigel's re-election.

Throughout 1992, I routinely worked seventy-to-eighty hours a week. Every night and through the weekends, I oversaw the details of Jim's campaign or accompanied the senator to an event or went door-to-door with him. I shed twenty pounds. Time with Carolyn and young Jack suffered, and I developed an untreated ulcer. Asthma, bronchitis, and pneumonia flared up, requiring nebulizer treatments and new prescriptions on top of the daily blood pressure and migraine pills. Each of these drugs had side effects that further challenged my energy at a time when I needed everything my body could give me. I refused to let my weak constitution stop the mission at hand: returning Senator Weigel to another term representing the people of York County.

With Jim at an event one evening, we ran into Stanton-Fisher, and his campaign manager Nicholas Cole, a tough and experienced Democratic operative assigned by the Senate Democrats to direct Stanton-Fisher's efforts. As Weigel and I walked by them—civility gone and handshakes between the candidates no longer exchanged—I overheard Cole say, "You're failing, old man. You should've retired. Now Tom and I will destroy you at the polls next month."

I'm not sure whether Senator Weigel heard him or not. I couldn't let it pass though. On edge and ready to explode from months of hyperactivity, I turned violently on Stanton-Fisher and Cole and shouted, "Shut your mouths. Where's your decency? I realize that's something Democrats don't have." I lost it and took this smack talk way too personal, losing any perspective. Walking away would've been the smarter move. As the incumbent, Weigel maintained a lead based on what our tracking polls showed. But I'd let them get under my skin despite these advantages.

Cole knew of my straight-shooting reputation and temper since I'd become well-known in Harrisburg by that time. He pushed the right buttons. "What's the matter, Curran? Worried about losing your cushy job? Maybe we can find a page job for you." Only about five-five with longer hair and an earring, something foreign to the son of Big Joe Curran, Cole foreshadowed what the "hipster" would look like in the future.

Instead of punching him, I settled for a finger in his face. "I want to knock the shit out of you, but I won't. You and Stanton-Fisher will go back to living your dreary existence when this is all over." Senator Weigel grabbed me to put some distance between us. Fortunately, Kostantin Pokornin wasn't around to cover the event. Or I would have caused the campaign a major embarrassment and been the subject of a banner headline. Never a good thing for a chief of staff and campaign manager.

After the tantrum passed, I apologized. "Sorry, Senator. I should've controlled myself. It won't happen again."

"You're working very hard, Jack, and I appreciate it. We'll be fine." Ever the optimist, I didn't share his confidence. It wouldn't be until late on Election Day I'd relax and let my guard down.

The party traditionally hosted a victory celebration for its candidates, committee people, and supporters. Several hundred folks usually attended. We rented a room in the hotel where these faithful rallied. I wanted to analyze the returns near the action but without the distraction of lots of people milling around. I knew Jim might need a break, too, from all the folks who desired to talk with him about the race, or wanted his help with finding a job since seekers of patronage always hang out at these gatherings like leeches feasting on human blood.

Pacing around the room as I did, no surprise that Weigel stayed out in the larger ballroom to avoid my nervous energy. The numbers would come in, I would analyze where they came from, and find Jim to give him updates. He remained cool and calm during all this while I was a wreck. The city returns always came before any others, and Stanton-Fisher hurt us in York. Slowly, the suburbs came in, and the race became more competitive as the night wore on. Once the rural areas reported, we relaxed. With the final tally, Senator Weigel had survived a significant, well-funded challenge, winning by a smaller margin than any of his earlier elections, however.

As I circulated around the ballroom, I thanked our supporters and left to drive up to the Capitol to share the returns with Ben Walker and the leadership. They'd been concerned about our race but had their sights set on several other seats even more competitive than ours. I also needed to thank the senior staff for all their support for us in a tough re-election.

Fatigued and ready to collapse into a deep sleep, I pushed on when I entered the Capitol and signed in with the Capitol Police since the building was closed to the public that late at night. I spotted Kostantin Pokornin's profile near a staircase I was heading towards and tried to change course before he saw me. Too late.

"Curran, I need to talk with you."

"Not now, Kostantin. I'm dead-tired. How 'bout tomorrow?" *Does this guy have a tent pitched somewhere?* I wondered. *He doesn't seem to leave here.*

"It's got to be now, Jack. One of my sources called me." *You've got to admire this guy's persistence.*

"Okay, two minutes," I answered wearily. "Off-the-record, agreed?"

Setting the ground rules with reporters up front before engaging in any substantive conversation is always a good idea.

"Fine. I hear this is Weigel's last term, and he's not well. People are whispering that you guys pulled a fast one in this re-election."

My worst nightmare having this question asked so directly, by a reporter no less, when all I wanted to do is crawl in bed. "Kostantin, we hid nothing. Jim had and will continue to have a full schedule. He went door-to-door and attended lots of community events. The voters returned

Senator Weigel to Harrisburg because they know he cares about them and York County." I should've crossed my fingers behind my back when I answered this, but it wouldn't have done any good. It was all a carefully constructed mirage.

"Some names are already floating around on who will succeed him, Jack. Care to comment on them?" An alarm went off in my head, like a firehouse whistle. His "source" no doubt was someone already positioning themselves for a possible run. The sad reality as much as I couldn't bring myself to voice it: Senator Weigel was a lame duck, and he hadn't even been sworn in yet for the new term.

"Give us a break, will you, Pokornin? He just got re-elected tonight. I'm not engaging in any speculation. Jim Weigel's the senator for at least another four years. Have a good night." I walked away.

Over my shoulder, I heard, "I'll be making more calls about this. Count on it."

"I'm sure you will, Kostantin," I answered without turning back. *No rest for the weary*, I said to myself in self-pity as I continued to my destination in the Capitol.

THIRTY-ONE

Ennis Again, Lunch with Rob,
Sexual Harassment Training

"JACK, THE SENATOR needs you in the Senate Archives, the caucus is almost over." In the post-election session, the final stretch before a new session began in January, I couldn't wait until Christmas when things would slow down a little, and I had some quiet with Jim's re-election safely behind us.

"Okay, I'll be right there," I answered back over the intercom. My office remained on the first floor, making it easy to reach the archives to find out how caucus went.

An important House bill that had come out of our committee required careful management along with our counterparts in the House Democrat Caucus. I assumed that's why Weigel had summoned me.

Finely tuned, the bill contained things our majority wanted and items we agreed to that the Senate Democrats sought to bring them on board, too. The House signaled its readiness to concur in these changes, and the governor's office signed off. A divided government made these compromises necessary if we hoped to accomplish anything. An example of good old-fashioned horse-trading—many things could still go wrong to derail the measure.

On-and-off the phone almost continuously with the other caucuses, and interested lobbyists; so far, the complex work seemed to be holding through the legislative process. I kept Ben Walker up-to-date on deals we made and he appeared satisfied with the approach. The legislation needed to get through the caucus and the floor vote. It would be up to the House to finish the job.

With Jim's fading memory, the caucus made me nervous. As his staff, we could not be at the closed-door gathering, so we did our best to prepare talking points and remarks. Nothing compensated for having someone seated next to Senator Weigel if he needed to be reminded of a point when members had questions on the bill.

Agnes greeted me with a wave when I entered the archives. Still in the same place only with a fresh stack of tabloids that joined those from the eighties that sat beside her desk. The blaring headline "FERGIE SPLITSVILLE WITH PRINCE ANDREW," spread out in front of her was certainly far more interesting than anything the Senate might be doing. "Hi, Agnes, what's new, my friend?"

"Not much, Jack. Need to catch up on reading," she responded. *There is comfort in her consistency*, I admitted to myself.

Jim sat waiting at the big table—the same spot Ennis O'Reilly had me vacate years before. "Hey, Senator, how'd it go in there this morning?" I asked, pointing to the caucus room. Several members passed us, the sign they'd finished up. An early meeting was rare since the leaders wanted to wrap up session sooner than usual. Otherwise, caucus occurred normally much later in the day.

"Uh, Jack," he began. "There are amendments to that bill we're interested in."

"You mean the House bill, right? What changes? Everything got negotiated in committee. The goal is to keep the measure clean on the floor. You know that, Jim." I was impatient, but Weigel didn't deserve this interrogation. When not in the passion of a legislative battle, it pained me to watch him not be able to articulate and defend his position like he used to.

"You must speak with Ennis. She did most of the talking during the caucus and I don't remember all she said." Not one of her favorites—I think my candor wasn't always welcome in her presence.

My mind whirled with the possibilities. Finally, I answered, "Okay, Jim. We'll figure out how to make this work. Maybe Ennis knows something I don't." Senator Weigel did the best he could under the circumstances. I waited patiently for Ennis's exit. She breezed out the door dressed in a new generation of Armani suits. Not much had changed since that first time she shushed me away over seven years ago. "Ennis, can I talk to you a minute?"

"What's up? I'm needed on the floor," she answered brusquely.

"Senator Weigel asked me to check about amendments to our House bill. The bill needs to stay—"

O'Reilly cut me off. "Yeah, one of the members has a problem in his district, and I had my policy shop put an amendment together. We're tacking it onto this piece."

"I'm aware of the issue," I said a bit exasperated since it was my job to be aware as the staff manager of the bill. "The plan is to find another House bill or move a separate piece for the senator because we haven't vetted his problem in committee yet. Everything's been negotiated with the House and relevant interest groups. Everyone's on board. With a new proposal introduced, I'm afraid this'll blow up."

"Look, Jack, the House will take what we send over. This is the best way to get this done for one of our members with a problem. Make it work." To the hallway she cruised. Her red hair and freckles appeared more pronounced than usual, probably because I'd annoyed her. Ennis's wardrobe had changed little since dressing in designer suits seemed to be the expected fashion in Washington, D.C., where she worked formerly for the Republican leadership—her employer was Bob Michel, the long-time minority leader before Newt Gingrich rose to power.

"Sonofabitch," I said too loudly, causing Agnes to glance up from her tabloid. "Sorry, Agnes, for my language." I didn't expect her to respond. A survivor, she kept her mouth shut. Ennis may have had her reasons for the change—with a view of a bigger picture than I had—but it still stung.

I got busy on the phone with other staffers involved with the negotiations and explained the fresh, unexpected development. The call I most dreaded was to Molly MacQuaid, my counterpart in the House. We had forged a close friendship despite working for separate parties. I respected her great intellect and integrity and she didn't react well to the call. "We've had nothing to do with this 'new issue,' Jack, and your caucus better not dump that amendment in there," she warned. As staff for a Democrat from Philadelphia, Molly could be tough but always fair and I didn't blame her for being pissed off at a classic blindside I had no control over.

"O'Reilly did this in caucus, and I can't get her to back down on the change. The amendment's going in," I said with a sigh. In an earlier time, the amendment would be dead because Jim Weigel would've shut it down in twenty seconds but that was then. A new reality required different tactics, causing lots of frustration for me because there were limits to my power as a staffer. In no position to dictate terms to Ennis, I had to eat shit on this one. Even if I found myself in such a spot, she was usually three or four steps ahead of everyone else in the legislative process because of her intelligence and willpower.

"The bill's probably dead over here, my friend," Molly concluded. "All those changes negotiated between the four caucuses and the interest groups are gone, too. There's no way my leadership will accept this. Tell your leadership good job killing months of hard work." Molly hung up the phone, and I rested my face in my hands in defeat. We'd have to start over in the new session, another bill down the drain.

My ruminations were interrupted by our receptionist. "Jack, Rob is on line one."

"Thanks. Get it in a second." I took a moment to compose myself before picking up the phone. "Hey, Rob, how've you been?"

Because of the session and the election, we had seen little of each other. Rob had left the House the year before for the more lucrative side of the legislative process—lobbying. The public accountants picked him up to represent their interests in Harrisburg.

"I'm okay, but you sound down though. How about lunch? My treat. I suppose you want to meet at your favorite deli." Rob remained one of the few people I'd eat with, preferring to grab food from the Capitol cafeteria most days.

"That sounds good. A laugh or two would be welcome at this point. The deli would be nice. You know me, nothing fancy. Before you called, I was fuming about a bill that's going down the tubes."

"Which one? Never mind, not worth talking about. There's always another day in Harrisburg, Jackie. See you at the restaurant around one. Later, pal."

After making more calls, I was accused further of killing the deals and couldn't wait to leave the Capitol. Frustrated and dejected, the few blocks in the brisk cold of November did a lot of good to erase the disappointment, frustration, and anger I had about months and months of work being to no avail.

I arrived at my favorite deli on Locust Street. Small and informal, it served great New York-style sandwiches at reasonable prices. Somehow, the restaurant survived competition from more well-known establishments that catered to legislators and lobbyists. The crowd seemed more "real" than what I thought was the fantasyland of the General Assembly and state government. The charge consistently leveled at us: the legislature and staff are "out of touch," an assessment I shared—one of the reasons I continued to do constituent work, even though I was in the top position and could've delegated the job to other staff. Fielding calls from angry folks could take one down a notch or two as appropriate ego control.

The hostess gave me a table back in the corner with a little more privacy since I expected Rob to gossip, one of his favorite pastimes. He entered shortly after I did, and we shook hands. Rob had put on weight—the good life catching up with my friend. He continued the entertaining circuit that I avoided. "Jack, you look like shit. How much weight have you lost, fifteen pounds?"

"Thanks, brother," I said sarcastically. "Down almost twenty for your information." I suspected Carolyn had called him about my health, the two conspiring to protect me, since I didn't take care of myself, consumed with protecting Jim Weigel.

"Seriously, you gotta slow up and let your body heal. When's the last time you and Carolyn had a vacation?" Rob knew the answer. It was obvious where he hoped to take this conversation. The waitress arrived to take the order. I chose my usual Reuben and a diet Coke; Rob, a pastrami on rye with an iced tea.

"We got away to Sea Isle this past summer for a week," I said. "Carolyn and Little Jack had a nice time. I was on the phone with the office and campaign staff a lot. Couldn't avoid it."

"That's not a vacation, Jack," he said. "The election's over. You did a great job getting Weigel over the finish line. Everyone knows his health isn't good. You guys withstood a shit storm from the Democrats. Time to chill, okay?"

I protested. "We're just wrapping up session. There are lots of letters to get out. Jim still has phone messages to return after the election. And we need to redraft Jim's bills to introduce in January. Maybe I'll take a few days around the holiday." Carolyn wanted me to take the full week between Christmas and New Year's. I kept putting her off.

"Since I've known you, you've always had these damn lists. Enough already. There's nothing left to prove to anyone. You're a chief of staff with a reputation for being a hard worker, honest, loyal, and smart. Revel in the win from November." Rob didn't let up. I knew he was right and needed it told straight. No one could talk to me like Rob did.

"Fine, Rob. You win," I said. "I'll take a week around the holiday. Maybe Carolyn can get her parents to watch Jack, and we'll book a trip to the Caribbean or something."

Placid broke out in a big smile, victorious once again at getting me to relax. At the mention of my in-laws, he couldn't resist a dig. Rob had experienced my father-in-law at our wedding and several holidays when he joined us for dinner with the Gianellas eating at our table. "How's Pop Gianella doing anyway?" he asked. "Remember the evil eye he gave you when he handed Carolyn over at the altar? Thought you were going to turn to stone or something. Thank God for Jack Daniels, huh, buddy?"

I chuckled at the memory of downing a shot before saying "I do." "He and I have an uneasy relationship. Frank didn't exactly welcome the marriage with open arms as you saw firsthand. On a happier note, Carolyn is pregnant again. We're due late summer."

"You sat on that big news this long. Congratulations, buddy. Give Carolyn a kiss for me." The food arrived. I realized how hungry I was— soup and crackers my usual lunch fare than the meaty sandwich I couldn't wait to wolf down.

"Let's eat. By the way, if we have a boy, we're naming him after you. Not my idea, but Carolyn's. I think you two are in a permanent alliance against me."

Rob Placid deserved this honor. And much more. I counted on him in a variety of ways. When it came time to move to our larger home, Rob helped organize the packing and drove the U-Haul himself. Without complaint, Rob sweated with me for several weeks in the summer evenings as we painted our Victorian house, outdated when we purchased it. While I had a cordial relationship with my brothers, they had their own lives. Rob filled that role, blessing me as only a close friend can do.

The lunch talk shifted to the gossip of Harrisburg. I had no "scoop" to share. Placid thrived on this stuff, picking up tidbits from the bars and Rotunda where lobbyists congregate and from a network of friends and acquaintances scattered throughout the Capitol. My chum's web rivaled Kostantin's in its breath and intelligence-gathering. "Did you hear about our favorite senator with the big comb and tall pipe, Dalton Schwemmer?" Rob asked. "The secretarial staff complained to leadership about his sexual advances on them. That guy will shtup just about anything."

Leaping out of his chair, Rob's hand high over his head as he sought imaginary recognition, gesturing wildly, he mimicked this short senator with a good imitation. The nasal whine Rob used grating to the ear. "Mr. President, Mr. President, over here if you can't see me, I rise to object to these very fallacious charges. Yes, I'm standing, Mr. President, I said over here. I touched no one, I swear. If you have a stack of Bibles, give me them." Despite myself, I laughed from deep within my belly, purging my bad mood. "As vertically challenged and bald as that guy is, he thinks he's some Don Juan. I dated one of his secretaries, and she alluded to his advances. Not surprised the news is out," Rob concluded.

I hadn't come across any of this scuttlebutt, but would soon sit in hours of sexual harassment seminars—mandatory and necessary for caucus employees to participate in to highlight the sensitivities of this serious problem. All because this legislator allegedly pawed female staffers. Very few seats remained when I arrived for this training. I sat by a middle-aged employee—a real joker—who took the subject matter lightly, causing the seminar leader to admonish us more than once. Her patience wearing thin, she threatened us with letters of reprimand in our personnel files. Guilt by association for being next to this hellraiser.

THIRTY-TWO

The Hoopla, Kim and Temptation,
Party Treachery

EVERY YEAR, our caucus held one of its largest political fundraisers, the Hoopla. Several hundred lobbyists, wealthy business people, and many of the Senate Republican staff would attend—invited to take part at a "reduced" ticket price of seventy-five dollars per person compared to the actual ask of five hundred skins per. "Highly encouraged" to go, it would have been illegal for the leadership to force us to pay, something known as "political macing." I participated as one of the few functions I went to each year as did Jim and several other members of the team, including Gloria.

The food plentiful, served by the senators themselves, included bags of steamed clams, hamburgers, corn on the cob, peach cobbler, and ice cream. Cold kegs on tap made sure attendees had a constant supply of beer. And live music made for a lively crowd. A wide creek, not more than a few inches deep, lumbered by the party site with some adventurous staffers splashing each other to cool off from the sticky summer air.

Rob had a large contingent of friends and fellow lobbyists that surrounded him at these events. Always the life of any party, I would join him since I didn't like working a crowd. And me? Grave Jack Curran going through the motions only. Carolyn stayed home with young Jack and carried Robert in her womb, so I kept my time at these things to a minimum. Mingling with people I saw every day at the Capitol wasn't high on my list of priorities. This event occurred in June, the busiest month with the budget deadline. It irritated me to be out another late night—in a month of many long evenings and early mornings, seventy-to-eighty-hour workweeks the routine drill.

As I went to leave, one of my fellow staffers named Kim grabbed my hand to lead me onto the dance floor. Taller and perky with brown hair and long bangs covering her high forehead, she had only graduated from college months ago. She wore small black shorts that revealed much of her legs with a pink halter top to show off her flat, toned belly and a red choker necklace that highlighted her delicate neck. Kim reminded me of the Abington cheerleaders in her dress and mannerisms.

In the past few weeks, she'd been coming to the office a lot to talk with me about issues the senator spearheaded, which could have been handled over the phone or by another one of our staff people. Kim made me uncomfortable during these meetings. It felt like flirting. I wore a wedding ring and thought it was common knowledge I didn't go out to the bars. Mentioning it to Gloria after one of Kim's visits, she laughed, "Don't flatter yourself, Jack. Kim's not interested in you."

Kim had obviously too much to drink as she tried to move me in rhythm to an older disco song the band played. Not in my genes to gyrate; even Carolyn had a hard time getting me out on the dance floor when we went out. I didn't want to be rude to Kim either since we worked together. Trying to disengage from her moves, I pleaded, "Kim, I have to be going. My pregnant wife and son are waiting at home for me." She wouldn't relent and lifted one beautiful long leg up onto my arm as I tried to balance my gyrations to the music. Panic and lust set in as that erotic limb brushed provocatively against me.

Kim's scent mingled with the twilight summer air, and she smelled good. Really good. *Sing the national anthem, maybe that will help. Okay, that didn't work. Recite your favorite lines from some of Lincoln's famous speeches.* Nothing worked as I fought a losing battle against a certain male impulse that didn't give a damn what my brain focused on.

"C'mon, Jack, lighten up. It's a party. I was a gymnast in high school. Wanna see my moves?" Kim's jade eyes sparkled as if they were casting a spell over me. *This is crazy, beyond insane. How do I get away from this woman without insulting her? How do I hide this tent in my khaki shorts? Please God, help me,* I prayed silently.

"I'm sure you were great, but I'm not comfortable dancing with you. I'm happily married you know." *I sound like a witness before a Senate committee made up of Methodist elders. Keep talking that way, Jack, maybe that'll cool you off.*

"I know that, silly. Everyone knows that. How old were you when you got hitched, seventeen? You were probably a child groom." Now teasing me, Kim tossed her head back with a throaty, suggestive laugh that sent shivers down my spine. "Let me teach you the bump, Jack Curran. That'll limber you up."

At that moment Rob passed us, and I saw my way out of this spider trap. I grabbed him by the arm and wouldn't let go. With quick introductions of, "Kim, this is Rob. Rob, this is Kim. You two finish up this dance." Out of there in a split second, I held my hand in front of my crotch to shield my embarrassment.

Before I was out of earshot, she asked Rob, "What's wrong with your friend? Why's Jack so serious all the time? Can't a girl have some fun?" Kim had maneuvered him into the bump although she didn't rest her long leg on his arm. *Good, he's much better at this stuff, and more important, Rob's single,* I noted.

Gloria's table seemed like a safe haven and I asked if she had seen the scene with Kim. "Okay, Jack, yes, she's flirting with you. I missed the signals. Doesn't happen too often though."

"I told you so. When it comes to women, I may not be a genius, but I know that behavior when it's aimed at me. Kim comes to the office again, the senator's door remains open when I meet with her. I'm not going to be in any compromising positions."

"Don't worry. Carolyn knows how devoted you are. Besides, Kim and Rob seem to be doing very well together," Gloria observed.

My quick thinking and introduction of them became a longer match than I expected—the two dated and married six months after the Hoopla. Honored to be Rob's best man, when it came time to congratulate Kim, she got only a dutiful hug and kiss—the memory of that long leg up on my arm still too fresh and troubling, stirring something in me I preferred to keep well submerged.

Another late night in June and another missed opportunity in tucking Little Jack in. My favorite time was with him snuggled in my arms as I read stories and sang lullabies. Crooning some classics every evening—and later to our younger son after he was born—soothed him and me as he rocked back and forth with his head resting on my shoulder, falling asleep, safe and secure in the knowledge his daddy would protect him. I made a vow when the children came along that they would not grow up without quality moments with their father.

Unlike Big Joe, I would balance my career and bound up those granite steps, with being their dad, and try to be a good husband to my beautiful wife. Not always successful, I'm sad to admit. But I usually didn't miss soccer, baseball, basketball games, scouting events, and school functions. Even if it meant dashing back to work after spending time with them, I strove to be there for my kids.

Once I got home from the Hoopla, Carolyn had poured me white wine, not touching the stuff herself since she became pregnant. We sat

out on our deck that overlooked the little run flowing through the back-
yard, the water trickling over the rocks, the only sound of that peaceful
good night. A waxing crescent moon provided the perfect light. I lit our
outdoor fireplace and leaned over to kiss her and told her the "Kim" story,
as it became known. We had no secrets although, for obvious reasons,
I left out the sexual feelings Kim stimulated within me. Very pregnant
now, my wife didn't need the emotional turmoil.

Her first reaction was to give me a light smack on the arm. "I think
you enjoyed that attention, Jackie boy." Carolyn saw through me like no
one else could, and it disturbed me she hit my ego head on with a sharp
arrow. Do I acknowledge the truth or deny it for the sake of her feelings
and the safety of our baby, not to mention my own safety? At that moment,
I played along, regretting the deception, but knowing the fullness of my
experience would devastate the woman I so deeply and completely loved.

"Yep, I did. It's hard for a man to get any attention with a little rug rat
in the house and one on the way." I reached over to rub her belly tenderly,
our baby now seven months along in the womb.

"Curran, you're too much." As she said this, her eyes twinkled; the
sign we'd passed safely through a pivotal moment in our marriage.

Resolved to love and cherish her more, I held her determined to sink
the erotic sensations stirred by another woman earlier in the evening.
Watching the dancing flames—the world could only be right when the
two of us were together. I prayed silently for forgiveness and murmured,
"Thank you, Jesus," for my wife. Rewarded with Carolyn's adoring
gaze—her angelic face softly lit by the glint from the moon and fire, I lost
myself in those soulful eyes. Truly my sanctuary in an unforgiving and
harsh society.

June came and went, the state budget completed by the deadline.
Our family returned to Sea Isle City for a week of relaxation; I promised
myself I would not call the office or return emails that entire week, a
pledge I didn't totally keep. With seven years under my belt as Senator

Weigel's chief of staff, I relaxed a little, developing a perspective that had been lacking in the early years. My point of view always got deeper when at the seashore—the salt and sun, a tonic to restore my soul.

The Capitol had this way of both frustrating and exhilarating me. The ups and downs of the legislative process were not helpful for someone as intense and prone to self-doubt as I could be. A good juncture to assess my career, while we were doing all right financially, we were careful since Carolyn stayed home as a full-time parent. We respected working parents but believed our son needed his mother all the time and wanted our second child to have the same opportunity.

Several firms had approached me about leaving to join the lobbying circuit. I resisted these overtures and enjoyed my work for Senator Weigel, elevating him in my mind to the same level as Ronald Reagan, Big Joe, and Dr. Moran, the men I admired most, but burn out from legislative staff work was a real problem. Failing rapidly, Jim had a lot of time left in his current term. *Can I leave him, Gloria, and the staff? Is it selfish of me to want a new start? A different venue might lift the exhaustion?* These were the thoughts running through my mind during that vacation.

That fall session's events would make the final decision for me. As we approached the third week in September, when we would return to session after the summer recess, scuttlebutt continued that the Democrats were courting one of our members, Senator Dunn Stuart O'Shea, to switch parties. This legislator, like Senator Madison and one or two other members, voted with labor and couldn't always be counted on to stick with the caucus on "tough" votes impacting on unions.

He and his staff enjoyed the immense attention they got from our leadership, who had heard the same rumors. As they gave him more, O'Shea wanted more. If the Democrats could convince this senator to switch, they would be the majority party, the lieutenant governor casting the tie vote for control of the chamber. That status would bring better office space, the appointment of the chairmen and committee slots, more funds for staffing, and the daily calendar decision on votes to expect and bills that wouldn't be voted. The stakes were thus very high.

Rob had heard these same whispers as he made the rounds in the Capitol and on the evening circuit. He warned me that the Democrats and O'Shea had struck a deal—the switch expected the first day we returned to session. Holed up in his office with only his staff and Democratic leaders the Monday we came back, the turncoat wouldn't see our leaders. Confirmation that Rob's sources had been right.

As the gavel fell into session that Monday afternoon, a hush descended over the chamber. Senator O'Shea stood for recognition. Once given, in his deep baritone voice, he announced with a flourish, "Mr. President, I declare I am a Democrat. I can be much more effective with my colleagues," his hand swept towards the left side of the magnificent room, "than with the conservative, I might note, now minority party. I will protect my labor friends from this new...more powerful position."

Mayhem exploded as the Republicans booed and reporters scribbled stories from their seats in the gallery. The Democratic leader scrambled to his feet at once to demand a reorganization of the Senate, stunning our leadership and Ben Walker, who no longer had the votes and could do nothing to stop the transfer of power away from the Republicans to the Democrats. Not articulated by either Senator O'Shea or his new majority colleagues: what about the betrayal of his constituents that thought they had elected a Republican in his last re-election campaign?

It would be our time to serve in the minority: the opposition party controlled the governor's office, House, and now the Senate. We'd have to change behaviors as a caucus, and in Jim's office, primarily reacting on the calendar, rather than driving the agenda, searching for ways to promote Republican principles and ideas via amendments to Democratic bills, holding policy hearings and press conferences of our making. As a minority, opportunities would be limited unless we pushed hard to remain relevant.

Almost immediately, the Democrats threw the GOP out of the prime real estate of the Capitol. Boxes, furniture, and carts clogged the hallways as they moved from their smaller spaces to Republican territory and vice versa. A complete waste of time and chaotic, but part of the spoils of war and the victor wasn't about to stay put.

Shortly after the change in power, the leadership notified us that personnel had to be fired due to our new minority status and more limited funding. We would have to end the employment of at least one staff person. That job fell to me. In normal times, the senator and I would've decided together. Not now. I consulted with Gloria, trusting her counsel more than anyone else's, other than Carolyn's and Rob's. The first time I had to terminate someone, and I carried the load alone.

I asked one of the Senate's lawyers to join me as I called "Debbie" in. My face telegraphed what was to come, and she knew immediately. "Debbie, I'm so sorry we have to let you go because of the reorganization. You've been an outstanding, loyal staffer to Jim." I felt like we had cut off an arm—that's how close-knit our team was. "The Senate is offering you a severance and I've written you a letter of reference." With my head down, I slid the documents across the desk to her.

"I don't understand, Jack. What have I done to deserve this? I'm married and have a child." Her anger spilled out at the injustice of this political action. For all of those who work in this profession, however, this hazard is well known and always just below the surface.

"I can't say anything more, Debbie. I'll do everything I can in phone calls if you have any prospects. Whatever support I can give you, count on it. We need you to sign the release if you want the severance." I struggled to hold back my emotions as she signed the document in disgust.

That night I experienced the frequent internal struggle. *Do I belong in this profession? What'd compelled me to choose politics?* I felt like I'd been sucked in too far, with a wife and children to support; the only path available—keep moving forward. This conflict would be with me until the last few years of my service when I saw the prospect of retirement, my light at the end of the tunnel. I often wondered, *What if I hadn't volunteered in that campaign? Would I have been happy in accounting?* I would never know. When the political bug bit as hard as it did, I was hooked, decisions followed that would chart my course, right or wrong.

THIRTY-THREE

Doc, Architects United, Leaving Government

ONE DAY SOON after the Democrats seized control of the Senate, I left the Capitol to take a walk to the river over the lunch break. This stroll would lead to my departure from state government. To the private sector and lobbying I would go. At the top of the granite steps, I stopped to enjoy the vista; the stately maple and oak trees that lined the street were turning a brilliant red, yellow, and orange, ushering in the fall season. Down the same stairs I'd bounded up over eight years ago. It was a good time to ponder what my next moves would be.

So many tough issues and challenges and the pace Senator Weigel set for all of us until his health declined had caused burn out. "Team Weigel" had been in an automobile doing seventy miles per hour, and the brakes had been slammed on hard. Jim would not be running again, and the GOP found itself in the minority. This placed the caucus in the position of reacting to whatever the Democrats led with, strategizing on how to stop or amend whatever the Democrats pushed and scheduled for votes in committee and on the calendar. What a change; from being the leader to bringing up the rear.

Carolyn continued to cope as best she could with a tough schedule. Robert had joined us. A much bigger baby than Jack Jr., he topped over ten pounds and twenty-two inches and a difficult labor for my wife that included biting me on the shoulder during one of the more painful contractions when I leaned in to comfort and remind her of the breathing exercises we had practiced. Felt like God's way of paying me back for the insensitivity I showed when I left my dear wife in the car when her water broke, and contractions began during Little Jack's birth. The OB/GYN nurse made direct eye contact and scolded her, "No biting, Mrs. Curran." Like a man, I took the pain, realizing the tiny discomfort she'd inflicted couldn't compare to her agony. But back to my river walk.

With my head down and lost in deep thought, I walked by a friend without so much as a hello. "Yo, Jack, how's it going?"

"Oh, Aaron. Sorry. In my own world right now," I answered. Aaron was a respected lobbyist in town and had been of invaluable help in Weigel's tough re-election. Like me, he'd started out as a Senate staffer and served now as a managing partner for his firm. Part of Jim's first election, he knew the district and assisted with raising money since the '92 re-elect had been so expensive—exceeding over ninety thousand dollars from our campaign alone.

The battle lines of a modern campaign and the chaos and pace that comes with a competitive race makes for a kindred spirit that isn't replicated in too many places—with the significant exception of combat and warfare. That bruising re-election had strengthened our bond and friendship. "No sweat. Good to see you, brother."

I clasped his hand and gripped his shoulder. "Always great seeing you. Thanks again for everything. Couldn't have done it without you."

"How are you? You survive the transition okay? How's Jim?" Aaron asked. Since he knew Weigel so well, Aaron understood how much the senator had declined so I didn't need to be as circumspect with answers as I normally would be with outsiders. The wall of denial, silence, and protection remained in place and a part of me continued to be in conflict over the key role I'd played in an election ruse.

"Hanging in there. Although it remains a challenge with the senator's memory as it is. I'm a little restless, to be honest, and burned out."

Not the first time he had heard this, Aaron nodded his head in sympathy. "That's understandable after last year's contest. Serving as staff in the minority isn't easy either. There are decisions to make, Jack. You can stay on the staff long-term or leave to lobby. Those are the paths available at this point if you stick around this town." While those seemed to be the options, a nagging voice inside flashed caution about the lobbying side of the profession.

Aaron continued, "Our meeting today may be a good thing. I got a call yesterday from an old friend of mine, Victor Pearl, or Doc as we call him because he'd been a sociology researcher at Temple University. He's searching for a lobbyist. How about I have him contact you?"

"The name sounds familiar. He was a Senate staffer years ago, right? Who does he work for?"

"Yeah, we were on the staff together. Doc is head of the Architects United up on Second Street. Great guy. Unmarried all his life. A little eccentric, I'll warn you. Very devout in his passion for the Jewish faith, he lives in uptown Harrisburg where he can walk to synagogue on the Sabbath. You're religious, too, aren't you? At least I heard you might be." Not wishing to discuss my spirituality since I preferred to keep that part of me private, I remained silent. "Anyway, you'll like Doc. Has a lot of charm."

"Thanks for the background. Sure, ask Doc to call me in the office. Jim and Gloria realize I'm looking at other possibilities. There are no secrets."

We said goodbye, and I continued to the river as Aaron proceeded to the Capitol Building. *Is it the right time to leave? Am I wired for lobbying as much as I hate the entertaining, begging, and pleading for action? A change might just rejuvenate me. The architects are an attractive profession, something I might comfortably represent on the "Hill."* All these thoughts raced through my mind as I walked over the Walnut Street Bridge, an iron truss overpass that connected to City Island and the West Shore before the river carried away a span in one of the more damaging floods.

Around the northern half of the island, I took my time ambling along the path that led down to the Susquehanna. The geese and egrets fed at the lapping water's edge; no doubt bulking up before the river froze and deprived them of a food source. Bicyclists, skateboarders, and other pedestrians were on the same path. I enjoyed the slow pace and the sunshine on my face, soaking up the rays, savoring the reprieve from the constant hustle and bustle of the Capitol.

By the time I returned to the office, I'd decided to at least listen to what Victor Pearl had to say. The notion of a pay raise to support two kids dangled out in front of me. Lobbying is more lucrative than staff work. Rob had transitioned well, lived in a nicer home, and drove an expensive convertible, while Carolyn and I had a Ford Escort and an old 1976 Buick Regal as our second car. The auto didn't move in a heavy snowfall; its rear-wheel drive, and the fact it weighed three tons, made it immovable during most of the winter.

Around five, Gloria buzzed me that Victor Pearl was on the phone. She and Doc had worked together before he left the Senate staff. Gloria and I were tight, bonding from all the legislative battles and our shared purpose of protecting the senator. She didn't want me to leave. But would never stand in the way. My colleague understood I was fatigued, restless, and uneasy about money with a larger family now to provide for.

"Hi, Victor. Appreciate the call."

"Hello, Jack. Aaron's told me a lot about you. Call me Doc."

"Okay, Doc it is."

"My lobbyist here is retiring. The association needs new blood, new ideas, new energy, and I hear you have a lot of that. Why don't you come in? We can discuss the position, compensation, and my group. Based on what Aaron's said, we might be a fit."

"That sounds good, Doc." We agreed to meet in a few days; I had a little more time in my schedule since we weren't in the majority.

One of the old Harrisburg brownstones converted into commercial space housed Doc's office. Handsome and dignified from the outside with ivy attached to the walls, a large sign adorned the building that read "DESIGNING A BRIGHT FUTURE, ARCHITECTS UNITED." Later, I would learn they were a rival group to another association of architects. For lawmakers interested in who to negotiate with on legislation relevant to architects, it made it difficult to discern exactly who represented the profession.

Doc showed me around to meet the staff before we entered his cluttered space filled with political memorabilia, piles of papers across the desk, on the library table, side chairs, on the floor, and even within the old stone fireplace. As I gazed around the room, I remembered he was formerly a university researcher before entering politics. Explained a lot about the office.

The disorganized look did not complement his impeccable appearance. From a shaved head, to dark, bushy eyebrows, to a three-piece suit, Doc's suave look reminded me of Telly Savalas from reruns and movies I had watched as a kid. The significant exception from this famous actor: two earrings on his left lobe. Like this celebrity, he originally hailed from Long Island before relocating to Philadelphia.

From all the memorabilia, he was obviously a veteran of several political campaigns. Posters, bumper stickers, and buttons filled the wall space. At once, I sensed the presence of a genius—bright and unfocused. Big Joe, Dr. Moran, and Senator Weigel were my examples: focused, disciplined, and organized. Piles of papers never littered their tidy offices.

Doc cleared off both side chairs, and his second-in-command entered to join the interview. I had not met her during the tour. While she appeared to be only in her forties, a much older manner weighed her down, almost as if life had been very difficult. Her graying blond hair had a bob to it, eyeglasses perched on her nose, an unflattering blouse and skirt, capped off with an unpleasant demeanor, all this not setting the right tone from my point of view. She clearly wasn't happy about being pulled into the conversation. In her defense, she probably had to be super-organized to make up for Doc's idiosyncrasies. He introduced her as "Iris." When we shook hands, the lack of warmth she conveyed continued. Iris didn't make eye contact, an important marker for me.

The impressive leather portfolio I carried that bore the "Senate of Pennsylvania" seal contained copies of my resume and I handed one to each of them. Doc waved it off, while Iris scrutinized it carefully, no doubt scanning for typos and possible fraudulent entries. In another life, I saw Iris with the FBI the way she eyeballed my credentials, hoping for an "aha" moment to have me whisked away by a G-man for detention and interrogation under a bright light and perhaps waterboarding if I didn't cooperate enough to her liking.

"Jack, Aaron speaks highly of you. Says you've done a phenomenal job for Senator Weigel. Incidentally, I bought a car from him years ago. Gave me a good deal I might add. You ever shop at Jim's dealership?"

Strange question to ask so I ignored it. "Appreciate the compliment, Doc. Aaron's been a mentor. Very helpful in the re-elect, especially to me personally as I ran Jim's campaign." Iris peered up from the resume, now openly glaring. I dropped eye contact with her. Doc asked me to interview for the job—Iris was his problem, not mine.

"You've been Jim's chief of staff for over seven years, right?"

"That's correct. Before that, I interned for Senator Young and had one congressional campaign I volunteered for in Montgomery County. I also served on a county transportation council," I said, summarizing most of my resume since he didn't take one.

"Any experience with architect issues?"

"The senator sits on the Consumer Protection and Professional Licensure Committee that considers the bills that impact on architects. Another staffer handles the committee, but I've kept a close eye on the agendas. I've interacted with several of the members on the Republican side; none on the Democratic side, however."

"That's okay. You're obviously a quick study. Knowledge of the profession will come although I'm still not real knowledgeable, am I, Iris?" Iris frowned deeper when Doc said this but did not answer. "Aaron probably told you I served on legislative staff like you before leaving the inside to work for Architects United. The architects wanted my connections to the 'Hill.' Grasp of the issues just happens along the way, sort of from osmosis, trust me."

This association was not unlike any other in Harrisburg or Washington, D.C. Mastery of substance would come later; relationships and the ability to open doors to the powerful were what counted in state government and the U.S. Capitol.

"If you offer the position, Doc, and I accept, I'm prohibited from lobbying the Senate for one year under the Pennsylvania Ethics Act." *A smart prohibition*, I thought. This put distance between staffers that depart and the members and staff of the chamber where they worked before.

"Yeah, that's no problem. I still have a lot of connections in the Senate. You'd focus on the House and on contacts with the Pennsylvania Congressional Delegation." I perked up when Doc mentioned Congress, a return to a venue I'd been away from for over eight years.

"Ever hear of Citizens for Conservative Priorities and Common Sense during the Reagan years? I interned there so I have familiarity with the city and Capitol." A photo of President Reagan adorned the wall. Highlighting that connection seemed to make sense.

"Yeah, I know of them. Good. A group of architects and the staff go down there several times a year for nothing but dog-and-pony shows, but our members enjoy the D.C. thing, walking the halls of the Capitol, having big dinners down there. Meetings back in Pennsylvania when the congressmen are home and focused, I believe, are much more productive. These events would be part of your responsibility, too." The job duties seemed better and better, although I didn't relish the idea of travel, becoming more of a homebody the older I got.

"How much travel is involved besides the D.C. trips?"

"I think most of the meetings in Pennsylvania would be one day only. As far as entertainment of legislators, something the current lobbyist likes to do, we don't have the budget and entertain only if necessary." Iris's nose wrinkled with the mention of the current employee and his expenses. I was getting the picture. It wasn't necessarily me as Iris's problem, but the government-relations department. I tested my theory out.

"Doc, when does he retire? Who would I report to—both you and Iris?" I hoped the chain of command didn't include Iris. I tried to work with everyone, but this one might be tough.

"To me directly. Iris is here for budgetary reasons. Your interaction with her would be limited to submitting expenses for her review and approval since she makes sure the bills get paid and we get paychecks." *Oh crap, I would have to interact with her after all.*

"The current lobbyist, when does he leave?" Doc jumped around a lot, so my eyes got a good workout as I tried my best to follow him.

"Oh, you asked that, sorry. He's gone in two weeks. I need someone almost immediately. Let's get down to it, Jack. How much do you earn? Our benefits are good but not as great as the Senate's. I'm sure you understand that. We do have a twenty percent employee contribution for benefits." Iris smiled ever so slightly. Obvious she had instituted this budget-saving practice.

"Thirty-eight thousand a year. I understand the benefits thing, although we pay nothing for coverage now, so the package would have to be right to move forward if I have a new, out-of-pocket expense in this position."

Doc turned and looked at Iris. "Okay, I want to offer Jack forty-nine thousand a year to get him to jump. Will this work?" Sure their more experienced lobbyist earned more, I would save them money. A big plus for as lean an operation as they appeared to be.

For the first time, Iris spoke up. "Well, Victor, I've made my opinions plain." *Odd, she didn't call him Doc,* I noticed. "I would prefer we not have these expenses. The rest of the staff works very hard to bring in revenue; the lobbying operation is a drain and waste of resources. What money do they generate? I can think of better ways to spend our limited funds." My sense had been correct.

"We've gone over that, Iris. Our competitor has a robust government affairs department, and we can't afford to get left behind. The members expect the same from us...one of the biggest reasons they pay membership dues. No members, no dues. Will that figure work under the budget or not?" Doc asked this sharply; Iris's challenge to his leadership had crossed the line.

"Yes, Victor, I can make this work." She said this with a big sigh, emitting a large breath. Whatever toothpaste Iris used failed that day.

"That's the offer. I'd like an answer as soon as possible, okay?"

"Understood. I need to talk with my wife and get her thoughts. She's aware we're meeting," I added.

"That's the way it should be. How many kids, and how long have you been married?" Doc seemed interested in my family.

"Two sons. Carolyn and I've been married for seven years. Shortly after I joined Senator Weigel's team, we wed."

"Great. I love family, and this is a family-friendly place, right, Iris?" Doc asked. She didn't even bother to look up with that comment. I had to consider whether I would leave an office where I served as the top dog on staff to work with Iris, who would not relent on her bias regardless of how hard I might try to charm her. And I could be charming when necessary. But I was sure Iris would be a real test.

"Thanks, Doc, for even considering me." I ignored Iris. She hadn't even tried to be gracious. "Be back in touch soon." I shook hands with Doc. Iris had left out the side door to an adjoining space. *What a miserable woman*, I commented to myself.

I called Carolyn and Rob when I returned to the office to give them a report and filled Gloria in on the interview. Subdued, it unnerved me that my office colleague wouldn't provide me with advice.

Carolyn arranged for an impromptu dinner with Rob that evening, knowing I would need to talk this over. I thought Rob would be all in since he'd made the jump to lobbying. Wrong. We sat down for Carolyn's famous noodle beef casserole and a large Caesar salad and said grace; Rob and I each had a beer with the meal.

"Jack, I realize you feel burned out," Rob began. "The money is better. But this isn't a good move." I was rowing in a different direction at that point, warming up to the idea, despite the vibes from Iris.

"I thought you'd like the idea, me going to the outside, maybe relaxing some, making more."

"Sure, I want that for you. You can't change who you are, man. The evening drill will kill you, and you won't like the travel. While Doc said it's only several times a year, I know you...you'll hate all of it."

"The travel doesn't sound bad. Doc said the eating out would be minimal. I can make it work. It's a change, Rob; I'm really tired out."

"I know, buddy. If you make this move, make it worthwhile because you're going to have to change your stripes, something you'll have a tough time doing. What Doc offered is a nice salary hike, but a larger firm would give you much more. Someone with your experience is worth more on the private market than his offer. Add another ten, at least, to that number."

Rob turned to Carolyn for her opinion. She replied, "I want Jack to be happy and worry about the same things you do, Rob. I don't want him to take the job just for the money. We're making ends meet."

"We have two kids, honey. The extra salary will help fix the house up more, allow us to get rid of the crappy Buick." The car's odometer had turned over. Over seventeen years old, the vehicle's rust and decay had defeated my attempts at patching and painting. "I don't wanna work for a large firm. A group based on one profession has more appeal," I whined.

"The car's running fine, Jackie," Carolyn said. "Listen to Rob. He knows you, and he knows what lobbying is like."

"I do," Rob added. "And I enjoy the hell out of it. I don't think it's a fit with your personality, Jack, but you must make this decision. No one else."

Dinner finished, mostly in silence. Rob and I went into the den, and I made us both scotch on the rocks. Rob knew I had to brood over this, so we drank the whiskey and watched a ballgame on television. After we downed the drinks, Rob said goodnight to Carolyn and our sons. I thanked him and walked him out to his sexy, late-model convertible that sat in the driveway next to the long in the tooth Regal with multiple patches, peeling paint, and those awful whitewall tires that yelled out the 1970s. *What a contrast*, my jealous psyche said, *the rich, private sector guy versus the government public servant.*

I kissed Carolyn goodnight and tucked Little Jack into bed and rocked Robert for a few minutes to help tire him out; later retiring to the den to have another scotch and to pace. I'd have to turn this decision over and over, probably until the morning. Carolyn recognized that was my way. It made no sense for both of us not to sleep—she had two boys to take care of during the day.

Is Rob spot on about my character? Can I make the transition to lobbying without compromising my integrity? I probed myself. Some lobbyists can represent even the most questionable interests; much like a good defense attorney can represent known criminals. They can flip the switch on their conscience as if it were a radio that could be turned on-and-off. I saw a nobility in the work of architecture that would allow me to advocate for their interests without losing more sleep than normal because of my habit of worrying so much.

I got to bed around four that morning and would take the job, wondering whether I had made the right decision. The hardest part would be leaving Jim, Gloria, and the staff.

THIRTY-FOUR

Capitol Bound, Photo Ops and Sound Bites, Jezebel's Joint, Henrietta Again

WASHINGTON, D.C., *look out, Jack Curran's coming back*. Upbeat about my return to the nation's capital, the new job improved our financial situation as I motored our Ford Escort onto the George Washington Memorial Parkway, a scenic route along the Potomac River. The Buick Regal got scrapped for a brand-new station wagon because Carolyn needed more room for the boys and I drove the Ford.

It was March. Doc and I were preparing for one of the lobbying visits with Pennsylvania's Congressional Delegation. About fifteen of our members would join us, along with counterparts from across the country. The national association, Architects United, would run us through several informational sessions so that all the state delegations worked off the same points to discuss during the Capitol stops.

Doc was right. These were dog-and-pony shows and nothing more, with not much accomplished. When we had a visit with one of the members of Congress, the staff aide would shuffle us along for a photo-op and *perhaps* a minute or two of light conversation. The staff took most of the appointments, and even these were abbreviated. Each office tried hard to make the meetings a matter of minutes per stop. In fairness to the aides, they had to meet the demands of their bosses, answer constituent calls and mail, research complex issues, and visit with lots of groups, like ours, that wanted access and face time.

It's no wonder these people in Congress have no ability to solve the nation's problems, I observed to myself, while we consulted the map and navigated between the office buildings. Constantly on the move with no time to think and debate. Our national governance reduced to sound bites, photo ops, and social media posts. With the reality that the bureaucracy of staff and lobbyists run the legislature and make the decisions—when decisions are made at all. Press releases, Twitter, fluff, misdirection, and bitter partisanship have supplanted real leadership with both parties at fault. *Where is Harry Truman's "The buck stops here" when our country so desperately needs it?* I mused.

Doc thrived in this environment as a talker. With a flourish, he'd highlight one or two points about architecture to impress our members. I had dug into the profession to be up to speed on the federal issues that mattered to architects, so I filled in the blanks if any congressional office had questions about our positions.

Away from home three or four days was something I didn't enjoy—keenly aware that Carolyn had little boys in diapers that kept her on the go all the time. Because D.C. hotel rates were so expensive, Doc and Iris wouldn't spring for two rooms. Now almost thirty years old, I didn't appreciate having to share a room with my boss. The lack of privacy irritated me to no end as a light sleeper. Not to mention getting dressed and undressed in front of my boss not the way I wanted to start or finish each day. To be fair, I'm sure Doc wasn't thrilled with doing the same in front of his subordinate.

Rob's advice and instincts couldn't have been more correct on that night we had dinner to discuss the job offer. I had undersold myself for the position given the increased demands. Iris gave me a hard time even about expenses that Doc had pre-approved, and I entertained far more than Doc had let on. While I tried to limit my outings to lunches, sometimes the evening stuff couldn't be avoided.

Most of all, I dreaded the political fundraisers. One after another, blurring into another, and another, and another with the invitations pouring into the office in a constant flow. We received twenty to thirty a week, and we only had a little PAC, funded through hard-earned personal dollars raised from our architect members. Even though I didn't sign the checks for the politicians, Doc did that job; I recommended who got the money.

As a bipartisan trade group, we gave to both parties—a tough pill to swallow as a dyed-in-the-wool Republican. With the passage of time and, perhaps, wisdom, I have mellowed and find plenty wrong with both parties. Nor am I nearly as conservative as I once was. The world isn't as black and white and hard and fast as when I started my political venture.

Checks were either delivered personally to members of the legislature or provided as the "entrance fee" to the fundraisers. A steady stream of breakfasts, lunches, dinners, and select events, like golf outings and boat trips, took place while the General Assembly gaveled into session and over the summer recess. At each event, I'd see the same folks—ordinarily my fellow lobbyists—on the same circuit between the restaurants, bars, and hotels in Harrisburg. The same small talk and gossip shared at each stop.

Rarely did the "guest of honor" at these events discuss anything of substance because protocol demanded they greet the revolving door of people coming and going. Nor did I like talking business after handing over a check. It didn't seem right, even though the contribution was given freely, with nothing expected in return. But the reality as famously uttered by Jesse Unruh, a California politician, is so true: "Money is the mother's milk of politics."

After our visits concluded, we hosted one member of Congress and his staffers at a swanky French D.C. restaurant. Along with our architects, there'd be almost twenty for dinner. The only thing enjoyable about this affair—Iris would curse the darkness when I turned over the corporate credit card receipt to expense the dinner for our group. Because the government-relations department had one employee, Iris assigned the blame for these excesses to me. The reality: I thought they were a waste of time and money, too. But she had to have someone to castigate, so I became the easy target. Forced to endure her line-by-line scrutiny and commentary on each diner's menu choice and drinks, Doc knew how to pick his battles. He'd disappear when it came time to review expenses and never endured the cruel and unusual punishment inflicted by Iris.

The congressmen at dinner that night represented Northeastern Pennsylvania. A personable enough fellow, very smart, a huge guy in his early seventies, he enjoyed the wining and dining associated with legislative life in Washington, D.C. Over 325 pounds, the congressman ordered a jumbo steak, rare, covered with Bordelaise sauce, which he gorged on, sipping red wine in between each large bite while discussing with our table the latest tome he read recently on the fall of the Roman Empire. I remember thinking to myself—*We are in the empire's last days before the Huns sacked Rome*. These dinners and photo ops symbolic of how far afield the Republic has wandered from what the Founding Fathers intended.

After finishing his meal, once again we had the requisite pictures for our member newsletter back home, so we looked powerful and effective at representing architects' interests. After the photos, Doc left me to pay the bill as a few of our members lingered, enjoying big cigars and after dinner talk. They felt good from the group's Happy Hour and drinks while dining and pulled me aside as I signed the credit card receipt.

"Jack, we noticed a few strip clubs on the way into D.C. Take us over there, would ya? The party's just beginning. 'Jezebel's Joint' has some tantalizing billboards. Those women are worth checking out," one guy said lecherously. I swear it looked like he drooled when he mentioned the highway teasers.

Noticing "Jezebel" and her brothel of women on the same poster, I couldn't help but think about the one time I ventured into one of these "establishments." In this instance, the club sat on a lonely road in sub-urban Philadelphia. Famous for drag racing, adult bookstores, and the "gentlemen's club" that evening that served as the host location for a high school friend's bachelor party, after exiting the place, I wanted to dip myself in a vat of acid and solvent to ward off whatever might grow in this place of ill repute. Drinks for ten bucks, the "ladies" should've been on a Russian dance exercise video from the '70s. For an extra fifty, Catharine the Great's descendants would gyrate on your lap. No guarantee you wouldn't leave without a broken bone or two if you opted for this "bonus recreation" that didn't include shock absorbers for the body blows. But back to Jezebel's Joint.

Okay, how do I keep my job and maintain the sanctity of my marriage? I asked myself. Carolyn was at home, no doubt tired. *Start with diplomacy.* "We have more meetings in the morning before heading back. How about we call it a night? All that walking around the Capitol has me bushed."

"Nah, you're young. A couple of hours at the clubs won't hurt you," said the leader of the pack.

Okay, time to ratchet up the response. "Sorry, guys. Those places are not my thing. I'll help you hail a cab if you want to go yourselves." A reason-able middle ground, right? Wrong.

"Not good enough, Jack. You're supposed to be taking us to these clubs. It's part of your job. Doc and the executive board will hear about this." The most senior member of the group now had his face close enough to mine that I got a blast of whiskey.

Time for the gloves to come off, my blood pressure rising, I said, "Respectfully, it's not my responsibility to take you to a sex den. You pay me to represent you in Harrisburg and Washington, not to be a nursemaid and copulation chaperone. Go to 'Jezebel's' yourself." I whirled around and handed the credit card receipt to the headwaiter with the phony French accent as I stormed out of the restaurant.

Doc never brought up the matter nor did these guys after they sobered up. Having met many of their wives during social receptions, I'm sure this subject remained better left undiscussed.

Finally, I returned to Harrisburg after sleeping very little in the hotel bed. A stack of messages, fundraising invites, and plenty of emails to answer waited on my desk. Doc and Iris wouldn't pay for a Blackberry, so I might keep up with email. I would work several late evenings after these D.C. trips, just to catch up on the Pennsylvania routine.

A message from Representative Henrietta Hoover, my first encounter with her, jumped out from the pile. The note demanded I call her back "immediately." Hoover sponsored a bill Architects United opposed. Since the legislation hadn't moved yet, Doc and I left well enough alone. We would activate if the proposal got traction and the committee chairman listed her bill for a vote.

In a nutshell, her plan required the Department of Education to create a clearinghouse of prototype architectural plans for school districts to avail themselves for new construction of buildings. In this way, schools wouldn't need expensive, customized designs; instead, their contractors would follow the blueprints prepared by the state. The hammer to Henrietta's proposal: if schools wanted reimbursement by the Commonwealth for their construction, they had to use a clearinghouse plan.

Under the law at that time, if the project qualified for compensation, districts developed their own architectural plans. Most school districts relied on Pennsylvania to fund new projects. As a result, any change to state law would have a tremendous impact on school building plans.

Architects opposed this proposal for obvious reasons. By forcing use of a clearinghouse, hundreds of unique projects designed and billed by architects would cease as districts instead used the cookie-cutter plans maintained by the department. As a fiscal conservative, I had to subvert my opinions to support the "party line." I silently agreed, however, the individual blueprints were wasteful and unnecessary and commended, to myself, Hoover's introduction of the legislation. But I had to suck it up and do the job, regardless of my personal views. Far from the sexy issues I'd staffed for Senator Weigel, this bread-and-butter stuff was the reason the architects paid my salary.

The first day back in the office, I reached Henrietta, and we didn't get off to a good start. "Representative, I'm returning your call. Sorry it's been a few days. I was in Washington, D.C. for a national lobbying event."

"I don't care where you were, Mr. Curran. Doesn't your office give you messages when you are out of town?" I quickly saw why Henrietta had the reputation for being so difficult. Emboldened further since the GOP in the House had taken over the majority, her caucus had convinced a conservative Democrat from Northeastern Pennsylvania to switch over to the Republican Party (as Hoover had done early in her career). Henrietta now sat in the catbird seat, spreading her rigid conservativism on a more powerful basis.

"I had back-to-back meetings and events, but we're talking now so what can I do for you, Representative?" I felt empowered not to take too much of her nonsense since we had very few members in her district. If she'd been close to architects back home, I'd have tread more cautiously for fear of receiving a backlash from those architects.

"Why haven't you been in to see me about my clearinghouse bill? I hear your outfit is opposed. Why haven't you come in? Why do I learn secondhand of your opposition? That's not the way Harrisburg works, Curran; maybe that's how the Senate operates where you used to work, but not in the House. I'm trying to save taxpayer dollars, and YOU PEOPLE are getting in the way! Republicans are now in the majority and I control a large block of conservatives if you haven't heard."

What a mouthful, I thought, waiting as patiently as possible until she came up for air, hitting the mute button so I could laugh at the reference to "you people." I guess as a small city guy—far removed from her rural district—I might have been from the Bronx from her standpoint. I observed that I no longer merited the courtesy of a title in front of my name either.

"Representative, respectfully, we are opposed but have put nothing out officially," I said. "If your bill has any sign of moving, we, of course, would see you before we issue a paper. We'd be glad to meet with you now to discuss our concerns. I can bring our president, Victor Pearl, and a few of my members when it works for your schedule."

Her voice rising to a fevered pitch, she said, "Too late, Curran. The damage is done. I don't want to meet with you, or Mr. Pearl. He has quite a reputation over here by the way." She didn't explain what "reputation" Doc had, so I launched.

"What'd you mean by that? Because he's Jewish? You better back off, Representative Hoover."

"Don't you accuse me of bigotry, you pompous ass. I support religious freedom for everybody. It's because of that shaved head and those earrings. I looked up some papers he wrote at Temple and I don't like what I see. Too liberal," she added. *Chalk up a big positive for Henrietta,* I admitted to myself, *she's not a bigot.*

"I sincerely apologize but assure you our president is an honorable man and a solid Republican, devoted to providing quality representation to our organization. That isn't what we're talking about, however. Do you want to meet or not?"

"Forget about a meeting. Why would you assume my bill isn't moving? I intend to have the education chairman list the legislation for a vote. Now I'm even more determined to teach your group a lesson."

"Well, Ms. Hoover," I dropped the representative since she was so offensive, "we'll have to oppose the bill if it's scheduled for a vote.

Again, we're happy to discuss our concerns, or testify at a public hearing, if the chairman plans one. I know the school boards are opposed, too. They'd probably welcome a public airing. Or perhaps a joint meeting could be held."

"Oh, you speak for them," she noted sarcastically. "I've talked to those birds. They're dead wrong. My bill will save taxpayer dollars and they should care about that." There wasn't much left to say before I got too candid and shot her a good taste of my Scotch-Irish temper. Our exchanges in later years would become virtual shouting matches. Had someone suggested mud wrestling to settle our differences, I likely would've been pinned solely because I could never match her will power and determination to prevail.

"I don't speak for them, Ms. Hoover. We've talked several times. That's what they've communicated. Thanks for reaching out. I'll make sure our group is aware of your passion for this issue, and we'll send you a courtesy copy of anything we put out."

"You do that, Curran. By the way, I intend to let the chairman and leadership know how insulting you people are and how you've slighted me." *Bam*, down went the receiver on her end. Two "you peoples" in one conversation.

Walking downstairs to Doc's office, I briefed him on the call and suggested we put this on the agenda for discussion with the architects' legislative committee. I suspected we'd need to discuss amendments for a possible compromise. My experience told me the chair may schedule the bill just to shut her up. And then let the leadership deal with her until she tormented them until they, too, relented. Many times, persistence does work in Harrisburg.

I needed air after that call and walked up to the Capitol. The ten-block walk would help bring my pulse rate down. Never one to let confrontation and conflict slide by easily, Rob instinctively knew lobbying wasn't for me. He was right. I didn't like the bowing and scraping that lobbyists are forced to do. Staff people had to take guff, too, but if one worked for a good member, as I had, this pettiness remained manageable.

Once in the Capitol, I went over to the Senate side for a quick visit with Gloria and the staff to help lift my spirits. I hadn't seen Jim's car as I walked up the long winding hill, so I knew he was out at a meeting. Another former colleague approached, and I mumbled under my breath, "This day just gets better and better."

Ennis O'Reilly and I passed one another, and I greeted her with a simple, "Hello," and a nod of my head. *Damn, she looks taller than I remember. Ah, it's the heels. Makes her even more intimidating*, I said to myself.

"Hi, Jack. Aren't you still under your one-year prohibition under the Ethics Act? Surprised to see you over here." *Don't let her get under your skin. Answer with a smile.*

With the broadest grin I could manage, I replied, "Sure, I know that, Ennis. Strictly on a social visit to Senator Weigel's office. The law allows social visits, doesn't it?" I asked with feigned innocence.

"Of course, it does, Jack. Just checking. I wouldn't want to see you in any trouble," she noted.

"Thanks for your concern, Ennis," I said drolly. "It's great seeing you. Take care." Henrietta and Ennis in one day. Fortunately, I didn't bump into Iris on the return to the office. Otherwise, it would've been the perfect trifecta for difficult encounters.

At Senator Weigel's suite, I got a big hug from Gloria and several other staffers. Seeing them made me realize even more that I had made an awful decision—one I would have to live with, at least for the time being.

THIRTY-FIVE

Summoned, Negotiating with the Immovable

"**P**LEASE GET OFF THE PHONE, Jack. I need to talk with you." Doc interrupted a call with the House majority leader's staff on the clearinghouse bill.

"Listen, Steve, can I call you back? The boss needs me for a minute. Really sorry for the interruption. Okay, bye."

Doc had an annoying habit of doing this during meetings and conferences and my tone reflected such. "What is it, Doc? I'm trying to negotiate to get us to neutral on Representative Hoover's legislation. What's so important?"

The conversation he disrupted was particularly sensitive. As I feared, Henrietta had badgered her leadership to get a committee and floor vote scheduled. They appeared to cave in and desired to appease this persistent member. The House leaders wanted no opposition, so they could send her bill over to the Senate.

"This is important, too. That other thing can wait. The Republican nominee for governor needs bodies for a fundraiser for his fall campaign. I want you to represent us. Something unique for a fundraiser instead of the usual pabulum. The campaign has commandeered a train to run

through Lancaster County. Carolyn, Little Jack, and Robert may like it."
The event sounded different from the drone of receptions. And Doc was
right; the boys loved trains.

"That shouldn't be a problem. I'll talk with Carolyn."

"Here's the information. The campaign is expecting you." He handed
me a small piece of paper, full of scribbles about the train ride. "Iris sent a
check over from the PAC to cover this. The congressman has been a good
friend to our profession. The trip will give you time to network with him
and his people."

"From your notes, it's only two days from now," I said. "Carolyn might
have a doctor's appointment or have another obligation with the kids. Let
me see if we can make it work, okay?" Doc had this habit of sitting on
stuff. It's possible he'd just been contacted, or the piece of scrap paper
might have sat on his desk for a week. I suspected the latter; campaigns
worked the phones for an event typically more than two days prior.

"If there's a conflict, rework it. I want us represented." Doc turned
and left my office satisfied he did his job in leaving the matter entirely in
my hands. An influential staff person in the Capitol back in the day—his
management style was more autocratic than mine. Fortunately, Carolyn
loved to have an opportunity for the family to be together and after I said
goodbye to her, I had an email from Steve in the House, summoning me
to a meeting with his boss—Noah Johnson. The school boards and architects were expected to meet in his office in thirty minutes to talk about
the Henrietta Hoover bill.

"Dammit to hell," I said out loud. That interruption from Doc caused
this summons. The discussions over the phone seemed fruitful; now they
wanted a face-to-face. I hustled out of the office to my car. A parking spot
near the Capitol would be a challenge since the House was back in for the
fall session.

After finding parking on State Street, at the Capitol entrance a new
security guard scrutinized my lobbyist badge carefully and let me pass.

The majority leader's suite sat off the main hallway to the right of the Rotunda. A receptionist guided me through the ornate brass swinging gate to the conference room that housed a large mahogany table, ornately carved, handsome and imposing. Waiting there, the advocate for the school boards, Dominic Campi, and Representative Henrietta Hoover in the flesh. To begin a new start, I walked around the table and extended my hand of friendship to her, "It's good to meet you, Representative."

Hoover did not accept the gesture, refusing even to press a little of her flesh. "Well, Curran, the majority leader shouldn't have to call a meeting for you to introduce yourself. I told you this bill would be moving, despite your efforts to stop it." Henrietta's focus turned to the legal pad in front of her and I noticed the pre-printed quote from Ayn Rand emblazoned prominently at the top: "The question isn't who is going to let me; it's who is going to stop me." My heart missed a beat. I stood at the threshold of combat with someone who took no prisoners. I feared this would be like a visit to the proctologist without Vaseline.

The school boards' lobbyist—our ally in this fight—and I exchanged glances, and he winked at me. Evidently, he'd received the same treatment. For about five minutes of deafening silence, broken up only by the incessant ticking of the grand mahogany clock that graced the conference room wall, we sat and waited.

From an adjoining space, the door opened. The majority leader bounded in, along with his staffer, Steve. A shorter man with a receding hairline, Noah Johnson carried himself as the retired Marine officer he was: back straight, square jaw jutting out, suit carefully pressed, shoes spotless without a smudge. One could easily see him conducting a white-glove military inspection. When he entered, I jumped out of the chair and he and I shook hands. Self-conscious we had not met yet, despite towering over him, I felt smaller in stature next to this man. I remembered what Rob said almost ten years ago when we interned that Johnson was a pit bull, highly partisan and hard-charging.

He got right to it. "Thank you for coming in, Jack and Dominic. I know you both have had preliminary conversations with my staff about Representative Hoover's legislation. Let me be clear this legislation is a priority for our leadership to move over to the Senate. We believe this measure will save precious taxpayer dollars. Now, what can your organizations live with to get this done?"

Henrietta had a big smile, like that of the Cheshire Cat, getting this sort of attention from her leader. They had no choice. Like finger nails scratching against a chalkboard, she would continue until they begged for mercy and realized no path lie ahead, except to accommodate her demands.

Dominic took the lead, which was fine with me. Architects opposed the legislation because school construction was a big-ticket architectural item, but the school boards didn't appreciate Hoover's attempts at limiting them to off-the-shelf plans. They stood against her bill because they had almost total freedom in the design of school facilities and, as a principle, resisted anything that infringed on local control over public education.

"Leader Johnson, thank you for inviting us in. We've had some conversations with Representative Hoover and the education chairman about this legislation. We can't support it in its current form. Architects United and the other architects' group stand with us in this opposition." Dominic had to restate the position for the record since this was the first discussion with the majority leader. I nodded my head when he referred to my group.

"I've been briefed on all the discussions, Dominic. I know your groups are opposed. But saying no will not cut it. There are two paths available here: compromise or I'm prepared to slug it out in the Education Committee and on the floor. Look at my record. Haven't lost too many battles once I push forward. I would rather this go smoothly, however." Johnson's eyes were a bluish-gray, and he had a piercing gaze that made it clear he meant what he said. Picturing him in combat, I envisioned him ordering the troops to storm a hill, regardless of how well defended it might be. To his credit, this "Devil Dog" would blow the bugle and lead the charge. Retreat would be met with severe consequences.

"Jack, your rival representing architects seem to be able to live with a compromise position my staff developed. We want to know if you agree." This caught me completely flat-footed. I squirmed around in my seat. Saying "no" to the majority leader over one of his priority items—while the most conservative and pesky member of the caucus sat there—was not in our long-term interests. There is always another day, another fight, that comes in Harrisburg.

"What's the compromise, Leader? We really would prefer current law." Now I sounded like a total idiot.

Henrietta slammed her fist hard onto the leader's conference table and yelled, "That's unacceptable! Do you hear me, Curran? Existing law is inefficient and costly to the taxpayers. There's no reason for spending tax dollars on all these Taj Mahal school buildings. Other states that have clearinghouses have proven the idea works. Education used to take place in one-room school houses for heaven's sake. Those didn't require any building plans."

As old as Hoover appeared to be—her official bio listed no birth date—I wanted to blurt out that her school building while growing up probably lacked indoor plumbing, too, but I kept quiet. I could feel my face turning red as my body tensed up, ready for a fight. No time to lose my temper; the majority leader of the House was trying to hammer out a deal. Even though Henrietta might have been schooled in a small building back in the day, worn and tattered *McGuffey Readers* the curriculum when she wore pigtails—that bullies didn't dare dip in their inkwells—there were bigger principles at stake.

I locked my eyes on hers and replied, "Representative, I didn't raise my voice to you. Can we keep this civil?"

As a good staffer and mediator, who knew he had to defuse the tension, Steve cut in. "The compromise is if the clearinghouse design is made voluntary with an added incentive built into the reimbursement formula for districts that use a clearinghouse plan, the other group says they can live with that...at least they'll try to sell it."

Henrietta snapped. "I told you, Steve, I don't like it. Not enough. Why should I have to step that far back?" Henrietta rarely bent in the legislative process, one of the reasons most of her bills went nowhere. If the Ayn Rand quote on the legal pad that lay in front of Hoover had been a "scratch and sniff," she would've clawed at it for magical help and inspiration. But her heroine had never worked in the Pennsylvania General Assembly where compromise, *in my opinion,* is essential if legislative measures are going to make it through both chambers and to the governor for approval.

Dominic interjected with an important observation. "Steve, I've talked with the Senate. The Democrats don't like the mandatory aspect of Representative Hoover's bill. I can't commit that they'll accept this compromise, but I believe the House might have an easier time convincing the other chamber to move the measure with the incentive you're proposing." Since I couldn't talk with the Senate because of the one-year waiting period under the Ethics Act, Dominic had spoken with them for both organizations.

The leader saw a ray of sunshine and aimed his force of will at his colleague. "I know you want your original bill, Henrietta. But this is real progress. The incentive will be a good reason for districts to use the clearinghouse as opposed to compelling them to do so. Besides, Dominic makes an important point about the Democrats in the Senate. The list of bills stuck over there because of their intransigence is growing. I'd rather not add another one."

Hoover went from a beaming smile to a huge glower with this turn of events. "I want your groups and that other architects' group to be supportive of my bill if I agree to this compromise. Neutrality isn't enough. On the record in the Senate for the change, if I agree to it." Emphasizing the "if" twice, I thought she went too far. There's no way I could convince Doc and our leadership to be a "yes." Architects would be livid if we agreed to that. Dominic and the school boards were in the same place.

In a trance, as I stared at the large oil painting on the leader's wall that depicted General Lee surrendering to General Grant at Appomattox, I was in no mood to capitulate. My turn to push back, and I focused on Johnson and his staff, knowing he wanted to get this done to move on to the many other fires he had to put out. Since the conference room door remained open, I noticed a group of lobbyists waiting to see the leader. They represented interests with bills and amendments also demanding attention. Several major pieces of legislation, besides the annual budget, dominate the calendar and garner lots of media scrutiny. At the very same time, many second and third-tier proposals take up most of the legislature's schedule and care. This was one of those times.

"Sorry, we can't do that, Leader. Architects will never agree to be supportive. If you have our rivals on board, I believe I can promise neutrality on the bill if the compromise is accepted." Negotiation 101 learned at the side of Big Joe when he haggled with Big Sweet over old junk—don't appear to be *too eager* to settle.

Representative Hoover threw her pen onto the table and it shot out like a cannonball and barely missed me as it whizzed by. Her tantrum scratched the old wall clock, and I hoped the Capitol Preservation Committee would send her an over-inflated restoration bill. While stuffing her big tote with a fuzzy image of Adam Smith stamped on it, Henrietta rose from her chair—her signal the meeting had concluded, and combat would follow.

"Henrietta, please sit down," the leader commanded. "We want to get this done for you. If these groups aren't neutral, we might pass the House. However, if the Senate won't move your bill, what's the point?

Accept this compromise and drop your demand that Jack and Dominic be supportive." The majority leader bore into Hoover this time. *Wow, I wrote on my legal pad, does this guy understand his caucus! And knows that while he should try to keep Hoover happy that doesn't mean he must give in entirely either.*

Any leader walks a fine line. Even though Henrietta dominated the conservatives of the caucus, the majority leader couldn't empower her too much. Smart and savvy, he maintained his own channels to the right-wingers in the caucus, outside of Hoover, in the event they clashed in the future, and he needed more than persuasive abilities to rein her in. In the end, a leader rules when he has the votes. And Johnson could count heads better than any legislator in the General Assembly.

"Noah, I don't like this. If you think that's the best we can do, I guess I'll go along..." Hoover had her head down in defeat. The attempts at blustering deflated—she accepted that the leader had signaled the time had come to settle for a small victory, rather than the Armageddon she usually waged.

"Thank you, Henrietta." Pointing at Dominic and me, the leader continued, "Okay, gentlemen, all the groups need to work the final language out with Steve. He'll share it with Representative Hoover and the education chairman. I expect that when you sign off on the wording, there will be letters of neutrality from all three groups. In fact, make it a joint letter, please, so the members know we've paved the way for the bill to pass."

With that pronouncement, Johnson stood up and left the room. Henrietta didn't bother to shake our hands, snapping at Steve that she wanted to see the draft language before he shared it with us. Out of the corner of my eye, I saw Steve roll his eyes after the representative turned her back. So, it's not just lobbyists she pummels. Staff is fair game as well. Both of us thanked Steve as we left the conference room.

I had work to do to convince Doc and our group to accept the compromise. On my return to the office, I briefed him on the meeting and downplayed mention of our rival, knowing this usually triggered an outburst.

His reaction was explosive. "*Lecherlech!*" I knew this from previous contentious discussions as Yiddish for "ridiculous."

"We're boxed in, Doc. The school boards seem to be okay and the other group. We gotta accept this." After thirty minutes of cajoling, I convinced him that we had no other options since we both knew there would be another battle to fight on the "Hill." Whenever that might be.

THIRTY-SIX

The Train Ride, Rob is Attacked

"**C**'MON, LITTLE JACK, we don't want to miss the train," I held my son's hand tightly. The Curran gang entered the old-fashioned steam locomotive as it prepared to leave Strasburg for a scenic ride through Amish country and the farmlands of Lancaster County. Packed with supporters and Republican State Committee people, we sat on original wood benches that were uncomfortable. Festive with red, white, and blue bunting draped throughout the passenger cars, the iron horse would make almost a half-dozen stops in small towns jammed full of local Republican committee people, volunteers, and folks just curious to see the GOP nominee for governor.

After almost eight long years of Democratic rule in the Governor's Mansion in Harrisburg, Republicans were enthusiastic to have a rugged-looking, tall congressman from Williamsport, who'd beaten two other candidates in the spring primary to represent the party. Rich with Republican voters, Lancaster remained a key county in any statewide campaign to help offset the solid Democratic vote that consistently comes out of the big cities of Philadelphia and Pittsburgh.

Torn about the nominee, while I applauded his military record, I didn't care for his pro-choice stance and attempts to be a "moderate" on other social issues. But he was the GOP standard-bearer, and the Democratic candidate for governor had too many liberal positions for most voters. And for me.

For a thousand bucks from the architects' PAC, my family and I rode on this train that reminded me of the old whistle-stop campaigns from long ago. Probably President Harry Truman the last to use this method of reaching people. Determined to enjoy the ride with Little Jack and Robert on my lap—the kids blew on the wooden toy whistles the campaign staff handed them when we boarded. Brightly stamped with "Jump on the Train for Prosperity and Security," these themes were at the center of the congressman's effort, a response to a languishing economy and crime spike the Commonwealth had endured under the current Democratic administration.

Discussion of social issues, like abortion, would fracture the various parts of the GOP (the establishment types, fiscal and economic conservatives, and party activists for whom the sanctity of life remained preeminent). Congressman Samuel Collins proved adept at unifying Republicans while appealing to the so-called Reagan Democrats, who lived primarily in Western Pennsylvania. Without support from this bloc, any GOP nominee faces a tough battle to win statewide because of the significant registration advantage enjoyed by Democrats.

The leaves had changed again, and Lancaster County's rolling hills and green pastures were tranquilizing as the locomotive progressed slowly to the first stop. Carolyn and I played a game with the kids that they name and mimic the sounds of the various animals we passed as they grazed and fed on vegetation that grew in the most fertile soils in the world. In their plain black clothes and straw hats, the Amish made me long for a quieter, a simpler time. One without modern technology and the hassles that come from living among the "English," as we are known to this religious and fundamentalist sect.

Working his way through the cab, Congressman Collins greeted guests with a wide grin and iron grip that crushed the hands of many lesser men. *Very charismatic,* I admitted to myself as he approached us, *almost cut out of central casting of how a gubernatorial candidate should appear.* Collins stood well over six feet, dark and handsome, towering over most folks with his physical appearance and a square jaw that signaled Collins meant business.

When he reached our seats, I rose to shake the candidate's hand and introduced him to my family. During one of the trips to Washington, D.C., we had met for a brief photo-op, although I doubted the congressman remembered me. "Hey, Jack, good to see you again." The aide traveling close behind must've reminded him of my name, a job I had done for my bosses over the years. Blessed with a photographic memory, I had stored many faces and names—always pulling them out at the right moment when needed. I would whisper in the senator's ear, just as the young buck who trailed behind the candidate did.

"Glad you could come. Is this your beautiful wife, and who are these little fellows?" Collins kneeled to high-five Jack, who slapped his small hand as hard as he could against the congressman's enormous palm. Robert received a pat of affection and a tousling of his tiny sprig of hair.

"Congressman Collins, this is Carolyn, and our sons, Little Jack and Robert. Thanks for having us on the train," I added, although it was weird to thank him after our group's PAC had given a significant contribution.

"Enjoy the ride, folks. Appreciate your support." Collins moved on to the next group seated behind us.

"The congressman's good-looking and friendly, Jack. I haven't met the Democrat, but I understand why people like Collins as much as they do." A shrewd judge of individuals, I didn't like the attention Carolyn paid to this hunky man. Jealousy crept up, watching the way my wife

gazed at this broad-shouldered candidate. Around politics herself for over
a decade now, I trusted her instincts. She had the advantage of being able
"to see the forest for the trees," something I sometimes lacked. Being
too close to personalities and issues in daily professional life sometimes
caused me to miss the big picture.

"Abortion is a problem, honey, although he's unified the party with a
strong anti-crime package and the pro-business platform he articulates.
Tony Molinaro's helped to advise Collins on policy according to Rob,
who's still wired into Tony's activities."

Pennsylvania's Abortion Control Act passed in 1989 and the Supreme
Court upheld the law in 1994. The law provides for parental consent for
minors who seek an abortion; women must be given information on the
gestation of the baby and dangers of abortion to the woman's health; and
supplied with facts on the alternatives that are available to this "choice."
Abortions in the third trimester are restricted to cases where the life
of the mother is threatened. Having staffed Senator Weigel during his
strong support for this major restriction, I was proud to be of assistance
to him as he and other Pennsylvania legislators reined in the open wide
abortion pathway that *Roe v. Wade* provided before the Commonwealth's
law passed.

As we got up to exit the locomotive at the first stop, I spotted an old
acquaintance from the Senate staff, talking in the congressman's ear. *She
must be on the campaign team*, I thought. I found Joan Otten not too far
from the train platform before Congressman Collins started his stump
speech to the gathered crowd and said hello to her. We had worked
together as colleagues on the Senate staff.

"Hey, Joan, where've you been? It's great to see you." Before the
party switchover in the Senate, I'd lost track of her whereabouts. While
Harrisburg is a small company town, it's impossible to run into everyone.

"Jack Curran, what a pleasant surprise. The campaign hired me almost a year ago." She added, "Heard through the grapevine you left Jim Weigel's office to lobby."

"Well, that explains why we haven't bumped into one another. Congratulations on the move." Reluctantly, I confirmed my jump to lobbying.

I liked Joan. A striking woman with dark hair, beautiful black eyes, high cheekbones, and sensual lips, she had just the right amount of makeup on to heighten her lovely features. She and her husband, Jonathan Otten, were influential on the Capitol scene, both coming from wealthy families and known to be large contributors to both parties. Joan covered the Republican side; Jonathan doled out dollars to the Democrats. The ultimate power couple—a merging of old-money interests—they understood to keep wealth, they had to be politically active and connected.

My thoughts drifted back to when we first met. Our bosses had a quarrel over legislation Joan's senator wanted, but mine didn't. Even though I pushed hard for a compromise to address Weigel's concerns, each time she responded with, "The answer is no, Jack. Sicilian people don't surrender." Eventually, we compromised. Joan proved to be a terrific negotiator.

"Congratulations on your leap to the 'dark side,' Jack," she said in jest. "I heard how hard you worked for Senator Weigel and how tough the last re-election was to get through. So sorry Jim isn't doing well. Nice man. Listen, if Sam Collins is successful in November, and I believe he will be, call me. Senior staff will need capable people with extensive government experience as part of our office. As a person of integrity with a strong work ethic, we could use you on the Collins team." At the time she said this, I wondered at once if this might be the pathway back into government and away from the "dark side" as Joan put it.

"Wow, I'm flabbergasted and honored you'd even consider me. I'll definitely get in touch. All the best the rest of the campaign. Terrific seeing you." Joan shook my hand in farewell and turned to greet a wealthy GOP contributor from Chester County.

Carolyn busied about at a table of refreshments, getting snacks for Jack and Robert, who were restless and ready to get back onto the train. Their toy whistles were a diversion for their boredom as I hustled them away from the crowd to avoid interrupting the speeches.

I listened to the candidate with one ear deliver short remarks while quietly filling my wife in on my encounter with Joan Otten. Carolyn knew of her through conversations with Rob when he came to our house. Rob didn't care for Joan because she was good friends with someone he'd dated before he married Kim. Their relationship ended on a sour note. Placid sensed that Otten held this breakup against him when he'd been in to lobby her on issues pending in the Senate.

"Rob hasn't had good interactions with her, has he?" Carolyn's pert nose crinkled as she asked this, a sign she didn't like Joan because of Rob's bias.

"They've skirmished, yes. Rob blames it on a bad relationship with one of Joan's friends. I'm not so sure. Policy disagreements might be at the root, but who knows. Harrisburg can be petty. Joan has always been fair to me," I emphasized, already positioning Otten in a positive way in case the career move came to pass.

Congressman Collins finished up his remarks, and we got back on the big iron horse. We followed pretty much the same routine during the next five stops. By the time the train arrived at the last stop, the Curran gang was tired and ready to head home, the campaign shuttling everyone back to Strasburg via charter buses they'd rented, only adding to the crankiness of our kids. I'd enjoyed the whistle-stop ride as something different from the standard fundraisers.

Lost in thought as we drove on Route 30 to York to feed the kids and do the nighttime routine of baths, brushing teeth, bedtime stories and lullabies, several times Carolyn asked again about Joan's relationship with Rob. I brushed the attempts off.

Around ten that night, sipping on white wine in front of a fire burning in our stone fireplace, the phone rang. Rob struggled to catch his breath, "Jack, you gotta come up here now. Kim's unhinged."

"Calm down, buddy. Tell me what's going on." I had never heard Rob this exercised. Normally the unflappable one, the rock I leaned on needed me now.

"I got home a little while ago, and she grabbed a steak knife and lunged at me..." Out of breath, he paused, and I worried about the silence.

"Are you okay, Rob, did she hurt you? So help me if she did." I told myself to notch it down. An angry fit wouldn't do Rob or the situation any good.

"Kim got my right shoulder...nicked the tattoo I got in college of our fraternity letters. Seems to be just a flesh wound."

"Hold a compress on it tight. Where's she now? What's she doing?" I asked in rapid fashion.

Anytime the four of us ate dinner together or visited each other's homes something about her eyes worried me. Kim also drank way too much. After marrying her, Rob sold his Harrisburg brownstone and purchased a center-hall Colonial for the two of them in a fashionable section of Camp Hill, a bedroom community of the State Capital, across the Susquehanna River.

Placid left the accountants to lobby for a much larger firm that made him a junior partner, drawing a more generous salary now. His responsibilities expanded considerably, including wooing clients, and traveling to Washington, D.C., since the firm also lobbied Congress. Obviously, he was away from home a great deal.

"Out in the driveway now. She's slicing and dicing the convertible top and tires. What the hell will our neighbors think? These are our friends at the country club. What am I going to do, Jack?"

"Rob, forget the fucking club and neighbors. Call 911. Kim's a risk. On my way up there now. Be there in thirty minutes. Call the cops, okay?" I wasn't sure what I could do other than give Rob moral support. In the meantime, he had to stop her from doing something dangerous. Not that wounding Rob with a blade wasn't savage enough.

"Get up here, please," he begged.

As I hung up the phone, Carolyn came into the kitchen with jeans, a sweatshirt, and shoes, having heard my end of the conversation. Dressed in only boxers and a tee-shirt before Rob called, I quickly filled Carolyn in and threw the clothes on and grabbed for the car keys. Pecking me on the cheek before I hurried out the door, she said, "Take care of Rob and call me when things settle down."

As I drove up the interstate, the sky opened somewhere around the hills of Newberry. Rain the size of dimes pounded the windshield, making visibility a problem. Still, I pushed on, hydroplaning several times. "Not now, dammit," I said out loud, wrestling with the wheel for control. The lightning became more fierce the closer I got to Harrisburg.

The police and an ambulance were on the scene when I arrived. A lightning bolt struck nearby, illuminating Kim's tortured face, as the cops struggled to handcuff her. She refused to go quietly into the night. Rob's convertible top and tires were in complete shreds. Neighbors were out in front of their homes, witnesses to this sad spectacle. With my booming voice, I yelled, "Go back inside, folks, the show's over."

Pushed into the back of the police cruiser before the door slammed on her freedom, Kim wailed out, "Screw you, Curran. What a twisted bastard you are. Always ice cold and proper. This is your fault for rejecting me. All I ever wanted was you...not him...then the asshole has an affair on me, spurned again. Burn in hell, you motherfucker."

Other than keeping my distance from her while at the Capitol, I remained polite and appropriate, remembering the impulses she had stimulated in me during that fateful dance. She was the twisted one. I felt horrible for my friend. Married only nine months. It appeared their union was over.

I entered Rob's back door and found him in the family room, sobbing. The crude compress soaked with blood on his shoulder worried me. But first I hugged him and then checked the wound. Rob had refused treatment from the medics. I made us both scotch neat silently praying for comfort for my friend and healing for Kim. Although she appeared mentally ill, she was my best friend's wife and didn't deserve this anguish and torment.

"Here you go, buddy. Take it easy. We'll sort it all out." A wreck, Rob gulped down the drink. "I'll make you another one, Rob, but slow down and breathe." At the bar, I made this drink on the rocks. Rob had downed a few earlier, no doubt while entertaining a legislator or staffer. "All right, tell me slowly, what happened?"

"Did you see the convertible top, Jack? Kim destroyed it. There's shattered china all over the kitchen floor." I noticed the chunks of porcelain when I walked in. These physical items could be replaced. Rob's emotional state and putting the pieces of his life back together—that remained to be seen.

"I'll clean that up. Everything is replaceable. What set her off?"

"She yelled...hysterical when I got home...accused me of cheating. No way I'd do that, I swear." Rob held his head in his hands. "She spotted me downtown with a gorgeous female lobbyist I work with, Natalie, and just assumed we're fooling around. All we do is work together. Took a break for lunch. That's it." he stressed. I let Rob talk. Good therapy for the emotional trauma he'd experienced, plus I planned on writing the sequence down later in case he needed it for the legal battle to come.

"Carrigan's downtown, you know the place with those big storefront windows? That's where all the shit started." I nodded yes to encourage him to continue. "Anyway, we'd just wrapped up a meeting with Senator Harshburger. You know what a prick he is to lobbyists and staff. I took

Natalie along, figuring it might soften ole 'Hash and Smash' up once he laid eyes on her. It didn't, by the way. That guy is like a stone." Rob stopped to take a big swallow of Dewar's. Ironically, Harshburger and Hoover—although hard-right and kindred spirits—detested one another as they fought for control over which legislator set conservative priorities in the Commonwealth.

"Where was I? Oh right, lunch. Kim sees us in the window, comes up to the table. I try to introduce my colleague to her, and she calls Natalie a 'slut' and me a 'cheater.' Natalie jumps up, and a little catfight breaks out with the two pushing each other. John, the proprietor, you know him, right?"

"Never been in there, Rob, but go on."

"He comes over and orders Kim to leave, threatening to call the cops. I should've left with her, but too pissed off. So, I said, 'we'll talk about this later, babe,' and I tell her to leave. I did nothing against Kim. You got to believe me, Jack."

"We go back too long for me to question your character. Messing around on your spouse isn't your thing unlike some others in this town. Have you guys been spending much time together?" I knew Rob traveled a lot and circulated in the bars, but hoped he reserved Saturday and Sunday for his wife.

"Not really. The schedule's crazy since moving to the firm. On the weekends, there's stuff to do in the yard and house, and I need my gym time. Look at this belly, Jack. It's got to be pulled in." At least he hadn't lost his sense of humor although I couldn't blame him if he did. "Kim's been spending time with her parents a lot lately." *Uh-oh*, I thought. *Not a good sign*. Not that I excelled at picking up Carolyn's cues, but Kim at her parents' home, when they should have been together, wasn't healthy.

"I called you right after she ran at me with the steak knife and left to tear the outside up. All this happened so quickly. The venom just poured out." I nodded in sympathy, experiencing a small part of the demons she carried deep within her.

"What did the cops say? She didn't go quietly as I arrived." Fortunately, I'm sure they saw the physical damage she did and her emotional state. Rob had kept his cool and had done nothing back.

"The police pulled up while she went psycho on the tires and arrested her. I think she also took a swipe at an officer. I'm sure it's why they roughed her up the way they did. One of them asked me lots of questions."

"Rob, you need to call a good lawyer tomorrow. Don't let her come back to the house after she's released. Kim's parents will probably post bail. Talk to your attorney about a restraining order, too."

With a pat of encouragement on his good shoulder, I asked if he had a camera I could borrow. He pointed to a drawer in their entertainment center. I went into the kitchen and snapped photos of the damage Kim had done in there. Then out to the driveway for pictures of the convertible. The last picture I took was a close-up of Rob's wound. The lawyer would need evidence for the civil litigation that would follow, or the pictures might be necessary to get the court order to keep her away.

After cleaning the kitchen, I put Rob's torn convertible top down since the storm had passed. No sense continuing to telegraph to the neighborhood the turmoil happening in the Placid home. Once I knew Rob could get to bed, calmer because of my presence, I headed home. He had a long, painful haul ahead. Divorce at the young age of thirty—I felt guilty, thinking back how I'd grabbed him at the fundraiser to dance with Kim, as my escape away from my own desire and temptation. On the ride home, all I could think of—*This could've been my life.*

THIRTY-SEVEN

The Flipperpalooza

DOC SENT WORD through Iris that I was to come to his office. This was how he communicated after I broke the news of my departure to work for Governor-elect Collins. He'd pushed back hard over my decision and our relationship was now rocky.

"Hey, Doc," I said with as much cheer in my voice as possible.

"I got a call from Herm Filipowski, our friend and chairman of the House Professions and Credentialing Committee."

"What'd he want?" Herman Patek Filipowski wasn't a friend by any means. One of the few legislators for whom I had nothing but disdain for the way he conducted himself in public life, Herman trampled on the voters he supposedly served.

"Herm's made a reservation for himself, his staff, and seven of his 'closest' friends in the caucus at his favorite dining establishment. Filipowski didn't ask we host the dinner, he demanded it."

"Okay," I paused, knowing something bad was coming. "What's that got to do with me?"

"I told him you'd be the host. Call Rob Placid and ask him to split the bill. We can't afford that kind of tab alone."

"I've got less than a week left here before I head over to the governor's office. Can't you entertain the group? The governor-elect's crew probably wouldn't like it if I did this kind of thing." Hanging out with Chairman Filipowski, or the "Flipper," the name many in the Capitol used behind his back because he lacked any core convictions, signaled potential trouble. Infamous for holding these lavish affairs at some poor sucker's expense, sometimes the spirit moved Herman to have his staff arrange golf at one of the swankiest country clubs in Harrisburg. Some sap of a lobbyist always nailed to pay for his amusement.

To avoid having to foist these extravaganzas on the taxpayers, the Flipper and his team kept a list of groups that had legislation pending before their committee or would have a legislative interest at some point. Our "turn" to host dinner had come. Filipowski enjoyed wining and dining at the best restaurants in the Harrisburg area, using these events to keep his power with the lobbyists he controlled and the members of the committee—on the receiving end of this "free treatment."

From Pennsylvania's hard-pressed coal region, his constituents struggled in an economy that had seen the decline of "Big Coal." But that didn't matter to Herman—out of touch with the conditions back home. My stomach turned over and over thinking about the crass and uncaring Flipper. His penchant for unchecked power used for his self-interests— and not the people he purported to represent—sickened me.

The Flipper's taste consisted of very expensive suits (whose tailoring had trouble hiding his considerable girth), and several gold rings, likely paid for by someone else. With dirty fingernails, not from working hard with his hands, but I thought a sign of how dirty he was as a politician, the Flipper liked heavy cologne. Probably to mask the body odor trapped in the flabby folds that even a girdle couldn't restrain.

Harrisburg's lobbyists shed no tears when the feds hauled him off to a federal penitentiary for public corruption crimes he committed. Filipowski lost an otherwise fat state pension with a judicial conviction so justice had been done. The federal judge, having been on the bench for over fifteen years, told Herman she was "disgusted and offended" by his behavior, handing down the maximum sentence as she banged the gavel with fervor to send him away to make license plates for ten cents an hour. But back to the dinner at hand and my push for Doc to take this one.

"I'm busy, Jack. You're the lobbyist."

"So much for not entertaining that much. Remember that promise you made in the interview? I do."

"Stuff happens. Not arguing about this with you. You're on the payroll another week."

"Family's a priority, Doc, until it conflicts with your needs," I retorted, a comment met with a sharp eye from Pearl. Ignoring his angry look, I continued, "Carolyn and I have plans with the kids. Dinner with Filipowski and his accomplices as they get drunk isn't high on my list of things to do."

Doc got the final word: "Do your job." I walked out of his office, recognizing I had to do the affair or there'd be a black mark against me. Carolyn wasn't thrilled with the last-minute notice but sensed my frustration and I shared with her verbatim how much I pushed back.

The next call was to Placid. "Rob, have any plans tonight? How do you feel about co-hosting a dinner with us for the Flipper? Herman called Doc and reservations are made."

"Nothing concrete. Yeah, I can join in. Have even more time now that Kim and I separated. The firm needs a better relationship there. What time?"

"Six o'clock sharp. You'll have to sit on me and my temper. Not happy having to do this on the way out the door. Thanks, buddy."

"No problem. See you then."

Rob and I arrived at the same moment and found the small room hosting the Flipper and his staff and legislative guests. We were only there because we had the corporate credit cards. As the official hosts for the "Flipperpalooza," we walked over to Filipowski and greeted him.

"Mr. Chairman, welcome," I said. "You know Rob Placid. He's my co-host this evening." The Flipper's chief of staff flashed me a look that conveyed his anger that I hadn't cleared bringing Rob into the mix. He must've had them on the list for the next night's gala affair.

"Curran, glad you could be here," Herman belted out. Obvious he'd already downed two martinis on the association's tab with more to follow. "You're a good boy, Jack. Sorry to hear you're leaving to work for Governor-elect Collins. Who's your replacement so we know who to call?" he asked. Filipowski patted me on the head and I could feel my face turning red from the humiliation.

Rob saw the signs of a blow up coming and wanted to avert a scene that would hurt his firm. "Mr. Chairman, it's our pleasure to do this. Jack's successor hasn't been named yet. Make yourself comfortable and enjoy the evening. Let us know if you need anything." Rob grabbed my arm and pulled me to the hallway outside. "What the hell was that about, Jack? Just because you're leaving for a better position doesn't mean you can tell Herman off. Some of us still have to work with him. Have a scotch and cool it before this guy screws my firm and the architects."

The Flipper and his team were quite capable of burying legislation our groups supported or posting bills we opposed. He'd been around a long time—vengeful and petty with a large staff that helped him do unsavory work. Time to act like a professional with a job to do as distasteful as it was. "All right, I'll bite my tongue. You know I hate this shit and the good old boy's network."

"Told you not to jump to lobbying but you wouldn't listen because you're so damn stubborn. Sit back and let me guide the night," Rob urged. The success I enjoyed came despite not making the circuit in the bars or playing lots of rounds of golf (who has time to chase a little white ball around the course anyway?), two hobbies engaged in by some legislators, staffers, and lobbyists. The rest of the evening I heeded Placid's directive and witnessed the surreal scene that followed.

The affair was what I envisioned a Roman orgy looked like. Tray after tray of food and drinks were consumed by this "elite" gathering. All it lacked were large chalices, ornate columns, togas, and scantily clad women feeding these guys grapes, servants with wicker fans cooling them as they lounged around, deciding the fate of the empire they governed. While the "little people" toiled hard in the fields and streets so they could pay taxes to this privileged class.

About two hours in, Rob told me to quit squirming in my seat. "This is how part of Harrisburg works. How lots of business gets done, at least by some members. You want to talk only in the Capitol, not the watering holes and haunts of legislators and lobbyists. Much better to ply them with liquor, dude, and the conversation goes smoother, and they become more agreeable. We could sell these guys just about anything right now. Look at 'em."

Swapping war stories about sexual conquests disgusted me. From serving in the military, I thought I'd heard it all—my Army buddies would have learned a thing or two, however. "Now that we've had multiple courses of food and the biggest steaks and shrimp cocktail I've ever seen, are the strippers gonna be jumping out of a big cake? Do we need dollar bills for their striptease?" I asked Rob.

Rob let out a throaty chortle. "Nah, that's not coming. The sign that we're wrapping up will be when they puff on big cigars and swirl brandy in sifters, congratulating each other on how powerful they are."

That moment eventually came as Rob predicted. The waiter handed us the eight-hundred-dollar tab—the poor bastard had earned his tip— and we gave him the two company credit cards to split the bill. As we signed the receipts, the Flipper's smarmy staff pulled me aside. "You gotta take a member home, Curran. Too drunk to drive."

"Can't we call him a cab?" I asked. The last thing I wanted to do was to drive "Representative Here's Mud in Your Eye" to his apartment. One more toast from that guy and I would puke.

"Cabbies talk in this town, Curran. You're doing it since you've barely had anything to drink."

"Fine," I said like a little kid unhappy he had to eat his spinach. "C'mon, Representative, let's go." I guided him out of the restaurant and into the passenger seat of my car, closing the door. "Okay, where do you live?" I asked him as I strapped myself into the driver's side after making sure his belt was secure. The last thing I needed would be for this drunken legislator to fall out of my car when I turned a corner.

"14008 Prospect Street. Who're you?" he gurgled out while his eyeballs danced around in his head as he tried to figure out my identity.

"The guy who paid for the night and your driver. Go to sleep till we get there."

Navigating through midtown Harrisburg, I heard this gagging noise like a cat with a hairball stuck in its throat had relocated to my car. "Don't you dare vomit in my car, Representative. We're almost to your place. Barf there if you have to." A false alarm, fortunately.

I found his place and woke him up, roughly guiding him up the outside concrete steps to an upscale brick townhouse. He fumbled around for his keys, finally handing them over. After three tries, I got the right one and opened the door. With a push, I shoved him through and threw the keys onto the chair in the living room. "Don't forget to lock up, Representative," I said as I closed the door behind me. He might've wanted to be tucked in, but that's where I drew the line. The older I got, the more I detested drunks, a reaction to Big Joe's alcoholism, which extended to my brothers, too.

The rest of the week with Architects United went without fanfare. I gladly filled out the expense report for the "Flipperpalooza" and tossed it onto Iris's desk. With the perpetual frown saved for the lobbyist of the office, she looked up and asked, "What's this? Who authorized this kind of bill?"

"Ask Doc." I couldn't suppress the sweet smile of justice on my mug as I turned and left the building for the final time.

THIRTY-EIGHT

Dinner with Sally, Inaugural Ball

"WOULD YOU HELP ME with the bow tie, honey?" the antique tuxedo Big Joe gave me years ago, out of the "junk" as we called it, looked good on me. From the Roaring Twenties or so, it had style and a certain timeless grace. Purchasing the accessories for the old tux, I struggled with the bow tie that Carolyn was now straightening out.

Looking at her reflection in the mirror, I whistled. "You are stunning, babe." Dressed in a black-and-gold evening gown, her thick reddish-brown hair professionally done earlier in the day, the moment had arrived to present a new necklace as my love gift for this special night. Pulling it out of my jacket pocket, I slipped it around her delicate neck but fumbled with the clasp not made for large fingers.

Carolyn kissed me softly in gratitude. I suggested that maybe we skip the party. With a husky laugh, she said, "No way, Jackie. I don't get to dress up too often, and my parents drove up from Abington, so we could do this. We're going. Cool it, big boy, till later."

We went downstairs greeted by the boys tackling one another in a game of football being supervised by my father-in-law—this time sitting in *my overstuffed chair*. A scowl meant for me soon changed after Carolyn gently kissed his forehead. Gianella's heart melted at receiving affection from his baby girl dressed to the nines for this once-in-a-lifetime event made possible by her ambitious husband.

Our eyes locked. Like tigers in a cage circling one another—prepared to pounce for a shred of flesh—we were two stubborn men, vying for the same woman's attention. We called a truce to this contest of wills because of the boys, who asked me to join in the football game. "Daddy, play with us," they begged in unison.

"Sorry my little chiefs, Mommy and Daddy are going out. Grandpop is in charge tonight." As I opened my arms for wonderful hugs, I stared hard at Frank Gianella, the intent clear: *Remember these are my sons. Their last name is Curran, not Gianella. Mind that, too, old man.* His glare back said: *Even during your greatest career triumph to date, I won't congratulate you.*

In the back of my head always lingered the troubling notion he would've been happy had Carolyn married a garage mechanic from Abington, instead of the driven kid with little hometown roots. The teenager who purposely chose a life in public service as his pathway, rejecting the antique business his father founded. For several years after we wed, I sought my father-in-law's approval and tried to be solicitous. No longer. I stood as my own self-made man and owed no explanations or apologies to Frank Gianella. Or anyone else for that matter.

With the inaugural tickets and outfits, we spent over nine hundred bucks for this big night. Carolyn and I would be guests along with several other thousand people gathered to celebrate a Republican governor, Sam Collins, sworn in earlier that day. Proud to be a staffer in the new administration, Joan Otten hired me during the transition. In the morning, I would start bright and early to take my extensive legislative skills to the executive branch, one of many young people inspired by the governor's vision for energizing a Pennsylvania that had been mired in economic malaise and rampant crime, and a magnetic personality that made you believe in him as a leader.

Rob had reservations for dinner before the ball and wanted Carolyn and me to meet his new girlfriend, Sally. Shortly after Kim went berserk, he filed his divorce papers. While lobbying Congress, he met Sally. From Northern Virginia, she was the daughter of a wealthy contributor to one congressman from suburban Washington, D.C. That congressman hired Sally to serve as a receptionist in his office.

As we entered the elegant and stately Hotel Hershey, our reservations were in the Circular Dining Room, my thoughts went beyond the celebrations to my job in the new administration. Work never far away even during a grand evening. Another colleague and I would be deputies to Joan, who would serve in a senior staff role for Governor Collins. The first responsibility would be to help her and the governor with getting his cabinet nominees confirmed by the Senate. I felt ready for this role since I had experience taking part in that process on the other end as a Senate staffer when candidates visited with Senator Weigel seeking his support for confirmation.

Rob and Sally welcomed us when we walked into the hotel. As Rob and I shook hands, he introduced us to Sally. In a tight-fitting, sequined gown that accentuated the feature she seemed most proud of—given the amount of cleavage the dress showed—her hair bleached platinum blond, bling surrounded Sally's neck and wrists. With dangling hoop earrings and heavy makeup, the contrast with how classy my wife looked couldn't have been starker.

After Carolyn and I hugged Sally, determined to make our best effort, Rob pulled me aside as the ladies chatted. He effused, "What do you think, Jackie? Crazy about her, man." I could tell he was. *Don't judge this book by its cover, Jack*, I warned myself.

With a note of caution, I answered, "Sally seems very nice, Rob, and I'm glad you're happy. Just take it slow, okay? The divorce isn't final yet." While the blame for his introduction to Kim fell squarely on me, I could be impartial in counseling a yellow light in this new relationship.

"The divorce is moving along. Kim will sign off if she gets something out of the marriage. Like she deserves much after only nine months. Whatever. The four of us are together. Let's get seated. A Republican is in the Governor's Mansion. Time to celebrate!" Rob did a little jig as he said this. And I couldn't help but laugh at his antics.

The perfect setting for the festivities, the Circular Dining Room overlooked a blanket of snow on this cold January night, lit up by soft spotlights outside of the dining room. In the spring, various colors of English roses would be in full bloom against the backdrop of a neatly trimmed hedgerow, greeting diners enjoying the panoramic vista in warmer weather.

Our table sat on the outside wall—the view spectacular—while the waiter came to take drink orders. Rob told us to order whatever we wanted. Dinner was on his firm through justification to the other partners that Placid needed to "nurture" a relationship with a new staffer in the administration with connections to the cabinet heads. Laughable in so many ways, I let it go. Rob knew how I approached any job, trying to be as straight as an arrow. He certainly didn't need to nurture anything with me.

Carolyn dawdled over her beverage choice, and I thought about ordering a single malt scotch. Rob believed the affair called for a bottle of wine to start, grandly telling the waiter, "We'll take Cabernet, your best recommendation, my good man." As a big-shot lobbyist, Rob relished his role in one of the most glamorous settings in Central Pennsylvania.

Sally made a face when Rob placed the order. "Sally doesn't want red, Robbie. Why do you always order red without asking me?"

"Whatever you want, Sally, we'll order it," he assured her. "Jack and Carolyn are flexible, aren't you guys?" My wife and I exchanged glances over this hissy fit mixed with a reference to herself in the third person. We didn't care what kind of wine Rob ordered. Neither of us could be called a "wine snob," preferring a cheaper bottle of white. Even an eight-dollar bottle of Riesling would do.

Sally held up the wine list. With her finger—weighted down with a large, gaudy emerald ring—she pointed to a Chardonnay from Toscano, Italy, and said, "Sally wants that one, waiter." He complimented her on the choice.

I leaned over and whispered to Rob, "That's almost eighty dollars."

With his menu held up to shield our conversation, he said, "I know it is. I want this to be a lovely evening. The wine will go on my personal credit card. Stop being so uptight." Rob clearly had his hands full with his new, high-maintenance girlfriend.

"What're you two boys conspiring about? We're here to celebrate, right, Robbie?" Sally asked. Neither Carolyn nor I had ever heard our friend referred to as "Robbie." Carolyn couldn't help herself but giggle. *This is going to be a long dinner.* I nudged Carolyn's knee under the table with my knee to signal such. With a sharp eye in return, she warned: *Behave yourself, Jack Curran.*

Despite my earlier pessimism, the food and atmosphere were fantastic. Sally simply bubbled over her wine choice, and one of the most expensive entrees on the hotel's menu. Some French dish that cost over fifty bucks. I stuck with my usual New York strip. And Carolyn had a pasta dish.

Time for us to head over to the ball; I didn't want to be late for the introductions of the governor, first lady, senior staff, and cabinet. Joan needed to see me present supporting the new administration, so I got off to a good start with her and the senior staff.

We entered Founder's Hall in Hershey, a magnificent tribute to Milton and Catherine Hershey, revered icons in Central Pennsylvania. The hall the perfect location for an inaugural celebration with its rotunda and a grand staircase that hosted Governor Collins and his big shots as they were introduced to the crowd. The applause raucous for our new leader after eight long years of Democratic rule.

Carolyn and I mingled about, saying hello to many acquaintances and friends from the Capitol, the ball being a veritable Who's Who of Harrisburg and the legislative scene. There were Ennis and her long-time boyfriend from the nation's capital. *He has movie star good looks and they are a handsome couple*, I thought with envy. Rather than an inaugural ball, I could envision them walking the red carpet on opening night in Hollywood or on Broadway as the stylish white cape Ennis wore with a matching tiara caused the paparazzi to snap pictures.

Even on a grand evening such as this, we worked to avoid Henrietta and the unpleasant exchange that would follow. "Why does she hate me so? I'm probably as conservative as she is but not as inflexible," I whispered to Carolyn. "What's up with Rob's girlfriend, referring to herself in the third person? Who does that other than politicians with big egos?" I asked with a mischievous grin on my face.

Carolyn elbowed my ribs and admonished me. "Stop it, Jackie. Try to be a good boy tonight. I know it's hard for you."

"Every day is a trial working with some of these people, honey. You see them once a year or so." Patience may indeed be a virtue, but I had little for some in the Capitol crowd. Not that I overflowed with it to begin with, even as a child. My tongue was sharper, too, from all the years in politics.

"No, I just have to listen to you complain every night about them. Did you ever really try to sit down with Representative Hoover? As far as Sally goes, Rob likes her and he's your best friend." Gently tussling my slicked back hair—blacker than usual because of the hair gel I used to control my longer hair I had let grow out now that my Army days were over—she added, "Smile, you're a new staffer for the governor."

"If you say so, dear," I rolled my eyes while saying this. Carolyn's voice was essential in keeping me real and from descending too far down into the gloomy hole my nature gravitated towards.

Many Republican members of the General Assembly attended, enthusiastic that the election had produced majorities in both the House and Senate. The top of the ticket had proved popular and reliable in assisting Republicans to get elected and the air bristled with excitement. The Grand Old Party had complete control of state government. Leaders and members alike dusted off their lists of policy items to push through when the session began in earnest in several weeks.

Sorting through these conflicting priorities would be a challenge for Collins and the leaders. There is simply not enough session and calendar time to address every member's wish list. Setting an agenda is much like cutting film from a movie while it's in editing. Some scenes don't make the final cut. Just as some legislative items fall by the wayside because of time constraints or because somewhere in the process an insurmountable choke point develops, and it's necessary to move on to other agenda issues. That immovable obstacle might be a powerful special interest or chairman, steadfast in their opposition.

Despite not enjoying large crowds, I was having a good time. Carolyn even got me out on the floor for a song we both liked. I didn't need much coordination to join a crowd that jumped to the music, shaking the floor and rattling the chandeliers. Sorry to disappoint, folks, but this is as raucous as a bunch of GOPers get when we gather.

As the evening ended, I spied Ben Walker alone, a rarity since nothing of any great substance occurred in the Senate without his knowledge and involvement. He usually had a line of people waiting to see him, especially now that Ben had returned as the majority counsel, out of the minority wilderness where power is limited. Walker congratulated me on the new role as we shook hands. He'd been a mentor, maintaining an open door anytime I had an issue or concern to discuss. Fond of Senator Weigel, Ben appreciated the job I did as Jim's chief of staff. We were straight shooters with each other.

"How did Doc take the news of your departure, Jack?" Ben and Doc had worked together years ago on the Senate staff.

"Okay, I guess. Groused and snapped and didn't let me leave before I had to entertain that fat slob Filipowski and his entourage for over four hours." Ben rolled his eyes since he knew of the Flipper's reputation for fleecing lobbyists. "Doc's disappointed I stayed for only a year, but he'll survive and break in a young 'un in no time to fit his mold." Ben laughed, aware of Doc's patterns. "Any tips, Ben, on the confirmation process since I'll have half the cabinet to guide through the Senate?" Joan's other deputy and I planned on sharing the responsibility.

"You've been on the Senate end and understand how arduous a process it is. Stay in close touch with me each week on how the visits are going. Each nominee must visit with all fifty senators unless the members wave off the appointment. The standing committees will have public hearings devoted to each candidate. Once you're close to wrapping up the meetings, the candidates will appear in caucus to answer questions senators may have."

Much like the U.S. Senate's confirmation process, it is exhaustive to make sure each person is vetted thoroughly before the state Senate casts votes of confirmation. The standing presumption is a governor deserves to have the cabinet of his or her choice. Rarely are candidates rejected. Senators use the opportunity of a personal visit to discuss concerns they may have with that agency, often bringing to the table unresolved constituent or district cases not addressed through regular bureaucratic channels.

The clear understanding: nominees should do their best to address issues senators have; sometimes the member's vote is hinged to an outcome or decision. Unless the leadership believes that to be unreasonable of the member. Then they try to talk them out of making that condition. Staffing Senator Weigel through most of the Democratic governor's administration, I stood on the other side of these visits. And felt well prepared to guide the governor's nominees based upon my depth of experience.

The other deputy and I would join them as much as possible for each of the meetings, a physically challenging endeavor since eighteen cabinet-level agencies required separate Senate votes with fifty stops for each nominee. This amounted to the staggering number of a possible nine hundred visits through the halls and offices of the Pennsylvania Senate. All carefully cultivated.

"No surprises, Jack," Walker emphasized. "If any of the nominees have issues in their background or if any Republican members have serious concerns, flag that at once. I'd rather hear up front if there's a problem, so we can work through it. And make sure the paperwork is in order." Each nominee would be required to fill out financial disclosure documents by the Pennsylvania Ethics Commission and separate forms by the Senate with necessary biographical information. I remembered at least several candidates over the years—who tripped up and didn't cross the finish line because of incomplete or false filings.

"Thanks, Ben, for the words of wisdom. We'll stay in close touch. Appreciate all the support you've given me personally over the years." Grateful for the sage counsel from this decent man, I genuinely meant these words.

"You're welcome. Have fun and remember where you came from," he said this with a wink, a reminder of my start in the Republican Senate. Ben understood my loyalty to be to Governor Collins, but I was a staff product of the Senate, too, and he expected me to conduct myself so.

By the time we left the ball, we were both exhausted from the social networking and fake smiles these events often required. On the way back to York, my thoughts raced with the enormity of the responsibilities that lie ahead with the most demanding career challenge I would yet face: serving the new governor of the fifth most populous state in the nation.

THIRTY-NINE

The Cabinet and Saving Carlisle Davin Kelso

WORKING FOR A GOVERNOR, I had many new "best friends," including individuals who had never said hello in earlier jobs, the two-faced nature of politics an aspect I didn't appreciate. Some in the Capitol crowd contrived of a hierarchy in Harrisburg—at least in their own minds. I tried to treat everyone as I wanted to be treated. While there can be sharp philosophical and political differences, there is no substitute for basic human decency to govern conduct. Admittedly, I didn't always meet my own standard, particularly if the staff role required me to be extra tough.

Many a lobbyist or staffer rued the day they were rude or arrogant with a secretary in an office, who later ascended to be the gatekeeper to a powerful senator or House member. They might find themselves at the bottom of the list when it came time for an appointment request.

The fifth floor of the Finance Building (built in the Depression-era) across the street from the Capitol served as the location of my new space. By happenstance, I discovered a little-known route that allowed me to slip over to the governor's office on the second floor of the big building without bumping into many people, particularly the buddies I didn't budget requests. Often contentious, these hearings remained one of the best opportunities for the Democrats to pick apart the priorities of a new Republican governor.

A diverse group of men and women from the Commonwealth and outside the state filled the positions with some agencies harder to fill because of the required ability needed. Or sometimes because Governor Collins had a policy focus that might require a non-traditional nominee to lead that agency. Madeline Donovan from Philadelphia, designated to lead the Department of Labor and Industry, had a high-pitched voice and her persona alienated senators, so we did our best to counsel her, as diplomatically as possible, to soften her tone. And we were not always successful in that counsel.

Arnold Dexter, one of those non-traditional nominees, headed up the Department of Education. He hailed from a university setting, eminently qualified because of his expertise in higher education governance. Because Dexter didn't come from the school teacher or administrator ranks—the usual place secretaries of education came from in earlier administrations—the establishment did not embrace him.

The job challenged him even more so because Governor Collins supported choice in education, views Dexter shared coming from a university, where options in Pennsylvania are robust among public and private colleges and universities. And yet, school choice remained anathema to the education establishment any secretary of education is forced to work with. The state's post-secondary grant program became the model for giving poor students a basic education grant to allow their parents to choose the best school setting for their children, regardless of where they resided.

Major General Gerald Theo, the first African-American to be named Adjutant General, was one of my favorite nominees since he'd served in Vietnam. An imposing figure who earned his two stars and a Silver Star awarded for valor in battle, Theo wore the uniform proudly as a "soldier's soldier." Having interacted with my fair share of officers during my military career, which ended in 1993, General Theo did not have a negative air about him for enlisted men and women. But the general commanded respect. As a former enlisted man, Theo had not forgotten what it was like to be down in the trenches.

A tall Scots-Irishman named Carlisle Davin Kelso or "Carl" became my absolute favorite cabinet nominee (we compared notes on our common heritage!). Hair kept cut close on the sides with a cluster of vibrant natural orange on top earned him the childhood nickname "Carrot Top." Charming and funny with engaging blue eyes and Crow's feet—maybe gained from the years Kelso spent helping to run New York's welfare system, Governor Collins named him to reform Pennsylvania's Department of Health and Public Assistance. I learned that Carl could spin yarns better than anyone I'd ever encountered. These stories were sometimes not PC, and I'd worry that someone might be offended by Kelso's off-color wit. For sure, he didn't telegraph "typical bureaucrat" as part of his demeanor.

While intelligent, Carl had no previous exposure to Pennsylvania's government and the powerful politicians in the Senate's leadership. Typically, when we began the confirmation process, we'd start the visits with the leadership, then proceed to the committee chairs, committee members, and finish up with the rank-and-file senators. As we walked the halls of the Senate, I'd brief Carl, impressing upon him who was who, and what to avoid or highlight during conversation in the meetings.

Our first stop: Senator Marco Corvi, the president pro tempore. In that position for many years, except for when the GOP found itself in the minority for that one session when a member had flipped sides (triggering my departure to lobby), my old "friend" Bruce Bauer joined the meeting. As Secretary-designate Kelso went to introduce himself to the pro tem, he made the mistake of addressing him as "Senator Pumfrey," an honest snafu. Pumfrey was on the list for visits that afternoon as a member of the

Public Health and Welfare Committee, responsible for considering the nomination through a committee hearing.

"Senator Pumfrey! Am I Senator Pumfrey, Mr. Secretary? You're leading one of Pennsylvania's biggest agencies, and you don't even recognize I'm the president pro tem." Usually unflappable, Carl found himself rattled as he sank down into the leather side chair from this tirade. The pro tem knew how to wield power, demanding respect. With an ego as large as the Capitol Rotunda, he let loose on Kelso and me. "What's the matter with you, Curran, didn't you prepare your nominee for his visits? You should know better. All those years working for Weigel..." he said, shaking his head in disgust. The exaggerated disdain—because he still held a grudge from Jim's property tax reform stance when Weigel bucked the GOP and crossed party lines.

Bruce jumped in, always one to pile on when the pro tem was wound up. "Yeah, Jack, you should understand how this process works. How could Secretary Kelso here," pointing to Carl, "mistake my boss, the pro tem," as if this needed emphasis any further, "for Senator Pumfrey, who is much older and from a different part of the state?" Bauer's long, gangly arms were up in the air, as he punctuated the obvious.

"Senator Corvi, my sincere apologies. Of course, I know you're the pro tem. Jack briefed me on leadership. There are so many visits and Senator Pumfrey's name just spilled out. I'm really sorry..."

"You should be," the president pro tempore retorted. Time for me to jump in. *Enough already beating up on this poor guy*, I said to myself.

"Senator, Secretary Kelso has apologized. Can we discuss his agency and any suggestions or concerns you may have?" Coming into my own as a man of experience and stature, I had limits to how much I'd be pushed around even by a big shot like the president pro tem.

The pro tem settled down although my interjection caused Bauer to glare. We never got along well while on staff together. I was the "enemy" now that I worked for the administration, even though we were all supposed to be one big, happy family as Republicans. The reality: something different as the executive branch would learn in upcoming battles—the GOP legislature eager to assert its own prerogatives, regardless of whether a Republican sat in the Governor's Mansion or not.

After about twenty minutes, the meeting wrapped up. Bauer asked me to stay behind while Carl waited in the outer office. "That's the best the governor can do for the Department of Health and Public Assistance? Really?" he asked. "We intend to push through welfare reform and need someone at the top of their game to lead the effort. This guy isn't ready for prime-time and should go back to the Empire State."

"I assure you Secretary Kelso is very accomplished. He's well-regarded in New York for his efforts at streamlining the bureaucracy and trimming public assistance benefits. Governor Collins has complete confidence in him." I locked my eyes on Bauer, my way of impressing upon him that the governor stood behind this nominee.

"Well, Kelso didn't get off to a good start here. We'll be watching him carefully *if he gets confirmed*." A hollow, pointless threat, we both knew it. After I left Bauer's office, I told the new nominee to give me a few minutes, so I could share with Ben Walker what just happened. Ben understood the pro tem and promised to speak with him, recognizing that simple mistakes happen.

"Sorry, Jack, you got your ass chewed when they asked me to step out." Not his usual gregarious self, the incident clearly bothered Kelso.

"It's okay, Carl. Seriously, shit happens. Too many egos in this building—the pro tem has one of the biggest for sure. We'll keep moving forward. Send him a little note on agency stationery, thanking him for the visit. Stress your door is always open." Petty stuff like this distracted from the serious policy discussions and debates that should be the total focus. Some politicians in Harrisburg wait for a slight to use as an excuse to sidetrack an issue or bar a lobbyist or official from talking with them until they had been "taught a lesson." This bullshit drove me crazy in all my years of service as a legislative staffer and during my time working for the governor.

Secretary Kelso and I would have larger problems than this rocky start with the president pro tempore, however. Shortly after this incident, we got calls from reporters who had received *anonymous* tips alleging Carlisle Davin Kelso had sexually harassed subordinates while in New York. With these claims as a foundation of "truth," a liberal female senator attacked the new Republican governor without waiting to learn the facts, another demonstration of the lack of bipartisanship in Harrisburg. We had a firestorm on our hands. All this happening before the public hearing on Carl's nomination began.

It fell to me to call Secretary Kelso to confront him with the charges—Joan and the senior staff wanted distance if they and Collins had to jettison Kelso because of the uproar. Rather than a face-to-face confrontation, I phoned instead. This would be difficult enough having to repeat the things written by the reporters. I genuinely liked and respected the guy as we had spent so much time together in the halls of the Senate for our visits. "Mr. Secretary, you probably know why I'm calling. This is an awkward conversation to have, but it's got to happen. Are the allegations, uh, true?"

"Dammit, Jack, they are complete fucking bullshit. Why would you guys put any credence into anonymous attacks? I made enemies up in New York because I shook things up, and now it's time for revenge by spreading this nonsense. Destroying my character in the process. These so-called subordinates were likely people written up for not showing up to work. New York is rife with a bloated bureaucracy I had to cut."

"Understandable that you're pissed, and I hate even repeating this crap. Governor Collins just wants the facts. We've been blindsided, and our press office is hounded on the hour to respond officially. At your hearing next week, we should address this in your statement and put this fire out." I assumed the governor and senior staff wouldn't be pulling the plug on the nomination.

"Why should I have to mention this garbage? Why are we even having this fucking conversation?"

While I liked the guy, I had a job to do and didn't appreciate the over-the-top reaction. "Carl, listen to me." I paused to emphasize my patience had limits. "We're having this discussion at the direction of the governor and Joan so settle down, okay? We need to hit this thing forcefully. I believe what you're telling me that the allegations are nonsense and will share that with Governor Collins and senior staff. Stay off the phone with reporters and let the press secretary manage this. Together, we'll craft a statement for the hearing and have our news people sign off on that, too."

"I guess...I don't deserve this character assassination. If I had known this would've happened, I would've remained in New York. Bye, Jack." I felt bad for the guy with enough experience to realize that once this stuff spilled out, the perception became a reality. Regardless if cleared, chances are these allegations would hang over him any time the name "Carlisle Davin Kelso" was mentioned.

Joan and the senior staff were anxious for my report. I conveyed Carl's anger and emphasized I believed him to be telling the truth. I also shared the explosion of profanity, not that I was by any means innocent in that regard, remembering how I even F-bombed my own mother.

After delivering my findings, our secretary buzzed that the governor was on the phone. As a new staffer in the governor's office, I had little interaction with Collins, reporting through Joan so this call intimidated me. "Hello, uh, Governor." A big guy, extremely confident, I shrank around him—as did many men.

"Jack, thank you for having that conversation with Secretary Kelso. I also want you to know I called to tell him that my cabinet officials don't swear at my staff. Unacceptable behavior. Carl will call you to apologize."

"Honestly, Governor, it's, uh, fine. His profanity wasn't aimed at me. I understand his anger at having to respond to these, uh, charges. I appreciate the support, though, sir." My military training came out, especially when dealing with a superior.

"Keep up the good work. I'll be meeting with Secretary Kelso to discuss the allegations and decide after that on whether to stand by him or not. See ya, Jack." The phone went down, and the governor's concern touched me.

The next day, he and Carl met. I anxiously paced the hallway outside of the governor's office, waiting to learn my new friend's fate. Would Kelso be given a political lifeboat or not? As he exited the ornate reception room used for ceremonial purposes, Carl flashed a grin. Shortly afterward, the press office released a statement that Governor Collins would move forward with the nomination, determining the allegations to be without merit.

Secretary Carlisle Davin Kelso would be confirmed and do an outstanding job at the department before returning to New York. I soon counted him as a good friend and enjoyed the "shoe leather" he and I had worn out together as we traveled the hallways of the Senate during his confirmation process. The governor stuck by Carl Kelso, and I had a small part in that decision. Other staffers wanted Governor Collins to cut him loose. I stood by Kelso and was proud my boss had as well. If he had "resigned" (the way these things are handled), Carl's reputation would've been damaged. Equally important, the Commonwealth would have been denied his ability and quality service.

A vivid lesson on how character assassinations are launched and fueled by the news media and partisan politics. In this new era of social media and "fake news," it is very easy to destroy someone's reputation with anonymous allegations and tips, which is one of the prominent reasons many highly qualified people refuse to enter public service.

FORTY

Vouchers Again, Nine Votes Short,
Electronic Board Failure

"**G**OVERNOR, the senator's staff is on the phone. They want to know, yes or no, are we going to make the deal or not?" the stakes were high, and the governor's legislative team wanted Governor Collins to deal. A sweeping school voucher program stood before the House and a vote could come at any time. Governor Collins had proposed this choice plan earlier in the spring. As part of the governor's education reform team, I was heavily involved in working with the cabinet to advocate for the voucher proposal.

Launched with the governor's 1995–96 budget proposal, we established the goal of tying the money and overall budget with school choice to give us a chance at navigating the legislation through the General Assembly. In this way, the budget provided the governor with a tremendous tool to leverage in negotiations with legislators. To allow him to use various grants and projects to trade for votes, a rather common practice in Harrisburg *if* our boss employed this tactic.

Secretary of Education Arnold Dexter had been confirmed and he and I had developed a strong working relationship through that process.

But until the Senate voted, we limited his exposure on the voucher issue. Not that we hid our support for choice in basic education; we didn't want to risk a negative vote on confirmation. Or make his Senate vote a test case on vouchers before we had our ducks in a row.

Once we had a favorable confirmation, Secretary Dexter became the face of the administration and a vital cog in the overall effort to bring school choice to Pennsylvania. Across the state, Dexter met with community groups, editorial boards, colleges and universities, and especially legislators, extolling the virtues of the governor's plan. We had an uphill battle to secure enough votes in the House. And our strategy—build support on the outside to pressure legislators on the inside.

The decision had been made to work the House first. More than anything, the Senate appeared stronger in its support for school vouchers after passing a broad-based measure back in 1991. The same plan my former boss, Senator Weigel, supported at great political risk to himself before his 1992 re-election campaign. If we could push vouchers through the House, we believed the Senate would follow suit because of its previous action.

Under the governor's proposal, state dollars would be available to students living in about one-third of the poorest school districts. The grants would range from seven hundred to one thousand dollars for high school students with lower amounts pegged for elementary pupils. Students could use the grant at any public or private school of their choice. The initial price tag: over forty million bucks, expected to balloon when implemented fully in all 501 school districts in Pennsylvania (there are currently 500 districts in the Commonwealth).

Not since the General Assembly had mandated back in the sixties the consolidation of over two thousand districts into the present configuration had there been anything as comprehensive and controversial proposed by any governor in the education arena. An unholy alliance of public and private sector unions, school boards, parent-teacher organizations, left-leaning churches, and school administrators mounted a fierce and sustained opposition. The teachers' union, Teachers for Fairness, had its massive PAC available to support opponents of the plan and to intimidate supporters of choice. Or any legislator on the fence wavering until they saw which way the wind blew.

Advocates for choice included conservative Republicans, like Senator Weigel and Representative Tony Molinaro—the latter would dramatically announce his support for vouchers. Some African-American legislators and community organizations from the larger urban districts in Pennsylvania joined with these Republicans because they tired of failure in their neighborhood schools. And these leaders were fed up with excuses. If only the establishment of board members, teachers, and administrators, had more money, better buildings, more equipment, *blah, blah, blah*, learning would improve. I have heard this refrain for so long as generations of kids fall by the wayside, tragically destined for welfare or jail, and complete and utter hopelessness.

Parochial schools in these same areas stood in stark contrast as diverse in make-up with far fewer resources to work with. The statistics showed they did a much better job in educating the smaller percentage of children they had in Catholic schools. Plus, these schools could take many more kids in their buildings because they had excess capacity at that time.

In large part because of a provision carried forward from the nineteenth century, designed to ban public support for sectarian institutions, Pennsylvania's Constitution remained a significant hurdle. The wording has roots back to the Know-Nothing party—anti-Catholic in its stance. Legislators who clung to this language conveniently forgot to mention this discrimination lodged in Pennsylvania's governing document.

As we lobbied the legislature, we found that legislators representing suburban school districts had two concerns: one, well-articulated; the other, hidden in the dark shadows of fear. Educating the children living within their boundaries, the demand and outcry for choices didn't come from these communities since parents were satisfied that their kids were learning and safe. This latter point is often a driving force for parents wanting to enroll their children in parochial, other nonpublic schools, and charter schools since we were successful in authorizing their establishment in 1997. Many public schools in urban areas resemble armed camps. Metal detectors, chain-link fences, and security officers pack guns as they rove the hallways looking to prevent mayhem and crime.

No constituency existed in these suburban districts. And, in fact, because of opposition from school boards and the union—even those areas not affected in the earlier stages of the program's implementation were forcefully against vouchers. Legislators from these regions found themselves in a safer place politically by being a "no" vote, regardless of the consequences for kids trapped in bad schools.

In my humble opinion, the other reason—and it represented the ugliest and most offensive trends in American society—was fear and race. White suburbanites didn't want African-American and other children of color living in urban areas, using voucher grants to come into their schools. In speaking with school district officials and legislators in these areas, we found that suburban communities argued that their buildings were "at capacity." In this way, if vouchers passed and survived the court challenges that would follow, districts would certify to the Department of Education that "they had no room in the inn." Leaving minority kids confined like prisoners in failing schools.

Many school choice proponents, including the author, believe educational opportunity, or the lack thereof, is the civil rights issue of our era. Government's efforts to subjugate children of color will in the end fail. The winds of freedom will blow and the metaphoric Berlin Wall erected by the education establishment will finally fall. No longer will a child's zip code determine their fate.

While not present at this meeting that happened during this debate, several of our legislative team were, and the story circulated within the administration and with voucher supporters as an illustration of the racial undertones of this debate. The legislator represented white suburban school districts that bordered a large urban area, except for a geographic division that required bridges to carry traffic between the communities. Like most cities, the area had suffered from "white flight" in the sixties and seventies, causing significant segregation of schools between the cities and suburbs and substantial differences in academic achievement and safety.

Taking a legal pad, the legislator drew a large river, saying to our folks, "There's a reason we have that river separating our districts from the other shore. We don't want those kids over here." This member was far blunter than most strident opponents, who would cage their arguments in a much more politically correct way.

I had good relationships with many House members in Central Pennsylvania and took it upon myself to host several of them for dinner, on my own dime, to explain why I passionately supported school choice. I had hoped my relationship and a talk among conservative Republicans, who presumably believe in competition and free markets forces—breaking bread together—could move the needle on their opposition. It didn't.

A "safe harbor" existed for joining the union and school boards. You earned praise from the establishment. Even more important, they left you alone in the next election cycle if you joined in opposition so long as you took a blind eye to children trapped in bad districts. And so long as you ignored your philosophical underpinnings that competition between schools would be a good thing, leading to innovation and efficiency. And the monopoly in public education controlled by the union and school boards is a bad thing, helping to perpetuate failure due to bloated bureaucracies and lots of inefficiencies, spending huge amounts of precious tax dollars with no regard to where the money comes from. The taxpayers, that's where!

Support for vouchers would bring condemnation, and an opponent recruited from the teacher, administrator, or school board ranks in your district. While the pressure, particularly from the Catholic Church, remained significant, it wasn't enough to push most folks over into the "yes" camp.

As we prepared to have a test vote in the House of Representatives, the governor made the somewhat unprecedented decision to appear before the House Republican Caucus in a closed-door session. The purpose: to pitch school vouchers and answer questions.

Before making this trip, an internal debate broiled about the political wisdom of such a move. If he failed, some staffers believed Governor Collins would appear inept. Emotional in asserting why he needed to appear, the governor articulated a compelling point: I'm a combat veteran and not afraid to stand before my GOP colleagues and argue for opportunity and choice after enduring warfare in the jungles of Vietnam.

I tried to see the world through his life experience in the context of this crucial political moment. When you're eighteen years old, sent to the hellhole of Vietnam, scared shitless, doing your duty because there's no other choice. You keep moving forward, you tell yourself. Is the next bullet fired or booby trap rigged meant for you? What if you can't escape the constant notion of terror you might never kiss or make love again to your sweetheart? Will your mom collapse when the Army staff car pulls up in front of your home to deliver the news no parent should ever have to receive? What if your face is blown off so bad that the undertaker won't be able to repair it for a viewing?

Those of us who have never faced combat, as Governor Collins did, can understand these emotions. One of the ballads in my limited Army training comes to mind. Every time I sang this, I got tearful. *You're standing in a foxhole. You watch your buddy die. You wish that you could help him. But all you do is cry.*

Annoyed with the vocal opposition coming from his senior staff, Governor Collins asked each staffer present, "Does anyone support this move, speak up if you do?"

Guess who spoke up. Inspired by his genuine passion and reference to combat, I urged the governor to follow his instincts. "Governor, it seems to me, the administration is all in on this fight. I don't see what you have to lose, and you might pick up some folks once they personally experience the depth of your emotion and realize what's at stake." Several staffers greeted my remarks with a glare since I had the gumption to speak up as only a junior staffer. I didn't care. A true believer in school choice, I couldn't have been prouder of Collins for his leadership.

The governor went into that caucus. And he came away with one convert—who would eventually become one of Pennsylvania's most articulate and capable champions of school choice—Representative Tony Molinaro. Tony was a loyal conservative Republican and a close ally of Governor Collins. When the governor described his reasons for the comprehensive voucher program, Tony left the caucus a "yes" vote. He asked to see several of us in the administration so we could help draft a press release to explain why he had changed his position.

Molinaro hailed from one of those areas in York County that had good suburban schools. He could have easily remained an opponent as many of his colleagues were. That would be disloyal to his governor—under Tony Molinaro's political ethics and integrity.

Intellectually, the representative also understood the governor's argument that large-scale failure in urban districts has huge budgetary consequences for the welfare and prison systems. Better educational opportunities give poor kids from cities a chance at a good education. And helps ease welfare, juvenile justice, and prison resources that consume a great deal of Pennsylvania's budget with an untold human element in the thousands of kids lost. Their potential gone forever from America.

Opponents fall back on the argument that not all families will use the voucher. Or will qualify for school choice grants. They reason—what happens to the children left behind in a failing building? Only in education is the assertion made that a school failing to educate or offer a safe environment for learning, more money and resources should be provided to keep that school open. Regardless of the consequences to the children and families trapped in that building. Close it! That's the answer.

Through payments to successful, surrounding school districts, move the children to a school that works and is safe. Where there's a will, there's a way. If, and it's a big "if," the will exists to push through the political obstacles and barriers preventing these kids from reaching their God-given potential. Every child has talents and intelligence and deserves a chance to explore his or her abilities. Regardless of where they live.

Unfortunately, while Tony's support helped the public appearance we'd gained ground, it brought no other votes to the "yes" column. We checked and cross-checked our vote tallies with each other, and with the House Republican leadership, who carried their own vote count, and determined we were nine votes short of the 103 we wanted to pass a bill.

While a constitutional majority in the House is 102, we wanted an extra vote for good measure. Legislators voting "yes" didn't want the tag in the next election as "the lawmaker that put vouchers across the finish line" by being that 102nd vote. Or so they feared this argument would be made in political mailers by their cunning opponents and the campaign committees housed in Harrisburg.

Senator Pete Agresti had enormous influence within the Philadelphia House Delegation. The senator controlled over ten votes he promised would be given over to the governor's voucher program *if* Governor Collins would deal with him on his legislative and City of Philadelphia priorities. I never learned what those issues were but heard the governor resolutely say he would not deal with Agresti to get those ten votes. He pledged to pass the voucher bill on its own merits—holding his own party's feet to the fire.

Our internal discussions were interrupted with word that Majority Leader Noah Johnson and Speaker Leonard Duda wanted to see the governor. An old pol from Southeastern Pennsylvania, Duda was of medium height with thick white hair and a quick wit. He had grown up in the machine politics of another era. A funeral director by trade, he used his contacts with families; first to get elected to the House and then steadily rose in leadership after that until his colleagues chose Duda to be the speaker.

Both Johnson and Duda wanted to see the governor succeed. They knew much more than a voucher program was at stake—the governor's credibility and political capital to govern the Commonwealth also hung in the balance. A defeat would hamper Governor Collins's effectiveness in future legislative fights, including the ability to pass an annual budget, the single most important act of any governor and the legislature.

Our leader looked and acted every bit a chief executive; some would say even presidential as he leaned against the massive oak desk that had served Pennsylvania's governors for over a century. "Show them in, please." Governor Collins greeted his colleagues with a big, lopsided grin and a signature, crushing handshake. "What can I do for you, gentlemen? How goes the battle for vouchers?"

"We're nine votes short, Governor. If you don't cut a deal with Agresti, there are no other votes available. Except for Molinaro, Central Pennsylvania won't budge," the majority leader noted.

The speaker added, "Look, Governor, we don't want to see you fail. How about we hold the vote over and work this more? That's our recommendation."

Collins didn't pause with his reply. "I'm not cutting a deal with Agresti. We've come this far; I want to hold these Republicans accountable. Make them vote against poor children trapped in bad schools. Dammit, guys, how can they live with themselves? There's just got to be more votes in Central Pennsylvania. What about the Black Caucus for Pete's sake, we're rescuing minority children? Can't we get more than two votes from them?" Governor Collins asked. They had been down this road several times. The governor articulated a frustration shared by the leaders. Seasoned legislators, these leaders knew intuitively when an issue could be voted. They didn't agree with Collins on the timing but would give him his vote.

"There are no more votes to find, trust us. Without Agresti on board, the city Democrats won't break. Too afraid of the unions. We'll hold the vote. But I won't let you be embarrassed, Governor. Count on that," said Speaker Duda.

As we huddled close around television sets in the governor's office, the speaker prepared to call the vote. The dramatic phone call came from Senator Agresti's staff. "Did the governor want to deal or not?"

Our legislative team wanted to do so, pushing the governor one last time for perhaps a new answer. The reply—the same as before. No way. Period. End of discussion.

Through the television we heard, "Have all the members voted? Have all the members voted?" Speaker Duda and his staff surveyed the floor from the high rostrum that provided them with a unique vantage point, hoping the added time would give the leader and whips the chance to turn more votes as they walked the aisles of the chamber seeking to change minds. The extra time didn't matter. The vote stood at ninety-four "ayes" for vouchers—nine short as predicted.

"Mr. Speaker, the 'yes' votes are abandoning ship," said one of the speaker's senior advisors. As the reality dawned on the rank-and-file that there were no more votes to be found, members switched to "no" before the final vote could be sealed by Speaker Duda. A herd mentality, quickly analyzing their own survival, drove the negative vote up. A sea of red circles overtook the green ones, causing even further panic as the "green" guys moved to red on the large electronic board that dominates the walls of the House chamber.

"Leonard, we've got to stop this," said Leader Johnson. "Collins will look like a fool and we can't let our guys be left on the hook for this vote."

"I've got this, Noah," Speaker Duda said, the air of calm about him signaled this was not his first legislative rodeo. With a simple command to his staff, the speaker had the power struck to the electronic board that records the roll call votes. "Members will be advised that there has been a malfunction to the big board. Our technical team is checking the system. No further votes will occur today."

A sigh of relief went up from those legislators who hadn't switched their votes to "no." With the "malfunction" as the official excuse, there never was a voucher vote that could be used against those who stood for the plan. Theoretically, this gave the governor another opportunity at a vote in the future.

We never got the second chance during the governor's term in office. But our Republican chief executive of the '90s got a school scholarship program funded by business tax credits and charter schools, two huge school choice wins for poor children. These wins required compromise or we would have won nothing for families trapped in bad schools. And, significantly, he won reforms on sabbatical, tenure, and continuing education—three areas grossly in need of structural changes to save taxpayer dollars and improve public education.

FORTY-ONE

The Old Lion Retires, A Job Offer

DEEP IN THOUGHT, my office door was closed. I needed time to think and brainstorm. Education Secretary Dexter would be testifying at a public hearing in September on a package of bills sponsored by the Senate Education Committee chairman—not an ally of the governor's.

While a good and decent man, who I liked very much, the chairman generally followed the lead of the establishment in running the committee. Introduced as an alternative to the governor's voucher plan, the chairman's legislation followed the same tired, old ideas of reduced class sizes (translation: more teachers to pay union dues), full-day kindergarten, pre-kindergarten, and higher state spending foisted on the taxpayers. Principles dusted off from previous playbooks; this time these "solutions" would serve to distract from the drive for school choice.

The notes on my legal pad started out broadly and got more specific: *1. No Retreat; 2. Stay on the offensive; 3. Mix in mandate relief to try to split the school boards from the unions; 4. Stay focused on the "customers" of education as the governor and secretary call them—parents and children, not the adults working in the system.* Rather than react to the chair's ideas, I and others on the team wanted the secretary to talk about the administration's plans. Ignore the package of bills. And keep the focus on the governor's goals.

One of our secretaries in the Finance Building knocked on my door, despite my request I not be interrupted. She wanted to tell me Gloria West wished to speak with me. She rarely called unless it was important. I picked up the phone. "Hi, Gloria, everything okay?"

"No, Jack, it's not. Jim and Diane are in his office right now. Can you please come over?" Gloria said this with an urgency I'd never heard before.

"Sure. Be over in five minutes. Bye." Even though the General Assembly remained in summer recess, I rode the elevator down to the basement to use the tunnels to enter the Main Capitol. Weigel's office was now on the first floor so I popped in unnoticed by any staffers or lobbyists that might lurk about. This intrigue might've been unnecessary, but my experience had been plenty of folks hang around the hallways, looking for signals of what may or may not be happening.

Gloria greeted me with a hug that conveyed deep emotion and showed me into the senator's office. Jim and his wife, Diane, were seated. I shook hands with the senator and hugged Diane. A strong woman, she'd been through an awful lot as a politician's spouse. Jim absent a great deal because of a grueling schedule for most of their married life—his health problems presented her with new challenges.

Diane led the discussion as the senator remained quiet. "Jack, we've decided it's time for Jim to retire." Peering into Weigel's gentle eyes as she said this, I welled up. This man was like a father to me and the model for public service I'd try to emulate for whatever days God granted me for this purpose.

Even though I realized this moment would come, it still walloped like a blow to the abdomen. I stuttered, "I...I...understand, Diane. What can I do?" I remained part of Jim's inner circle and tried to shake off the emotions. *Focus, Jack. Jim needs you again to protect him.*

"Please let Ben Walker know of the decision and handle the press end," she said.

"Sure...I'll take care of everything." In my head, I quickly outlined a strategy and suggested we'd need a press release that would focus on Jim's love for the job and his accomplishments. I also proposed one interview with a newsman of the senator's generation. Someone who understood Weigel wasn't well. This television reporter would do a story, highlighting all the positive things Jim accomplished for York, Central Pennsylvania, and the Commonwealth.

Now was not the time for Kostantin Pokornin, who would be merciless with probing questions and jibes, or even the bombastic radio host, David Cortes. The senator needed to go out with dignity and grace. His legacy secure in his various deeds and achievements to help people rather than a story that focused on his health decline.

Diane and I embraced again, and I went around the senator's desk. Jim rose to grasp my shoulder. As I leaned into his left ear, I murmured, "You're doing the right thing, boss. Whatever you need, I'm here. I can never thank you enough for what you've done for me." Weigel had hired a young man with little experience. He took a great risk, particularly coming off the firing of a chief of staff who'd betrayed him and the public trust. I'd be forever grateful for Senator Weigel's confidence.

"Everything will be all right, Jack," the senator said as he struggled to hold back his own tears. I didn't share his unceasing optimism. His retirement marked the end of an era for York County. And for me. At that moment, I felt like I'd experienced a death in the family.

I proceeded to Ben Walker's office. Ben and the leadership went into action after I alerted him. The leaders would need to call a special election for the victor to serve the remainder of the senator's term once they received Jim Weigel's official resignation letter. Scheduled with the off-year races planned for November of 1995, the county and municipal offices normally dominated the ballot. Not this time with a senatorial contest joining the cycle.

I asked Ben whether we should give Tony Molinaro a quiet heads-up as the senior House member of the York Delegation. Besides the immense respect we had for Tony, both of us knew several other possible candidates were circling like vultures, hoping to succeed Weigel. We agreed I would visit Tony with this confidential news, so he could have a little additional time to think about running or not. This would be crucial if Molinaro sought the seat against others, who'd be caught flat-footed with the announcement of the resignation.

Before doing so, I huddled with the ever-capable Susan on the staff to talk about the points I thought should be articulated in the resignation letter and press release she'd draft for my review, and that of Ben Walker. *Everything will be done right to honor this great man*, I promised myself.

As I made my way across the Capitol Building, I kept my head down to avoid interaction with anyone. "Somber" doesn't describe my mood correctly. At Tony's office, I asked to see him. He was in. After we shook hands, the representative inquired, "What brings you here, Jack?"

"I have confidential news to share, Tony. It's not to go further than you and your wife, okay?" I paused for emphasis; my face graver than usual.

"Understood. What's up?"

"Jim's retiring. The announcement's in a few days, and the election will be scheduled for November. We want you to have extra time to decide on whether you're running or not." Jim and Diane were comfortable with Molinaro being the senator's successor. Politics what it is—this became both an end and a beginning. And I, the messenger and conduit. The senior House guy, Molinaro had been more than a worthy opponent when the two had fought for the nomination years ago. It was important to me that someone who would respect Weigel and his work get the nod.

"I'm not sure what to say. How're Jim and Diane doing?" Tony asked this with genuine concern. While they had been rivals, they were colleagues, too, and Molinaro understood the moment called for empathy. Not the equivalent of political handsprings because the brass ring on the carousel was now within his grasp.

"Doing okay. Diane is a rock and taking good care of Jim. It's been a tough day, to say the least. Look, I hope you run. Once we draft the press release and resignation letter, I'll share it with you before the stuff goes out. Maybe you can call Jim after the news is out. He'd appreciate the gesture." I stood up, shook his hand, and left the office.

Susan did an outstanding job with the writing as Ben and I reviewed it and changed very little in the documents. A few days later, we were ready to release everything. Having kept the circle of people involved in the planning to a minimum, thankfully the story hadn't leaked out. The television interview would be the exclusive story on the retirement and we'd take no other press calls. Senator Weigel would not be subjected to uncomfortable questions that might tax his memory.

Health questions were off-limits for the story and I trusted this reporter completely. I had been burned by several in the media, so it wasn't easy to achieve this confidence from me. The focus would be Weigel's accomplishments and love for public service. Period.

Out of the way in the corner of the senator's office, I burst with pride in the senator. The old lion did a terrific job answering the newsman's questions, articulating how much he loved being a senator and loved his constituents. Vintage Weigel, he'd summoned up from deep inside the ability to finish with grace.

The tears flowed watching my former boss in action. Entering a new phase like my other hero, Ronald Reagan, had been forced to endure, this would be a time harder for the loved ones who would hang onto memories about the goodness and accomplishments of this great and decent man. As his dimmed in the twilight of his life.

Now that the public part of the senator's retirement announcement was over, I said goodbye to Gloria and Susan and headed home. It was the right thing for the senator to do, exiting while he could with his head held high. Yet, it still hurt deep in my gut.

Carolyn met me at the door with an embrace and drink already made. Little Jack and Robert ran at me with the game we played. They would come fast towards me, yelling, "Ramming speed on Daddy." Their antics involved trying to knock daddy over. Only four and two, I could take their blows while laughing hard. My family always the tonic for my soul when politics pulled me down emotionally.

Several days after the resignation, Rob called. He asked to meet across the street from the Capitol for a hot dog from our favorite vendor. Placid continued to grow in power with the major lobbying firm he was a partner in. And he kept seeing Sally.

After picking up hot dogs and soda, we walked down to sit on a bench near the Susquehanna River, a view I never tired of. Harrisburgers often say the river is a "Mile wide and a foot deep" because of its shallowness. A brightly painted riverboat, *The Pride of the Susquehanna*, slowly powered by as several jet skis darted around the surface on this humid summer day. A light breeze blew off the water and provided some relief from the heat.

We exchanged pleasantries and small talk. After that, it became clear Rob had an agenda, so I asked, "What's up? There's something on your mind."

"Tony called me. He appreciated the way you handled Weigel's resignation. He's running. Will you be his campaign manager and chief of staff if he's successful?" Caught off-guard by this ask, I enjoyed working for Governor Collins, especially as his liaison to the Department of Education and Secretary Dexter. Education reform remained a passion even though we hadn't been triumphant with vouchers. Now Tony and Rob wanted me to return to the arena where it had all begun.

"Surprised, Rob, and a little speechless. Never thought Tony would be interested in me. There are some people up in the Capitol who are familiar with the district and could do the job. I'm Weigel's guy. Tony's okay with that? Not the way it usually works, old friend." It said a lot about Molinaro that he'd overlook my loyalty and service to Jim.

"Tony's an astute politician and has watched you in action a long time. Someone knowledgeable about the district, inside and out and who knows the Capitol. That's the combination he wants. And you fit that bill. Plus, you'd be comforting to the Weigel camp of supporters since they know you. You're a link to the past."

True, I understood the Eighth District from all the years staffing Jim and we lived in York. Jim's group within the party trusted me as their go-to-guy when they couldn't reach the senator and needed aid. Or had a gripe with something he did or a position he took. Often more likely to share those concerns with me than with Weigel.

Unfortunately, I recalled many late-night phone calls from folks venting because I was an easier and more accessible target and didn't have the title "Senator" in front of my name. I had a reputation for getting things done and the more problems I fixed, the more my business boomed from Weigel's network.

Tony needed to nail down the nomination with the Republican committee people, including those in the Weigel camp, and then win the special election. Well-skilled to help him with both, the representative recognized I could hit the ground running in November since the district remained relatively safe for Republicans to retain. A tight timeline from August to November to secure the nomination, organize a fall campaign, win, and hire talented individuals to staff his offices.

"Is this a move down? I'm in a prestigious position; a return to the Senate might be viewed as a demotion. People in this town will talk." The gossip that would follow: "Curran had to leave the governor and Weigel and Molinaro cut a deal, so he would have a job." Or something to that effect. The Capitol crowd never lacked subjects to whisper about.

Thinking for a bit after I asked this, Rob answered, "Tony Molinaro will not be your average freshman senator. He's seasoned, smart, a member of the House Republican leadership, and a staunch ally of the governor. You get to prove you can manage a twelve-week campaign, from start to finish, a real notch of accomplishment, buddy. No decision is needed right at this moment. I've been trying to lure you guys to my new house on Long Beach Island. It's been a helluva summer between vouchers and Jim's resignation. Take several days down the shore to think this through."

The Jersey Shore remained a special place for our family. We usually vacationed where I had spent some of my teen years—Sea Isle City. Long Beach Island is north of there. As Rob described it, quiet and more residential. The commercial honky-tonk of some New Jersey beaches didn't appeal to us.

"Good idea. I'm floored and need to process all this with Carolyn. Can you tell Tony I'm thinking through the generous offer? Once I talk things over with my wife and return after a few days of rest, I'll call him."

"Sure. Molinaro will understand. This job offer isn't a move you have to make. It's a decision to mull over, for sure. You guys don't have to pack much for the trip; the house is fully stocked. Enjoy and ponder the career thing."

While eating our hot dogs, he brought up Sally, probably because I'd been silent in not asking about her. "It's getting serious, Jackie boy. Every weekend we're either in Harrisburg or D.C. Mom wants to meet her, too." Rob's mother, Gladys, still lived in Sharon—in the same small home he grew up in. His father passed away when he was only ten years old, forcing Gladys to be independent and strong-willed.

"Wow, a trip to Sharon, that's huge." A special lady, Mrs. Placid invited me to their place during many college breaks when there was no other home for me to go to. As conservative and plain-speaking as I knew her to be, I couldn't imagine how she would receive a blond bombshell like Sally.

"Take it slow, okay," I urged him. "No need to rush in. This time, remember the prenup, man." A standing joke between us, Rob vowed never to have to buy back his house again; Kim became the financial recipient of the value of the home and part of his pension savings to settle the divorce.

With a punch to my arm, he laughed. "No worries there. I learned that lesson the hard and expensive way. Before we head back to our offices, have to catch you up on the scoop around town." Gossip remained one of Rob's specialties.

"Wouldn't be lunch without me bitching about several of my favorite people up there and you sharing scuttlebutt. Go ahead, what do ya got?" I tried not to engage in this stuff but couldn't help it with my pal. This is just what we did.

"On the Senate side, the word is two Senate security guys have been stealing stamps from Senate offices. They sell their loot on the streets of Harrisburg for cash," Rob explained.

"Has the story broken yet?" I asked.

"Soon. Law enforcement's on it. Charges are coming."

"How the heck do you hear about this stuff before everyone else does?"

"I'm friends with the secretaries, pages, storeroom and mailroom guys, and security," he said. "When I pass them in the hallway, they just share the news. I keep my ear to the ground, too, man. Never know if a staffer wants to trade stories. That's one way I pick up on the real legislative developments, by sharing scoop. Doesn't hurt to have juicy material if I have to nudge someone along, too." Rob was well-liked up on the "Hill" and good at what he did.

"I connect with those people as part of my approach, too, particularly the secretaries," I said. "None of them share this junk with me."

"Everyone knows how serious you are, Jack. Even when you smile and laugh, there's just this serious aura about you. Been there probably since you came out of the womb."

Grinning, I said, "Not that far back but definitely as a child. My parents and siblings always said I was 'ten going on forty'...I guess that makes me about seventy now, huh?"

"You're an old soul, no question. Okay, last story. This one you have to play the guessing game, agreed?" Rob asked. Placid liked playing this challenge with me. The contest protected his sources and tested my knowledge of the members in the Capitol.

"All right, shoot."

"This House member is tall, broad-shouldered, big guy, a mane full of silver hair, fancies himself a real ladies' man."

For a moment I pondered and his name came to me. "Has a large ugly mole on his forehead, should have its own zip code, right?"

"Yep, that's him," Rob confirmed.

"I lobbied him on school choice, and he wouldn't budge. Real chicken lacking any c...c...c...courage." I stuttered for dramatic effect.

Rob smiled and continued, "That guy has never cast a tough vote in his political life. Up there to live high on the hog and stay in office as long as possible. Not as bad as the 'Flipper' but close. Behind his back, his colleagues call him 'Tiny Bubbles.' Fits, doesn't it?"

The image of this big lug tagged with small testicles caused me to spit out my soda. "Next time, hold that shit until after I've finished my drink, Rob. Honestly, the crap people say lightens things up. Come to think of it, doesn't he have another nickname he wants to be called? I can't remember it."

"Yeah, he does but the other label fits better."

"Okay, I should return to work already. Enough gossip."

"I'm not done. The salacious part is he's having a wild affair with a staffer of the other caucus, not his own."

"Oh well, that makes it acceptable then. He's a real bipartisan guy." I said this with as much sarcasm as I could muster.

"There's more. House Security walked in on them in his office. Too funny, right?" I rolled my eyes. This stuff happened at the Capitol as I suppose it does at any large institution where people interact closely with one another.

I pictured this legislator as he glided through the halls of the Capitol. His stroll seemed to be feigned like he practiced it so he looked fresh and collected at all times. Holding an ornamental walking stick at his side (who does that?), through the halls of the Capitol this guy would glide. Glad-handing lobbyists and fellow legislators, a fake smile—that sported straight white teeth—always glued on his face, he was on the prowl to make new friends and allies with an ego that sought constant gratification.

Rob and I said goodbye after I thanked him for the hot dog and soda and we walked back towards the Capitol. Placid proceeded into his firm's office on State Street, while I vigorously walked up my favorite steps, no longer running them as I did back in the day. I felt torn about leaving the governor. But a return to a chamber I loved, to work for someone I admired for his gutsy and principled leadership, enticed me as an attractive notion. Time down the shore would be restorative, and a chance for reflection to make my next career decision.

FORTY-TWO

Jersey Shore Renewal

"JACK, REMEMBER the shovel and umbrella. I don't want the kids burning on the beach." We had this routine of digging a big hole for the boys to play in, covered by a huge umbrella, to protect their fair skin from the rays of the sun. Both Carolyn and I had been sunburned as kids; a time when children were lathered up with baby oil at best.

After loading the car, we headed to Rob's vacation house on Long Beach Island, New Jersey. In reading about this Jersey Shore destination, I learned that the barrier island is eighteen miles long, connected by a causeway from the mainland to Ship Bottom. Rob's home was in Brant Beach; in a more residential section of the island.

With about four hours on the road, stopping only to get the kids a snack and a potty break for everyone, I saw the bay. "Honey, pop in something fun." I wanted music playing to sing along to when we headed onto the island. Several funny faces that I made during this Karaoke attempt caused my precious bunch to laugh hard.

The window all the way down, I inhaled deeply. "Smell that family. That's the scent of my youth and happiness." Instantly, all the aggravation and strain faded away.

"Daddy, it stinks like fish," Little Jack said.

"That's the fishery we're passing on the right, son. That's a good aroma, too. We'll rent a small boat from there to go crabbing. The blue claws are big I hear. Might even be bigger than you and Robert." Little Jack looked at me quizzically, not sure what the heck I meant by this reference to the crabs, famous at the Jersey Shore.

Originally an old fisherman's bungalow, Rob had his place refurbished into a three-bedroom house with a nautical theme and modern amenities. He'd done quite well at the lobbying firm. On track now to become a full partner. His home sat on the ocean block, a short distance to the beach; a lower deck led off the kitchen and a rooftop platform gave the house views of the open sea. Truly an ideal setting for us to relax and have fun as a family.

After unpacking, I fired up Rob's charcoal grill on the lower deck and cracked open a Coors Light. The kids were inside playing, so Carolyn joined me, pouring white wine as we enjoyed some peace. The solitude pleasantly interrupted by the cawing of seagulls, this sound brought back memories of my childhood and early teen years.

"Penny for your thoughts? You've been pretty quiet about the conversation with Rob." Carolyn understood how I internalized everything; her way of drawing me out: to engage at the right time. She knew the offer from Tony was churning over and over in my mind. My trusted advisor in all matters, yet I wouldn't share my thinking until she initiated the conversation.

"Really wrestling with this, babe. I like the work with Collins, especially on education reform and I've developed good relationships with the cabinet after the grueling confirmation process in the Senate. Working for a governor is one of the most prestigious jobs in my career. Now I'm being asked to take a step back...to a position I held with Jim, with a former foe of his."

"I thought Jim and Tony mended fences? Apparently, Tony thinks so, or he wouldn't have asked you to be his chief of staff."

"They've both mellowed, and Molinaro appreciated the heads-up. The perception will be from Jim's supporters that I turned on Weigel to join Tony, right or wrong."

"Jack, honestly, who cares what they think. What do you want to do? That's what matters. Some of Weigel's folks didn't like it when you went to work for a pro-choice governor. You made that decision despite their gossip. If you've drilled anything into me, it's that Harrisburg likes to talk. If they're not discussing Jack Curran, it's someone else." Carolyn was right. The senator was solidly pro-life. Joining the governor had caused accusations of being a turncoat. While I hadn't changed my pro-life stance (and never will), I did not serve in a policy position where abortion was part of my portfolio as a deputy director. Had it been, I would have said no to Joan and Governor Collins.

That is a line I'd never cross. My conscience wouldn't have allowed promoting or implementing pro-abortion views. The law was settled (until the Supreme Court changes) after the bruising battles of the late eighties and early nineties, which Weigel and I took part in. Governor Collins had pledged not to work to overturn the restrictions successfully imposed by the pro-life majority in the General Assembly. That pledge had comforted me and many other pro-lifers—who were nervous until he articulated it.

"Loyalty in politics is important. The Weigel camp may think less of me if I accept Tony's offer. On the positive side, as Molinaro's top guy, I can work to protect Senator Weigel's legacy without being disloyal to Tony. The two of them have similar views on just about everything, except abortion. If Molinaro stood differently, and I didn't see this as a step backward, it would be a no-brainer." Tony later would have a profound personal conversion and become pro-life, something I applauded after it occurred. I knew it wasn't my place to interfere with the struggle Tony underwent on one of the most emotional issues of our time.

"You're the sum of your experiences, sweetheart," my wife wisely observed. "Each experience has strengthened your resolve to succeed and be a good man. If you go back to the Senate, you won't return as the same guy. Think about how much more you'd bring to the job after service with Collins, and as a lobbyist. How many Senate staffers at your age can say that?"

There weren't many folks, for sure, who return to the Senate after serving a governor, so Carolyn was right. I'd be in a unique position. York County also occupied a special place in my heart and I missed the daily interactions with constituents.

As a staffer in the executive branch, I felt removed from collaboration with real people. Regular communications occurred only with the cabinet, fellow staffers, lobbyists, and legislators. I fretted that I'd become insulated and arrogant from the real problems of ordinary Pennsylvanians. It was all too easy for "the governing class" in Harrisburg to be distant, which in my judgment, can lead to callousness, to a lack of connection to the voters that send the elected officials to Pennsylvania's capital city.

The grill burned ready for the burgers, and we planned on taking the kids on a boat ride after dinner. In one brochure I picked up, an older vessel called the *Snoopy* drew our attention. It looked to be a more family-oriented ship, painted a flamboyant red and white, ideal for the first time the boys would be out on the Atlantic Ocean.

We finished up eating and drove north on the island to the end, Barnegat Light, anchored by a distinctive lighthouse known as "Old Barney." It had served as a beacon to many sailors, navigating the treacherous Atlantic. The boat moved through the choppy inlet that connected the Barnegat Bay and ocean. For about three hours, we cruised off the island. Jack and Robert squealed with delight as we stood on the bow of the boat, watching it slice through the water, while it splashed up sea spray on the other passengers and us.

Mellow, the pressures of the budget season, vouchers, the Kelso confirmation fight, and Jim's retirement all faded away with the sound of the Atlantic pushing against the *Snoopy*. Perceptive to suggest this small vacation before I reacted to Molinaro's offer, Rob knew I needed to let my body and mind heal. My style: keep driving, regardless of what the stress, time pressures, egos, and twists and turns of the legislative process did to my health. Squeezing Carolyn's hand, listening to the excitement of the kids, my spirit renewed.

The next morning, while the boys and Carolyn slept, I got up to take a run on the beach. In front of a full-length bamboo mirror with fish netting surrounding its edges, I noticed the small paunch sitting over my black boxers. *Where is that young kid in a toga, I wondered? And the college stud, where'd he go? He's been replaced by a near middle-aged man on too many prescriptions with two kids and a big mortgage*, the mirror seemed to answer back with ugly malice.

I pulled on tan and blue board shorts and sucked in my gut to draw the string tighter as if I had a girdle on. Out of my bag, I found a ratty Steve Miller Band tee-shirt I picked up in college and threw on my frayed Army cap to complete the "I'm on vacation and don't give a shit how I look" attire. I walked across Beach Avenue and climbed over the dunes to the beach, taking my time, enjoying the feel of the pearly white sand that—unlike other beaches—was soft to the touch.

Pushed forward by an inner sense that the sea is a safe place to think about where I had been in my life and where I hoped to go, I at first pounded the sand hard, scaring the sandpipers along the surf. And then slowed up to a jog, luxuriating in the aches of my thighs and calves, a reminder of being alive and well.

While this Jersey Shore kid involuntarily left for Pennsylvania as a teenager with one of the many moves ordered by Joe and Annie, the ocean had never left me. In such a wild dash focused almost madly on succeeding, time for me and my needs was never a consideration. Something had triggered this drive and the loneliness I experienced. Although happily married and full of love for my family, I had let no one completely into my inner soul. Even Carolyn knew she had a tough time penetrating what made me tick.

The events of my youth had formed my essence—an overachiever and a loner (common traits for adult children of alcoholics), in a stressful profession that can chew up any person. I fought to maintain my integrity. To be the man I thought God and Big Joe wanted me to be. I had a terrific wife and two sons to carry on the Curran name, hugely significant to my ancestors, and to me.

Supporting my family as a good provider remained more important than anything else. Carolyn and I wanted the boys to attend Christian school to honor the Lord. I trusted God that He would provide as He always had since that day Annie walked out and I stood on my own. The Lord had never failed me.

Governor Collins would likely be re-elected. That was the tradition in Pennsylvania for incumbents, but he'd be finished after that because of term limits. I didn't want to return to lobbying. That experience did not fit my character and temperament. Tony was still a relatively young man (in his late forties at the time) and I had to be focused on putting food on the table in a profession where at one moment you stood on top, the next unemployment and shame. Through no fault of your own, other than a bad election cycle.

"To the victor go the spoils," I barked out. A passing female jogger gave me a weird stare. I named her "Bambi." Bambi looked like she came from Staten Island with a bad spray tan of burnt orange, instead of copper brown. With big frizzy hair that most women left behind in the eighties—a decade when fashion and taste didn't warrant an afterthought—Bambi's tight purple leotards did not flatter her. A sackcloth would've been more proper. Bambi probably thought I wasn't much of a prize in burgeoning board shorts, holy shirt, and Army cap tilted backward on my head. Sweating like a pig, I'm sure I didn't smell good to her either.

A jetty of massive rocks jutting out into the sea looked inviting. I slowed down to walk out, the green moss slimy on my bare feet. The mist of the ocean against my face as the waves battered the boulders and beach—in a cycle that in the end, the sea will win—I decided that I wanted to return to the Senate, to work for Molinaro. I liked leading a team in a common goal of serving a public servant as he or she served his or her constituency. Even though I had significant responsibilities with the governor, I worked as only a junior guy and missed the direct link I had previously as a chief of staff to Senator Weigel.

The shore loomed large as the only special place for me to think through where I wanted to go and who I wanted to be as a man and as a professional. *Back in the Senate would be much more fulfilling,* I concluded. To celebrate my decision, I shucked off my shirt and cap and dove off the jetty into the surf and swam out to the breakers. As a kid, I was a pretty good body surfer but my exuberance at that moment clouded my judgment. I mistimed the wave's crest and tumbled about until I hit the beach hard.

After sheepishly collecting my clothes and looking around to make sure Bambi hadn't seen my crappy athleticism, I slowly returned to Rob's place. Keeping a sharp eye out for Carolyn's favorite thing to collect, I found several pieces of amber and magnesium blue sea glass, lapping away in the ocean wash. A rare find, smooth from tumbling around in the surf for who knows how long, I liked the feel of the glass, a reminder that the sea can tame anything man makes.

When I returned from my run, I handed these treasures from the deep to Carolyn and my wife beamed with joy. I told her of my epiphany during the trip out onto the rocks. Without hesitation, she said, "I support you, Jack, if this is what you actually want." It is, I answered.

The kids wanted to go to an amusement park Carolyn found in another brochure. "Hartman's Entertainment" promised, via a simple advertisement "Family fun or we'll refund your money." Driving south on Long Beach Boulevard, we passed quaint "shotgun" cottages, two-story bungalows, Dutch Colonials, and blocks and blocks of Cape Cod houses, varying only in color or additions homeowners constructed. Many of these homes sadly have been demolished and replaced by huge monstrosities that scream out "nouveau riche." Bar after bar appealed to a younger crowd, including Sylvester's, with a sign that trumpeted "SYLVESTER'S—WHERE DRAFTS ARE A BUCK DURING HAPPY HOUR."

Locating Hartman's, I had to park the car about a mile away since everyone apparently wanted to take their kids to the park that day. Robert's little legs couldn't keep up with the pace, so I hoisted him up onto my broad shoulders. Jack registered his complaints about the lack of equal treatment. F. Lee Bailey would've been proud of our oldest son's persuasive abilities. In the heat and humidity, I bitched about not being on the beach. The grounding force in my life said, "Stop it, Jackie. We're doing this for the kids."

A tall blue and white slide anchored the park, and we watched adults and children in brown burlap bags glide down the smooth ruts. A fat guy got stuck in the middle, requiring a beanpole of a teenager to shimmy on up as he strained to push on the big man's back despite gravity being in favor of the effort. Callously, I pointed to him and laughed; joined by Carolyn, who normally wouldn't let me poke fun at someone else.

Jack and Robert wanted to go on flying helicopters that rose thirty feet in the air and dropped suddenly with the height and speed of decline governed by a chrome bar each rider manipulated. My fear of heights never left me. The memory of falling off the Army rappelling tower during training a vivid reminder of why it is always best to stay planted firmly on the ground.

"How 'bout those boats, boys, instead?" I asked with over-the-top enthusiasm. I remember throwing in the super-size blue cotton candy as an inducement. These vessels remained safely in a concrete basin in a circle of water only eighteen inches deep. We want the flying things they yelled back; said with far more fervor than I could ever muster for the boring little ships whose only exciting features were little bells rung with a small pull string. Dad lost that debate. After leaving the copter ride, Carolyn made me drink a Diet Coke, hoping it would restore some color back to my face.

My complexion turned ruddy when we rented a small Sunfish after Rob's neighbor offered to babysit the kids for a few hours. Rob assured us this kind, old lady, who raised four of her own children, would take good care of our precious ones. As a young lad, I had taken sailing lessons and maneuvered the little boat around the bay. I first tacked into the wind, so we could enjoy the return ride when the breeze blew at our back.

Going about, I forgot to tell Carolyn to duck, and the light boom hit the side of her head. After making sure she was all right, I said, "That's for smacking me during labor." She whacked me again with a chortle I cherished; Carolyn needed this vacation as much as I did.

After several more days on the beach and taking the kids crabbing over on the Barnegat Bay, my wife was the only one brave enough to dump the clawed beasts we caught into the boiling water. Too chicken to watch those sad, bulging eyes extinguish, I still enjoyed the crab meat we carefully picked out and ate.

After this feast, we sadly packed up to head home. We fell in love with Long Beach Island and Rob's house. Not ostentatious at all and decorated with seashore colors, it was designed to be comfortable with pine crate furniture and white shabby chic complementary accent pieces.

I applauded Rob's success. He'd paid the price for this affluence though. Failure in marriage and drinking probably more than he should since much of his profession's work and the relationships he formed and maintained were around the bars of Harrisburg and Washington, D.C. I had consciously rejected that life back when we started as interns and reaffirmed that rejection after working for a brief period lobbying for the architects. I would continue doing things on my own terms, avoiding the temptations that come with those places.

On the way off the bridge to the mainland, I told Carolyn, "We will have our own place someday, count on it." And I meant it. Years later, after we were financially secure, we found one of those little shotgun shacks, falling in love with its vaulted ceiling, cedar planking, and dark pine floors. In a town right out of scenes from the 1950s, we hit the jackpot, finding a house by the bay. But that stood in our future, and the present required me to react to Molinaro's offer.

The next day home, I reached Tony in his law office and agreed to be his campaign manager and chief of staff if we were successful. I would have to give less than a month's notice to the governor. I felt terrible about that. It was August, and in a little over three weeks, the party would meet to nominate Tony to be the GOP's standard-bearer to replace Senator Weigel. And then the fall campaign would begin. But I had one ask of Representative Molinaro.

"Tony, you've got to give up your calendar. I can't manage your campaign and the office with you keeping your own schedule. It's awkward and inefficient. We'll bog down when we need to be chugging along." I had broached a sensitive topic. Unlike many officeholders, he kept his calendar, something that Jim Weigel had not done even back while running the auto dealerships.

"That's asking way too much. I like the control that comes with saying yes or no to what I do each day. Why can't we continue to work that way?" Tony held fast, and if I had been in his position, I suppose I'd have done that, too.

"That won't work. The Senate district is much bigger than your House district. Between the campaign, your House duties until you're elected and sworn in, and the law office since you're going to continue to practice, it will be too cumbersome. We'll never keep up with all the invites that pour in. How 'bout if Colleen maintains your calendar?" Colleen, his long-time trusted secretary at the law office, was capable and could handle the schedule. I could reach her easier than if I had to run everything by Molinaro. I hoped Tony would go for this compromise.

"Okay...I guess we'll try this with Colleen holding the calendar," he said. "If I feel like I'm losing my independence, Jack, I take it back." The reluctance dripped out of him, but I appreciated the willingness to compromise.

"Absolutely, Tony. Nothing goes on that you might not care for. If something is questionable, either Colleen or I run it by you. And we'll keep blocks of time to think, I know that's important, too. We won't overschedule you, I promise." Gloria and I had done an excellent job managing Jim's time. I was confident Colleen and I would do the same for Molinaro. Proper and efficient time management is more critical than almost any other element in a political office.

FORTY-THREE

Whatever Jack, Returning to the Arena

WITH GREAT TREPIDATION, I knocked on the door to Joan's office in the Capitol Building. Because I'd interrupted her morning routine of a bagel and café expresso, she appeared annoyed. "Hi, uh, Joan, do you have a minute to talk?"

"I guess my breakfast can wait, Jack." The breakfast tray was pushed away. "Okay, how was your vacation? Your family went to the shore, right?"

"Yeah, Rob Placid gave us his beach house to use for a few days. Very relaxing time." Joan made a face when I mentioned Placid. She didn't care for him, but that wasn't on the agenda for today.

"Oh, how nice he has a place at the shore," she said. "Why am I not surprised? Rob Placid's become quite the lobbyist here in town. I realize he's a friend, so I won't say anything more. What's up?"

"Well, I have something difficult to tell you."

"You're not leaving, are you?"

Here goes. This exit felt almost as enjoyable as the preparation I'd gone through for a colonoscopy since I'd suffered from abdominal issues that the doctors attributed to stress. "Yes, I am. Tony Molinaro's running for Jim Weigel's seat. He's asked me to manage his campaign and become his chief of staff if he wins." I tried to maintain eye contact with Joan while I said this.

"Aren't you happy working for the governor and me? Certainly, we like having you on the team. Tony Molinaro? He's a hothead." The representative had that reputation. But, so did I. Surprised at Joan's reaction to Tony, he was, after all, a close ally of the governor's—time after time demonstrating his loyalty to Collins.

"Joan, I like staffing you and Governor Collins, I really do. But I understand this district. The party's got to keep Weigel's seat." I hoped the reference to GOP loyalty would mean something. It didn't.

"This isn't a good career move. You've been with us for less than a year and going back to the Senate will be viewed poorly, count on that." Joan had a vast network of friends she could influence, and she was taking this personally when she shouldn't have.

"I appreciate everything you've done for me. Being Tony's chief of staff just seems right. Think about what Tony and I can do for Governor Collins in the Senate. The administration has few close allies over there. This is a positive." I meant what I said to her and hoped she recognized my sincerity. We could be of great help in the upper chamber, particularly on education reform, where the governor most needed aid since the chairman of the committee remained somewhat hostile to the governor's agenda.

"Effectiveness is a question of degree. Comparing the Senate with the highest office in Pennsylvania is ridiculous," she lectured me. "I won't beg or grovel. I'll let the chief of staff and Governor Collins know you're abandoning us. They'll be disappointed."

"One more thing, Joan." Now it seemed like the damn hernia exam we were forced to endure for high school sports. All of us athletes lined up only in our tighty-whities. The gross, old doctor with bad breath the school district used—probably a relative of a board member—executed these very invasive manipulations of our balls with a little too much interest when he ordered each victim to, "Drop your drawers and cough." But back to the departure that wasn't going well.

"Sorry for the short notice, but Tony's campaign will be launching hard after Labor Day. I'll need to leave in two weeks."

"Whatever, Jack," she said. The ultimate kiss-off. "Hope this works out for you. Have a nice day." She dismissed me by returning to her now cold coffee and breakfast.

The relationship would never be the same after that nor would it be the same with a few other staffers I thought were my friends. They viewed me as a traitor and used some of the same lines that Joan did: "Molinaro has a temper. Molinaro's too ambitious for his own good."

Ironically, the same charges were leveled at me. No turning back from this move, however, and I'd be less than honest if I didn't disclose that when we got to the Senate, I had an attitude about the administration and carried a grudge for the way they reacted. That bitterness would cause me to sit sometimes on my hands when they or the governor needed help. One of my many faults is having a memory like an elephant.

To spare campaign funds since Tony's coffers were not exactly overflowing, I set up an office at home, using the den in our old Victorian house for the unofficial Molinaro headquarters. I'd plan and execute the effort from there when I wasn't at Tony's law office or Republican State Committee headquarters in Harrisburg. The party and caucus had a keen interest in keeping Weigel's seat for the GOP, and we were the only important race that election cycle, except for the municipal and county races occurring across the Commonwealth.

With only twelve weeks until Election Day, I dug in with all my energy, experience, and enthusiasm, and wrote a detailed memo to the representative on how I intended to organize and carry out his campaign. The Curran plan addressed fundraising. He had less than fifteen thousand dollars in his fund. I expected we would need over a hundred thousand to have a positive impact and to scare off a challenger in 1996 when Tony would have to turn around and run again for a full four-year term. The memo also included door-to-door outreach, yard signs, advertising, and poll watcher coverage.

After receiving the suggestions, Tony called me to the law office. "Jack, I won't micromanage you. It's not my style since I have a lot of confidence in you. The plan is good, but I have two reactions. Add door knocking in York City. I've never represented the city before and need to get familiar with the people and leaders there."

I protested. "There aren't too many Republicans in York. I live there. As popular as Jim was, we never cracked twenty percent in any of his elections."

"I know that," Tony said with a touch of frustration. "I'm not as concerned about the vote out of the city as I am convincing people I understand I'm not just a guy from the suburbs any longer. York is the hub of the region. Some community leaders and big money people are wary of me as a suburban House member. We need to allay those fears." The light bulb went off with his explanation. There were powerful community and business advocates highly loyal to the city that Tony needed to get acquainted with. I knew them from my work with Weigel, but his name would be on the ballot, not mine.

"Sure, I understand now. I'll add areas in York, and I'll plan on joining for as much of the door-to-door as possible."

"Great. Last thing. Representative Henrietta Hoover is a close ally. She and I came into the House together in the Class of '80." *Uh-oh, like a bad penny, she keeps coming back into my life.* "Hoover's the leader of the conservative caucus in the House and can be helpful with right-wing groups that might want to give money to the campaign. Make an appointment with her, brief her, make her feel ownership. You're to keep her updated at least weekly after that." *Oh crap, I said to myself. It must be a face-to-face and would be ongoing.*

"She and I don't enjoy a good relationship, Tony. When I lobbied for Architects United, she took an intense disliking to me. Maybe you should do this one yourself." I didn't try to avoid work for the sake of avoiding it, but I also didn't want to hurt Molinaro with a conservative ally. Even though, ironically, Henrietta and I agreed with each other on almost every issue. I just didn't agree with her entirely unyielding way of approaching the legislative process. "Compromise" was always a dirty word to her.

"No, Jack. Do this yourself. Henrietta will be fine. As a House member myself, the number one rule will be we treat House members with respect. There are too many House members who leave for the Senate but forget where they came from. It must be that rarefied air over in the Senate." Good that Tony wasn't going to forget where he came from. But did it have to be *Hoover* as the first use of the Molinaro Doctrine?

"Okay," I said reluctantly. "I'll do the best I can with her and will share this memo with the senior staff in the caucus and with the state committee, so they're aware of the general game plan, all right?"

"Sure. I've talked with several of the leaders already. The pro tem called last week, and they'll fully support us. They seem to be very excited I'm running." Thinking to myself, *I'm sure they are.* Leadership never forgave Jim Weigel when he voted against their direction on the procedural motions during the tax reform fight back in the eighties. That was in the past, and I tried to approach the leaders and my former staff colleagues with a clean slate.

"Here's a list of suggested calls for fundraising, boss, and suggested amounts for the 'ask.' That will need to be one of the priorities. We must get early money in to ward off the Democrats as much as we can and pay bills for start-up." Tony grimaced when I handed him the list. One of the tougher aspects of being a candidate is asking for dollars, even though most politically active, big money givers expect to get these "asks."

"I'll do it, but I hate these calls. They're demeaning and cheap."

"Understood. They're a pain in the ass, but you've got to do them. Just have Colleen track commitments, and I'll ask her to keep me informed. See you soon, boss." Back in the role of working directly with an elected official felt good. I missed the relationship more than I realized at the time.

Returning to my home office, I had a message to call Gloria. She'd remained to staff the senatorial office on a skeleton basis until Jim Weigel's successor took office. I called her back and could hear the sadness in her voice. Gloria and the senator had worked together for so long, and she had been his trusted assistant in building a multi-million-dollar enterprise and then as a successful state senator.

"Hi, Jack. Have news."

"How're you holding up, Gloria? How're Jim and Diane doing?" I owed my former boss a visit and vowed to myself to stay in close touch to keep Jim connected to the local and Harrisburg news. Everything was moving much too fast.

"As good as can be expected. Jim's driving Diane crazy. He still compiles lists of things to do." *Some old habits die hard*, I thought. "I'm doing okay, too. It's quiet in here and in the skeleton district office. Going to file my retirement papers in the fall. It's time. There's no more joy in doing this job, not without Jim…"

"I'm really sorry. I know this is a tough time. Glad you can retire to peace and relaxation. You deserve to be happy." Like a big sister, I loved this extraordinary woman.

"Information for you I picked up here in the Senate. Bruce Bauer is on unpaid leave to oversee the special election for our district." Not good news at all. I didn't need this guy looking over my shoulder.

"You're kidding, right? Is this from a good source?" What a dumb question since Gloria's information was always golden.

Annoyed, she answered, "Of course. Confirm it with Rob. I'm sure he heard it, too."

"Well, shit, at least it's only a short cycle. I'll do my best to avoid Bruce and his Monday-morning quarterbacking."

"You know this district better than just about anyone. Just keep driving forward as I'm sure you will."

After we said goodbye, I faxed copies of the campaign plan to the state committee and the Senate Republican Campaign Committee. Keeping the leaders and senior staff apprised of our general plans was important. I left a message for Henrietta Hoover to call me back, requesting a meeting at state committee so I could brief her on the election contest.

After several days of ordering yard signs, talking with party people about the nominating convention, and tending to many other details (after Labor Day would be a sprint to November's election), I had a message from Bruce Bauer to call him at state committee. Here we go. Shades of the first meeting in his office so long ago when he put me in short pants over tax reform.

After he answered his phone, there were no pleasantries exchanged. In his most officious voice, he began, "Jack, I'm the liaison for your campaign with the leaders. They can't afford to lose this seat, so you will report to me daily. Now... let's start with this so-called plan you *attempted* to write."

"Hold on, Bruce, I don't report to you. I work for Tony Molinaro in this campaign. Let's get that straight right now."

"If Tony wants money from our campaign committee you'll do what I tell you, clear?" the only game going that fall, he was bluffing. Both of us realized they had to keep this seat heading into the '96 cycle when the GOP would have several vulnerable incumbents to defend.

"Crystal. Couldn't be more certain of anything. Let me call Tony and tell him you're hijacking *his* campaign from Harrisburg. Notice how I emphasized his campaign, threatening to withhold funds. I'm sure he'll be on the phone to the leaders right away. Good day, Bruce." I began hanging up and heard his screeching retort.

"Wait, Jack, you don't have to lose your temper over this. Just keep me informed of what you're doing, and that'll be enough." Bruce folded like a cheap tent as I knew he would.

"Fine. What else do you want?" I wanted him to squirm now that I had the upper hand.

"We think going door-to-door in York City is a waste of time." Use of the royal, "We," he didn't clarify exactly who else he represented. "In analyzing Weigel's returns there, he did poorly in the city. Tony needs to expend more efforts in the suburbs and rural areas that he hasn't represented in the House." *Why didn't I think of that?*

"Made the same arguments. That was Tony's add. There are leaders down here that care deeply about the city. Tony must prove to them he understands York is key to this district. He also needs to understand what the issues of concern are to people living in York. Sorry...we're not negotiating over this item."

"Well, waste of time. Make sure you have plenty of door knocking elsewhere, got it?"

"We know the district. How about you and the leaders raise money and leave the local stuff to us, okay? Bye, Bruce." I slammed the phone down on its cradle and threw my stapler against our wood floor, causing Carolyn to come into the den to ask me if I was all right. Nothing but extreme frustration due to Harrisburg micromanagement, I replied.

Gloria's advice would stay foremost in my mind: just keep driving forward and make Bauer and others play catch-up.

FORTY-FOUR

Curran the Leftist, Nominating
Convention, Anna Christianson

THE REPUBLICAN STATE COMMITTEE's headquarters, located on
State Street, is a stone's throw from the Capitol Building. As I walked
up to the three-story office, I said a little prayer for patience before I
met with Representative Henrietta Hoover and Alexandre Brest to discuss the race.

Brest and I knew each other from encounters at different functions
where I'd represented Senator Weigel. Well-known in Harrisburg, he
was a self-appointed conservative leader. Authoring many articles and
appearing on talk radio, Brest also attended lots of events where conservatives congregate and talk among themselves—but not with too many
other people outside their immediate ideological orbit.

Hoover and Brest were waiting in a conference room. With as much
charm as I could muster, I beamed and extended my hand, "So happy
to see you, Representative, Alexandre." With bushy black hair, bulging
brown eyes, and a thick mustache that curled up at the edges, his stache
reminded me of Rollie Fingers, the great reliever and Hall of Famer.
Proud of his French heritage (his middle name of "Destin" only added

to his total essence as a Francophile), Alexandre sometimes wore a gray beret and mixed in French words into his conversations. One had to stifle a laugh with the unlikely pair of Henrietta with her curly hair and Alexandre with his jaunty beret.

Brest shook my hand, and his handshake lacked strength and purpose. Something Big Joe always emphasized—a man needs to shake hands like he means it. Henrietta didn't bother with any formalities. I remained a pariah to her. We worked from the campaign plan I'd sent them, and I opened the meeting with an invitation to questions and a desire to have their input into the election contest.

Hoover launched right in. "There's nothing in here on the themes Tony plans on emphasizing in his Senate run, why not? Is he moving to the left now that he has a big city in his district?" Henrietta asked. *York, a big city? Your job isn't to argue with her, Jack. Stay calm.*

"No, Representative, he'll talk about the things he's always stood for since election to the House fifteen years ago when you both were elected, issues I know you care about, too. Free enterprise, limited government, lower taxes, law and order, and now educational choice. Nothing has changed other than his desire to knock on doors in York to meet city residents. We believed this to be understood. This plan is more about the elements of the campaign rather than the themes. But I will add this and appreciate the good suggestion." Putting my lips on Henrietta's substantial ass as much as it pained me wasn't beyond the realm if that meant helping Molinaro.

"Fine. What about abortion? Tony and I've never agreed on this. What's he going to say? You agree with him, too, don't you, Curran?" *I'm on trial now for my conservative credentials.* I took a deep breath and mentally counted to ten. *Don't lose it, Jack.*

"No, actually I don't, Henrietta. I'm very much pro-life. The representative understands that. Just once, could you please use my first name? It's Jack, by the way."

With a sour face, she snapped, "Could've fooled me about your abortion position. I thought you were a leftist or socialist, and I didn't say you could call me Henrietta? I'm your elder...show me respect if your mother even taught that. And I'll call you whatever I want to." *Look at that bucolic watercolor painting on the wall. Cows are grazing by a stream, hot air balloons and billowing clouds are floating serenely, a farmer is operating his old red tractor—all untouched by city life. The moon is visible during daylight.* The artist's rendering was my escape from Henrietta hell and her assault on Annie—who I dearly wanted to defend from this old crank.

With her arthritic, crooked fingers in my personal space, she snapped them incessantly, "What're you staring at, Curran? Pay attention to me!" Hoover brought me out of my trance of self-imposed exile.

I couldn't help the deep sigh she invoked. "Representative, I've been a conservative all my life from when I learned about politics in Reagan's first election in 1980 and my parents were Goldwater voters if that means anything to you. Unlike you, I've always been a Republican. President Reagan inspired me into public service. What I stand for doesn't matter, okay? We're here to talk about Tony Molinaro, not his chief of staff."

Hoover began to retort especially since I'd hit a raw nerve alluding to how she originally had been a Democrat, but Alexandre interrupted. "Jack, I have to agree with my *cher ami*, Henrietta," he said with a flourish. *Oh, it's all right they're on a first-name basis, and she warrants "dear friend" in French*, I said to my snarky self. "It's a shame Tony's not pro-life. Raising money statewide would be so much easier if he championed the unborn." Henrietta nodded her head in agreement with such vigor I thought her creaky ole noggin would fall off.

"Tony's record is well-known," I began. "Especially since he's been the policy chair for the caucus for years now. Representative Molinaro's comfortable with the current restrictions on abortion in Pennsylvania law, believing the matter is settled. He will not lead any effort to overturn those regulations. If he had a different stance, I wouldn't be a staffer for him. That's all I can say."

"That helps, Jack. *Merci.* If Tony would write me a letter on what he stands for, I'll circulate that to my conservative network. It might elicit financial contributions to him." I thanked Alexandre for his support and promised that correspondence.

The gathering had been largely a success. I hadn't gotten cross with Hoover. Other than my dig at her original party roots, I'd respected her as a powerful woman on the Harrisburg scene. Unless you were a member of the right-wing caucus or a conservative outsider like Brest, who believed she could do no wrong, connecting with Henrietta was never easy.

On the return to York, my thoughts were on the nominating convention as our number one focus. Discussions continued among a small group of Molinaro and Weigel supporters we convened to make sure Tony had the votes. And there would be no surprise nominations. We wanted this event to be a coronation of Tony as the sole heir to Jim Weigel. The goal: to use the assembly to propel Molinaro through to victory in November.

Tony and I met in his law office and I reported on my conference with Henrietta and Brest. We discussed such details as who would nominate him at the convention, and checked, and rechecked the vote totals.

The big question mark remained what the city chairman, Harry Cline, would do? An old disciple of George Dimple, who had long since left the York political scene after Molinaro beat him when he first ran for the House, the few remaining Dimple associates, including Harry, never forgave Tony for taking on the old man as publicly as he did back then. Once Dimple lost power, his followers did, too. That meant government jobs, contracts, and the spoils of politics were no longer available.

Weak and ineffective, the city committee comprised more "paper" GOP people than anything else. Convinced to run for the position (usually unopposed), these folks signed over their proxies so that Chairman Cline might vote these at any countywide gathering, giving him the *illusion* of power. With Harry controlling so many votes, we had apprehension he might nominate someone just to embarrass Molinaro, even though we remained confident we had the nomination locked.

After thorough discussion, we used an emissary to approach Harry. A retired judge, who maintained a decent relationship with Cline, made contact. The judge reported back that the city boss realized Tony had the votes and knew it would be unwise to challenge Molinaro at such a public gathering. That allowed us to breathe a sigh of relief as the big day came.

Held in a suburban high school, the nominating convention consisted of committee people living in the Eighth Senatorial District. If they couldn't attend, they could sign a proxy. Any Republican living in their precinct could take part and vote on their behalf. Non-committee people could observe the process, so I floated around to ensure everything was in good order. At the entrance, a huge banner that read "Molinaro for Senate, A Strong Voice for York County" welcomed delegates.

We had yard signs, brochures, and buttons available and volunteers recruited to hand out these items. Tony circulated, greeting people with a broad smile. I had called Diane Weigel and asked if Jim would be up to attending the convention. He was. Honored to transport him to the event, I did my best to catch up the senator on Harrisburg news. I handed Jim a large Molinaro button that he put on his suit lapel as a demonstration of support for Tony. The clearest way yet we could assure the Weigel camp it was okay to be for Molinaro.

A Republican gathering like this at the local level is truly a sight to behold. As a long-time people watcher, I saw teachers, realtors, homemakers, small business owners, truck drivers, landscapers, courthouse officials and their employees (one of the few places of actual patronage left), nurses, bartenders, and retirees. Indeed many walks of life were represented. Unfortunately, the party of Lincoln still struggled to recruit minorities to run for local committee positions. We were a rather white gathering as a result.

The role didn't have the allure it once had with the advent of the civil service system. Government jobs were not as plentiful nor were committee people paid "street money" any longer. In the old days, the GOP had plenty of funds. Each committee person was compensated for working his or her precinct, particularly on Election Day. Strictly a volunteer position; now one of the few perks available included free attendance at party fundraisers and picnics.

I spotted one committee woman wearing every pin and button possible across her front and on the large straw hat she wore. She had buttons dating back to Richard Nixon and Ronald Reagan displayed. With the Molinaro button now part of the collection, this committee woman became a living, walking billboard among the crowd. Later, she would go on to serve as a state House member, rewarded for faithful service to the party over many years of attending these types of events and working her polling place for Republican candidates. Kostantin Pokornin sneaked around as he sniffed out gossip to write about for the *York Tribune* and its sister paper, the *Harrisburg World*.

Friendly to us, the county chairman wanted the event to go as smoothly as possible. After the several hundred folks in attendance said the Pledge of Allegiance and sang the National Anthem, he recognized Senator Weigel for his service. The senator stood and smiled, and the crowd applauded with a standing ovation. Seeing my old boss rewarded in this way brought tears to my eyes.

A cross section of individuals from the district nominated Tony for state Senate. We had prepared and distributed each speech—leaving nothing to chance. Nominations closed and voting began. Almost unanimously, the convention voted for Tony. A few negative ballots cast probably came from what remained of the Dimple faction. My new boss rose to give his acceptance remarks, magnanimous in thanking Senator Weigel for his accomplishments. I paused a moment to savor how well the day had gone without a glitch. In politics, one never wants surprises, and we had none.

Our attention turned immediately to defeating the Democratic opponent—a retired school teacher from Molinaro's House district. Anna Christianson, an elementary educator for many years, had been active in the union: Teachers for Fairness. From a local union steward, eventually, Christianson rose to serve on their statewide board until she later stepped down from an active role in the association's politics. She and Molinaro were friendly for years. Christianson's family had always displayed his yard sign in front of their home.

That changed when Tony voted for the governor's voucher plan. Anna became a vocal enemy, writing letters to the editor and organizing phone calls to Tony's district and Capitol offices. Representative Molinaro tried, to no avail, to explain his reasons for supporting Governor Collins.

But Christianson wouldn't budge. As a suburban school teacher, who had never taught in the city district, Anna refused to accept his logic for vouchers, especially in poorly performing urban school districts. Her community routinely topped the charts for student achievement test scores in York County. As a result, Christianson wasn't exactly in touch with the state of education in the York City School District. Anna would have resources from the union's PAC and the Senate Democrats would at least give her seed money to make the race somewhat competitive even though the GOP had the advantages of greater registration and voting patterns.

Almost at once, we knocked on doors. While Tony had great visibility in the news media, there were plenty of areas in the larger Senate district where he wasn't well-known besides the city. I refused to delegate door-to-door organization since I prided myself on knowing York County's various neighborhoods. Tony and I would canvass during the week with a larger group of volunteers joining us on the weekends, so we'd cover more territory.

One weeknight, Tony and I walked neighborhoods for two hours. After finishing, he learned it was my wedding anniversary. Another family commitment missed because of a lack of perspective about work. Few people realize that Molinaro is a sentimental man. After he discovered the missed milestone, Tony sent a card and penned a lovely note to Carolyn, something she treasured receiving.

On one occasion, we met in a large suburban development of upper-middle-class voters and seniors. A gated community, I finagled permission to work that neighborhood. We needed this bloc of the electorate to get out and vote. Tony and I dove in. I knocked on a door with Molinaro across the street. Our pattern: I would point to him, so the citizen would know Tony was in the neighborhood. If the voter wanted to speak with the representative, he'd finish up his conversation and join me.

But we didn't get that far before Molinaro spoke with a lovely older woman. The representative went into his standard pitch. "I'm Tony Molinaro running for the Eighth Senatorial District. I'd appreciate your vote and would be glad to talk about any concerns you may have."

The lady smiled in return. "I know who you are. I've seen you on the six o'clock news. Harold and I would love to support you but can't."

Tony had a perplexed look on his face. "Why not?" he asked.

"We live in Adams County, not York. Didn't you know the development straddles county lines? Two blocks over you left your district. Senator Tillingsworth represents us. Good man, by the way."

"He is, ma'am. Well, you have a nice day. Sorry to have bothered you." Tony walked across the street to meet me on the sidewalk before I proceeded to my next house. "Jack, you have us in the wrong district. Let's go back to York County." Pissed, he hated wasting time, a trait developed during law school and a successful legal practice that followed before he ran for elective office.

"I'm so sorry, boss. Thought this development went to the county line. Won't happen again."

The rest of the campaign would be a sprint to the finish and I'm happy to report there were no other snafus. As a perfectionist, I beat myself up anytime I made a mistake.

FORTY-FIVE

Election Night, Senator Anthony Edward Molinaro, Flaunting Her Legs

"THE FIRST RETURNS are coming in, Jack. Tony's getting slaughtered by Christianson," one of our young volunteers came rushing in out of breath. We were in the home of Molinaro's closest supporter—with him since the very beginning of his political career. Stationed all over the district, our poll watchers had orders to report their totals as soon as their polling places had tabulated results.

"Thanks, Chris, let me look." Tony sat over in the corner of the living room in a large oak rocking chair with a scotch in hand, relaxing because he knew I'd sweat the details.

The returns came from the city which reported its results earlier than the suburban and rural areas. Despite intensive canvassing and Tony's attendance at many community events, it appeared that Molinaro would mirror Jim Weigel's numbers at around twenty percent of the vote in York City. Admittedly, a disappointment. But not unexpected for a GOP candidate running in an urban area in the late twentieth century.

"Only York so far, we're okay," I said to assure everyone, and, frankly, myself. A bundle of nerves, I wouldn't rest easy until victory was assured.

Our hostess came by to refill my scotch and water, the fourth time she or her sister had done so. "Sit down, Jack, and loosen up, see how Tony does it," Betsy said with a deep, raspy voice. A chain smoker, she organized volunteers and precincts better than anyone. I understood why Molinaro relied on her so much.

"I'll take another drink after everything comes in, Betsy. Tonight is our first election together. I gotta pace around, just my nature. If I didn't have asthma, I'd probably ask you for a cigarette to help calm me down."

"Well, we'll keep your drink fresh. Now that the election's over, I told Tony I wasn't sure about you because you were Jim Weigel's man and everything and I advised Tony not to trust you because of that. For years, it pissed me off that Senator Weigel beat Tony the first go-round. It worked out, didn't it, Tony?"

"Seems so, Betsy," he said as he gently rocked in the chair, dog-tired after working hard in the election, while maintaining his responsibilities in the House.

A pay raise vote happened in the fall, always unpopular with the electorate. House leadership gave Molinaro a pass, and his peers griped because of it. As a member of leadership himself, Tony had to put up tough votes. Salary hikes ranked at the top of that list. Senate leadership convinced their fellow leaders in the House, however, that the GOP had to keep the seat to maintain its majority in the Senate.

Tony voted "no" only weeks before the election. We didn't talk about this subject. These compensation votes are deeply personal things, only for discussion among the members, much as leadership votes are when legislators caucus to decide upon their leaders each session.

"I still disagree with what you did on the tax delinquency issue, Jack," Betsy said. Even on election night, she wouldn't let it go. Being the top staff dog made you subject to almost constant second-guessing.

"As you said, everything worked out, Betsy. Couldn't have done this without you." As the campaign manager, I was already looking ahead to the next fight. Keeping Betsy happy remained important. Our opponent had been delinquent on some taxes. The information came to us and I refused to leak it from our campaign. It came out on its own, however. As the front runner, I just didn't see the need for the Molinaro campaign to dirty our hands. If our polls had showed otherwise, that would have been a different question and I would've justified the decision to my conscience that the voters deserved to have this information before voting in a Senate contest.

My cell phone buzzed from one of our volunteers from the city. He had stopped by several polls to get results for us, and his news disturbed me. "Jack, you're not going to like this. I found sample ballots with our race and Tony's name sliced off the bottom. In a city alley, a big trash barrel full of them." An old trick to depress votes from loyal party voters that followed the sample ballot religiously, it appeared to be evidence of a dirty deed as voters discarded the ballots at each polling place. I believed it to be the work of what remained of the George Dimple faction of the party. They couldn't get even at the nominating convention, so they tried to sabotage Molinaro's numbers in York.

"Those lousy sonofabitches." Said too loudly, the representative glanced up with a quizzical look. "Nothing I can't handle, boss," I assured him. Betsy and I would confer with a few of our most influential people and figure out how we'd respond to this foul tactic. At the very least, the Dimple group would be frozen out from access and meetings with Tony and our network. Or we'd put up folks to run against them in the committee races next spring with the goal of putting loyal people in place. A slight like this couldn't be ignored.

But we couldn't be too harsh with another election around the corner. For sure, it was a balancing act to punish without prompting a primary from Dimple's remaining followers. The next batch of returns came in. We'd pulled even with Christianson. Some suburban areas offset Anna's lead in the city, causing me to forget about the sample ballot. For the time being.

Carolyn's parents thankfully watched the boys, so she might join me. She gave me a "good luck" kiss and a squeeze of my hand to convey her pride in me. Working from my home office the last twelve weeks had been a blessing. I took little breaks to be with her and the kids. "Slow down on the drinks, Jackie," Carolyn whispered in my ear. She knew I didn't drink other than socially and must've smelled the many scotches on my breath.

"Honey, Betsy's filling 'em. She and her sister must've bet on how quickly they can get me drunk."

At that point, more numbers came in. The rural areas were going seventy-to-eighty percent for Tony. He'd pulled ahead with victory assured. Walking over to him, I extended my hand, wanting to be the first to wish him well with his new title. "Congratulations, Senator."

We shook hands and the senator-elect responded with a pat on my shoulder and praise, something very rare. "Good job, Jack. Now the real work begins."

A flurry of calls came in from Senate leadership, House members, and other political figures around the state. All conveying their best wishes. To her credit, Anna Christianson phoned to concede the election. Checking my cell phone, I had missed several messages from Bruce Bauer, demanding returns. I was glad to ignore him.

The York Tribune also called with a request to send a reporter and photographer over to the house to interview and snap pictures. I said, sure, come on over. We couldn't afford to rest on our laurels with a new election to prepare for only a few months away in 1996. As the newly elected incumbent senator, there would be little time before a Democrat lined up to challenge Tony. I did a quick mental calculation that we'd have to circulate petitions to have the senator-elect's name on the primary ballot in less than ninety days. The whole process would start over again!

Betsy came by with a new drink after giving me a congratulatory hug, and Carolyn stepped in. "Jack's good, Betsy. How about you and I toast the victory with wine? I appreciate all you've done for my husband this fall." Carolyn ran interference, thank God.

As the campaign manager, I circulated through the house to thank volunteers and supporters and we headed home. I would be up bright and early: thank you notes needed to be written and mailed; yard signs had to come down and be stored for the next election; campaign finance reports had to be filed with the state; Tony's House office would have to be packed up and moved; I had staff to hire for the Capitol and District offices; and we had to prepare for a swearing-in ceremony. All within ten days. Senate leadership wanted to get back up to full strength right away.

"How does it feel to be a chief of staff again, Jackie?" Carolyn drove since the drinks had taken effect.

"Good, babe. Tony's a very decent man, and we've clicked well. There are lots of things to do, however. Got to be at it bright and early tomorrow and I suspect there'll be a hangover to deal with. My breathing is tighter than usual. I hope bronchitis doesn't come on."

"You need to take a few days and rest. You've been driving yourself into the ground. Bask in the win and let some other people step up." Drained as she said this, I'd worked seven days a week and joined Tony for canvassing as much as possible. I was an extra set of hands when we walked the streets, plus it gave us time to get to know each other better for the challenges that would come in the Senate.

Our first staff hire was Kate Jones. Senate leadership highly recommended her, and I was glad they did. Organized and computer savvy with a take-charge persona, I entrusted her with Tony's schedule. Kate would serve as his assistant and mine. Coming back to my hastily furnished office in the Capitol, she interrupted my phone call. "Jack, we have a long line of people checking in for the swearing-in. I need help out here." Another staffer and I went out to assist.

Molinaro's ceremony was the only thing happening. Plenty of space on the floor and in the gallery permitted his supporters, friends, and committee people to come up to Harrisburg to watch the big event. We also had arranged for a catered reception in the caucus room. Again, since Tony would turn around in '96 to run for a full four-year term (he was finishing out the end of Weigel's term), we needed to keep our supporters and network energized.

Of course, everyone wanted floor seating close to the action. My unenviable task—decide who got choice seating and who had to sit up top in the gallery. Inevitably, I angered many people. Part of the job though. The day belonged to Tony and his family. His wife, grown children, and mother all in attendance, he'd brought along an old Bible. Handed down from his mother's side—an old German family whose name "Haas" Molinaro referenced as much as he could when campaigning in York County to highlight his deep roots—the senator-elect's hand would rest upon this ancient heirloom as he repeated the oath of office.

After we seated everyone, the ceremony began. In a rare moment of pulling rank, I reserved a choice seat near Tony and his family. As I looked around the Senate chamber, it felt like I'd never left. Ennis O'Reilly, Bruce Bauer, Ben Walker, and many other staffers I worked with during my last stint all in the same places as before. More prepared this time with lobbying and governor's staff experience under my belt, I was determined to be more patient and wise.

The festivities wound down, and we bid Tony's family goodbye. Tired from playing host to a large crowd of several hundred Molinaro supporters, anyone who has ever been in that role understands how exhausting it can be, time for the senator and me to relish the moment in the solitude of his office.

I mixed two Dewar's on the rocks as we both gazed out the window with a view of the East Wing of the Capitol Building. Kate interrupted the silence and relaxation to say that Rob wanted to see us. He had sent regrets that an obligation in D.C. prevented him from attending the actual swearing-in. The senator gave Kate the go-ahead to bring Rob back from the reception area.

With Rob was an associate of his firm. Tall with long copper-colored hair, she had a curvy figure, green eyes, and full lips. Other than a touch of lipstick, this lobbyist avoided cosmetics, relying upon olive skin that looked perhaps Mediterranean in origin. The contrast of a darker skin tone with her Northern European ancestry highlighted a unique and eye-catching beauty. I remember Placid mentioning her hire some months ago. His company had employed this young woman right out of college after she had successfully interned with them.

After introductions, she moved over to the senator's empty chair. Her hips swayed as if she found herself modeling down a runway. A skintight, short dress underscored a sexuality that oozed from every pore of her body. Too dazed to say anything, we all watched this stunning woman cross her long legs up on the senator's desk. A mischievous smile graced her face as she did this.

When I looked over at Rob, I noticed sweat forming on his brow, a sign of his obvious embarrassment. Sitting in a side chair, Senator Molinaro had turned to his Blackberry to check email. None of us wanted to stare directly over at her as she flaunted natural legs that probably had never seen pantyhose.

A woman is needed to handle this job, I said to myself. I quietly slipped out of the senator's office to my adjoining space. Into the intercom I whispered to Kate to get back pronto.

Entering the office, at once Kate knew what to do. "Get out of the senator's chair now. Your appointment is over. Rob, happy to see you again. The senator and Jack must drive back down to York. Thanks for coming by." This lobbyist leaped out of the chair and scurried out—Kate had left no room in her voice for her to do anything but that. Placid was crimson-red as he trailed behind, and I suspected he and his new associate would have a stern conversation. At least, I hoped they would.

"What's the matter with you two?" Kate asked. "Need to be rescued, huh? Big babies." I liked her straightforward style. Direct but not disrespectful. An older African-American woman, who stood no more than five-three, she reminded me of an Army drill sergeant—perfect to be our gatekeeper. Proving in this first instance that she took no guff and would protect the senator and me.

"Seriously, Kate, she doesn't get an appointment unless she's with Rob or someone else from the firm. Talk about flirtatious. She'll get a reputation on the 'Hill' quickly."

"You think so, Jack? Acting like she did, the word will get out," Kate concluded.

FORTY-SIX

The Speech, Peddling Death

THE SWEARING-IN would begin many years that I served Tony as his chief of staff; by far the best and most productive of my career. While Molinaro and Weigel shared many views, they were different in their approach to the office. Jim was a people person, who loved that aspect of the job. Tony did the community events and interacted with constituents. His real love: shaping public policy to make the Commonwealth a better place for citizens to live and work in. I watched and learned from a master of the legislative process, and it was gratifying to be part of his success as a state senator.

In now representing the York City School District, Senator Molinaro would develop an unbridled passion for education reform, serving as the governor's chief ally in the Senate to remake public education in Pennsylvania. I would be by his side in all the battles we fought against the establishment that uniformly resisted any change other than the consistent behavior, "Give us more money and get the hell out of our way because we know what's best."

Shortly after being named to the Education Committee, a loose-knit group of school boards from urban areas asked the senator to come to one of their meetings to be the keynote speaker. This group invited Tony as the new senator and a member of the Education Committee. Perhaps they thought the olive branch would bring him back into the cozy fold of: "Do what we say on education legislation and we'll leave you alone next election cycle." Boy did they regret that invitation after Molinaro gave the speech.

His commentary would be a long explanation of Molinaro's tenets on why public education deserved a failing grade, especially in urban districts, and why the governor deserved support for his efforts to shake up the status quo.

At the Western Pennsylvania location where they met, over two hundred school directors from urban districts welcomed the senator and me. The emcee for the evening warmly introduced Tony, and that warmth ended about five sentences into Molinaro's speech. By the end of the remarks, they booed him. The elected officials of these school boards couldn't stand to hear things weren't as rosy as they all liked to believe.

One excerpt from his remarks: "You need to look at the Catholic system of education for efficiencies and success in educating children with far fewer dollars available to them."

The catcalls are worthy of mention. "Whose pocket are you in?" "They (the Catholics) get to cherry pick their kids (ignoring the reality that many parochial schools are in urban areas open to non-Catholic children)." And my favorite, "Who put you in charge?"

For many school board officials, there is no higher power or authority than themselves even though school districts are nothing but instrumentalities created by the Commonwealth to deliver educational services. In the lexicon of today's political culture, they supported a set of "alternative facts" on the state of education in Pennsylvania's urban school districts.

While Tony served in office, we referred to that as "The Speech." The only time he was ever booed publicly for calling it the way he saw it. One of many reasons I was proud to work for this courageous man of high integrity.

After the senator moved over to the Senate, his views transformed on abortion, causing former advocates for abortion rights to turn on him. One of those pro-abortion leaders was new to Harrisburg and represented a fringe group with its headquarters in the nation's capital. Louisa Smith-Diaz of Fighting for Our Rights and Bodies Alliance (FORBA) hailed from California. In her early thirties, she had pasty skin, spiked-up blond hair and a bulimic appearance. I observed to myself, *She should've remained in San Diego for sun treatments and extra- fattening milkshakes.* Despite the modern hairdo, this advocate wore a traditional flower-patterned dress, appropriate in length, with tasteful flats.

Louisa knew Tony championed reproductive rights previously and hadn't given up hope he might yet be persuaded to return to their side. Lobbying against a measure in the Senate that further restricted the period in which a woman may have an abortion and clamped down on abortion clinics by applying more state inspections, Louisa came knocking on our door. As Tony's chief of staff, he asked me to join because of the potential for the meeting to be contentious.

The leader of FORBA wasted no time in launching a direct verbal assault as she faced Tony's desk from a side chair. Our first meeting with Louisa, I'd done some intell by calling around to my colleagues. They forewarned me that Smith-Diaz could be abrasive.

Resting her wrists on the senator's mahogany desk, she didn't try to avoid having her large bangle bracelets *clang* against the surface. Louisa began, "What happened, Tony? How can you go from being one of our most passionate leaders and strategists in the House to this radical antichoice position? We hear you're voting for this ridiculous bill that would make it more difficult for women to have control over their bodies?"

The right buzz words flowed out of her mouth like honey. The Golden State's radical politics prepared Louisa well. But this was Pennsylvania, far more conservative and traditional than the Left Coast. "The voters do not approve of waffling or changing positions on what is one of the most personal choices of our time. Come back to our side, Senator. It's not too late," she urged him.

Senator Molinaro intuitively knew what the people of York County would stand for or not. He had served many years in the House and successfully made the move to the Senate, winning with over sixty percent of the vote in a Republican-leaning district. "Enough, Louisa," Tony replied. "My change of heart is deeply personal. And based on research on how science has advanced. Life begins at conception. Don't give me the consistency line. I've been consistent on most issues and very open on why I changed my mind. The voters in my district accepted this, despite how much money women's groups gave to my female opponent trying to defeat me." Tony's voice rose a few decibels, a sure sign Louisa had hit a raw nerve.

"Well, Senator, you may have changed your position, but this will be the first legislative vote since you turned on us. We'll see how the voters react if you follow through with supporting this intrusive bill. Because of your leadership in the past on women's issues, I'm doing my best to hold our people back. But if you vote for this, I will not stand in the way." Pointing her finger in the air for emphasis, the bracelets slid down her bony arm and the implied threat was clear for us to understand.

Time for me to jump in as the senator's senior staffer. Tony and I often played "good cop, bad cop." I purposely asked a flammable question. "Tell me, Louisa, how does it feel to peddle death?"

As I tossed this verbal grenade into the room, I looked right into her pale blue eyes. Molinaro gave me a look I had gone too far, but retreat wasn't possible now.

"Do staff in Pennsylvania talk like this? In California where I come from, this behavior wouldn't be tolerated, Senator," she said indignantly. "I won't sit here and be insulted by a man. You have no uterus, Mr. Curran, and have no right to take a position on women's issues. Who are you and the government to tell a woman what she may or may not do with her body? How dare you!"

With a quick glance down at my junk, I nodded in agreement that I was indeed a male. Leaning over closer to her, I said, "Once pregnancy begins, Ms. Smith-Diaz, the uterus holds an unborn baby, alive and growing. That permits a civilized society that values life under a Constitutional framework to impose restrictions. Otherwise, we cheapen life and where does the killing stop?"

Leaping out of her chair, a red leather briefcase loaded with abortion propaganda became her shield and weapon which Louisa whirled around recklessly as she let loose a high-pitched war cry. "This isn't over, you know. We have people in the senator's district. They will learn about my treatment here today."

Having done some research, I knew as a fringe group they had little presence in York County. Armed with this information, I pointed *my* finger at her as I rose from the chair—after making sure I wouldn't be hit by the briefcase—and emphasized, "Threats get you nowhere here. Your kind threw a ton of money against Tony and lost. Try it again," reiterating Tony's earlier point we wouldn't be intimidated. I wanted to borrow one of Clint Eastwood's famous lines, but that would have been way too theatrical for the moment.

"My Mexican-American husband, he's brawny by the way, would have some words for you, Mr. Curran."

"Yeah, what's that?" I let my curiosity get the best of me.

"*Estiércol de burro.*" A Spanish-speaking friend later translated that Louisa had called me "donkey dung." On that note, Louisa turned and began to leave.

With a broad smile, I said to her retreating form, "Welcome to Pennsylvania."

When she was safely out of earshot, Tony scolded me and rightfully so since this wasn't one of my better moments. "A bit much, Jack. You didn't have to antagonize her like that. I should have known you were prepped to attack the way you sat on the edge of your chair."

"Sorry, boss, but she came in with guns blazing." To defend myself, I mentioned another Harrisburg pro-choice lobbyist. "I have no problem with Judy Lemko. She and I just agree to disagree on the subject."

"Judy's an old hand and knows her way around the building. I guess Louisa got a lesson that Pennsylvania is a little different from California. Ok, who's next on the schedule?" Tony didn't want to talk about Louisa or abortion any further. Like most members, he hoped the majority leader would schedule the bill for a vote soon.

For issues of this nature, the best course is usually to vote as quickly as possible. The longer the issue hangs out there on the calendar, the more grief members face from both sides. Even the pro-life people checked in all the time to make sure Tony remained on board—this trying our patience, too.

"Women Against Alcohol and Vivian Ulrich are waiting to see you, Tony."

"She's still alive? How did they get on my schedule?"

"They wanted you to come out like Jim—" As soon as these words left my lips, I regretted them.

"I'm not Jim Weigel, Jack. If you and Kate don't want to chase me for the schedule, be mindful of that and mindful that my time is valuable."

"I apologize, Senator. Their visit is fifteen minutes only. Message understood, loud and clear."

"They'll probably beat me up for supporting privatization. This day can't get any better," Molinaro added.

"Maybe focus on underage drinking, your stance against expanded gambling, and your support for the crack down on child porn," I suggested.

I had crossed a line several times and deserved the reprimand from Senator Molinaro. A chief of staff is only as good as the trust they have from their member—I had stretched mine that day.

FORTY-SEVEN

Nervous Breakdown, Antiques 2.0

"**W**HAT'S WRONG, what's the matter, baby?" Carolyn found me hunched over in the fetal position in the corner of our den, sobbing in the blackness and loneliness of two o'clock in the morning. Her arms encircled me as I shook and convulsed, years of stress and pent-up emotions released into the darkness of the night.

"I'm so tired, honey." I uttered this over, and over, and over again.

Carolyn continued to hold me, removing her pajama top to use it to wipe my eyes and nose gently. She rubbed my neck, whispering, "I love you, Jackie. *Shhh*, you're safe. Everything is going to be okay."

Little Jack, now a teenager and not so little, came out of his room and asked, "Mom, is Pop okay?"

"Go back to bed, Jack. Daddy's all right. Just a bad stomach ache. Get some rest."

After years of strenuous and stressful service as Tony's chief of staff, we had been through two more re-elections (1996 and 2000). Tony also was considering a run for governor; a challenge for any Republican from Central Pennsylvania to undertake since party nominees typically came from the major metropolitan areas of the Commonwealth. This added to my responsibilities, juggling an office and a much more aggressive schedule for Molinaro since we had his Senate and district duties to continue to cover and his attendance at events around the state to explore a possible candidacy.

Carolyn was a stay-at-home mom, and both boys attended a Christian school. These conditions created enormous pressure to cover tuition of over six hundred dollars a month and all the other bills. Foolishly, I volunteered for many community endeavors, holding leadership positions that required extra time and generated additional stress, but no new money.

Big Joe was in bad shape—financially and emotionally. Remarried, he and his second wife moved to North Carolina to be closer to her family. Because of poor personal and business decisions, they teetered on the edge of bankruptcy. Carolyn and I sent five hundred dollars a month to help them stay afloat, money we really couldn't afford to part with. Dad would call almost every evening, unleashing his soul about the regrets he had as a husband and father. His speech slurred from too much scotch, I told him I loved him, assuring him he was a good dad and provider.

At the core, Big Joe never gave up loving Annie, the beautiful woman he'd met in that Philadelphia park so long ago. In his tortured mind, there were many failures—starting with his first marriage and ending with time lost with his children that could never be recaptured. At the end of his life, all he sought was emotional affirmation that his seventy-plus years had been of some value.

In many ways, his depression helped launch mine. The drowning man took down another man, who didn't have the mental and emotional strength to save the victim. Or himself. Family burdens, Big Joe's, the senator's, and ten other staff people for whom I felt responsible, all rested on my shoulders. Everything came crashing down around me and I suffered a major nervous breakdown.

Carolyn found a Xanax the doctor had prescribed for me along with a stern warning issued from him—again—to slow down. Which I ignored to my great peril. My wife continued to hold me, assuring me I wasn't alone. Whatever I faced, we'd face it together. As she guided me back to bed, I clutched her tightly; a lifeline then and since we were teenagers. Carolyn had never seen her strong husband emotionally collapse. But this didn't deter her from knowing I would need her strength to get through the most desperate times I've ever experienced.

The morning routine of getting the kids off to the bus occurred without me as I slept through the alarm and hustings of the household. Carolyn called Kate at the office to say I wouldn't be coming in. Next, she placed a call to Tony, and he answered right away. "Hi, Carolyn. Everything okay?"

"No, Tony, Jack's not doing well. The stress and constant worrying have finally caught up. While he's resting now, we had a very bad night." For sure, this wasn't an easy conversation for my wife to have. To this day, I'm in awe of her quiet strength.

"Tell Jack to take time off. Should I stop by later this afternoon to check on him?"

Carolyn waited a moment and replied, "Probably not a good idea, but thank you for your concern. I'll keep you posted. Jack said something before going to sleep that his deputy can run the office."

"We have an excellent staff. Jack hired and trained them well. He needs to get back on his feet." Tony was right. Highly competent, the team understood their roles. I'd always stressed to them, "If I ever get hit by a bus, you all will carry on for the senator's benefit."

The deep depression I fell into indeed felt like a bus splattered me across the roadway. Into chaos and despair I descended, withdrawing from church and community organizations and neighbors. During this time, I stayed in bed a lot; the covers wrapped over my head like I was in a cocoon, hiding from the bogeyman. I interacted only with Carolyn, the kids, and Rob. And found out who my friends were and who forgot I even existed. Rob stayed in close touch and avoided talk about work. Even so, he confided in Carolyn that the scuttlebutt network remained alive and well in Harrisburg. Many people gossiped about how Big Jack Curran had crashed and burned. Some delighting in my demise and fall from power.

As an aside, I received one note that touched me. From Henrietta, it read: *Dear Curran, I hear you're under the weather. Get back to the Capitol. Our skirmishes aren't over. Regards, Representative Henrietta Hoover.* In her own way, she'd expressed concern and acknowledged me as a worthy opponent and I treasured receiving it.

After months of one-on-one therapy to discuss the trauma of my youth and recognition of how anxiety had always controlled my life, attendance at Al-Anon so I could better understand how Joe's alcoholism had hurt me, and a prescription for an anti-depression drug to correct a chemical imbalance, I would slowly recover to my old self. A valuable, but horribly painful lesson had been learned. By refusing to take care of myself and pretending to be some sort of superman for twenty-plus years, my body and soul gave way.

For a time, not much remained of Jack Curran. I thank God and my family for pulling me through the darkness that enshrouded me. Many times, wide awake in the middle of the night, I cried out to the Lord to save me from despair. I asked Him to point me in the right direction, any direction, rather than the feeling that my life had no meaning or purpose. Carolyn would hold me as I stared into the edge of the abyss, wondering if I would ever be normal again.

A return to the Senate and political life was out of the question. At least at that time. My recovery too fragile, Tony reluctantly filled my job as I went on leave and then temporary disability. After all, he had an office to run and ambitions to pursue, so I don't blame him for having to move on. Everyone is replaceable, particularly in politics.

When ready to work again, I returned to something familiar: the comfort and familiarity of the antique business. Carolyn and I would start an enterprise from scratch. Subconsciously, I suppose I followed in Big Joe's footsteps when he, too, walked away from a commanding position in corporate life to launch his own venture. Profitably occurred as we grew to several locations in Central Pennsylvania. I worked harder physically than at any time in my life and enjoyed every moment of it. Liberating to be away from government and the pressures of public service, I enjoyed having freedom over my schedule. I kept a small hand in politics by consulting on the side, providing us with a steady income when the business would hit a drought.

Driving along in my big white cargo van, sipping coffee and munching on dry roasted peanuts (one of my vices), I stopped at junk shops in York and Harrisburg, establishing a rapport with the mostly African-American owners, much as my father had done twenty-five years before in Philadelphia. Climbing around in basements and attics, finding long-lost treasures to bring to market for a new generation of people to enjoy, we developed a reputation for providing our customers with unique and reasonably priced items.

On one such occasion, I checked in with "Bill," one of my regular suppliers, who owned a small "clean-out" business in Harrisburg. We'd become good friends and Bill trusted me to be fair. At each visit, I would comb his shop, outside porch, yard, and basement, and pull together a pile of things to buy. Like Joe and Sweet, we haggled and always arrived at a just price. Behind his counter that day, Bill had a large wooden airplane propeller blade. He moved it out to the middle of the shop, so I could see it. "Any interest in this, Jack? Not a thing my customers want to buy."

I looked it over carefully. Dubious about its value, I needed to keep Bill happy. "Really not something we'd sell in our shops, Bill, but sure, I'll take it. How much?"

"Forty dollars and it's yours. Came from an estate so I got nothing in it." Two Jacksons later, it belonged to our business.

After some scrubbing, polishing, and taking photos for the internet, I discovered a beautiful, lighter wood, maple in finish—under sixty years of grime and fifth. With its original manufacturing decals and brass tips and rivets, the propeller became a handsome piece. While tempted to keep it for our house filled full of antiques, there were bills to pay. Up it went on the web, sparking a bidding war with the final buyer spending almost eight hundred dollars, a terrific profit margin.

We eventually expanded the business to reproduction garden items we imported directly from China, mixing these things in with the antiques and had a faithful flock of customers—who appreciated our pricing and variety. As Big Joe had taught me the antique business, Jack and Robert joined me, learning the value of hard work. I cherished this time with them much as Big Joe seemed to love our time together. It felt right to be off the government payroll, and I suppose this chapter of my life had to happen. Proving I could be successful in free enterprise was part of my DNA. My blood coursed with the trials, tribulations, and successes of operating a small business from when Big Joe first lifted me up into his truck to join him every weekend.

FORTY-EIGHT

The Dream

OVER TIME, the physical work beat down my body. As a man in my forties, constantly lifting, standing, crouching, took its toll. One night, I came home wiped out and plopped myself down in the hot tub we'd splurged on. The 101-degree heat and pulsating jets were wonderful on my tired joints. I sipped on a single malt scotch—I believe it was a low-land—and savored its feathery-light taste.

A train rumbled by in the background since our property was only a half-mile from the railroad line. A neighborhood dog barked. Carolyn worked in the kitchen. Dinner had to be prepared and she and her mother were talking on the phone. Through the window, my wife smiled at me. I grinned back, appreciative of the time she gave me to relax. Jack and Robert played hoops in the alley. The methodical *thump, thump, thump* of the basketball the last noise I heard before falling into a deep slumber.

The little boy stares into a mirror. He sees not himself but a man, tired, gray, withered. Someone's voice is telling the man, "Go back; they are waiting..." A raging river sweeps the man away as he fights to grab something, anything, to stay afloat and keep from drowning. A large hand he does not know pulls him up. He is comforted by a warmth, a love, that envelops him. Deposited onto the top of a tall building, the man is safe from the rising water. In the distance, he sees a small light blinking, on-and-off, on-and-off, on-and-off. A new voice calls out, "It's not over." The man calls back but cannot hear his own voice. He struggles to say anything. A woman's voice cries out, "There's more." The man looks back into the mirror and sees the little boy again—this time at the bottom of a steep staircase.

"Wake up, Jack. You're dreaming. Shouting something about drowning and a little boy. You've been in the tub for over thirty minutes." I rose unsteadily; my legs felt like marshmallows. While my dreams had been more vibrant lately, nothing like this one with imagery and messages I struggled to understand. Carolyn handed me a warm towel which I wrapped around my body, now chilled from the cold November air. "Maybe you better slow down with the drinking, honey," she said. "You've been brooding about something and taking in a lot more alcohol. Anyway, dinner is ready." Carolyn called out to the boys, and I slipped off my shorts and pulled on a pair of sweats and a sweater.

We made it a priority to try to have dinner as a family, a credit to Carolyn. An excellent cook, she made sure we had this nightly ritual. As an antique dealer, I had more flexibility with my schedule and enjoyed this time with my crew. That night, I wasn't that talkative other than to ask Jack Jr. to make me another drink.

"Here you go, Pop," Jack said as he handed me the glass. I caught a look of disapproval from Carolyn, mindful of her warning several minutes before.

"What's bothering you? Can you tell us about the dream? Something's eating at you," my wife said. The boys munched on the homemade calzone Carolyn had prepared, so I slowly recounted the dream, struggling to remember the sequence and what was said. "For over a week now, you've been sullen. What's going on? I've said nothing because I figured you were just tired from the physical labor," she observed. "Talk to me, Jackie, please."

"After the election last week, I called Tony to congratulate him on his rise to Senate leadership. We had a good conversation. The senator asked me if I missed the Senate and staff work..." My voice trailed off. I wanted to avoid this conversation.

"Okay, what did you tell him?" Carolyn asked.

"Jack, pass me the salad." As I scooped up greens onto my plate from the bowl my son handed me, Carolyn waited patiently. She would not be deterred. Her blue eyes bore into me. "I told him, yes, I missed it. I also said the work in the business is wearing my body down. Tony asked me if I'm ready to come back. Robert, how'd fall ball go this afternoon?" I asked my youngest son, trying to change the subject.

"Good, Pop. Hit my sixth home run of the season," he said. Robert was a robust and natural athlete, competing in baseball as he prepared for a high school career in the sport.

"Proud of you, son."

"What did you tell Tony? I can't help you if you don't open up." Carolyn was now losing her patience.

"That I'm ready to return. He offered me the chief of staff job back since he has expanded responsibilities now as a Senate leader." I stared down at my plate, rattled about Carolyn's possible reaction.

"I won't nag you or warn you about what could happen to your health if you return. I know you never want to be back in the place you were in four years ago when you collapsed. None of us can go through that again." Carolyn's voice, even and judgment free, made the points I knew needed to be made. "I think you know what this dream means, and you have to confront whether you want to return to the political life or not."

For several minutes, I remained silent as the kids talked about school that day and Carolyn filled me in on her mom's health. Frank Gianella had passed, and Mrs. Gianella suffered from poor health. After we'd finished the small talk, I told Carolyn about my decision. "I'm going back, babe. Stewart wants the business." He was a dealer we worked with and had recently made an acceptable offer for the inventory, truck, and building that housed my workshop and goods. "Tony wants me to start the beginning of the year when the session begins if I have your support. I miss the public policy work, and I should plan for college for the boys. There's not nearly enough money saved up."

"This shouldn't be about the money. We're doing okay with the business."

"We are but just paying the bills. There's not much left each month. I'm tired physically, honey, and yes, I'm drinking too much. I need to be careful of alcoholism because of my father. The dream seemed real and obvious. I must go back. My work there is unfinished." Carolyn accepted my decision as she had many others through our years of dating and marriage.

When I returned to the Senate for the third and last time in my long career, many talked about the political resurrection of Jack Curran, who seemed a different man, working smarter, and who was more judicious, wise, and a little more patient.

I understood there were limits to what I could do, realizing that I had to put boundaries on for the sake of the people who depended on me to be their provider, husband, father. Duties that since Carolyn and I said, "I do," were the most important ones, regardless of what daily pressures I faced.

As I reflect on the vivid images from that dream, I believe the large hand lifting me up from certain destruction and death was that of God. The comfort I felt could only come from Him, saving me, giving me a sign that I needed to go back into public service; to finish what we started, to keep climbing those metaphorical steps, especially in education reform for the sake of poor kids, who needed to be saved themselves.

FORTY-NINE

Back to Retirement

"YOU'RE DAYDREAMING, Jack. C'mon, my call's finished. Let's head back to the party." Rob shook me to bring me out of the intense daydream I found myself in. We were in the Rotunda after slipping out of the retirement reception at Placid's office.

"Just thinking about the past again, pal. Did you resolve your client's issue?"

"Nah, but at least we have a strategy on how to stymie the legislation in Congress. Proponents will want to move on to something else after I stir up enough trouble. The big moving companies are regulated to the rafters as it is. Killer amendments will poison anything they try to do."

We walked back to Rob's office and entered the conference room. The party continued like we had never left. I searched for Samantha Tinsdale, my colleague and a staff lawyer we recruited from private practice. Unlike some lawyers, there wasn't a shred of arrogance within her. Very smart and sensitive, her compassion for people set her apart from most legal practitioners I've interacted with—qualities I thought made her more successful at writing legislation to help people. Pretty and conservatively stylish in dress, Samantha could've been a literature teacher or librarian. Her command of the English language was second to none.

An accomplished staff team, I generated the "big" ideas and strategy. The much tougher job: putting these concepts into policy and bill form to make them cogent, understandable, and able to pass judicial muster. Senator Molinaro needed an attorney to offer him legal opinions he could rely upon once Tony ascended into a leadership position.

Samantha and I often argued over my ideas. My focus: help Tony shape legislation to get out of committee and through the legislature with the minimum twenty-six votes required in the Senate, and 102 in the House. Sometimes Sam had to push back, explaining that the courts would never uphold my idea if someone challenged. Since we worked together in education reform, usually a party stood ready to sue against our policy proposals, from the teachers' union, to the school boards, to the school administrators, the adults who guarded their turf zealously.

Finding my colleague, I put my hand out to clasp hers. "I'll miss you, Sam. You were the brains behind our success. I came up with the crazy ideas, sometimes throwing stuff against the wall to see what would stick." We both enjoyed a laugh, knowing this observation to be accurate. Looking back over a lifetime as I said this, Otto von Bismarck's famous quote came to mind: "Laws are like sausage, it is better not to see them made." I'd participated in more sausage-making than I cared to admit.

"You're welcome, Jack." Samantha took my retirement decision hard. In moments like this when I sensed someone else hurt, even a little, I overdid it.

"Seriously, your genius was somehow channeling my bursts of creativity and insanity, making it work on paper."

With an understanding smile, she nodded. "Really...it's okay. Your health comes first. I understand. So does the rest of the team." Samantha had heard me many times express my love for shaping public policy to help people.

But the signs of burnout were telling. She had seen me at my best, and at my worst, with most of the theatrics portrayed during negotiations. Sometimes I could abruptly end a parley with a party who wouldn't negotiate in good faith, slamming my fist against the table for added effect. Or other times when I could charm the other party to keep talks going, I would use humor to lighten up the discussion. Dramatically conceding a point so the other side would have a "win." After so many years of negotiating contentious issues, I developed a sense of when someone might walk out of the room. And yet I needed them to stay for fear the discussions would collapse. The goal—to keep talking. Rarely did quitting and going back to the drawing board help solve an impasse.

Any successful negotiation requires an understanding of the pressures the other party faced; what did they need for it to be a good deal to declare victory? What could I sell to the people I represented and their colleagues as positive for our side? In the end, the aim is to reach an agreement that results in positive public policy with enough votes cast on the big board to get the job done.

"Tired of all the bullshit, pettiness, and oversized egos. Yanked in multiple directions day after day, putting fires out all the time. I can't do it anymore, Sam. I won't do it."

A younger staffer I hired as an intern several years before interrupted the conversation, and Samantha seemed relieved she didn't have to engage further. He slapped me on the back a little too hard, causing me to spill my beer and asked, "Did you hear about the latest scoop, Jack?"

I took the bait. "Okay, what news?"

"One member got beaten downtown tonight."

"Oh, that's terrible," Samantha observed.

"Yeah, but get this," my former intern said this with too much fervor given the topic. "This legislator was with his aide. The beating happened outside of Renegade Away." A bar that caters to the sizeable gay population of Harrisburg.

I cut him off. "What about it?"

Despite the intended rebuke, my young associate continued, "There's been a persistent rumor he and his staffer maybe swing the other way so this kind of firms it up, right? Wait until his wife hears about this!"

"Don't jump to that conclusion. How do we know what's true, or not true? Frankly, it's none of our business either. I hope they're okay. If he's cheating on his spouse, that's between him and his wife. The Harrisburg rumor mill just doesn't quit," I said this too forcefully, given the occasion. Clenched fists were a sign of my rage. His face crestfallen, I patted him on the back, realizing I had come down too hard on my protégé. "Only the three of us here so don't sweat it, man. Let's drink to a long, successful career for you. Appreciate your coming." We raised our glasses to one another.

Out of the corner of my eye, I glimpsed Gloria West approaching. Always well put together, Gloria wore a tight skirt, stylish blouse, and the highest heels made on the market. Her frosted brunette hair topped it all off, always done as if she had just left the hairdresser.

Samantha whispered, "When she worked with you, how the heck did she walk in those heels over the tiled floors of the Capitol? Flats are even challenging."

"How about that email scandal?" Gloria asked after hugging us. This topic was the latest wrongdoing in Harrisburg, the talk of the town, including at my party. "I heard something about pornography and other inappropriate stuff being passed around in the Attorney General's office over some staff email."

"Yeah, I read that in the paper today," I agreed.

"Heads will probably roll, but what do I know, I'm retired and away from a scene best left to young people," she said, though I recognized this modesty to be false—Gloria maintained contact with many folks in the Capitol.

Gloria had a sixth sense about people and had been around a long time that I'd never bet against her when she made these predictions. As a young man, I benefited from her wisdom and patience, particularly when I was about to step in "it." She saved me more than once from making a huge mistake and knew the signs when I appeared ready to charge into a situation without thinking it through, my emotions guiding me instead of logic. Her counsel slowed me down enough to think about my next moves more carefully.

"Where's Carolyn?" I pointed to my wife in a far corner of the room and realized where this appeared headed. "How'd she put up with you all these years?" Gloria asked. "At least you listened when we worked together and bought nice gifts for her birthday and your anniversary. That woman deserves a medal for patience and suffering."

"No disagreement from me there. She deserves that and much more." Carolyn mingled about so easily, relieved she wouldn't be sharing her husband any longer with the Capitol. "I'm not the easiest guy to live with. I'm my father's son, warts and all for the world to see. Did I ever pretend to be anything but who I am?"

Gloria laughed and pecked me on the cheek. She knew I tended to beat myself up. "You're all right, Jack. Your friends want you to relax. If Jim were here, he'd be proud of what you accomplished and the man you became." Her reference to Senator Weigel caused me to well up again; my emotions continued to bubble just below the surface. If anyone had earned the privilege to proclaim what Jim Weigel thought and felt, it was Gloria West. She moved on to the next group at my party.

"Pop, there's someone waiting to see you," Jack Jr. said. As I turned around, there stood my little sister Carol and her husband John. They had driven in from Cleveland. Estranged for years because of my stubbornness, I hugged my sibling, clutching her and drawing security from her presence.

"I can't believe you guys are here. Where're the kids?"

The night was now complete. Less than eighteen months difference in age, we grew up together as best friends. Events had pulled us apart, but the bond, even when ripped by conflict and sharp words we both regretted, had never completely broken. We always knew the other one was there; siblings and survivors who had walked through the fires of hell through no fault of our own. Still the children of Joe and Annie Curran.

"Jackie, we wouldn't miss this for anything. The kids are staying with John's parents. Credit Carolyn for making sure the Curran family is well represented." Carol was crying, too. An inspiration for what she'd overcome, championing babies since she had suffered from two abortions during high school and college. While I had always been pro-life, my sister's influence made me appreciate more the pro-life network and its commitment to unborn children. Her abortions made the issue much more personal for the family and me.

Stepping back from my sister, it was like I had seen a ghost from the past. Carol looked so much like our mother, aging beautifully and gracefully, as our mom did before cancer took her from us. The resemblance startling like Annie stood before me. There for one of the biggest moments of my life even though she'd died years before.

I choked back my sobs of joy and pain from the years lost to past conflicts; unable to utter my thanks to Carol for making the party. With another hug and a gentle nudge towards those waiting to greet me, Carol said, "Our siblings wanted to be here but couldn't swing it. Go mingle. This is your well-deserved night."

FIFTY

I'm Sad, Carol Accosted, Tony Toasts

GABRIEL WALKED UP TO US, hesitating in his step. Jack Jr. turned away, sensing my third "adopted" son wanted to speak with me alone. I waved him over. We didn't have the chance to talk much in the car, and I wanted to catch up. "How are you, bud? What's new? Talk to me." His countenance reminded me of when we first met—that of a funeral face rather than a party for a good friend.

"I'm sad, Jack," he said with a childlike innocence that was so endearing. The lightbulb went off in my head. We were the closest thing he had to parents and our moving three hours away troubled him. It reminded me of how I felt when Big Joe died. Like an orphan.

"It's okay, son. We'll stay in touch. Carolyn and I are so proud of you... proud of everything you've overcome. You'll be all right."

"I...I guess. I just want to..." His chin was down, touching his chest while he said this.

"Gabriel, look at me," I whispered, a line of folks waited to see me, and I didn't want to embarrass him. As he looked up, I whispered again, "We love you, kid."

He moved towards me, loosely wrapping his arms around me. I hugged him and kissed his forehead. "Thank you...for everything, Pop."

For the umpteenth time that night, I shed a tear, especially over his use of this familial title, and allowed it to dry on my cheek. Why try to hide or wipe away my tears? No need to be "Bad Boy Jack Curran" any longer. Mission accomplished. No one left to protect, except my family. And no more legislative battles left to fight.

Choked up, I could only sputter, "You're welcome, son." He had come a long way from when displays of affection were impossible. Nor was eye contact or a firm handshake. The first time we shook, it felt like I had grabbed hold of the first fish I reeled in as a young lad off the Atlantic coast, a *Ling*, limp with little fight. I corrected this back when we met.

"Look at me, Gabriel. Clasp my hand firm like this." I demonstrated the technique. "Now, look me straight in the eye and greet me like a man. If you have sweaty palms, try to wipe your hand discreetly on your pants. No one likes to be gripped with a wet palm."

My party was a step back for Gabriel in confidence and self-esteem. He and I shared this sentiment as we were both moving into the unknown. To buck him up, I said, "Before we both blubber too much, go find Jack and Robert and have a shot of tequila with them. You guys won't be driving back to York. Carolyn will drive since I'm going to have a scotch. Rob's paying after all." We high-fived, and I got a thin smile from him before he moved on.

Gabriel's success stood front and center for me. I'll never know how many disadvantaged kids I played a small role in saving—never. Visiting many charter and private schools, as part of my job, I saw children bursting with enthusiasm. Happy, safe, and learning. As a wise principal once told Tony and me on one of our many tours, "You can smell learning when it's taking place in a building." And I'll take the liberty of adding, we saw plenty of failure in some public school buildings we visited where little education occurred, and students went to school every day afraid for their lives.

For these children, we fought hard. Staking out bold positions—inevitably, we were forced to compromise. Again and again. I was mindful of Reagan's advice: get something that will make a difference. Or go down in flaming defeat and get NOTHING but perhaps accolades for fighting the good fight. For some, that's enough.

But not for the governor and two senators I staffed. They never forgot the faces of the kids we tried to rescue from certain failure or death before the violent streets took their lives. Along with our legislative allies and groups on the outside, we secured enough votes to pass major school choice bills that made a real difference for low-income families so that they had the opportunity to flee poorly performing public schools.

The celebration came to an abrupt halt when all heads turned to two women engaged in a heated argument. Even the harpist stumbled on the strings because of the brouhaha. A younger female lobbyist on Rob's payroll known to be rabid in her support for abortion rights accosted my sister. Someone must've pointed out Carol to her. As an author of a book on the trauma and suffering abortion causes women and families, Carol often became a convenient target for feminists of a different view.

"No one tells me what I can do with my body, especially you...you prolifers! You hear me? Why don't you put that in a book? You make me sick."

Carol was more than capable of standing her ground although my brotherly instincts kicked in as I motioned to Rob to back his employee off or I would be in her face protecting my own. Before he intervened, the other Curran at the celebration, the youngest daughter of Big Joe, set the record straight. "Am I insulting you? I'm sorry you're wounded. If there's anything you want to talk about, including counseling for post-abortion trauma, here's my business card. I'll never apologize to anyone for fighting for unborn kids. Now back off. This is my older brother's retirement party, and you're making a fool of yourself."

Carol's work brought her into contact with many women, grieving over the abortion choice they made and later regretted. Lashing out to justify the "choice" was one possible tell that the lobbyist may have aborted a baby. The exchange was a visible sign that some guests had too much to drink, as the woman hurried off to a neutral corner, afraid of my baby sister. Passions can and do run high over divisive public policy issues even during a going-away party.

While I appreciated everything Rob had done, the night had drained and humbled me since I didn't like being the center of attention. The verbal assault on Carol only reinforced my decision it was the right moment to depart from state government since I had no patience left for conflict and the time and energy it takes to resolve disputes.

Before Placid could wrap up the night, Doc strolled up to Rob and me. We both nodded hello. "Great party, Rob," Doc said. Our host acknowledged his compliment. "Quite a spread you have here."

Rob simply answered, "Jack and Carolyn deserve a great send-off." While Placid was wealthy, dressing the part of a powerbroker and living in very nice homes, he didn't like to talk about or flaunt his financial success other than when breaking my balls. Having grown up in relative poverty, no one would have blamed him for doing so, however.

As usual, Doc remained as dapper as ever. Sporting a white dinner jacket, his head shone as if it had just been shaved before the party. While he had aged a great deal since we worked together, he remained graceful and elegant.

Turning to me, he said, "Congratulations, Jack. To be honest, didn't think you'd make it this far as hot-wired as you are."

"Thanks for the overwhelming vote of confidence, Doc," I replied in reaction to this backhanded compliment.

Shifting gears, he announced, "Well, gents, I'm moving to a new life as well."

"How so?" Rob asked.

"I'm selling everything and moving to Israel. Have a buddy who lives on a kibbutz, outside of Jerusalem. There are exciting things happening, and I want to be part of it as a former sociology guy."

We both wished him well, and he walked off to catch up with Gloria West.

"Okay, Rob, it's time to call it a night. Can't take too much more as much as I'm grateful for the evening."

"Understood. Senator Molinaro's going to speak. I thought you'd appreciate that."

Glad Rob planned on ending the event that way, I had enormous respect for Tony as everyone in the room did. Seven terms in the House, four in the Senate, he'd earned grudging respect even from his many opponents. Molinaro tired of battling the powerful special interests he had tangled with, unions and trial litigators who controlled large PACs, dispensing millions of dollars each election cycle. Some of that money always found its way to Molinaro's opponents, forcing Tony to raise funds, something he did, but never enjoyed doing.

In my experience, asking for money isn't comfortable for many politicians. Some are pros, however, at squeezing dollars out of businesspeople, special interests, and labor leaders, the usual suspects for the two parties to hit up for big and consistent money. Tony wearied of the vicious campaigns and constant demands from constituents that came with the job. A quiet man, his shyness was mistaken for aloofness. But for those who got close to him, his high intelligence was matched with a wonderful sense of humor, very dry, almost British in nature.

When the senator called me into his office early one Monday morning to tell me he would not be seeking another term in the Senate to represent the Eighth Senatorial District of York County, we each tried to hold back the tears, too masculine to cry in front of one another. The water flowed freely when I called the rest of the staff into Tony's suite for the senator to share his news. My retirement came not too long after his. In part, my heart just wasn't in it without Senator Molinaro in the fight.

The time with him was demanding, but we had accomplished much together. I usually anticipated what he needed even before he articulated it. Thinking as he would, and Weigel before him, required me to subvert my own thoughts. After a time, I began to wonder what was left of Jack Curran's convictions and essence.

Rob and his people planned for everything. A microphone was hooked up for the occasion as the harpist stopped playing. Tony stepped up to the front of the crowd, without notes, when he always spoke at his finest.

"I believe everyone knows Jack worked for my predecessor in the Senate, Jim Weigel. Jim has been gone a long time now, but I'd be remiss if I didn't mention him as an important part of Jack's journey. Would it surprise anyone to know that Jack Curran was a serious young man back in the day? Not much has changed. We interacted a great deal in meetings when he represented Senator Weigel since my House district sat in Jim's Senate district. Jack carried himself a certain way with confidence, but humility. All of those who know him have seen the flashes of his temper and candor. I saw this as a passion and intensity that would serve me well as it did Senator Weigel."

"Admittedly, it was a little risky hiring Jack because of his long association with and loyalty to Jim. I couldn't be sure that would transfer over—it did, by the way. Jack left the governor's office from a good position when I asked him to run my Senate campaign. He attacked the campaign with his usual attention to detail. With Jack, I counted on him to always worry about the state of the election. And, later, when I assumed office in the Senate. Jack fretted plenty for both of us," Molinaro said this with a chuckle. The group aware of my nature, joined in the laughter.

Carolyn shouted out, "You're right, Tony, that's just what he did."

"I'm reminded of one of the most famous Teddy Roosevelt quotes, appropriate to end this occasion. 'The credit belongs to the man who is actually in the arena, whose face is marred by dust and sweat and blood; who strives valiantly...who at best knows in the end the triumph of high achievement, and who at worst, if he fails, at least fails while daring greatly, so that his place shall never be with those cold and timid souls who neither know victory nor defeat.'"

With his glass high in the air, the crowd following along, Tony finished. "Would you all join me as we toast Jack and Carolyn as they start a new chapter of their lives? To Jack and Carolyn..." My head down during the toast, I blinked away a tear to wink at the senator in thanks for the praise, something he did not often do.

FIFTY-ONE

Into the Sunset

BLESSED TO WORK for Tony Molinaro and Jim Weigel, my time with Victor Pearl and the governor was mostly enjoyable, too. As Carolyn had said to me so tellingly, I am the sum of my experiences. Shaped by Big Joe and Annie and the trauma of the Curran family and the turbulent times we lived through; shaped by two mentors in Sarah Hahn and William Moran; shaped by the Army; and shaped by the challenging professional positions I held.

The tapestry of my life has been rich, each strand connected and woven tightly. God is good to me, always. And I am content to be a blessed man, secure in the knowledge that I did the best I could, making many mistakes along the way, many times the result of the passion I had for work and a temper and tongue I have struggled to control all my life.

As the Bible wisely tells us, the tongue, when untamed, is a weapon. "But no man can tame the tongue. It is an unruly evil, full of deadly poison." (James 3.8). Mine was that and more. The harsh words and barbs I had for many I deeply regret and I'm sorry to anyone I might have hurt. Being in politics is a tough business. Like it or not, I played the villain most of the time to allow my boss to take the high road. Even the "Big

Three" of conflict during my career: Hoover, O'Reilly, and Bauer, earned my respect and admiration, despite tough words we had for one another and squabbles over approach or ideas. They were doing the best they could, too, under trying circumstances on difficult issues. I never doubted their sincerity and passion for doing what they thought was right.

All my life, I tried to emulate Big Joe. The reality is I'm wired much more like Annie: sensitive, quiet, and compassionate. I'm not sure I ever moved beyond that little kid, the bookworm, lost in the adventures and tales of great people. The model of manhood I had before me as a child fought against that notion, pushing me involuntarily in another direction. Toward a facade of toughness and a feigned masculinity with the belief that the world is harsh and unforgiving.

And the career path I sought demanded I be someone other than who I really am. That tug of war within my soul didn't stop until I retired to the quiet life I believe I was meant to live. But maybe this is all just psycho-babble. And the Gemini in me—my birthday is in early June—finds it only natural there would be the two faces of Jack Curran.

"Jackie, you have to see this sunset. The clouds in the background are so majestic, like mountains. Stop typing and get up here, please." Carolyn's voice pulled me back to reality and the present time, away from so many memories, both good ones and bad. Intentionally, or perhaps unintentionally, once again, she helped set needed boundaries.

After months of leafing through mounds of journal books and detailed entries, creating outlines of the most memorable experiences from which to draw upon, hammering away at the keyboard, it was time to join my wife. To be with my love, on the rooftop deck of our little cottage to marvel at God's creation, His landscape of brilliance there for us to enjoy and revel in.

We would walk arm and arm that night on our town's boardwalk along the bay, enjoying that sunset; a vibrant and appropriate symbol for one concluding phase of our life. Together, we'd face whatever the good

Lord intends for the next chapter. But for now, taking in a deep breath of the sweet salt air, the easterly breeze brought the ocean as if it were right next to us, listening to the seagulls, watching the sailboats gently rock and tug at their moorings, seeing the last lights shimmering against the swells of the water, I am forever praising God for giving me a good life and family. I trust Him for whatever may lie ahead with Carolyn by my side. Just as it should be.

EPILOGUE

JACK AND CAROLYN strolled the boardwalk that summer evening, mostly in comfortable silence, enjoying a life they never experienced most of their married years. This stage didn't last long, however.

Like a Greek tragedy, the terrible premonition Jack never really shook came true. With time on his hands, his heart grew stronger and stronger for the poor and destitute and he volunteered in a homeless shelter. From that service, several winters after his retirement, he contracted a protracted bout of pneumonia and never recovered. His body too weak from scarring of his lungs from an illness that plagued him since birth. And a refusal to take care of his body because there was always a mission at hand; a list of things to do; a need, never fulfilled, to please Big Joe.

Jack being Jack, he never liked his manuscript, constantly editing, adding, deleting, polishing, relentless in the pursuit of perfection, and unsure whether his story was worth telling.

It was left to me, Robert Placid, to see that his final professional and personal accomplishment made it over the finish line and into print. While Jack and I always joked that I would be the one to pull the plug and take him out of his misery, I will never forget the frenzied pace of health care providers trying to keep my friend alive and the doctor's words, "I'm sorry, Mrs. Curran, there's nothing more we can do other than try to keep him comfortable. Your husband's living will prevents use of a ventilator."

In Jack's final minutes, I clasped his hand and our eyes met. He nodded ever so slightly in recognition of our bond. I said, "I know what you want to say. You're grateful that I helped you take the stick out of your ass." Tears streamed down my cheeks as his eyes reacted with a dim twinkle and his lips parted in what I knew was his attempt at a smile while in such discomfort. I stepped back to allow Carolyn and the boys to have their goodbyes.

From the back of the room, I was in unspeakable grief as I watched him take his last breath—a death *gurgle* is the only way I can describe it. Carolyn and I embraced, and I vowed that she would always be taken care of. I knew my strength would have to carry her and her sons through the coming days.

My friend never liked a fuss and always lived life *his way*, avoiding the partying and good times in Harrisburg that I've certainly experienced. Despite my best efforts, he limited the amount of frivolity in college he allowed himself to enjoy. While the rest of us partied hard, Jack had to organize some meeting or lead some charitable drive. He was too determined.

Driven by a tortured childhood that caused him to attempt to live up to his father's expectations, and driven to achieve success, despite his mother's abandonment of him and his sister. I will not add any further to his commentary on the journey he and I took, other than to say we truly completed one another as best friends and professionals.

As our final goodbye, a small group of us, including his family, siblings, Tony Molinaro, the Hahns and Morans, and Gloria West, took my thirty-five-foot cabin cruiser out of Beach Haven, New Jersey, the following summer after Jack's death, for a committal ceremony. Finding a spot about three miles offshore, I cut the engines, and the air was heavy and sad with what we were about to do.

Joining hands as we stood on my boat's stern deck, Bill Moran led us in "The Lord's Prayer." Jack Jr. and Robert then scattered their father's ashes into the deep of the Atlantic. Carolyn, with Gloria's assistance, placed a large wreath of blue and white carnations—the colors of our alma mater—upon the sea. I had to will my right hand to open to ready Jack's Army dog tags, knowing how important it would be to my friend that they rest with him for eternity. With an almost reverent tenderness, I kissed the stainless-steel chain that had rested against Jack's chest for over thirty-five years and then tossed them into the ocean to join his remains and the flowers.

In a clear voice, Gabriel read Jack's favorite scripture, found in Ecclesiastes, "To everything there is a season, a time for every purpose under heaven: a time to be born, and a time to die; a time to plant, and a time to uproot what is planted; a time to kill, and a time to heal; a time to break down, and a time to build up; a time to weep, and a time to laugh; a time to mourn, and a time to dance; a time to cast away stones, and a time to gather stones; a time to embrace, and a time to refrain from embracing; a time to gain, and a time to lose; a time to keep, and a time to cast away; a time to tear, and a time to sew; a time to keep silence, and a time to speak; a time to love, and a time to hate; a time of war, and a time of peace." (Ecc. 3.1). Jack would've been so proud of Gabriel's poise and confidence as he said these words that my pal loved for their simplicity and beauty.

Sarah Hahn closed our little service by leading us in "How Great Thou Art," Jack's favorite hymn. I started the engines. At a slow pace, we returned to port, taking comfort in a sunset that blazed across the western sky. At his best when near the ocean, we allowed the swells of the sea and seagulls that trailed my boat to be the final sounds of Jack Hudson Curran's interment. As Jack would have said: "Just as it should be."

For the sake of Jack's readers, I'll wrap up his book by informing you where the folks are that influenced him and that he tried to bring to life in the previous pages.

CAROLYN CURRAN remained at the Jersey Shore, honoring Jack by living in the little town he loved so much. She volunteers for her church and takes lots of walks on the beach—collecting sea glass—something she and Jack never tired of doing together.

SENATOR JIM WEIGEL died over twenty years ago, but his legacy and integrity live on in the memories of those he touched with his good works.

SENATOR TONY MOLINARO moved to Gettysburg where he lives in a beautiful brick Colonial not too far from the battlefield. As a history buff, Tony is enjoying his part-time role as an adjunct professor at Gettysburg College. He actively volunteers for his church and serves as a mentor to young people with political aspirations. Molinaro spoils his grandchildren and takes them on lots of jaunts, hiking through the battlefields and woods of Gettysburg.

SARAH HAHN and her husband Rick have traveled the world. Her work as a teacher lives on in the many students she nurtured.

WILLIAM MORAN retired some years ago. He is a noted author and contributing writer of articles on the escalating costs of higher education. He is a lone voice in the wilderness on this important subject. Dr. Moran and his lovely wife Mary live in an old English Tudor, not too far from Ford's campus.

GLORIA WEST, when not traveling to sunny climates, volunteers in a shelter for battered women and cares for two rescue dogs she adores.

BRUCE BAUER retired from the Senate and replaced David Cortes as a talk radio show host. With his state pension to draw upon, he bought a new wardrobe and employed an expensive hair stylist with the goal of having his radio program podcast to a national audience. His former boss, Senator Marco Corvi, left the Senate with his appointment to a key engineering position in the federal Department of Transportation.

ENNIS O'REILLY married her long-time boyfriend, Seth Weisman, a high-powered lobbyist for a global conglomerate of interlocking companies. The couple live in a Georgetown mansion. An invitation to one of their many cocktail parties is one of the most sought after in Washington, D.C. Ennis occasionally returns to Harrisburg to participate in caucus retreats to teach the ropes to a new batch of senior staffers.

BEN WALKER retired and is an adjunct professor at the Dickinson School of Law in Carlisle, Pennsylvania.

REPRESENTATIVE HENRIETTA ZELDA HOOVER involuntarily retired to private life after being challenged in the primary after Jack left state government. Her opponent, a young female upstart, attacked Henrietta as remote and ineffective in representing the district. She beat Henrietta by only 326 votes. Hoover is now a guest commentator for conservative blogs and a right-leaning research foundation in Harrisburg. Jack sent her this note: *Dear Representative, I was sorry to learn of your loss. Even after all our battles, you remain a giant for me. I rest easy knowing you'll keep fighting for the principles you hold so dear. Ayn Rand would be proud. Regards, Curran.*

AGNES BONNEVILLE retired from the Senate Archives and spends most days at the local casino near Harrisburg. Her tabloid collection grew and grew until found hidden in an old copy room close to the archives, long after she had left the Senate.

VICTOR PEARL was true to his word and now lives in Israel as one voice in a newer kibbutz, assisting with administrative work.

KOSTANTIN POKORNIN suffered a massive heart attack one day while hanging out at the Capitol snack bar, waiting for tidbits to come his way. Newspaper editorials across the state memorialized his mountains of stories that kept politicians honest.

SENATOR CADDOCK PUMFREY passed away while sitting at his desk in the Senate chamber as he and Senator Harshburger (his only friend in the legislature) chatted away. But not before attempts by first responders to revive him from the stroke that took his life. In a twist of divine intervention, these health care heroes, African-Americans, tried valiantly to save Pumfrey. Doing their job, regardless of the color of *his* skin.

SENATOR MICHAEL MADISON's long and distinguished service to the people of the Commonwealth ended with his retirement. After his passing, a state office building was named for him and the people of his district erected a magnificent statue of the senator that graces the entrance of the suburban town he proudly called "home."

REPRESENTATIVE HERMAN PATEK FILIPOWSKI's reign of lobbyist terror ended because of an FBI sting. The Flipper did his time in federal prison for accepting bribes, dining in prison orange, instead of in the finest restaurants in the Harrisburg region. He is now rumored to be in a nursing home, long forgotten from the Capitol scene.

GEORGE YODER DIMPLE, the former GOP counselor, lived a long life. On his deathbed, he allegedly said, "Molinaro's the only one to beat me."

JOSEPH CURRAN JR. made his peace with Big Joe becoming a successful businessman and lay evangelist. He passed away unexpectedly before Jack did, leaving behind a wonderful wife and children. William, Emma, and Carol remain close, although they grieve the loss of their brothers. At family gatherings, the extended gang hears many of the stories of the Curran Seven. Some memories now bring laughter. Others are much too raw and traumatic to discuss—even today.

CARLISLE DAVIN KELSO had a distinguished career as Pennsylvania's health and public assistance secretary. After public life, he established a for-profit business that manages nursing homes and is reportedly a multi-millionaire.

LOUISA SMITH-DIAZ no longer lobbies for abortion rights in Pennsylvania, moving onto a national cable news network that solicits her views on women's issues. She returned to California and is purportedly also writing a book. Louisa finally gave up on Tony's office, knowing Senator Molinaro remained squarely in the pro-life camp.

ALEXANDRE DESTIN BREST ran for elective office on a Tea Party platform—he downplayed his "French" origins," shortening his name on the ballot to "Alex"—and became Pennsylvania's auditor general in a squeaker of a win, using the post to ferret out waste and fraud. Brest and Henrietta Hoover had a falling out over who is a more prominent spokesperson for conservatives in Pennsylvania.

JONATHAN AND JOAN OTTEN retired from the Capitol scene and now split their time between a trendy condo in a tony Manhattan neighborhood and an oceanfront property in Malibu.

SENATOR DALTON TABNER SCHWEMMER left public life after making a fortune in commodities trading. According to the Harrisburg rumor mill, he lives in a secluded villa in Belize with his mistress.

Finally, as for me, **ROBERT PLACID**, I married and subsequently divorced Sally. I should've heeded my friend's words of caution. After Jack's retirement, I met and married my third bride, Leslie. We purchased a small farmette in rural Perry County (near Harrisburg). I remain the senior partner in my firm, keeping my hand in Pennsylvania politics while enjoying the rigors of farm life with my wife, who is pregnant with our first child. If it's a boy, his name will be Jack. In honor of my friend, my pal, who enriched me far more than I could ever do for him. The hole in my heart will never heal.